GOLD

OTHER TITLES BY K.A. LINDE

GOLD

USA Today Bestselling Author

k.a. linde

Linde

Gold, All That Glitters, Book Two

By K.A. Linde

Copyright © 2015 by K.A. Linde

All rights reserved.

Cover Designer: Sarah Hansen, Okay Creations, www.okaycreations.com

Editor and Interior Designer: Jovana Shirley, Unforeseen Editing, www.unforeseenediting.com

Poem reprinted with permission © r.m. drake, instagram.com/rmdrk

Visit my website at www.kalinde.com

ISBN-13: 978-0996053075

16.99
11/19/15
DS

*so ask yourself if you are willing
to burn. because the moment you
open yourself to me, i will have
no choice but to scorch everything
that defines you. and without
regret, i will devour and i will
leave nothing behind.*

—r.m. drake

ONE

"HELL HATH NO FURY LIKE A WOMAN SCORNED."

That was the damn truth.

Bryna twirled her Harry Winston B diamond necklace around her finger and parted her pouty lips. She had decided on a gold glitter Chanel dress and hot-as-fuck black Jimmy Choos, and when she walked into Las Vegas State's local nightclub, Posse, all eyes turned her way—just the way she liked it.

She was still getting used to her new life in college. No annoying cling-ons. No obnoxious stepbrother. No wannabe stepmother. No reminders of what had happened her senior year when her life was shot to hell. No reminders of *him*.

Just her scarlet letter hanging around her neck and a new crowd to rule.

This was the life.

"Bryna! Over here!" Trihn called from the bar.

Bryna fluttered her fingers at her friend and walked her way. It was strange, in a way, to have friends. In high school, she always had Gates Hartman, her movie star ex-boyfriend, but that had crashed and burned. Otherwise, she usually considered other girls as either followers or competition. With Trihn, there was none of that.

Trihn Hamilton, a name she only used professionally, was model tall and exotic with roots in both Vietnam and Brazil. She had endless brown-to-blonde ombre hair and slightly upturned eyes. Plus, she could dance circles around everyone knew. Not to mention, she was the nicest, most sure-of-herself person Bryna had ever met. They had met in this very club the first week of school. Trihn had confidently commented on Bryna's next season Christian Louboutins. After a night of shots and dancing, a friendship had blossomed.

"Look at you rocking the Chanel tonight after the big game," Trihn said. She pulled Bryna in for a hug. "I think glitter is your color."

Bryna laughed. "Always. Look at you in your rocker grunge."

"Excuse me. This is designer rocker grunge," Trihn corrected her.

She wore skintight black leather pants, a ripped white crop, and strappy Gucci high heels she had probably gotten when she modeled for them last year. Bryna normally thought model types were dumb as bricks, so she was constantly surprised that they got along and that Trihn had a real personality.

"Ah!" a girl screamed, barreling into Bryna. "You look fucking hot!"

"I'm surprised you're not still in uniform," Bryna said.

Stacia Palmer was on the cheerleading team with Bryna. Her father was the head football coach at their biggest rival, the University of Southern California, and that would have made her the enemy, but she had come to LV State to stay out of her father's shadow. It also explained her obsession with football players. Her reputation as a jersey-chasing whore really endeared her to Bryna. She appreciated the honesty.

"Oh, please." Stacia flipped her bleach-blonde bangs out of her eyes. "All the guys here know I'm a cheerleader. Plus, Blaine isn't even here yet. I just made a circuit to see if I could find him."

Blaine was the starting quarterback of the LV State Gamblers football team. Stacia was determined to hook up with him. Her real goal though was to marry an NFL quarterback.

"You're ridiculous. How can you even stand college guys?" Bryna asked.

"Don't talk to me about older guys. Blaine is a senior, Bri. That's good enough for me."

Bryna arched an eyebrow. "Whatever you're into."

"Like Eric." Stacia sighed heavily. "I would be very into him if he were still playing."

Bryna's eyes wandered through the crowd of football players to where Eric Wilkins was standing. She *had* been very into him on her school visit here last semester. Sometimes, she still was when she forgot why they would never hook up. She was pretty sure none of her friends and certainly no one on the football team actually knew the reason.

Eric was gay. That was why he never tried to hook up with her on her visit and why he hadn't talked to her since.

"I don't think you're his type," Bryna said.

"Whatever. I heard the guys talking about how he dated that psychotic head case last year. What was her name?"

Bryna raised her eyebrows. She hadn't heard anything about this. Must have been one hell of a cover story.

"Audrey," Trihn said.

"That's it."

"Why did they break up?" Bryna asked.

Stacia shrugged. "Who cares? She was a crazy bitch. But now, he's on the market. We can all take our chances with him. What do you say, B?"

She laughed and shook her head. "I don't think *I'm* his type either."

"Bri, you're everyone's type," Trihn said.

"I appreciate the sentiment."

Normally, she wouldn't disagree with Trihn. Bryna had perfect long blonde hair, an impressive rack, and a killer body to boot. Most guys couldn't tear their eyes away from her, and she always enjoyed the attention. After her disastrous senior year, she had especially enjoyed that attention this summer while lying on various European beaches and hooking up with gorgeous exotic men whom she couldn't understand.

"So then, go ask him out." Trihn nudged Bryna.

Stacia cracked up. "Ask him out? You want Bryna to ask him out?"

Bryna rolled her eyes. "You know that's not happening. Do you know who I am?"

"The elusive Bryna Turner," Trihn said with a wink. "Come on. You should be confident enough to be able to ask him out. I'd do it."

"You do it then and let him turn you down. I'm not interested."

"Well, *I'm* interested," Stacia said.

The girls didn't get it. Bryna never considered herself a good person. In fact, she normally figured she was a class-A bitch. But she wasn't about to tell people that Eric was gay. He obviously wasn't out, and the last thing she wanted was for it to get back that she was the one who had outed him. She admired him too much to spew venom.

After all, as the defensive back, he had led LV State to a national championship before he'd completely blown out his knee, ending his career. Now, he was a student assistant coach for the team, which meant they always hung in the same circles.

She would keep her mouth shut and tolerate her friend's ridiculous behavior.

"You know what?" Bryna said with a smile. A plan was already formulating in her mind. "I'll go ask him out."

"Yes!" Trihn cried, thinking she had won.

"But...when he's not interested, you'll get a big, fat I-told-you-so, and you bitches will need to find guys to buy us the next round of shots."

"Easy for us," Trihn said. "There's no way he's not interested."

Bryna smirked. *This is almost too easy.*

She honed in on Eric. Tall and still built like he played ball with short-cropped dark hair and an easy smile, he was easy to spot, even in the crowd of football players. The guys he was hanging out with had a bunch of girls desperately clinging to them, but Eric was without one. He might have told everyone else that it was because of his psycho ex, but she knew the truth. *They always said all the hot ones are gay.*

"Hey, Eric," Bryna said, interrupting their conversation. "Can I talk with you a minute?"

She felt the eyes of all the other football players heating her skin, but she kept her focus on Eric. She wet her lips and looked up at him from under her long lashes. One of the other guys murmured something vulgar under his breath, and Eric shoved him.

"Sure, Bryna. What's up?" he asked nonchalantly.

Bryna pointed her French-manicured finger toward a more private location. "Mind if we talk over there?"

He nodded and then followed her away. The guys immediately catcalled to him.

He flipped them off before returning his attention to her. "What's going on?"

When she stared up into his honey-hazel eyes, her smile widened. *God, he is fucking hot.* She always thought so. *Too fucking bad.*

"Bryna?"

She snapped out of her trance and remembered why the fuck she was here in the first place. "Do you want to go out sometime?"

Eric blankly stared back at her. He looked surprised, but underneath the shock was something else. She couldn't quite put her finger on it.

"You're asking me out?"

"I know. Shocker, right?" She tried to play it off as if it wasn't a big deal. She had never done this before. Mostly because she didn't need to. She was hot, and guys flocked to her. She was just proving a point.

"Look, I…I don't think you're my type." He scratched the back of his head. "Nothing against girls like you, but they're not for me."

Bryna's mouth fell open. "Girls like me?"

"You know what I mean." His eyes fell to the floor.

There it was in his voice again. *Is that…disgust?*

"No, I don't think I do. I've been here for a month. What exactly is my reputation that makes you say 'girls like me'?"

Eric sighed, and his eyes found hers once more. "You know what people say about you…about all the cheerleaders," he clarified quickly. "No offense. I'm not into that."

"Them now and not just me?"

She had expected him to turn her down. She had expected him to say no, that he didn't want to go out with her. But she sure as hell hadn't expected him to basically call her a slut-bag whore.

Girls like me? What the hell did that even mean?

She hadn't slept with anyone since arriving at LV State. While she had flirted, she had been wary of getting too close to anyone. The last thing she wanted was for feelings to get involved and fuck her up again. She preferred meaningless hot sex. And it was harder to come by with someone who went to her school, knowing she could inevitably run into that person again.

"I don't want to get into it, Bryna. But it's…cute that you asked me."

Cute.

He had said it was *cute*. This had gone from irritating to humiliating with one word. *What an asshole!*

"Maybe call up your friend Gates. He seemed into you."

"We're not friends anymore, but thanks," she spat sarcastically.

Bryna turned to walk away, but Eric reached out and grabbed her arm.

"Hey. I didn't mean to upset you. I didn't know you two weren't friends anymore."

"Let me go," she growled.

Eric immediately dropped her arm. "Whatever."

He had that look again, like he was already disgusted with her, and her harsh tone had only made it worse.

Bryna stormed away, back to her friends. She struggled to find composure.

The thought of Gates irritated her to no end. He had been in love with her, and everything had gone straight to shit. She hadn't even talked to him since he kicked her out of his movie premiere, and now, Eric Wilkins had brought him up.

Ugh!

And that only made her think of one thing. Images flooded her mind. The most prominent of them all was *him.*

Jude.

She took a deep breath and shut down. She locked away the image of him. She refused to think about the man she had once loved telling her he was married with a son, and then him turning around, following his wife out of the banquet room, and leaving her forever.

She swallowed hard. This wasn't right. Jude's name held no power over her. Never again would he hold any power over her.

She shouldn't let this get to her. Gates was out of her life. Jude was out of her life. And Eric Wilkins didn't matter.

TWO

"SO, WHAT DID HE SAY?" Trihn asked. She planted her hand on her hip and gave Bryna an expectant look, thinking she had the cat in the bag.

"No. He said no," she said tightly.

"What?" Stacia asked. Her mouth dropped open in her overly dramatic style. "I can't believe it."

"Well, believe it."

"I mean…have you ever been rejected before?" Stacia asked. "I haven't. What was it like? Did it suck?"

"I'm giving you my big, fat fucking I-told-you-so. I knew he'd say no," she said as if everything else he had said didn't bother her in the slightest. "Now, where are my drinks, bitches?"

"Maybe we should verify," Trihn said.

Bryna shrugged her shoulders. "Confirm if you must, but Eric is going to tell you the same damn thing. I think a better use of our time would be to find some guys in VIP to buy me those drinks."

Trihn still looked skeptical but acquiesced to Bryna's suggestion. They walked across the room and to the upstairs VIP lounge. The bouncer checked them out first before allowing them access. In L.A., Bryna wouldn't have even needed a second glance. If the bouncer didn't know her, then her promoter friend, Max, would always put her name on the list. The scene was so different here.

Trihn swished her hair to one side and smiled at the bouncer. "Thanks!"

Bryna kept from rolling her eyes. Trihn, the eternally nice one.

"You don't have to talk to him," Bryna murmured.

"What?" Trihn asked.

"The bouncer. You don't have to talk to him."

"Ignore, Bri," Stacia said. "You know she's a bitch."

"I am," she conceded. "But I stand by my statement. Your approach to bouncers might be different in Brooklyn, but isn't everything?"

"Hey now. Brooklyn gets a lot of heat, but it fits my image," Trihn said with a smile. "Plus, you can't have a fashion photographer for a father without living in an artsy area. You all should be glad I ended up with the fashion side and not the artsy side."

"Trihn…you're a design major. Does that not scream artsy to you?"

"At least I *have* a major," she said, pointedly staring at Bryna.

"Whatever. I assume you lived your life like Dan from *Gossip Girl.*"

"I am not Lonely Boy!" Trihn cried.

Then, all three of them cracked up laughing at the ridiculous turn of their conversation.

"Drinks!" Bryna cried.

She ushered them away from the entrance. Once she reached the bar, she eyed the crowd and focused on her prey. She could see a couple of hot guys who would likely buy drinks for them with no more than a smile from her. The home game had brought in so many prospects.

Leaning forward against the bar, she let her chest pop over the top of her dress, and she winked at the bartender. "Maya!"

Maya fluttered her fingertips at them from the other side of the bar. The girls had quickly become regulars at Posse, and Maya was their favorite bartender. She finished pouring drinks for a group of frat douches and then sauntered all five-foot-ten inches of her luscious African-American caramel-toned body over to them. "Hey, babes. What can I get for you?"

Bryna pursed her lips and looked around the room. "Him and him and maybe him, too." She pointed out each guy in turn.

"You don't need help with them. Not if I know you," Maya said. "How about a dirty martini with three olives?"

"You know me so well," Bryna crooned.

"Trihni, my love!" Maya leaned across the bar and kissed Trihn on the cheek. "Gin and tonic, and something girlie for the cheer slut?"

"Perfection," Trihn said. "Just like you."

"I love when you talk dirty to me," Stacia said.

A minute later, all three drinks were placed in front of the girls. Before any of them could retrieve their wallets, a guy motioned for Maya to put it on his tab. Bryna raised an eyebrow as Trihn fawned over his generosity. He was good-looking in an LV State button-up and slacks that he had likely worn to the game. His appearance screamed wealthy alumnus, and even though everything in Bryna told her to back away, she couldn't help but be interested in older guys. Another unfortunate side effect of the Jude catastrophe.

"Why don't you ladies come sit with me and my friends?" he asked with an easy smile that said he had done this before.

11

"Oh! We'd love to," Trihn said.

Bryna's eyes traveled down to his left hand buried in his pocket, and she wondered if something was lurking on his ring finger.

"Bri," Stacia snapped, nudging her.

"Yeah. Sure," she said.

She met his gaze and saw that look she craved. Desire. He wanted her.

She licked her lips and smiled, slow and sultry. "Sounds fun."

She followed them across the VIP lounge. His friends had a booth right off of the dance floor, and Stacia immediately starting grinding on Trihn.

"Come on, Bri!" Trihn called over her shoulder.

But Bryna didn't have any interest in dancing at that moment. She shook her head and held up her martini. Trihn and Stacia were almost finished with their drinks already, working toward that state of oblivion. Bryna liked to get there slower. After that one horrendously embarrassing moment when she had gotten shitfaced on her college visit, she didn't like to let herself go like that. Being out of control didn't suit her.

"Hey, I'm Thomas," the guy said, sidling up next to where Bryna stood by the booth.

"Hey yourself," she said with a smile.

Yes, up close he was even cuter. Strong jawline and extremely dark eyes. She could see the expensive watch on his wrist, and she took that as a good sign.

"What's your name?"

This was a step in the right direction. "Brihn-uh," she said, deliberately drawing her name out. People tended not to pronounce it right.

"That's different. I like it."

"Me, too. My friends call me Bri though."

"Your friends seem to be having a good time. Are you guys students?"

Inquisitive one. She wasn't used to that. Her European hunks hadn't asked a lot of questions. And before that…well, Jude hadn't cared to ask or else they might not have ended up in that situation in the first place. At least she was legal this time.

"Yeah. Students. And you're an alum?" She plucked the Gamblers logo on his shirt with her fingers and leaned in closer.

His eyes landed on her lips, and then he nodded. "Yes. A proud Gambler."

"I can see that," she purred.

God, it was all a game. A very, very familiar game. And she wanted to hate herself for playing along…and even worse, for enjoying it. But she didn't. She couldn't hate something that made her heart race. She associated the mystery and danger with an unbeatable adrenaline rush and super hot sex. At the same time, she had an uncontrollable urge to watch with a smile as it all burned down in front of her.

He laughed and then offered her a spot at their table. They eyed her appreciatively and seemed impressed with their friend for not only finding one hot girl but three.

Shots appeared out of nowhere, and then they reappeared regularly. The girls were past tipsy and dancing sloppily with Thomas's friends. Bryna even relented to dance with them. She was sandwiched between Trihn and Stacia, shaking their asses as if there were no tomorrow.

Thomas grabbed her hand and pulled her away from her friends. Grinding their hips together, he leaned into her. She thought he might kiss her or something, but he never did.

The music changed, and they all crashed back into the booth.

Stacia pulled out her cell phone and groaned. "B, we have to go downstairs. Everyone else is here, and they're doing some kind of cheer thing."

Thomas's hand landed on Bryna's, and his lips grazed her ear. "Don't go. Stay up here with me."

She smirked at the attention. She craved it like a life force. "I'll come down later," she told Stacia.

Stacia gave her a knowing look. "Are you sure? It'll be fun."

"S, go!" Bryna nodded her head toward Thomas and raised her eyebrows. *Hello, I'm occupied.*

"Fine. Trihn, are you staying?"

Trihn wasn't even paying attention. She was animatedly talking to one of the other guys about who knew what. She was a happy drunk and suddenly found everyone interesting, not that the guy seemed to mind in the slightest.

"Hopeless," Stacia said with a shake of her head. She kissed Bryna on the cheek and whispered in her ear, "Be careful."

Bryna laughed off Stacia's warning, and then she disappeared through the crowd. Stacia was super cautious and paranoid about everyone, except for herself. The girl seriously knew how to let loose, but when other people did, she'd freak out for them.

"So," Thomas said, "you're a cheerleader?"

"Don't I seem the type?"

He let his eyes drag down her body. "Your friend seemed the type. You seem…different. More mature."

That was a new one. "I like that."

"I like you," he said.

"You barely know me," she corrected him.

And she was sure he wanted to keep it that way. It would be easier to justify the one-night stand if she was only a beautiful face in his mind.

"You're gorgeous and an LV State cheerleader. What else should I know?"

She let the hit roll off her shoulders. The fact that she had come into LV State with a 4.0 GPA probably didn't matter to him.

"Nothing," she said dryly. "That's all there is to know about me. What about you? What do you do?"

The question popped out of her mouth before she could stop herself. The way he had acted like anything other than her looks didn't matter made her want to act like nothing other than his money mattered. It reminded her of last year and made her stomach twist. This was the person *he* had made her. *Damn, Jude.*

"I'm a biomedical engineer," he said with pride. "It's technical and not interesting." He grabbed her by the waist and pulled her onto his lap. His lips settled into the crook of her neck. His hand crept up to her upper thigh. All the inhibitions he had been holding on to disappeared in the darkened booth with the help of the booze they had been downing all night.

She tilted her head, so he would have better access, and she reveled in the feeling of being wanted. She craved it like a smoker needed nicotine. And she refused to apologize for it.

As his hand snuck further up her dress, she reached down and grabbed it. She wasn't going to do anything more than this in the crowded bar. She'd go back to his hotel room before that.

"Aw, come on," he urged.

She crossed her legs and shifted. She wasn't an open invitation. He would have to work a little harder for this.

His friends were watching them from the other side of the booth. "Your friends clearly like a show," she said. It came out sounding like an excuse to stop, but she was more curious about their interest.

"Ignore them." Regardless, he pulled away from her. "They should mind their own business. Let's get another drink."

Suspicion crept into her mind. *Why would his friends be this interested in a girl he wanted to take back to the hotel?*

"Or we could get out of here," she purred.

She stood and reached for his left hand. Her hand brushed across his ring finger and found it empty, but she couldn't ignore the indentation where a ring used to sit. Her stomach turned, and she tried to rationalize that maybe he was divorced.

He hesitated a second longer than she'd expected, and her insides turned to lead.

He followed her to his feet as he made his decision. "You have a place nearby, or should we go to my hotel?"

She gritted her teeth and then forced a smile, wondering how far he was going to take this. "Probably your place."

"Yeah, my place," he repeated.

Bryna giggled and leaned into him. "Something wrong? Don't you want to take me back to your room and fuck me all night?"

Thomas groaned. "Yes. Yes, I do." He pressed forward into her and let their lips meet. "Fuck, I want you."

"Then, let's go," she encouraged like the devil on his shoulder.

He grabbed her and crushed his lips down on her again. She could tell he desperately wanted her at this point, and they hadn't even made it out of the bar. Maybe she should have felt bad, but she didn't. The guy was bringing this on himself.

"Come on," she urged.

"Wait," he said.

"What's wrong?"

"Nothing." He met her baby-blues. "Nothing's wrong."

Bryna withdrew. This game was over. Thomas bored her.

"It couldn't be that you're married?"

His eyes widened. "What?"

"And your friends are looking at us, wondering why you're a cheating scumbag making out with this whore?"

"What are you talking about?" he stammered.

"Please. An indentation on your ring finger, overly curious friends, and you being fidgety when I told you to fuck me. I should have guessed." She pushed him away.

"Wait!" he cried before she could turn and leave.

She curiously eyed him. *Did I misjudge him?*

"I've never done anything like this before."

She rolled her eyes. *Nope.* "Clearly."

Thomas was such an amateur. She couldn't believe how much it irritated her. He hadn't even made it interesting. If she was going to do this again, he'd need to be better than this, make it worth her while to try to wreck another marriage.

"Stay with me tonight," Thomas said softly, lacking all the confidence he'd had when he bought their drinks and flirted with her much of the night.

Ugh! Such a waste.

Bryna grabbed a half-empty cocktail off the table and threw it in his face. "You're disgusting. Go home to your Stepford wife."

She walked over to where Trihn was sitting with her mouth wide open. "Let's go."

Trihn immediately jumped up and followed her out of VIP. "What the hell just happened?"

Bryna sighed. "Jude happened."

THREE

"OKAY. THAT'S A WRAP, GIRLS. If you have any questions once you leave, send me a text message. See you tomorrow," the cheer coach said.

Bryna breathed a sigh of relief. *Finally*. After three hours of grueling rehearsal, they were leaving the practice facility to go home. She'd had class all morning and cheer all night. Her body ached from stunting, and she couldn't wait to shower, but at least they were ready for their first away game at the University of Oregon on Saturday.

Stacia swept her bangs out of her eyes and nudged Bryna. "Ready?"

Bryna nodded. She grabbed her cheer bag and followed Stacia out of the locker room. "That was one hell of a practice."

"You looked great. I'd die for your bow and arrow."

"Ugh! No more cheer talk. I can't think about it anymore before the game. I'm going to need some serious retail therapy."

"You need retail therapy for everything," Stacia said.

"Truth."

"I just need that." Stacia nodded her head toward the practice field.

The football team was filing out of the gate, still dressed in pads, about to hit the showers.

"Which one?" Bryna asked.

"All of them," Stacia sighed.

"Sounds like a porn. Cheerleader gangbanged by the football team."

Stacia tilted her head as if contemplating it. "Doesn't sound that bad."

"I hear they pay good money," Bryna joked. She couldn't help but egg Stacia on.

Bryna wouldn't put it past Stacia to join in on something like that. She wasn't selective. A small part of her understood where Eric had been coming from in regard to cheerleaders. Stacia was the definition of *that* girl. Bryna just took offense to him calling *her* that kind of girl.

"I wouldn't need the money. I'd be in it for the sex," Stacia said with a wink.

"Slut."

"Bitch."

Bryna raised an eyebrow and smirked at her friend. This was why she and Stacia got along. There were forty other girls on the squad, but most of them drove Bryna nuts or made her want to stab her eye out with a fork. Plus, she and Stacia were the only freshman flyers, and that pissed off enough people, so they had to stick together.

"Look! Blaine!" Stacia said.

Bryna narrowed her eyes and searched for the quarterback. "Where?"

"Right there," she said, gesturing toward the back of the line.

Stacia must seriously have a radar for the guy because Bryna could hardly tell the players apart in their uniforms. Blaine was exceedingly tall, which helped, but so was most of the team.

"Let's go say hi." Stacia dragged Bryna across the pavilion.

"What? They just finished practice," Bryna said.

She shook off Stacia's vise grip. The girl was nutso for Blaine.

What the fuck? Bryna had no interest in any of the football players. College guys, she was discovering, weren't much better than high school guys. She didn't mind flirting and fucking with the best of them but not right now when she needed a shower.

"Who cares?" Stacia said. She jogged forward and fell into step next to Blaine.

Bryna quickly caught up to her. Her eyes landed on the person walking next to Blaine, and she nearly groaned aloud. *Eric.* She hadn't seen him since their encounter at Posse. They uneasily eyed each other, but she made sure that she wasn't the first person to look away.

"Hey, Blaine! Good practice?" Stacia asked, her voice chipper.

Blaine smiled in an unabashed way that won over crowds. "Yeah. Great practice. We're ready to stomp some Ducks this weekend!"

"I know you'll be great," she crooned.

Bryna tried not to roll her eyes. *Jesus.* Was this how Stacia got what she wanted—by batting her eyelashes and purring to get attention?

Eric snorted next to Blaine, and Bryna saw that his expression mirrored her own. When they both noticed, they glared at each other and then turned away.

What an ass! She could be disdainful of her friend slutting it up, but he couldn't.

"Thanks, Stacy," Blaine said with that same smile. "We have to get to the showers. See you around."

"Bye!" Stacia cried as he left her in the dust.

Once they were a safe distance away from the practice fields, Stacia let out a heavenly sigh. "He wants me. I know it."

Bryna's eyes bugged out. "He didn't even call you by your real name."

Stacia shrugged. "I mean, technically, it *was* my real name, but I had my parents legally change it in high school."

"Why am I not surprised?"

"Anyway," Stacia said dramatically, "I think I'm going to make a move at the away game this weekend."

"Good idea," Bryna said.

There was no convincing her otherwise. She had her eyes set on the quarterback, and she wouldn't be discouraged just because Bryna knew Blaine wasn't interested in her. Not only was he not interested, but she knew he was also hooking up with some girl on the basketball dance team. Either way, he was going to the NFL next year and leaving both girls behind.

"You know, I saw that thing between you and Eric," Stacia said once they reached the parking lot.

"What thing?"

"The eye thing." Stacia wiggled her eyebrows up and down.

"There was no eye thing." The only *thing* that had passed between her and Eric was disgust that they'd shared an even remotely similar thought.

"Okay. Whatever you want to think."

Bryna rolled her eyes. One day, she was going to lay it on them that Eric was gay, and they were going to be so stunned that they wouldn't know what to do.

"Seriously, there was something," Stacia crooned. "I'm not sure I believe that he turned you down. It was a front, right?"

"Wrong," she said, exasperated. *Why do I have to keep defending myself?* "Maybe we were both amazed at how much you want to suck Blaine's dick."

"Why would anyone be amazed at that?" she deadpanned.

Bryna laughed. "You're such a slut."

"I only hope that I'll be as good at it as you are." She innocently fluttered her eyelashes.

"Doesn't everyone?"

"Pretty much. Speaking of," Stacia cried, "what exactly happened last weekend? I want the goods. Trihn said you threw your drink on that guy you were with."

Bryna shrugged, unperturbed. "He had it coming."

And it was true. He hadn't even had the decency to be honest. Not that Jude had ever been honest. But the whole concept just irritated her. She knew she should just brush it off and roll with the punches, but after the way Jude had played her, she was a changed woman. And not necessarily for the better.

"Hey, B." Stacia snapped her fingers in Bryna's face. "Hot guy? Cocktail in the face? What the fuck?"

"He didn't know how to play the game, so I gave him a lesson." She winked.

Stacia giggled. She retrieved her car keys from her bag and clicked the unlock button. Her giant SUV beeped across the parking lot, and she leaned on the hood of Bryna's Aston Martin while they talked. "That doesn't sound like *my* idea of a lesson."

"That's because you would have banged him."

Stacia tapped her lips. "True."

"Anyway," she said, popping open her door, "he was married."

"Oh," Stacia said in understanding.

Bryna wished that had been the real issue. But she had been there, done that before.

BRYNA VALETED HER ASTON MARTIN at Caesars Palace on the Vegas Strip and entered the Forum Shops for a last-minute shopping trip. She hated to admit that she was a little nervous about her first away game, but she couldn't help it. Jitters wracked her stomach, and the only way to calm those nerves—other than sex, which wasn't exactly accessible at the moment—was a quick shopping trip. She could use a new carry-on anyway.

Meandering through the designer boutiques made her heart happy and calmed the unnecessary nerves. She rounded the corner and entered the beautiful interior of Louis Vuitton.

A clerk immediately approached her. "Hello. Welcome to Louis Vuitton. How can I help you?"

"I'm looking for a new carry-on. Something sleek."

"I know just the thing," the woman said with a smile.

Bryna spent a solid hour with the saleslady. It was hard to decide on only one bag, so she ended up with two—a black carry-on with all gold accents and a new gold makeup bag. After swiping her daddy's credit card, she exited the boutique with every intention of returning to her condo to finish packing.

She pulled out her cell phone and scrolled through the messages she had received while occupied. There was one from Trihn, wishing her good luck at the game this weekend. Attached was a picture of her history homework with a sad face drawn on it. Bryna laughed and clicked over to the next message where Stacia had posed for a picture in her cheer warm-ups with a thumbs-up and added text underneath.

See you in twenty.

Bryna checked the time and realized she had missed that only a couple of minutes ago. She still had some time. Maybe she would peek into one more shop before heading out.

Knowing she only had a short time, she walked through the Forum, back toward the entrance, and scoped out where to make her stop. Her smile brightened at the next entrance where a security guard was posted on the other side of the door. She sighed.

Tiffany's.

She had a gold bangle with diamonds inlaid in the band from Jude. The smile slipped from her face for a split second, but she forced it back on. *Fuck him!* She was over that shit. The bracelet was the sort of thing she *should* be wearing, and it didn't matter that she had gotten it when he decided to make their arrangement more serious, only to pull the rug out from under her later. Tiffany's was too perfect to be tainted by him.

She brushed past the guard and into the large Tiffany Blue-and-white room. She marveled at the glass counters and all the sparkling jewels. Her heart fluttered. The diamonds called to her. She breezed past the engagement rings and went straight to The Atlas Collection.

Her eyes were immediately drawn to a pair of gold Atlas hoops with diamonds. She had gotten the ones without diamonds this summer in Paris, but she had been kicking herself for not getting the ones with diamonds, too. She needed them.

"Good choice."

Bryna startled. She hadn't realized anyone had walked up to her while she was salivating over the earrings.

She faced the stranger, and her heart stuttered. *Oh, yes. So much yes.*

"Well, I have impeccable taste," she drawled.

He smiled. "I can see that."

He was perfect. Older than even Jude or maybe the same age. Mid to late thirties and utterly delectable. High cheekbones, full lips, chiseled strong jaw, and gleaming light-brown eyes. What she noticed next was just as important—an indulgent custom suit that fit him like a second skin. With that kind of cut and quality, it had to be something straight out of London's Savile Row. A fine suit had all the same necessary characteristics as a diamond, and both should be worn as often as possible.

She shifted her Louis Vuitton bag to her other arm and faced him head-on. "It appears I'm not the only one with good taste." She wet her lips.

"You can never go wrong with diamonds."

She completely agreed. "You think so?" she asked, playing coy.

"Absolutely."

"And what exactly are you shopping for?" She was mesmerized by his cool exterior.

Their conversation was intense, and they had barely shared more than two-dozen words. He had a commanding presence with such little effort.

The man leaned in slightly. "Just browsing."

He looked her directly in the eyes, and she got the impression he considered *her* to be merchandise.

If the Harry Winston diamonds around her neck were any indication, she could be bought.

"I would recommend anything in Tiffany's," she managed to get out.

An easy smile crossed his face, and she wondered exactly what he was thinking.

"Thank you. I'm sure I'll find something that I like."

Goose bumps broke out on her skin. She needed to get herself under control. This man was too much. She hadn't even checked if he was married, and it scared her a bit to know that she wouldn't care.

He had done this to her. It was a slippery slope, and she couldn't get her footing.

She needed to make up her mind about what to do. She had thrown that drink in Thomas's face at the bar because he had played the game wrong. *Do I want to play at all?*

Her only requirement was complete control. She needed it to breathe, to survive. But under the right circumstances, she would let it happen. And this seemed to be the right circumstances so far. She would let the ball roll and see whether or not he picked it up.

"Are you here on business?" she asked none too discreetly.

"What? I don't strike you as a local?"

"Hardly!" She swished her hair over her shoulder and leaned forward. "You have that out-of-town-businessman vibe down pat." A vibe she was very much enjoying. That meant he wouldn't be around all the time, and she could have her fun.

"You certainly don't look like a Vegas local either," he admitted, evading her question.

"Transplant from L.A.," she told him.

"Now, *that* makes more sense. You have that Cali vibe."

Bryna looked down at her outfit—skintight black jeans, a black tank, and a gold belt around her waist. *Me?*

"Please don't tell me you think I look like a surfer," she joked.

It was what people always incorrectly associated with California when, in fact, there was so much more to the state than that.

"You look Hollywood or Beverly Hills."

"That's more like it."

"Ma'am," a clerk said, coming up to stand before them at the counter, "did you want to try on the Atlas earrings?"

Bryna chewed on her bottom lip, debating. She did want them, but she had already wasted her last precious minutes talking with this man—well, not truly wasted, of course. Still, she had to leave already and didn't have time to get them. *Another time perhaps.*

"No. Thank you though."

"Try them on," the man insisted.

He gestured for the clerk to take them out of the cabinet. She placed them on a black crushed-velvet pad, and they were even more stunning when Bryna could almost reach out and touch them.

She took the earrings from the woman and switched out the ones she had been wearing for the Atlas diamonds. She brushed her hair back to look at them in the mirror and sighed delightfully.

"I think you have to get them," he said.

"Is that so?"

"They're perfect for you."

She was about to agree with him when her phone rang noisily. *Fuck!* She dug through her purse and silenced the ringer. *Stacia. Oops!*

"Sorry," she said to the man and the clerk. "Give me one minute."

They both nodded, and she walked a short distance away to answer the phone. "Hey, S."

"Where the eff are you, Bri? I'm at your condo. We're supposed to leave for the game soon!"

"I know. I got held up. I'll be there in ten minutes. Let yourself in."

"Where are you? Why are you not home?" Stacia demanded.

"I'm at the Forum."

"You're seriously shopping right now?" Stacia shrieked. "We have to be on an airplane in a couple hours, and you just *now* realized you're missing something?"

"I needed a new carry-on," Bryna said. She was in no hurry to leave before getting the man's name and number. That was for sure. "I'll be back soon."

"A carry-on," Stacia said dryly. "You have a full closet of bags, and I've seen your Louis Vuitton luggage."

"Well, you can never have too many. Plus, I got sidetracked in Tiffany's," she confided. She wasn't used to having people question and command her like this. She was trying to rein in her inner bitch, so she wouldn't tell her friend to fuck off.

"Bri!"

"And there's a cute guy. So, I have to go."

"B, walk out right now. No cute guys. We have a game to get to."

"You ruin all my fun," Bryna said in a pouty voice.

"Blame cheer."

"Fine. I will," Bryna said. "You know I'm only doing this because my mom cheered, right?"

"Yes. Sure. Not because you enjoy it," Stacia said sarcastically. "Your mom was a cheerleader, and your dad was a star football player. Maybe if you didn't hang out at Tiffany's with hot strangers, you could meet one of those yourself."

Bryna glanced over her shoulder at her hot stranger and lowered her voice. "But then, how will I know they can afford my lifestyle?" She was only half-joking. Or maybe she wasn't at all.

Stacia laughed. "You have a fair point. I hate to concede to it, but it *is* you. And I do want a wealthy, hot NFL quarterback," she said dreamily. "We're not asking for too much, are we?"

"Definitely not. I really have to go. I'll come back soon."

"Hurry up," Stacia said before they disconnected.

Bryna dropped her phone back into her purse and then returned to the counter. Luckily, the guy was still standing there. It seemed he had purchased something while she was on the phone.

She went to take the earrings out of her ears. "Sorry. No time to get these. I have to head out. At least you found what you were looking for."

"Yes, I did."

The man held the bag out to her, and she stopped trying to fiddle with the earring clasp.

"What?"

"I told you that you needed them," he told her.

"I'm confused."

"I got them for you."

"You purchased the earrings?" she whispered in surprise. She had said to Stacia that she wanted someone to support her lifestyle, but she hadn't quite expected *this*.

"I couldn't let you leave without them."

"Wow." She took the bag from him. "You didn't have to do that."

Of course, she was thrilled. She had rolled the ball toward him, and he had picked it up and put it on a pedestal.

"No. But I wanted to."

It was official. This guy was too perfect. She wished she had more time.

"Thank you."

"You're welcome. It was nice meeting you."

"Bri," she said automatically.

He took her hand and firmly shook it once. "Nice to meet you, Bri. I'm Hugh."

He smiled and then left before her. She had no idea what to make of all of that. A guy didn't buy a girl twenty-two-hundred-dollar diamond earrings and then not ask for her number…or something more in return.

As she exited the store, she opened the blue Tiffany's bag and peered inside. There was a blue pouch with her other earrings inside and a crisp white business card.

HUGH WESTERCAMP

WC RESORTS

On the back, he had scribbled his number. But that wasn't the only thing that made her stomach tighten with excitement. WC Resorts owned casinos and resorts on the Strip as well as other locations. And the sole owner of the entire conglomerate and resort fortune.

Hugh Westercamp.

FIVE

BRYNA AND STACIA were going to be perfectly on time for the flight out to Oregon even though Stacia was complaining the whole way about Bryna being late. Her head was up in the clouds though, and she was tuning out Stacia's comments. No wonder she had thought the situation had all the right characteristics for her to be interested. The man was Hugh Westercamp.

Just the thought made her skin tingle with excitement. She would have to play this right. A man like that wouldn't accept just anyone. She was shocked he had even given her his number. He must have been so fucking confident that she would call.

Déjà vu hit her something fierce. She remembered leaving her number with Jude, knowing that he must have been interested after the incredible night they had spent together with their intimate deep connection.

She rolled her eyes. *What bullshit!*

There had been no connection. Just hot sex and a whole lot of deception. At least she could take what had happened in her past and make it work for her here. If Hugh was used to something happening, then she'd need to be unpredictable. The card weighed heavily in her purse, but she vowed to ignore it for as long as she could. Absence made the heart grow fonder. Or at least she hoped it would make his wallet fonder.

"So, tell me about the hot stranger," Stacia said. She hoisted her cheer bag out of the back of her SUV. "I see you have new bling. Atlas Collection. Obsessed!"

Bryna shrugged. She wasn't ready to reveal all her secrets yet. The girls knew how she was, but Hugh felt like an investment she would have to take seriously or else it could all slip away.

"It was nothing. He was cute."

"Older?" she guessed.

"Much. But I like that."

"I know. I think you want a guy who already has a job and a career, so you can fit into his life."

Fair assessment. "Nothing wrong with coming to college to get your MRS degree."

"Don't let Trihn hear you say that," Stacia said with a giggle.

They walked into the airport where they were meeting the team.

"We'd both get a lecture on how college is about more than just finding a husband."

"Of course it is. There are football, parties, drinking, dancing, cheer," Bryna rattled off.

Stacia giggled in agreement. "So, did you give the guy your number?"

"Nope." That was true. Stacia hadn't asked if she had gotten his number. "I told you, it was nothing."

"Well, you know what *is* something? Blaine," she said with a sigh.

Their eyes were drawn to the quarterback, who was laughing and making jokes with his friends.

"You are not hooking up with Blaine this weekend."

"Maybe. But my options are open. I bet we'll both find someone sexy to hook up with," Stacia said confidently.

Bryna's eye caught on Andrew Holloway, who was standing near Blaine, and he smiled broadly at her attention. Yeah. She was pretty sure she could do that in the meantime while her plans came together.

LV State beat Oregon by a field goal in overtime. Bryna screamed at the top of her lungs and excitedly jumped up and down. Stacia barreled into her and hugged her tightly. Leaving Stacia behind, Bryna threw herself at her base, Daniel.

"We won! We won! We won!" she screamed.

He picked her up and threw her into the air as if she weighed nothing. To him, she supposed she probably did, considering he hoisted her into the air with one arm pretty regularly.

"So fucking awesome," he said when she landed back in his arms.

The girls cheered on the sidelines toward the LV State fans who had made it out to the away game. The players raced past the cheerleaders and jumping over the barrier into the stands. The crowd clapped them on the back with congratulations. The press was all over it like a field day, snapping pictures and rolling the cameras.

In the mayhem, Bryna felt someone circle an arm around her waist. She looked up to see Andrew smiling down at her.

"Hey, Bri."

"Andrew! Congratulations! That was an amazing game!"

His hand moved a little lower, and he winked. "Maybe we can make it an amazing after-party?"

She smiled. "Maybe."

She wished he were someone else—Hugh preferably. But Hugh was a game, and this was just for fun. Stacia was right when she'd said Bryna should hook up with people while she waited for the prize. Some fun wouldn't hurt anything.

"Find me later."

And he did.

Even though the team was instructed to remain model examples as they were here representing their school, a raging party broke out at the hotel. Bryna was swept away with the energy from their victory and ended up disappearing back to Andrew's room.

Her head was fuzzy as she let him drag her into his empty room. The lights were off, and she ran into a chair, falling down, and landing hard on her ass. She broke into a fit of laughter as she tried to right herself. Andrew was there, lifting her easily from the ground and pushing her toward the bed.

His hands were on her body, pushing at the material of her slinky black dress and riding it up to her hips. He groped at her breasts, and she tried to relax into his touch. This was what she wanted. This was what she had done all summer with random strangers in Europe. She was glad she was drunk enough that she might not remember it in the morning.

This wasn't about love or passion. Just sex. Just fulfilling her needs.

Andrew's lips were heavy on hers as he forced her mouth open. His tongue was an invasion. He tasted like stale beer and cigarettes. She hadn't even known he smoked. *Whatever.* She wasn't going to think about it. She fisted his shirt in her hands and returned his kiss with enthusiasm.

"God, Bri, you're fucking hot," Andrew breathed. He twisted her breast and then grasped her bare thigh. "I knew I'd get inside this all along."

"You knew?" she asked.

He sat on the bed and yanked her down on top of him. "Yeah, babe. Now, let's get you out of this dress."

He pulled the material over her head, rolled her over flat on the bed, and covered her body. His hands were everywhere, drawing a road map on her skin as clumsily as he could. Then, he fiddled with himself, slid on a condom, and reached down to shove her underwear aside.

It had been a while since she had sex, and even though Andrew wasn't the person she wanted to be on top of her right now, he would have to do. He wasn't a conquest in the same way. He was more of a plaything, and she wasn't going to think about the fact that she could do better than him and had done so in the past.

Her body responded as if it had been starving for attention. Europe was a distant memory. When she came, it wasn't earth-shattering, but it did the job better than masturbating. And it was damn better than waiting around for Mr. Right to never show up. Otherwise, she would never have sex again.

Later, when she returned to the room she shared with Stacia, she wasn't even surprised to find it empty. Stacia had said she was going to find her own fun even if it wasn't with Blaine. Bryna changed into her silk slip and crawled under the hotel comforter. She didn't even crinkle her nose at the lack of quality compared to what she was used to. She rested her head on the pillow and tried to let sleep take her, but her heart constricted.

This was right. This was how life was supposed to be.

Love was an illusion. It didn't exist in her world.

She shouldn't expect it. There was no point in searching for it. All it had ever done was weaken her, turn her into an idiot, force her to make bad choices, and completely lose control.

She had the control now.

No matter how empty she felt on the inside.

The next morning, Bryna shrugged off Stacia's questions about her night. She didn't want to talk about it. It had been a while since she felt so low. And it made zero sense. After such a victory, she should have been unbelievably happy, yet she had lain awake for far too long, trying to fall asleep and chase the memories away.

She was not broken. Today, she would renew her calm confidence and forget about the momentary slip.

They were transported back to the airport, and she sank heavily into her assigned seat on the airplane. Her head was throbbing. She was in no mood to talk to anyone. It was too early in the morning, and she hadn't gotten enough sleep. As soon as the plane took off, she was going to put in her headphones and pass out. She wished she were flying private, so she would have a bed to sleep in. That would be ideal.

"Bryna!" Beth said, appearing in front of her.

Beth was a senior on the cheer team and a real pain in the ass.

"Hey, Beth," she said.

"You're sitting next to Greg, right?" she asked.

"Uh…yeah, I think so."

"Can we switch seats?"

Bryna arched an eyebrow. "Why?"

"Why do you think?" She flipped her dark brown ponytail and winked. "Plus, you'll be at the front of the plane, so first off."

Bryna wanted to ask what Beth was going to do for *her* if she switched, but it was a sign of how out of it she was that she didn't. "Fine. Where are you sitting?"

Beth breathed out a sigh of relief as if she had thought it was going to be more difficult than that. She handed over her plane ticket, and Bryna grabbed her bags and trudged up the aisle. She found her row empty and took the aisle seat even though Beth's ticket directed her to the window.

Bryna hated window seats. She hated the thought of climbing over people to have to get up. She hated waiting for someone else to get out of the way, so she could get to her bags. In fact, this was why she hated coach, too. If she couldn't fly private, then it absolutely should be first class.

She hoisted her carry-on into the overhead bin, retrieved her headphones, and placed her purse under the seat in front of her. She was blissfully unaware of her surroundings as soon as she closed her eyes and turned on her music. This was her Zen. As long as no one disturbed her, she might be able to control the über bitchiness that was bubbling right under the surface this morning.

A tap on her shoulder pulled her right out of her happy place. She yanked off her headphones and glared up at the person who had disturbed her.

"You're in the wrong seat," Eric grumbled.

Fucking great.

"We meet again," she said dryly.

"You're in the wrong seat," he repeated.

"I switched with Beth. She wanted to sit by Greg. I'm sure if I had *known* I'd have to sit by you on the way home, I wouldn't have been so generous."

"Generous," he said with a chuckle. "I've heard you're very generous."

She ignored the jab and rolled her eyes. "Just what I wanted."

Eric threw his bag up next to hers. "Seemed that way at Posse."

Bryna hadn't talked to him since that night, and if she'd had it her way, she wouldn't be having this conversation at all. Especially after the night she'd had, she was in no mood for this.

"Don't flatter yourself."

"Didn't have to," he said. He crossed his arms over his muscular chest. "You did that for me, remember?"

Bryna glowered at him. *Seriously, what is wrong with him? All this because I'm sitting in Beth's seat? Fuck off already!* "You have no idea what you're talking about, so I suggest you shut the fuck up," she said.

At her profanity, the people in the seats surrounding them glanced over, but Eric pointedly smiled at them, and they quickly looked away.

He leaned forward before speaking again, "Why don't you scoot over?"

"Um…no. I like the aisle. If I have to demean myself by flying coach, I'm staying in the aisle."

"Wow. Flying coach must be so rough for you," he said as sarcastically as possible. Then, he stepped over her legs and sank into the seat next to her. He pushed his backpack under the seat and removed his own headphones.

"I prefer to fly private," she said.

"Why does none of this surprise me?"

Bryna gritted her teeth. She had given him the benefit of the doubt earlier because she admired his football skills. But her temper was flaring, and she wasn't sure she was going to be able to handle this right now.

"What the fuck is your problem? You don't know anything about me."

"I know enough," he drawled, untangling the cord of the headphones.

"Clearly nothing important. What about you, Cowboy?" she joked, but it came out with venom.

She knew Eric was from outside of Dallas, and the Southern drawl sometimes crept into his words.

"What should I know about you, other than that you're a self-righteous prick who likes to try to humiliate people and pick fights?"

"A self-righteous prick?" He raised his eyebrows and then nodded. "Seems you already know everything about me. Not sure why you asked me out if you thought that about me."

"Ugh! It was a joke."

"Asking me out?"

"Yes!" she snapped. "It was a joke."

"You don't have to cover it up, Bryna. I thought you were quite proud of your promiscuity," he said the last word so casually.

On any other day, she might have not cared about what he was saying about her, what he was insinuating about her reputation. But she'd had sex last night with Andrew, someone she didn't even care about. She wasn't ashamed of what she had done.

"Slut-shaming? That's a new one."

"I wasn't shaming you. Just making a statement about the facts," he said.

Bryna glared harder and tried to keep from biting his head off. She took a deep breath and then worked for her hardened exterior. "Promiscuous has such a negative connotation, Eric. I like sex. Maybe you don't?" she suggested.

It was as close as she could get to saying she knew he was gay without saying it. Though she was sure he probably had a lot of sex with other men, too. That seemed perfectly normal.

"I like sex," he said in that sweet Southern drawl.

She swallowed hard. *Hot.* "Anyway, I am *very* picky, so our conversation *had* to be a joke."

41

"I'm sure."

"You seriously have a negative opinion of me."

"I can't be the only one. You seem to make it rather easy."

She wasn't sure why that offended her, except that she had never done anything to Eric. He had this god-awful impression of her that made no sense. So, she had slept with one of the guys on the team last night. Who cared? Stacia had slept with a dozen. Yet Eric's venom was specifically for Bryna. She never saw him act this way around anyone else.

"Most people find me pretty awesome actually," she said through gritted teeth.

"Do you tell them that?" He gave her a pointed look.

"What? No!"

"You think very highly of yourself, is all, and you're not afraid to let other people know how great you are."

"What's wrong with that anyway?" she spat. *How dare he judge me!* "It's called self-confidence. More people should have it."

"There's self-confidence, and then there's *you*."

Bryna beamed as if what he was saying was a real prize. "Thank you."

"It wasn't a compliment," he said in frustration. "Kind of hard to get through to you up there."

"Hard to get through to me? Are you insane? Talking to you is like speaking to a brick wall. Are you even going to graduate on time? Aren't all jocks idiots?"

He stared blankly back at her, but she saw something brewing in his hazel eyes. He was irritated. She was turning into more of an annoyance than he had bargained for. It was clear he was trying to antagonize her to make her leave, but she had no intention of doing so. Not now for sure.

Something changed in his face as if he was resolute. Bryna braced herself for his barb.

"All jocks are idiots? At least we got into school based on talent, not on our parents' booster donations."

"I had a four-point-oh in high school. I had the grades and clearly the talent to get in here. Why the hell did they keep you anyway? It's not like you have talent anymore." She leaned into him to deliver her killing blow. "Let me ask you, Eric, what's it like not having a functional knee?"

Eric cringed.

She knew she had taken it too far, but he had started this shit. And she would certainly finish it. He already thought poorly of her. What would it matter if she dug her own grave?

Eric's mouth hung open slightly, and then he snapped it closed. His eyes were hard, but what she hadn't anticipated was the look on his face. It wasn't anger or disgust as he had every right to feel but rather determination.

He was quiet when he responded, "What's it like not having a working heart? Must be hard to continue living with a black pit in your chest."

He had no idea.

She opened her mouth to respond even though she had no clue what to say. He was right. She didn't have a functional heart, and it constantly felt like she had a black pit in her chest. But she couldn't let him know that.

"Come on, Bryna. Throw more punches. Get in some more swings. I can go all day like this."

And he looked serious.

She didn't know what to make of that. No one went head-to-head with her and came out ahead. But she didn't know what to say. She had no witty retort.

Finally, she shrugged and faced forward. "Whatever."

She plugged her headphones into her ears and tried not to notice the victorious smile that spread across his face.

He hadn't won.

Right?

SIX

"OH, HIM!" Stacia cried. She pointed out a tall guy with blond hair in the pool near where they were lounging. "What do you think about him?"

On this particularly beautiful Sunday afternoon, the girls had congregated outside at the pool at Posse. This was the last weekend they would be open since the weather was becoming more and more unpredictable. Unable to miss a good party, they had decided to forego studying to spend the afternoon checking out hot guys and drinking daiquiris.

"No," Bryna said. "He is definitely on steroids, and we all know what that means!"

"No way is he that tall and has a tiny dick, Bri. I refuse to believe it," Stacia cried. "Why must you ruin my fun?"

"I can't let you go and try to attach yourself to someone who does 'roids and won't satisfy you. It's for your own good."

Stacia stuck her bottom lip out. "Are you sure I can't peek to find out? Then, I could have all sorts of fun."

Maya appeared with their drinks. Her sleek black hair was tied back into a ponytail, and she looked like an African goddess. She handed Bryna a replacement strawberry daiquiri and brought Stacia some super sweet fruity concoction that Maya labeled the Cheer Slut. Stacia approved. Trihn took a water from Maya and lounged back in her chair.

"Drink?" Maya offered Trihn.

"Next round," she said. "Thanks though."

"Now, who are you two going on about?" Maya asked.

"The blond with great biceps and washboard abs," Stacia said.

"Keith? He's a regular and a regular douche bag. He grabs everyone's ass and fucks everything that walks," Maya filled them in.

Stacia sighed and glanced hopefully up at Maya. "But does he have a small dick?"

Bryna burst out laughing. *Only Stacia.* "Get your priorities straight."

"They are!"

It felt good to cut loose and laugh with her friends. She had been tightly wound all week since the Oregon game. Even fucking Andrew again, twice, and winning their game this past weekend hadn't removed the stress from her shoulders. Today felt like a detox. Exactly what she needed.

Maya shook her head. "I'll ask around for you, S."

"Good, and thanks," Stacia said with a broad smile.

"Anytime. You know I like to take care of my friends."

"True," Stacia agreed.

"Hey, have you figured out the mystery with the owner?" Bryna asked.

Maya had told them a couple of weeks ago that the owner of Posse was some incredibly secretive man. He had purchased the property and built the best club in town but never took any of the credit. No one had ever met him, not even employees. He was the Gatsby of his own Vegas party—always watching from high up, but never letting anyone get near him.

"No!" Maya cried. She leaned into her hip and flipped her black hair to one side. "A group of us are trying to figure it out. We think a couple of guys in upper management might know something. One of the girls thinks she can get it out of them by sleeping with one of them."

Bryna laughed. "Sounds like Stacia's kind of plan."

Stacia shrugged. "I'd do it."

"I know you would. But no luck yet. All we know is that he was some hotshot in Atlanta before moving here, and supposedly, he's single." Maya winked at the girls.

"Who do I need to sleep with?" Stacia perked up at the thought of meeting the millionaire mogul who had created her favorite club.

"And I thought you wanted an NFL quarterback," Bryna said with an arched eyebrow.

Stacia sighed heavily in despair. "Blaine won't even give me the time of day. He keeps calling me Stacy."

"I told you!"

"Yeah, well, if he keeps this up, I'll start honing in on the backup. He's hot, and he will probably be the starter next year. I'll have a leg up."

"Oh, I'm sure you will," Maya said. She nudged her. "Isn't the backup Marshall Matthews?"

"Yeah," Stacia said surprised. "How do you know him?"

"I think I have a class with him."

"Maya, you know everyone!" Stacia crooned.

"I'm a bartender. That's my job. Speaking of my job," she said, glancing around, "I should probably make a circuit and then come back. Don't want the boss to get on me."

"Force him to take you to the owner," Bryna said.

Maya laughed and nodded. "Done."

"You know they won't say anything to you," Trihn said, finally speaking up.

"You've been in the clouds a bit, Trihni," Maya said with a smirk. "I wonder why that is?"

"What?" Bryna tugged off her Gucci sunglasses and gave Trihn a pointed look. "What are we missing?"

Trihn shrugged. "Nothing. I was just thinking. What were you talking about anyway?"

"Who is he?" Bryna asked. "No one thinks that long unless it's about a guy."

"Oh my God! Is he hot? Is he here?" Stacia's eyes scanned the pool perimeter.

Maya grinned wide. "You haven't told them yet?"

"Told us what?" Stacia bounced excitedly.

"Really, Maya?" Trihn asked, exasperated.

Maya cackled and then walked away with her hands raised as if she hadn't done anything.

"It's nothing," Trihn insisted. "No big deal, which is why I haven't mentioned it."

"If it's no big deal, then dish!" Bryna cried.

Trihn sighed. "Fine. You win." She sat up in her seat and placed her untouched water on the side table. "I met a guy last week while you guys were out of town. His name is Neal. He's a graphic design major in the art school. We actually have art history together."

"And?" Stacia asked.

"And...we went on a date. Okay, two dates this week."

"Two dates, and we're just now hearing about this guy who is no big deal?" Bryna asked. That didn't sound like no big deal to her.

"It didn't feel like a big deal until you spelled it out like that. He was just a guy."

"A cute guy?" Stacia prompted.

"Very. I guess we're dating. I don't know. We haven't clarified anything yet, but he's a great kisser," Trihn said with a smile.

Bryna smiled to try to keep from laughing. Of course, Trihn was the normal one, who went on dates with a guy and proceeded to kissing and then on from there. That was totally typical behavior. Instead, Stacia was spreading her legs up the ladder on the football team, and Bryna had fucked Andrew twice now without any interest in getting involved with him. *Why does none of this surprise me?*

"Kissing." Stacia giggled. "I'm not sure I kissed the last guy I was with."

Trihn rolled her eyes. "Of course you didn't, but you also didn't want to date him either."

"You're right."

"If it becomes more than it is, I'll let you guys meet him. But I don't want to scare him away. I kind of like him." Her glowing smile said she more than liked him. "And what about you, Bri? I've heard all about Stacia's wild rides…literally. What's with Andrew Holloway, huh?" She wiggled her eyebrows up and down.

"Nothing."

She wasn't surprised Trihn knew about Andrew. Everyone knew about Andrew because he had a big mouth. It was fine by her for now—as long as it was mutually beneficial. But it really meant nothing to her.

"Is that a thing now?" Trihn asked. "I didn't think you'd be into him."

Bryna waved her hand. "It's not a thing. We're having fun."

"Not the way I heard it," Stacia crooned.

"Of course, Andrew was bragging. He wants you to think it's something more than it is," Bryna told them.

"Okay." Trihn raised her hands in defense but didn't seem to buy it.

"Well, what about hot stranger?" Stacia suggestively raised her eyebrows. "You're into him."

"What did I miss?" Trihn asked.

Bryna quickly filled Trihn in on meeting Hugh at Tiffany's. Bryna had been thinking about calling him all week. Holding off this long had been harder than she had thought it would be. She had used Andrew as a distraction from her real plans.

"Wait! You didn't tell me he left you his number!" Stacia cried. "Have you called him?"

"No," Bryna confessed.

She really did want to make him wait. She knew being unpredictable was something that guys who had everything found irresistible. Bryna was good at that.

"What are you waiting for?" Stacia asked.

"Yeah. Why are you dicking around with Andrew when this Hugh guy is right in front of you?" Trihn asked.

These were all great questions. Her friends wouldn't understand the rules she had in place to guard herself. She hadn't told them everything that happened with Jude, and she never intended to. She never intended to tell anyone about what had happened. Her horrid stepbrother, Pace, knew some of it...the worst of it, and Gates knew everything. But they were both people she didn't see anymore, and she wanted to keep it that way. This was an all-new Bryna.

On the other hand, waiting felt like it was taking all of eternity. She wanted to meet up with Hugh again. She wanted to start in on this new adventure...start in on the plan she had made the night Jude left her. She wasn't wearing her scarlet letter at the pool, but she still had every intention of flaunting her gold-digger status like a new skin.

"Maybe I will call him," she said finally. She would break her rules just this once. "I'll do it now."

She pulled her phone and Hugh's business card out of her Bendel tote bag, slipped her feet into her sandals, and then trudged away from her friends. She walked until she found a place secluded from the pool and the music jamming through the speakers.

She dialed his number and twirled the card around between her fingers while she waited for him to answer.

His voice cut through the line after the third ring. "Hello?"

"Hey, this is Bri," she said. She left it hanging. No explanation. Surely, he remembered her.

"Bri." He let the name roll off his tongue. "It's good to hear from you. I'm a little surprised it took you so long."

A slow smile spread across her face. *Perfect.*

"It hasn't been that long," she cooed.

"No," he agreed. "But longer than expected."

"Glad I could surprise you."

"I don't like surprises," he said.

Her stomach knotted at the words, but she held back her retort. He might say that, but he was still on the phone with her, and he had sounded pleased to hear it was her. She figured men generally didn't know what they wanted until she gave it to them. Hugh couldn't be that different.

"But..." he drawled.

"Yes?"

"I am glad you called."

Good.

"And I'm glad you left your card. It would have been a tragedy for us to meet and have no way to get in contact with each other," she teased.

"Why is that?"

"Because," she said lightly, "then you wouldn't be able to take me out."

"You are forward, aren't you?"

"You're the one who bought me Tiffany's earrings and then left a phone number."

He laughed. "True."

Check...

"I'll be in town again in two weeks. Dinner?"

Mate.

"I'd love to."

SEVEN

TWO WEEKS FLEW BY with two more wins for the undefeated Gamblers football team. But instead of celebrating their winnings or using the time to study for her rapidly approaching set of midterm exams, Bryna was getting ready for her upcoming date with Hugh. She wanted to be on her A game. This was her first official foray into digging. At least the first time she had consented to participating. Whether or not Hugh realized what this was, was a different story.

He was handsome, but to her, it was a game. It was a way for her to feel in control and get what she wanted. No feelings. No emotions. No connections. He didn't even need to know about the game to participate. And if he turned out not to be the perfect target, she could find other ones here in Las Vegas. If she really went searching, it would be easy enough to find a guy who came into the city on business and wanted to take care of a pretty face.

But Hugh was the pièce de résistance. There weren't many sugar daddies out there who could top a resort owner. She would make it work.

Bryna fitted the Atlas diamond earrings into her ears and adjusted her Harry Winston B around her neck—the perfect finishing touches to her ensemble.

Since she wasn't sure where they were going, she had gone for a killer outfit but nothing too fancy. She wore a skintight racerback burgundy dress and black high heels with gold glitter bows. She had a matching black clutch. Her hair was twisted around the back of her head into a loose side ponytail where it flowed long and curly over her right shoulder.

She was prepared for anything that might be thrown her way. By the time the doorbell rang at her condo, she was cool and confident.

When she answered the door, Hugh was standing in the doorway in the hottest tailored suit she had ever seen. He paired it with a black button-up, no tie, and the top button was undone. He was freshly shaven and looked utterly delectable.

His easygoing smile was her favorite characteristic about him. He drank in her beauty but still held the self-confidence of a man who was used to getting his way. She found that super hot.

"Bri," he said. "Are you ready to go?"

"Yes. It's good to see you," she said, meaning it. She grabbed her clutch and followed him through the door.

Her heart was beating with excitement. She couldn't believe she was doing this—actually following through with her plan. It was exhilarating.

A black town car was waiting for them at the front of her building, and the driver held the door open for her to climb into the backseat. It was spacious and decadent, but a part of her had hoped for a sports car. Her father, Lawrence Turner, was obsessed with them and had passed that obsession on to her. She had learned to drive a stick at a very young age, and guys who drove them would get an automatic pass from her.

The drive was short, and soon enough, they were pulling up to the backside of the Paris Las Vegas Hotel and Casino. Bryna was surprised. She had expected a little more glitz and glamour from the man who owned his own resorts. She could go to a casino hotel any day of the week, not that she did. The only time she ventured to the Strip was when she wanted to go shopping. Most locals avoided the tourist traps.

"This way," he said. He took her hand and directed her through the glass doors.

A man greeted them at the entrance. "Welcome to the Paris Las Vegas Hotel and Casino. Allow me to escort you."

Bryna raised her eyebrows but didn't say anything. Maybe she had been too hasty in her assumptions.

The man took them through a side elevator not accessible to the public. Up, up, up they went. Still, Bryna remained silent. Anticipation was a knot in the middle of her stomach.

Where the hell is he taking me?

The elevator dinged open.

"Here you are," their escort said with a grin.

When Bryna rounded the corner with Hugh, her mouth dropped open. There were only a couple of upscale restaurants inside the Paris hotel, and she had kind of figured he would choose the best, but she hadn't expected this.

They were inside the Eiffel Tower Restaurant, renowned for its French cuisine. It sat over a hundred feet above the Vegas Strip, overlooking the Fountains of Bellagio, which were lit up at that very moment.

But the most incredible thing was that the restaurant was completely and totally empty. Not a single person was inside. Candles blazed on every table, and soft classical music filtered in through the speakers.

"What is all of this?" she asked breathlessly. More of her surprise came through with her question than she should have let on, but she couldn't help it.

Hugh had set a new bar for a first date.

"The head chef and I are close friends. When I told him of my intentions, he offered a special culinary experience unlike anything you've ever seen. I assume you like French food?" he asked casually, as if renting out the Eiffel Tower was no big deal.

Good God! Maybe it was no big deal.

She wasn't normally blinded by luxury. Her father was an incredibly successful Hollywood director. Her family always had money, but this extravagance for someone he had just met surprised her.

She tilted her head up and let the shock pass over her. She was worthy of this. She was fucking Bryna Turner. This was the treatment she deserved and the treatment she would continue to expect. This was her game after all.

"I spent half of my summer in France. Of course, I enjoyed their food." She sent him a radiant smile.

He seemed to be judging her reaction to the whole thing and was pleased that she wasn't freaking. Perhaps she had passed her first test.

A waiter appeared a minute later and showed them to their seats against the glass windows where a single rose sat in a vase on the table. She tried to refrain from crinkling her nose at the flower. Jude Rose had made her hate her once favorite flower. She should have realized all those thorns were there for a reason.

"I've never been here before," she confided.

"Well then, you're in for a treat," Hugh said. "The chef has prepared a special menu for us—five courses, all original creations."

Bryna raised her eyebrows. He was bringing out the big guns early. *Is he trying to impress me, or is this normal behavior?*

Their first course was paired with win that complemented the dish, and it was then when she finally felt like she could lead the conversation to more important things.

"So, this is all incredible," she murmured. "How is this even feasible?"

He laughed softly. "Anything is possible. I thought you would enjoy it."

"I am. I was just curious, what exactly do you do?"

She knew it was the fatal question. *Do or die.* It was the one that would seal her fate as a gold-digging slut-bag whore. But she'd asked it anyway, completely on purpose. She didn't want to be in over her head. She had chosen this, and she wanted to make sure Hugh wasn't about to walk away at the first sign.

Hugh raised his eyebrows. "You didn't look me up?"

"I already knew of WC Resorts. When I saw your business card, I knew who you were," she told him.

"Yet you didn't call right away." Surprise slipped into his voice.

She liked it. He knew that his name elicited a certain reaction, and she had deviated from that. *Good.*

"Well, I wasn't sure I wanted to."

"What changed your mind?"

"You did. I figured any man who was confident enough to leave his card with a girl deserved a phone call. It usually works the other way around," she teased.

"I figured a girl who was confident enough to call me back deserved the Eiffel Tower." His eyes were alight with humor. "It normally works the other way around."

She laughed lightly. "All it takes is a phone call?"

"For you," he said pointedly.

"Fair." She smiled at the compliment.

Clearly, he thought she was special enough to give her the star treatment, to offer her the Eiffel Tower.

"Besides taking me out to dinner, what does a resort owner's life look like?" she asked.

"All business. Little time for pleasure," he said the last word delicately. "I keep the business running, visit the various locations, meet with investors—that kind of thing."

"I see. You're not in Vegas all the time?"

"No. I live in Vail and work out of the resort there. I'm usually only in Vegas once, maybe twice a month," he said.

"I see." She made a mental note about that. It would only make this whole situation easier for her. Between cheer, classes, and her rather active social life, fitting in a digging situation would be difficult. This seemed perfect.

"What about you?"

"What about me? I live here. I'm here all the time," she said, playing coy.

"What do you do here?"

She sighed. *Time to take a cue from history.* She looked up at him from under her thick black lashes and smiled. "Do you really want to know?"

"I'm interested in you," he told her.

"Come on. Don't you like the mystery of it all?" It was so easy to slide back into the routine. "Isn't it more fun this way?"

Hugh eyed her curiously. "You're going to be a lot of trouble, aren't you?"

She gave him the most innocent look she could muster. "Me?" A smirk touched her lips, and she lost all pretense. "Not unless your idea of trouble is *a lot* of fun."

Turned out his idea of trouble *was* a lot of fun.

Bryna's body slammed back into the wall of the mirrored elevator. Hugh covered her, and his lips landed on hers without asking for permission. He claimed her like he had paid for this kiss with dinner. She didn't mind. His kisses were hot as sin. And she felt a sin coming on.

Her body heated to his touch. After an evening of clever banter and sexual tension that could have been cut with a spoon, it felt good to finally have his mouth on hers, to taste him.

His tongue ran along her bottom lip before entering her mouth, and she sighed with pleasure. This was what it was supposed to feel like—pure blissful tension and sexual cravings crashing down between them. Nothing like the stupidity that came with necessity from being with Andrew and none of the feelings of being with anyone else. Just the knowledge that, here, she was in control.

She ground her body against him, and his hands reached out and firmly grasped her hips. His fingers dug into her flesh to the point where it almost hurt. She might be bruised there tomorrow, and it only made her smile. Here was a man who knew what he wanted and how to take it. The pure self-assurance was like a shot of adrenaline to her system. Nothing was sexier than a man cocky with his cock.

The elevator stopped at the bottom floor, and Hugh glided away from her as if they hadn't been close to ripping each other's clothes off. She saw herself in the mirror then. Her hair was coming out of the ponytail, her cheeks were flushed, and even her dress was a little rumpled.

Dear God, they had only been in there for a minute. *I've fucking missed this!*

Hugh took her hand again, and they walked silently back to his town car. The energy between them was sizzling like a lit firecracker. She could tell how desperately he wanted her, his prize at the end of the evening.

She slid in beside him, and he drew her in close. His mouth found the curve of her neck. He kissed along the soft sensitive skin.

"I had a good time," he murmured.

She swallowed hard. "Me, too."

"I don't want the night to end."

She wasn't sure if that was a question, a statement, or a command. With him, it really could be any of the above.

"Me neither."

"Come back with me."

Now, that was *definitely* a command.

"I want to…" She let her words linger in the space between them.

"Then, do."

"But…" She hesitated.

This was where her powers rested. She knew what she wanted out of all this. She could tell *exactly* what he wanted from her. The longer she held out, the more he would want it. If she gave in tonight, she would be like every other girl he had probably done this with. She wasn't naive enough to think someone this smooth had never been with anyone else other than his wife…who she was also sure he had. She would never be naive like that again.

This wasn't about love. This was about lust and diamonds. The longer he lusted, the more diamonds.

"No buts," he insisted.

"I can't," she finally got out. "I want to, but I can't."

Bryna, the girl who had fucked Andrew for kicks and giggles countless times since their first foray as fuck buddies, was turning down someone she *actually* wanted to sleep with.

All for her games.

This had better be worth it.

EIGHT

"OH GOD," Bryna moaned. "Oh God, yes. Right there."

Her cries were elevating as Andrew finished, and she came right after him. She fell forward on top of his muscled chest. She was breathing hard and had probably just ruined the fifty-dollar blowout she had gotten earlier. The thought made her giggle. *Blowout.*

"What's so funny?" Andrew asked. He squeezed her waist and nuzzled her neck.

Okay. Enough. Enough.

"Nothing."

She hopped off of him and went into the restroom to clean up and check out her hair. *Just a little mussed. Nothing too bad.* Plus, her makeup was still intact. None of the flyaways and smudges that had come from a hot elevator make-out session with Hugh.

Bryna frowned at her reflection. In fact, she hadn't heard from Hugh all week, not since he had left her at her doorstep last weekend, even though she had given him her number and he had seemed interested in another date. She knew in the grand scheme of things, it wasn't that long to wait. But fear still gnawed at her. *Did I do the wrong thing in turning him down?* Sex was her biggest advantage in all of this. Holding out should have made him desperate for it. Maybe she had tried too hard to keep the cards in her hands.

No.

She wasn't going to doubt herself. She couldn't at this point. Hugh was interested. He was simply taking longer than she had expected. She wasn't going to think about it anymore tonight.

Her plans for the evening would keep her occupied at least. With the football team home for a bye week, they had decided to throw a huge Halloween party. Beth, from the cheerleading team, had taken the reins this year and was putting on the annual Slutfest at her house. Everyone who was anyone was supposed to be there, dressed up and ready to get shwasted.

Andrew had claimed that, last year, most of the guys didn't dress up in anything, except for their letterman jackets, but all the girls went all out. Bryna hadn't needed the encouragement to put together her outfit. She had decided on a rather appropriate Queen of Hearts dress, complete with a crown, red-heart stockings, and red high heels. She wouldn't be painting the roses red tonight.

She slid back into her outfit that Andrew had deftly removed earlier and added her crown. *Queen.*

"Hey, babe, maybe forget these?" he suggested, holding up her thong. "Then, I can have fun whenever I want to."

Bryna gave him an amused look. "And who says I'm not going to have fun elsewhere?"

"Because you had my dick inside you ten minutes ago."

"And?"

"Come on, Bri," Andrew groaned.

"You and I both know what this is, Andrew."

"Yeah, but it's so much fucking fun."

She shrugged. It was fun, but it wasn't completely satisfying either. At least it got her off well enough.

"We're fucking. Not dating. That means I can fuck anyone else at the party tonight, if I want to."

"Like who?" Andrew asked. "E?"

"What?" Bryna asked, taken by surprise. "Eric?"

"Yeah, Eric. I was there that night you asked him out, you know."

Bryna raised her eyebrows. "I'm not interested in Eric Wilkins, and he's not interested in me. That was a joke. I don't even like being around him. He's an asshole."

Andrew smiled at that as if she were making a joke. *What the hell is wrong with everyone?*

The doorbell downstairs tore her from her thoughts, and then she heard her friends' voices rising up the stairs.

"Bri!" Stacia cried. "Put your clothes back on, and stop fucking around. We saw Andrew's car in the driveway."

Bryna rolled her eyes. *Dear God.* "Anyway, get dressed. Almost time to go." She walked to the door.

"What if I lie here naked all night, waiting for you?"

She sighed heavily. "Then, you'll probably be waiting forever. At this rate of clinginess, I'm going to end up at someone else's place tonight."

"Mine?"

"No," she said. Then, she left.

She trotted down the stairs and into her living room.

"Hey, slut!" Stacia said. She was even more giggly and bouncy than normal in some slutty lingerie that maybe passed for a French maid.

Trihn was standing next to her, dressed like a rock star, in black cutoffs with a low-slung studded belt, a black bra, black leather vest, and thigh-high leather boots.

"Trihn, we said to dress up," Bryna said.

"Ha. You're hilarious."

Andrew trudged down a couple of minutes later. "Hey, Stacia, Trihn. You ladies look hot."

Stacia preened. "Thanks."

"Can you talk some sense into your friend while we wait?" he asked.

"No," Trihn said automatically. "Bryna wouldn't know sense if it punched her in the face."

"Wow. Thanks," Bryna said.

Trihn shrugged. "It's true."

"Harsh, Trihn," Stacia said.

"I mean it with all the love in my heart," she said. "Now, when is this group bus thing coming to pick us up? And do I have to hang out with football players all night?"

The doorbell ringing kept them from answering her.

"That must be them," Andrew said, bounding toward the door.

He opened it without waiting for Bryna's permission, and standing in the doorway was a relatively short man in a suit and tie with a large box in his hand.

"What's up?" Andrew asked.

"I have a delivery for Bri," the man said.

"That's me." She stepped forward.

He handed her the box, which she promptly transferred to Andrew.

"Sign here."

She scribbled her name down on the line. "Thank you."

Beep. Beep.

Her head popped up, and she saw the bus the guys had rented to transport them to and from Beth's house pulling up into her driveway.

"Come on, Holloway. Let's get the fuck going!" one of the football players yelled out the window.

"Put that on a chair, and we'll head out," Bryna told Andrew.

"That's a huge box," Trihn said.

"What is it?" Stacia asked.

Bryna shrugged. "I don't know. I didn't order anything."

The bus honked the horn twice more, indicating their impatience.

"Why don't you tell them we'll be there in a minute?" Bryna suggested to Andrew.

"Yeah. Sure."

When he disappeared through the door, she grabbed some scissors and cut open the box. The lid yanked free all in one motion. Inside was layer upon layer of silver tissue paper and a single red envelope. She reached for the card and turned it over to find a wax seal with a WC from a signet ring. Her heart fluttered.

Hugh.

She cracked open the seal and removed the cream linen paper. She read the short note, and it took everything in her not to jump up and down.

> BRI,
>
> CLEAR YOUR SCHEDULE FOR THURSDAY EVENING. I WANT YOU TO WEAR THIS FOR ME.
>
> SEVEN O'CLOCK?
>
> HUGH

"Well," Trihn asked, reading over her shoulder, "hot stranger worked out then?"

"Seems like it," she agreed.

"Oh my God, open it!" Stacia cried.

Bryna placed the card on the side table, and with shaking hands, she peeled back the layers of tissue paper. Inside was the most beautiful gown she had ever seen in her life. She removed it from the package, and it flowed with silky rose gold layers to her feet. The top was intricately hand-beaded with a series of tiny buttons to wrap up around her neck.

"Is that what I think it is?" Trihn asked. All her sarcasm was gone as she stared at the dress.

"I think it is," Bryna breathed.

Trihn delicately fingered the material as if she were touching pure gold. She turned the neckline in, so they could all see the tag, and they sighed in delight.

Alexander McQueen.

"This looks like an original, Bri," Trihn muttered in awe.

"Looks like I have a date for Thursday night," Bryna said.

She carefully hung the dress up in her closet, and then the girls hurried out to the bus. They chatted excitedly about the possibility of where she might be going in that beautiful dress.

Bryna slid into the seat beside Andrew, and he dropped an arm over her shoulders.

"Um, no," she said. She removed his arm and crossed her legs.

She was going to have to stop fucking him if he kept this up. She thought she had made herself clear.

"What was in the box?" Andrew asked, seemingly unperturbed.

The girls giggled but knew better than to answer.

"Nothing. It doesn't matter," Bryna said.

She wasn't going to talk about Hugh with anyone, other than the girls. People could think what they wanted about her, but she didn't need to encourage the dirty rumors that seemed to be floating around already.

"Nothing, huh?" Andrew asked, unconvinced.

"It was probably from one of her admirers," Eric said from the seat in front of them.

She hadn't even been paying attention to see that he was on the bus. There were about ten of them inside, and it was completely full. She suspected it would be dropping them off and then going back out to pick up more students. It would have been easier to go to Posse, but Beth had a big enough place that a lot of people would crash there, and Bryna had been told that things would get out of control.

"No one asked for your opinion, Eric," she snapped.

Eric leveled her with a look and shrugged. "Yes, Your Highness."

Even if she hadn't been wearing a crown tonight, she would have known he was mocking her. "Maybe if you treated people more like royalty, you wouldn't be such a prick."

Stacia made a playful scratching motion like a cat. "Retract your claws, B."

"Yeah," Andrew agreed. "Eric is the nicest guy on the team. He was joking."

Bryna raised her eyebrows and twirled her necklace. "I'm sure he was," she said sarcastically.

"Can't help it that you can't take a joke," Eric said.

His eyes were full of mischief, and she wanted to lean forward and smack that smile right off his face.

Here Eric was, the asshole, and she was the one catching flak because she had a bitch reputation. *Fabulous.*

Bryna plastered on her sweetest smile and stared right back at Eric. "You're right. Sorry. Thanks for helping to put this bus situation together."

"You're so bad at this," Stacia said, laughing.

"What? I'm being sincere!"

"My ass!" Trihn said.

"Fine. Forget being nice. It won't happen again. You all have totally ruined it." She glared at her friends. "It's not like Eric is even part of the team, so I don't know why he is even coming to this party."

"Babe, he's a student coach," Andrew said.

"Are any of the other coaches coming?" she asked.

"We're not doing this again, are we, Bryna?" Eric asked. "I busted my knee up a year and a half ago. I could still play if I wanted to risk it. I'm that good, but I happen to want to be able to walk when I'm older."

She pursed her lips. Arrogance was such a goddamn turn-on. She crossed her legs and tried to appear unaffected. She was not interested in Eric Wilkins because absolutely nothing could come from that. He was not interested. He was not interested in any women whatsoever. *Asshole.*

The conversation changed topics, and Bryna stayed out of it. She was trying to remember the Alexander McQueen dress waiting for her at home. That was what was important, not some stupid comments from football players.

The best part of it all was that, in the end, she had won this round with Hugh. Her game had worked out.

Tonight, she would get drunk with her friends and enjoy the Halloween weekend, but on Thursday night, she would be one step closer to the person she wanted to become.

And so the cycle would continue.

NINE

BRYNA TWIRLED IN HUGH'S ARMS around the crowded dance floor in the giant ballroom. They were at some gala for one of Hugh's business associates. It was a big affair with several hundred people all decked out in their best. So much wealth was all concentrated in one place. She didn't know what they were here for, but she didn't really care. It was an excuse to wear an expensive beautiful dress, and she would take any excuse for that.

The song ended, and Hugh escorted her over to a group of men standing around with their cocktails in hand, discussing business. Hugh jumped right in. The whole time, his hand rested lightly on the small of her back. In some ways, it was strange to be there but not there.

Arm candy.

Even when she had been with Gates and had purposely gone to events as his arm candy, she hadn't felt like this. She didn't mind, not really. But people seemed to *know* that was what she was, so they didn't talk to her. She was there to be looked at, not spoken to. She wondered if they thought she must be an idiot with a pretty face. Or maybe they didn't care.

Bryna shrugged the discomfort away. She was wearing an Alexander McQueen original and living the life she wanted. *Who cared if all the men ogled me? Who cared if they direct all their conversations to Hugh?*

Hugh finished whatever he was saying and then made some excuse for them to walk away. His hand still rested possessively on her back.

"Do you know how jealous every man in this room is?" he asked against her ear.

"How jealous?"

"Blindingly."

"And you like that." She knew he did.

"I like being the one to touch you in this dress when everyone else here is wishing for the same thing," he said.

He nipped at her earlobe, and she shivered all over.

Desire. It was such a strong motivator. It made smart men stupid. It was even more powerful than jealousy. But desire and jealousy combined? She might as well be carrying around his balls in her pocket.

"Let's go somewhere more private," he suggested.

Man, he really wants to get inside me.

She wondered what his colleagues thought of him bringing someone other than his wife here. She hadn't checked to see that he had one for sure, but she didn't really think she needed to. *Did all these men know he was cheating on his wife and not care? Or had he made some excuse about her?* It didn't really matter to her either way. Nothing was off the table at this point.

"All right," she agreed. Her nerves rattled a little.

She knew where this was leading, and she needed to make sure she could keep the ball in her court. When he kissed her, everything got fuzzy. It was easy to forget what she was doing with such a rush coursing through her body.

She knew Hugh had a room upstairs in the hotel, and she was sure that was where they were headed.

He had his arm tightly wrapped around her waist on the way to the elevators. They were walking down a darkened hallway with balconies overlooking the courtyard below. They had made it almost to the end when he stopped.

"On second thought." He grabbed her hand and pulled her into one of the balconies.

The curtains swished closed, partially obscuring the view into the hallway.

Her heartbeat skyrocketed when he looked at her. *Oh, yes.*

He was doing this. She could see it in the devious glint in his eyes that he wanted her right here, right now.

She slowly backed up until her hands hit the ledge of the stone balcony. "Anyone could see us in here," she said evenly. She tried to keep the excitement from her voice. Her whole body ached for him, and she had to somehow control her urges.

"I know."

"You're not worried that someone might try to look through the curtains?" She arched an eyebrow.

He took two paces in front of her. "Let them watch."

She swallowed hard. *Shit.*

"You seem nervous," he said.

She tilted her chin up. A haughty smile appeared on her face. "I'm never nervous."

"Good."

His hands landed softly on either side of her face, and then his lips were on hers. He tasted like scotch and honey and all things that made her melt on the spot.

How did he elicit such a reaction with one touch?

It had to be the forbidden nature of the affair. She needed it, craved it. It was too easy when she could have anything and everything she wanted on a silver spoon. She wanted more. She wanted power and passion and the knowledge that he wanted her more than anyone else in his life…if even for a moment.

Their kiss was electric, and he left her panting as his lips slid to her earlobe and then down her neck. She tilted her head back and breathed in the crisp, clean air, trying to right her senses. But when his hand reached down and grabbed her ass, she knew there was little hope for her.

How the hell am I supposed to keep from sleeping with him?

She had no fucking clue. And she wasn't even fighting it. Alexander McQueen had done the trick.

Her hands went to the waist of his pants, and she made quick work of the button and zipper. She forced her way into his boxer briefs and found him hard and ready for her. He roughly bit into her neck as she grasped him in her hand.

All hers.

"Fuck," he growled.

"That's what you want, isn't it?" she asked as she stroked him.

"Yes. But right now, I think I want you on your knees."

He pushed her shoulders down, knowing exactly what he wanted and knowing there was no way she could refuse him at this point. She struggled to her knees in a puddle of expensive fabric. She was both terrified that she would rip the outrageous gown and excited that he clearly cared so little for the price tag on the garment that he would risk tearing it.

He removed his cock from his pants, and she licked her lips.

His thumb traced the outline of her bottom lip. "I like that. Do it again."

She repeated the movement and swirled her tongue around his thumb where it rested at the corner of her mouth. He groaned and then seemed to lose control as he grabbed her head and shoved his dick down her throat.

She gasped around it and pulled back, so she could breathe. *Fuck!*

Hugh seemed unperturbed by her initial reaction and bobbed her head forward and back on his dick. She easily took up the motion, grasping on to his legs to steady herself. Her tongue licked up and down him as he filled her over and over again. She could feel her jaw locking up the longer he went at it, but she wasn't about to stop.

Bryna could hear footsteps and voices in the hallway, and it only added to the excitement. She knew she should have felt fear that some other guests from the gala might catch them at any minute, but she felt none of it. In fact, it only made her pulse beat harder and her core throb in time with their movements. He was going to need to do something about that after this.

Hugh grabbing her hair harder while shuddering was the only indication he gave before he came in her mouth. She swallowed quickly, taking him all back. As he watched her, she proceeded to lick him clean. He only moaned more at her touch.

She wiped her mouth with the back of her hand and then stood. He had already zipped his pants and put himself back together. She placed her hand on the balcony balustrade to steady herself. Her heart was beating a symphony in her chest.

Hugh circled her waist and pulled her in for a kiss. "Let's go upstairs, so I can return the favor."

She sighed into his embrace, wanting so desperately to let this be everything she was pretending it was. She wanted to be the girl in her boyfriend's arms, happy to go upstairs to let him ravage her all night. But she wasn't that girl.

"I've had an incredible night," she told him honestly. It was true. Even with the unexpected blow job, the night had been all but perfect.

"Good. Let's end it the right way," he suggested.

"I…can't stay the night."

"You don't have to."

She narrowed her eyes. "I'm not one of those girls."

"I don't know what those girls are, but I'm asking to spend more time with you. Is that really so bad?"

"Of course not. That's not what I meant."

"Then, stay," he persisted. His hands trailed to her neck where he slowly unbuttoned the top buttons of her dress. "I'll make it worth it."

Bryna nipped at his bottom lip and forced down the urge to agree with him. "Then, it'll be worth it another time, too."

His hand stilled at her neck, and he sighed. "You're one hard woman to pin down."

She smirked. "I think, in time, you'll come to find that is *not* true."

He laughed, and that easy smile, the one that had won her over the first time they met, came back on his face. She loved that smile.

"Maybe, in time, I will."

Hugh walked her back downstairs and then drove her across town to her condo. He gave her a passionate kiss good-bye that was so hot that she felt woozy while exiting the car. But by the time she got back into her empty condo, the feeling had worn off, and she was left empty all over again.

A part of her wanted to phone Andrew for a quick booty call, but she resisted the temptation. She would have sex with Hugh soon enough. When the time was right, she would move forward. At least, that was what she told herself as she brushed her teeth before falling into bed.

TEN

BRYNA STOOD OUTSIDE in her cheer uniform, holding her pom-poms. The weather was nice for the first weekend in November, but as the sun was setting, all the girls wore their black-gold-and-silver cheer jackets over their uniforms to ward off the chill before the annual homecoming parade.

Bryna was on her phone, lounging against the bed of a pickup truck. Andrew was texting her from his hotel room out of town with the rest of the football team, saying how boring it was and describing all the things he would rather be doing to her instead. It was a nice distraction even if he was getting really clingy.

Hugh had also been texting her semi-regularly since they had left the gala. He wasn't sure when he was going to be back in town again. She hadn't decided if this was a good thing yet. She wasn't anxious to find another excuse not to fuck Hugh, if she could even hold out any longer.

She wanted to fuck him. He was hot and wealthy and charming—everything she was looking for. He was Hugh Westercamp. He could have anyone he wanted, and he wanted her. That was what mattered.

"Bryna, come take a picture with me!" Stacia called. Three little girls were staring up at Stacia star struck.

"No, thanks. I'll wait right here."

Stacia pouted her bottom lip. "You can't be on that thing all night."

"I'll put it away when the parade starts."

"*One* picture? Please!"

As if on cue, Bryna's phone rang. "Sorry. I have to take this."

"Fine," Stacia spat.

Bryna glanced down at her phone in her hand and saw her father's name lighting up the screen. Her stomach dropped before she even answered the phone. "Hey, Daddy."

"Hey, sweetheart! How are you doing?"

"I'm great. We're about to start the homecoming parade. When should I expect you to be in town? Late tonight or really early tomorrow? You know what it's like," she said, babbling on. "We have to be at the stadium, dressed and ready early in the morning, so tonight would be better. Are you going to stay at the condo? Or did you get a hotel room? There's plenty of room at the condo, of course. I had the maid make up the guest room for you. On Sunday, I thought we could do brunch before you leave town. I'm dying to take you to this new place on campus. Also, Coach Galloway wanted me to remind you—"

"Bryna," he said softly.

"No," she stated firmly. "No. You're not doing this to me again! You promised me homecoming."

"I know, honey. But Celia has been sick lately, and she needs me here."

Bryna frowned. She despised Celia, her evil witch of a stepmother, for ruining her parents' marriage and then moving her Valley trash into her father's house—not to mention, for bringing her horrible stepbrother, Pace, into her life.

"So, you're choosing her over keeping your promise to your only daughter?"

Fire filled her veins. She couldn't believe this was happening again. He used to come to everything for her when she was younger, but ever since he'd married Celia and with his overindulgence in work, he hadn't come to anything. He had missed Christmas last year along with countless other important events for her over the years, but it had never been for something as ridiculous as this. And she had thought—after he had made it home for her charity function last year, even if it had been a fucking disaster with Jude there, as well as spending time together in Paris over the summer as promised—things would turn around. But no. She could never count on him for anything.

"Now, Bryna, that's enough! You're going to be there for three more years. I'll come next time."

"Sure you will." She ground her teeth together. "Why can't someone else take care of Celia? What is even wrong with her?"

He hesitated. "We're not sure yet. I didn't want to scare you, but she has to get some tests taken."

"What kind of tests?"

"We want to make sure everything is okay. Try not to worry about it."

"Okay," she said flippantly. "So, you're still not going to come then? Not at all?"

"I can't, Bryna, but I'm sending Pace in my place. He has some exciting news for you."

"Don't bother," Bryna growled. "I hate Pace, and you know it."

Her father sighed heavily on the phone. "He is coming up there for recruitment anyway. He doesn't even have to stay with you, if you don't want him to, but try to show him around."

"He can't go here, Daddy! You have to convince him to go somewhere else," she said, nearly hysterical.

"He's my son now, Bryna. He'll be a Gambler if I can help it. It's where he wants to go, just like you, and you're not going to stop him. Do you understand me?"

"He's your *son*?" She nearly gagged. "I can't even right now. That's seriously disturbing."

"Bryna—"

"You know what? Forget it. I'm sorry I'm just realizing that your new family is so much more important than your old family."

"Honey, you're overreacting. There would be serious implications for me if I left right now. I hate disappointing you, but you will always be my baby girl," her father said.

"Okay." She clearly wasn't getting into his head. The whole thing infuriated her. "Well, the parade is starting. So…bye."

"Bye, sweetheart."

She hung up the phone, even more pissed off than when she been talking to her dad. *How dare he!* With everything going on in her life, she had really been looking forward to spending some quality time with him, but no, he couldn't even manage that.

"Hey! Who was that?" Stacia asked, bounding over to Bryna.

"No one. Doesn't matter. Are you ready to go?" Bryna threw her phone into her pocket, stripped out of her jacket, tossed it on the back of the truck, and retrieved her poms.

"Yeah. Totally."

But it did matter, and Bryna couldn't let it go.

It only got worse when Pace showed up at her condo later that night.

"Hey, sis," he said.

He barreled inside, passing her, and she considered leaving to avoid him, but she couldn't even stay with Andrew, who was holed up in some hotel.

"Don't call me that," she spat.

"Don't tell me you're not excited that I'm in town," he said as if he didn't know she hated him. "You're going to have to get used to it because I have a feeling that I'm going to be here a whole lot more come January."

Bryna's face paled. "What do you mean?"

"Coach Galloway got the approval today. I'll officially be an LV State football player in January. I'll graduate high school a semester early and start classes in the spring. I won't get to play for this season, but I'll start practices."

She rested her hand on the couch to keep herself upright. "You're…moving to Las Vegas in two months?"

"Yeah. Dad said I could stay here until I got my own place."

Pace's smirk was so broad that she thought she might be sick. He was really serious.

"You cannot stay in my condo."

"Technically, it's Dad's condo, so—"

"Stop calling him that! He's not your dad!" she shrieked.

Pace dropped his bag in the middle of the living room and kicked back on the couch. He crossed his arms and stared up at her in a leering way she definitely couldn't miss.

"Keep yelling all you want, Bri. I like it when you yell."

Bryna's grip on the couch tightened as she kept from screaming in rage. "Just stay away from me and my friends."

"What? Think I know things about you that others don't? How many people know about senior year, Bri? How many know about Jude?"

She shuddered. "Leave him out of this. You have no idea what you're talking about."

"Oh, I think I do."

"Even if you did," she ground out, "senior year is long over, and I'm already tired of having you around again."

She stomped upstairs, trying to convince herself that she wasn't fleeing her sleazy stepbrother. *This weekend couldn't possibly get any worse.*

The next morning was a dry seventy-five degrees, and Bryna was cheering on the sidelines at the game. She could see Pace standing next to the team on the sidelines, and it infuriated her all the more. He hadn't even wanted to come to LV State until he knew she was interested in attending. Last year, he had made it his personal mission to try to ruin her life, and she was not looking forward to his reappearance since nothing had changed between them. He still wanted to torment her and also get in her pants. She wanted to get away from the reminder of what her father had done.

Right before the end of the first half, the cheerleaders were jostled closer to the football team to accommodate the marching band and all the alumni members of the football team, band, and auxiliaries—dance team, flag line, and baton twirlers. A figure moved to stand next to her, and she glanced up, surprised to see Eric.

"What?" she demanded. She was already on edge, and she and Eric did nothing but argue. "I'm really not in the mood today."

Eric frowned. "I was coming to see if your dad was here. Coach wanted to talk to him after the game, but he wasn't listed with the alumni players."

"Yeah, he's not here."

"All right. I thought you said he was coming."

Bryna closed her eyes and breathed out before answering, "My stepmother is sick, so he couldn't make it."

"I see. I hope she's okay," he said with sincere concern in his voice.

She rolled her eyes. "I hope she falls into a vat of acid."

"That's pleasant," Eric drawled. "What did she do to you?"

"Nothing. Broke up my parents, married my dad, and moved into my mother's house."

"So then, that's your stepbrother?" he asked, pointing to Pace.

Bryna nodded. "Unfortunately. Why?"

"They've been recruiting him. I think he's going to be here next year."

"Don't fucking remind me," she grumbled. "I can't stand the thought of that creep being here."

"He's a good ball player."

"So was O.J. Simpson," Bryna deadpanned.

Eric actually laughed out loud. He tilted his head back and closed his eyes. His whole body seemed to relax with it. "That's true."

Suddenly, Bryna felt uncomfortable. She wasn't supposed to be comfortable around Eric Wilkins. He was the prick who always picked fights with her. She knew his secrets, and he despised her for being *that* girl.

"Anyway, Pace is an asshole," Bryna said.

"I noticed that."

Bryna looked up at him in shock. Most people thought Pace was an angel. He put on a good act. She didn't think many other people could see through it. Certainly, no one in high school had. Her own father couldn't see through the bullshit.

"Well, have to go. Thought I'd check for Coach," Eric said quickly before disappearing into the crowd of football players running toward the locker room.

Pace approached her at the end of the game after the Gamblers had come out victorious, and she did everything she could not to scratch his eyes out. Being around him made everything worse. She was going to have to find a way to get him to leave.

"Good game," Pace said. "I'm really liking it here, sis."

He blatantly leered at her in her cheer uniform, and she momentarily wished she were more covered up. He was so disgusting.

"Don't get any ideas, asshole. You're not coming here next year." She hoped that saying it out loud would make it a reality.

"Oh, I have plenty of ideas," he said, looking her up and down.

"You're disgusting."

"Babe!" Andrew cried. He appeared at her side in that moment.

Without a second thought, he threw his arm around her waist and crushed his lips down onto hers. She breathed in the kiss in slight horror because Pace was watching. He had made it clear that he was out to sabotage her all over again. She didn't want him to sit around and watch everyone who was in her life.

She took a step back when he released her. "Hey."

"Who's this?" Andrew nodded his head at Pace.

"I'm her brother," Pace assured him.

"*Step*brother."

"Cool, man!" Andrew cried.

"I didn't know Bri was dating anyone," Pace said. He sent Bryna a questioning look.

"We're *not* dating," Bryna said automatically. She had been saying it since Andrew told everyone they were sleeping together.

Andrew seemed to believe her less and less.

"Same old, same old, huh, Bri?" Pace asked.

"Fuck off, Pace," she snarled. "Come on, Andrew. Let's get out of here."

Pace laughed at her retreating back. "See you tonight at Posse."

She shook her head and kept walking. She was not going to let him get to her any more than he'd already had.

"What was that all about?" Andrew asked once they were a safe distance away from Pace.

"Nothing. He's an asshole, but he wants to play football here next year."

"Cool!" Andrew said.

It was as if he hadn't heard a word she said besides football. *Ugh!*

"Oh my God!" Stacia shrieked. She rushed toward them and attached herself to Bryna's other arm. "Who was that guy? He's mega hot!"

"Stepbrother, S. Don't touch him with a ten-foot pole," Bryna demanded.

She stuck her bottom lip out. "You ruin all the fun!"

"He's still in high school anyway." *For two more months.* If she could help it, he wouldn't end up here.

Stacia shrugged. "Fine. Forget I mentioned it. Let's find Trihn and get ready for Posse tonight! Sorry, Andrew, I need to steal your girl."

"I am *not* his girl!" Bryna insisted.

"All right. Later, babe. See you tonight," Andrew said before planting a possessive kiss on her lips.

"Goddamn it. I can't keep doing this," she told Stacia as they walked away.

Andrew's insistence that they were dating was icing on the cake with all her other problems this weekend. She needed a drink something fierce to forget her own existence for a little while.

ELEVEN

POSSE WAS FILLED TO THE BRIM with students and alumni anxious to see the football players after the successful game. The bouncer wasn't admitting anyone else inside due to the fire code, but luckily, Bryna, Stacia, and Trihn were regulars, so they could bypass the wait.

Once they were inside, it was a swamp. She didn't want to deal with the crowds. She wanted to get wasted beyond comprehension and forget about this weekend, maybe even the whole week.

They finally made it to the bar where Maya was working. It wasn't often she was downstairs, but she was the best, and it was so busy that they must have needed her expertise.

"Peppermint Posse," Bryna called as soon as her friend appeared in front of her.

"Going for the strong shit tonight?" Maya yelled back.

"As strong as you can. I need it."

Bryna leaned back against the bar in her black sheer lace dress that left little up to the imagination, and she drank in the stares she was receiving. She had on her favorite classic red-lacquered Louboutins. She was ready to rule tonight. No more bullshit.

Maya handed her the drink, and Bryna promptly downed it as quickly as she could. She shuddered as the mint-flavored vodka martini set fire to her throat.

"Whoa! Take it easy. You have all night," Maya chastised her.

"Keep them coming," Bryna instructed.

"That's what she said," Stacia said with a giggle. She sidled up to Bryna at the bar, wearing a sapphire backless romper that tied around her neck. "Can I get something fruity?"

"Sure, sweets." Maya poured both of the drinks at once. "What about you, Trihni?"

Trihn shrugged. "The usual."

"You're looking particularly grungy today," Maya complimented her.

Trihn was decked out in a black leather skirt with a black sequined tank and studded combat boots. She had bangles on both wrists, almost up to her elbows, and onyx studs in her ears. Her makeup was especially heavy tonight.

Trihn ignored the comment, but when Neal appeared at her side, the reason for her extra effort became clear. He was cut and tall with shaggy brown hair and the same arsty look as Trihn. They looked like a matched set. It made Bryna sick.

"So, are you two officially dating now, or what?" Bryna asked. She reached for her second drink and guzzled it as if it was water and she had run a marathon.

"Bri, geez," Trihn said in exasperation.

"Just curious."

Bryna knew Trihn hated talking about her relationship. She was super private about it, and it made no sense.

Bryna and Stacia were completely open about theirs. *What did Trihn have to hide?*

"Are you and Andrew?" Trihn shot back.

"Oh my God, no! We're not even dating. This has to stop!"

She couldn't handle this anymore. *How many times would I have to say that Andrew and me aren't dating before people fucking figured it out?* They were fucking around, and that was all. She was going to have to prove a point tonight.

Bryna finished her drink and left it with Maya before abandoning her friends and heading straight to the dance floor. She danced with the first hot football player she could get her hands on. There was no Andrew in her life. At this point, he didn't fucking exist to her. Her head was full of vodka, and she was riding the wave on a surfboard.

After a few songs, Bryna had forgotten the faces of the different guys she had danced with. Someone had bought her a drink, something fruity that tasted like shit. She'd also miraculously done a round of shots with a group of people, but she couldn't remember what it was. She was wonderfully tipsy with her arms around a guy whom she strained to put a name to. All she knew was that he was cute, on the football team, and decidedly *not* Andrew.

His lips landed on hers, aggressive but sloppy. She ignored her own disgust and returned the kiss with vigor. Suddenly, she was wrenched back from the guy. She stumbled backward into another girl who cussed her out. Bryna didn't even bother apologizing.

Her eyes adjusted to what was going on. Andrew was all up in the guy's face, yelling profanities and holding his fist up as if he planned to punch him right then and there.

"Andrew, stop!" she shrieked, grabbing his arm.

"What the fuck, Bri? What is going on? Why did you have your tongue down this guy's throat?"

"We're not even dating. I can do whatever I want," she slurred.

"You're fucking joking, right?"

"No, I'm not."

"We've been fucking exclusively for over a month. What more do you want?"

"Who said we're exclusive?" she asked condescendingly.

"Well, have *you* fucked anyone else?" His eyes dared her to respond.

"Do you really want me to answer that?" she asked. She hadn't actually been with anyone else since she hadn't gotten that far with Hugh. But she had given a blow job earlier this week. *Did that count?*

"Fuck!" Andrew yelled. "Who is it? I'll fucking kill him."

"Get over yourself. This was supposed to be fun, Andrew, and now, you're making a scene. It's not fun anymore."

Andrew angrily shook his head and threw his arms out in frustration. "Sorry, I misunderstood. Enjoy your fucking night."

He stormed off, leaving her in the middle of the dance floor. All eyes were on her, and she felt their judgment from all sides. *Fuck, I'm so over this.* She needed another drink to stop thinking about her self-sabotage.

She made it back to the bar. Trihn was still with Neal talking to Maya. Both girls had concern in their eyes when Bryna returned.

"Another martini, Maya," Bryna said.

"Maybe you should slow down." Trihn lightly touched Bryna's arm. "What happened out there?"

"Pay attention," Bryna snapped. "Andrew and I aren't together."

"There you are, Bri!" Stacia cried. "I saw that shit on the dance floor. Are you okay?"

"Yes, I'm fine. I have *no* feelings for Andrew. I'm never going to have feelings for anyone ever again."

"But he has feelings for you," Trihn said. "It was kind of a bitch move to make out with someone else instead of just breaking up with him."

"We're not dating though!" Bryna rolled her eyes. *A bitch move. Great.* "Isn't that what everyone expects from me anyway? How is this any different?"

She was letting the alcohol and anger get the best of her, and she didn't even care. It was like every bit of emotion she had bottled up in the past eight months came rushing back to her all at once. She couldn't control it. She just rode the emotions like a train barreling off the tracks.

"We're trying to help," Trihn said. "You're kind of self-destructing."

Bryna shrugged unapologetically. "This is who I am. I'm the queen bitch. I accept my crown and title. Take it, or leave it. I've never pretended to be anyone else, and I never will."

She walked back to the dance floor to try to find someone else to buy her another drink. She had made a circuit on the floor when a hand on her shoulder stopped her in place.

"That was an interesting show."

Ugh! Pace.

"Fuck off. I have no reason to be around you, and I might turn homicidal if you remain in my presence."

"Oh, sis, you're such a sweet talker," he crooned.

Bryna reared back and slapped him clear across the face. His head jerked to the side. The sound ricocheted through the room. Her hand tingled from where she had hit him, and he roughly grabbed her wrist before she could walk away.

Pace bore down upon her as he laughed at the exchange. Despite that, she saw the unbridled anger in his eyes. He was furious with what had happened, and he looked like he was ready to take it out on her.

"Let me go!" she yelled.

"I don't think I will."

"Get the fuck off my campus, away from my friends and family, and out of my fucking life, you sick, twisted pervert!" she spat. She wobbled from the alcohol, and she knew her words hadn't come out completely right. But she didn't care.

"Okay," Pace agreed.

Bryna warily looked at him. Even drunk and sloppy, she knew that wasn't the right response. "Okay? Just like that?"

Pace gave her an once-over. "I'll leave and I won't come to LV State."

"What's the catch?"

He smiled. "It's really simple. I only want one thing."

She narrowed her eyes. "And what's that?"

"You. For one night."

"Oh my God," she cried, shaking her head. "Are you demented?"

He pulled her in really close, and she recoiled.

"We're not related, as you keep telling everyone, and anyway, I know you want me. Can't you feel all the sexual tension?" He ran his hand along her jaw.

She slapped it away. "There's *no* tension between us. Zero!"

"Let me have your body tonight, and then you can go back to doing whatever you want."

"Fucking you is quite possibly the last thing I want to do in this lifetime. I'm drunk, Pace, not a completely different person, and I would need to be someone else to even consider something that repulsive."

"And I thought you wanted LV State to yourself."

"And I thought you claimed not to want me. I always knew that was a fucking lie. You want me and my life and my family. You'll never get that. You'll *never* have me! Stay the fuck away from me." She yanked her hand out of his grasp and stumbled backward.

She got lost in the crowd, letting the sea of people direct her movements. She was more furious than ever.

Tears pricked at her eyes, but she pushed them back. She needed to drink more and forget all this shit. She wanted to black out and wake up tomorrow to find her picture-perfect life was all back in order, not lying on the floor in a scattered mess.

The angrier she got, the more the memories flooded her conscious. She remembered the devastating weeks after Jude had walked out of her life. As hard as her exterior was, she had turned into a zombie after he wrecked her. He'd entered her life, full of love, passion, and complete understanding. Then, several months later, after she had lost everything but her immense love for him, he had torn her apart. Even though she had still been the queen bee at school during the last few months, in her despair, nothing else had ever really mattered to her.

Now, the depression was settling back over her like a familiar dark cloak.

So, she danced with anyone and everyone as seductively as she could. She noticed another commotion with Andrew, who seemed pissed that she was dancing with another football player, but she avoided it. She couldn't deal with that tonight. Andrew didn't have anything to mend a battered, broken heart.

She felt like her walls were fracturing, and only immeasurable stress could crack the ice queen.

One of the guys brought her more shots, and she tipped them back without tasting them. Another pair of lips descended on hers. She let the intoxication muddle her mind. She didn't care anymore.

When she pulled back from the kiss, the guy backed up in surprise.

What is his name?

"Mind if I talk with Bryna for a minute?" Eric asked over her shoulder.

"Sure, man." The guy was already dancing with another girl.

"What the fuck, Eric?"

He sighed dramatically. "Can I talk to you? In private?"

"You already turned me down. Haven't you done enough? I'm not your type. Trust me, I know *all* about your type," she slurred.

"I'm sure. But no, that's not why. Let's just go talk, Bri."

"Didn't anyone tell you, only my friends call me that?"

"Well, you won't have any if you don't get moving and chill out. I'm doing you a favor."

"I don't need your fucking favors." Bryna slipped forward and landed against his chest. Instead of laughing, she felt a tear trickle out of her eyes. *Good God!* She needed to get it together. She wiped the tear away with the back of her hand.

"All right, drunkie. I didn't want to have to do this." Eric slipped his hand under her knees and picked her up as if she were as light as a feather.

"Eric!" she cried. "Put me down!"

But he wasn't listening as he carried her through the crowd and outside to the mostly empty patio. The pool was closed, but there was still water in it. It was a chilly night, and goose bumps broke out on her skin, but the coldness seemed to immediately clear her head.

Eric lightly dropped her onto a lounge chair. "You should be glad I didn't throw you into the pool."

"Fuck you!"

"I'm pretty sure you gave the impression that you wanted to do that with everyone else in the room tonight," Eric told her.

"Who cares? I'm *that* girl, right?"

He ran a hand back through his hair as if he couldn't believe he was dealing with this right now. "I was starting to think otherwise," he admitted.

"What?" she asked, honestly surprised.

"But you're proving that wrong tonight."

"I don't have to prove anything to you. Stop meddling in my life. I can do whatever I want."

He threw his arms out at her. "By all means, keep fucking up your life. You're not only hurting all the people you care about. You're hurting yourself, too, even though you seem to have little regard for yourself."

"What does it matter to you who I'm hurting? You've been nothing but an antagonistic asshole since I got here. I don't know what this knight-in-shining-armor routine is, but you can drop the fucking act."

"It's not an act! Andrew is my friend, and while I repeatedly told him he was too good for you, he wouldn't listen. So, you've fucked with my friend by being *exactly* the person I warned him about. What is your problem?"

"My problem?" she shouted back at him. "You have no clue. You just judge me. Don't feel bad for me. I'm fine. It doesn't matter that my father won't spend time with me or that my stepbrother simultaneously wants to fuck me and ruin my life," she cried.

Eric stiffened at those words and clenched his fists.

"Forget the fact that I get looked down upon when my fuck buddy decides to get outrageously clingy, and I do something about it because I'm a bitch, right? I'm just a slutty cheerleader!"

"Bryna," Eric interjected.

"Let's not forget the part where I have a judgmental asshole yelling in my face because I hurt his friend's *feelings*. I made it fucking clear to Andrew that we were just fucking around. I'm not interested in long-term anything. In fact, I'm not interested in *feeling* at all." Her eyes were hard and unwavering. "So, you can tell him that he fucking did this to himself."

Eric shifted uncomfortably.

She hadn't meant to spew everything that had been bothering her tonight, but it had all come out. The alcohol had been a part of it, but it had also felt good to unload on someone—even if it was Eric Wilkins.

"Look, you and Andrew are with each other all the time, giving the impression that you are together," he said as if that made it right.

"Whether I gave that impression or not, I said countless times that we weren't going to be in a relationship, and he refused to listen. That isn't my fault. I'm sorry, but he dug himself into a hole, and now, he's boohooing that I don't want to be exclusive. I might be *that* girl, but I'm honest about it."

"Well, I've always known you to be blunt with me," Eric said dryly.

"Anyway, if he had a problem with me, he should have been man enough to be out here, voicing his own opinion. He shouldn't have sent a lackey to do it for him."

"He didn't send me. I was concerned," Eric admitted. "I saw you talking to your stepbrother, and things looked tense. After that, you seemed to spiral more and more out of control."

Concerned? Eric was concerned? Yeah, right. And pigs could fly.

"Thanks for your concern, but I'm fine. No need to hover and stick your nose in other people's business," she said, flipping her blonde hair off her shoulders.

"Fuck. You've been pissy since you came to school. Sorry that I was fucking worried about you."

"Don't be! I'm a big girl. I can take care of myself."

"Clearly," Eric drawled. He sounded unconvinced. Considering he had carried her drunk ass outside, maybe he had a reason.

"Run along, Cowboy," she taunted, not listening to her own subconscious. "I have a few more people to piss off before this miserable fucking weekend is complete."

Eric shook his head in both disgust and pity. He mumbled something under his breath and then walked away. He made it to the door before turning back to her. "You know, you draw people in with your larger-than-life personality"—he sighed—"and then you kill them with it, too."

Bryna glared at him. "This is just who I am."

"I'm starting to think even you don't know who that person is."

TWELVE

A COUPLE OF WEEKS LATER, Bryna was packing for the trip to L.A. for the big USC game. Life had been such a blur since homecoming. Her friends acted as if her big meltdown at Posse never happened, but Andrew had been avoiding her at all costs. She missed having him around— or at least having someone around since she hadn't heard from Hugh at all. Even though she had been swamped with cheer and the end of the semester, all she could think about was whether or not her plan with Hugh was an utter failure.

The doorbell pulled her from her thoughts. She scrubbed her hands over her eyes and jogged downstairs. She wrenched open the door.

"Hey," she said to the deliveryman.

"Package for Bri. Is that you?"

"The one and only."

"Sign here."

She scrawled her name on the line and took a small box from him. After what the last package had contained, she couldn't control her excitement as she tore into the wrapping. When she saw the label, she bit her lip in delight.

AGENT PROVOCATEUR.

Inside was a black strappy bra and thong set, plus the garter belt and stockings. It even contained the matching black leather paddle. Her heart fluttered. She had always been a La Perla girl, but Agent Provocateur was overtly sexual and suited her very nature—especially around Hugh, who she assumed had sent the gift. However, there was no card.

Without a second thought, she grabbed her phone and dialed his number.

"Hugh Westercamp."

"Hey," she breathed lightly into the phone.

"Bri." He sounded happy to hear from her.

"Where and when do I get to wear my present?"

Hugh laughed. "It's good to hear you got it. Straight to the point."

"Always."

"Well, I'll be in town in two weeks. Pack a bag. I think, this time, you won't be leaving."

Two weeks later, a limo showed up at Bryna's condo. She had her Louis Vuitton luggage packed and had gotten an excuse to miss cheer for that night even though it was the week before the conference championship game in San Francisco.

After clinching the division, Bryna had suffered through her Thanksgiving holiday. Celia had tried too hard to make Thanksgiving perfect. Her father had seemed to hover over her more than usual, as if it wasn't bad enough that he had married her. Pace had proceeded to constantly annoy the shit out of Bryna while talking about attending LV State in the spring. The only people who hadn't bugged her were Celia's youngest children, the twins, and it was because they hadn't said anything.

She was most thankful that she'd had an excuse to vanish from home in L.A. and return to school for the University of Nevada versus Las Vegas football game, but then watching Andrew disappear with another cheerleader after the game hadn't helped her mood. She had been glad that she had this trip to occupy her mind.

As the limo drove her away from her condo to where she would meet Hugh, her anticipation grew. She smoothed out her torn black skinnies and flipped through the feed on her phone. The limo pulled up to a private airfield and straight out to the tarmac.

Hugh was waiting for her, his arms crossed, and his eyes locked on her arrival. The driver opened her door, and she glided out toward Hugh.

"Hello, beautiful." His smile was as bright as the afternoon sunlight.

"Hey," she said. She threw her arms around his neck, reached onto her tiptoes, and kissed him full on the lips.

"You're in a good mood."

"I've missed you."

After her blowup during homecoming, she'd had a lot of time to think about what she was doing. Part of her had realized that her time with Hugh, though different than anything she had experienced before, made her feel good, wanted, desirable, and appreciated.

He wrapped his arms tightly around her waist and gave her another kiss. "I've missed you, too. Are you ready to go?"

"Yeah," she said, following him onto the plane.

They took their seats next to each other on the private jet.

She leaned into him. "Where are we heading?"

"Somewhere you can't run away from."

She threaded his tie through her fingers and looked up at him under her lashes. "I don't plan on leaving anyway."

"Good. I can't stop thinking about you. You're driving me crazy."

"I didn't mean to," she lied through her teeth.

She hadn't known he was going mad over her. He had been decidedly absent from her life. She had been left wondering if they were going to get back together again.

"I want this to be a special trip for us," he said softly.

His eyes were so sincere. Chills broke out on her body.

God, he really meant all of this. She had him hook, line, and sinker...and she was wondering if perhaps a part of her was falling for him, too.

No...probably not. Just a warm wave of déjà vu.

About an hour later, they circled around the beautiful mountains and gorgeous lake a couple of times before landing outside of Lake Tahoe. Growing up, she had skied here once or twice, but her father preferred Colorado or Europe, so she hadn't spent much time here.

Once they arrived at the resort, a valet took their bags up to their room, and Hugh was immediately greeted warmly.

"Mr. Westercamp, what a pleasure to have you back on the premises," a woman in a tailored black skirt suit said.

Bryna wrapped her arms around herself to try to fight back the cold. She had been hoping for somewhere warm, and her mind went to the beautiful Caribbean feel of St. Barts. She cringed and forced herself to stop thinking about Jude. *Motherfucker haunts my thoughts.*

"Good to see you as well, Meredith." He wrapped an arm around Bryna. "You must be freezing." Ever the gentleman, he stripped out of his suit coat and threw it around her shoulders.

Meredith's smile never wavered as she watched the exchange. She stood by dutifully. "Please allow me to escort you around the resort." She continued speaking as she walked them through the luxurious resort lobby, "Will you be skiing this afternoon? There is fresh powder on your favorite slopes."

Hugh glanced over at Bryna. "I have dinner reservations for tonight, but I left our afternoon open. I wanted to spend some time with you. Do you ski?"

"A bit," she said. It wasn't entirely true. She was an excellent skier and had been doing it her whole life, but he didn't need to know that. "But I didn't bring anything to ski in."

"We have a fully stocked ski store on the first level," Meredith said.

Hugh raised his eyebrows as if he hadn't already planned for this. It wasn't what *she* had planned for, but it might be fun to try to relax with him. He was trying to make her comfortable here with him. This had to count for something, more than a dress or earrings.

"All right," she agreed.

"I think you took advantage of me," Hugh said. He was laughing as he walked through the snow with both of their skis and poles in his hands.

She gave him a sheepish look. "So, I might or might not be more experienced than I'd let on."

Red colored her cheeks, but she wasn't sure if it was from his scrutiny or the bitter cold from the slopes. Perhaps it was both.

"A little? I own the resort, and you were skiing circles around me."

"Not…literally."

"I bet you could though. Why didn't you pursue it?"

She shrugged but held her head up. "Los Angeles doesn't leave you much time to practice. It was something fun my father and I used to do. My mother was always too worried about hurting herself. She'd stay in the ski lodge and drink most of the day away. It was really my thing with my dad. We used to ski together all the time when I was growing up. He worked a lot more when I got into middle school, so I tended to spend a lot of time on the slopes alone."

She snapped her mouth shut before she got into her whole family diatribe. She hadn't meant to spill all of that to Hugh.

She didn't usually remember her childhood that way, but it didn't seem like much had changed. Her father still worked too much, and her mother, Olivia, continued to drink much of her life away. Neither of them spent any time with her.

Bryna and Hugh were silent as they trudged up the last hill before he grabbed her and softly kissed her on the lips.

"I like that you're sharing more of yourself with me," Hugh said. "I want to share more of myself with you."

She smiled languidly. She was sure there was a double meaning buried in there.

"This way," he told her.

He returned their ski equipment and then took her the back way up the elevator. It opened up directly into a massive penthouse suite complete with a perfect view of the mountains, an outdoor Jacuzzi, several bedrooms, and a grand kitchen. Every luxury was accounted for.

"Hungry?" he asked, kissing the soft spot between her neck and shoulder.

"Starving."

"Me, too."

She swallowed hard. "Maybe we should eat now…"

He gripped the top of her new jacket in his hands and peeled it off. "Yes, I'd very much like to eat right now."

She shivered against him. His hands ran down her arms and then gripped her hips. He lifted her shirt, so he could touch bare skin. The tips of his fingers trailed along the inside of her pants.

"By all means…"

"But we have dinner reservations," he said, taking a step back.

She looked at him, aghast. *Is he really stopping?*

"Go on. Get dressed. I have big plans for you tonight."

She was sure she was being punished for teasing him the last couple of times they had been together. Now, he was getting her all turned on and walking away. She'd had a great day with him…better than had been expected actually. He was an easy guy to be around. He always had a smile on his face and a ready laugh for all his stories. Being around him was like a breath of fresh air.

Bryna quickly showered off the hours of skiing from her skin, blew out her hair, and kept her makeup natural, enhancing her best features. Her black dress ended at mid thigh and flowed out when she moved in a circle. She paired it with leopard-print pointy-toe heels that killed her feet but looked fabulous. *The price I pay for beauty.*

She walked out of the bathroom, only to find the entire suite covered in lit candles. The table was set for two with a full buffet of food, and Hugh was drinking red wine in a stemless glass.

"I thought we had dinner reservations," she said, narrowing her eyes at him.

"We did." He walked up to her and wrapped an arm around her waist. "I decided I didn't want to share you."

"You're not sharing me."

"I like to hear that."

She hid her smile under her lashes.

"Dinner?" he asked.

Bryna sat down at the table, and Hugh took the time to personally serve her food. She was sure a man like him, with his wealth, didn't do anything for himself, let alone for someone else. They had a Gorgonzola spinach salad, braised chicken, grilled asparagus, and three-cheese truffle macaroni and cheese. Her mouth watered at the display.

She bit into the chicken and sighed at the incredible flavor. "My compliments to the chef. This is incredible."

"Well, thank you. It's my recipe."

She raised an eyebrow. "Friends with a chef and a chef yourself?"

He laughed. "Not exactly. I never went to culinary school, and I don't run a restaurant, but I've worked in a kitchen a few times in my life."

"Really?" she asked, surprised.

"I didn't have to, but during college, I was rebellious and decided I wanted to set out on my own. You work in a lot of kitchens when you do that."

"You seem pretty down-to-earth for someone who runs his own resorts."

He shrugged. "Life tends to knock you down a few pegs every time you think you're on top of the world."

"That's the fucking truth."

Maybe she had pegged him wrong. She had thought he was going to be…well, Jude. She hated admitting that she'd kind of hoped for that. Jude had been an asshole. Hugh kind of seemed like a nice guy, all things considered.

"So…mind if I ask you a question?" she said.

"Of course you can."

"Why me? Why did you pick me out that day? Why do you spoil me like this?" she asked in a rush.

The answer was an important one for how their relationship would continue to develop.

His smile was completely open when he responded honestly, "It's complicated. I noticed your beauty first, of course. How can I not notice? But there was something more. You clearly had good taste, expensive taste. I like that. Yet you weren't going to buy the earrings, and you seemed very appreciative when I got them for you. I don't mean for this to come out as offensive, but you don't seem like the type of person who wants me for my money...and I've met people like that."

Bryna swallowed and tried to keep her face blank. He liked her because she didn't seem like a gold digger. *Well, shit.*

"I mean, you knew who I was and didn't call me right away. We've been on several dates, and you haven't pushed for anything. You seem like a woman doing well for yourself in your own right while doing exactly what you want."

A blush crept onto her face. That sounded exactly like her...except that she had completely been playing him the whole time.

Knowing his reasoning almost made her feel bad about her motivation.

After dinner, Hugh cleared the table and suggested they take a dip in the Jacuzzi. She changed into her mint-green bikini that made her look even more tan and then met Hugh out on the balcony. He was already seated in the steaming water in nothing but a pair of blue swim trunks. This was the first she had seen of his sculpted body. She had known he was trim and must work out a lot, but really seeing him made her appreciate his body even more.

She jogged over to the Jacuzzi and quickly got into the warm water. "It's freezing," she said, her teeth chattering.

"Come over here, and I'll warm you up," he suggested.

In the warm water, she dipped her body up to her neck, and she gave him a flirtatious look. "I'm better now," she said, toying with him.

"You've been playing cat-and-mouse with me." He walked across the square Jacuzzi.

"Have I?" she asked coyly.

"Oh, yes." He stopped right in front of her.

Her skin tingled, even with the superheated water, just from the anticipation of him touching her. She was ready, very ready, for that.

"I've been right here the whole time." She licked her lips, knowing it would drive him crazy.

His touch lit a fire in her core. She had been waiting for him to come on to her since they arrived. Spending the day with him in a completely nonsexual way had made her sexual appetite all the more fierce.

His fingers skimmed along her wet torso and down to her skimpy bikini bottoms. "Right here but always running away."

"Maybe I wasn't ready," she whispered. In her voice, she heard the vulnerability that had never escaped her hard exterior.

"Are you ready now?"

"That depends…"

She leaned back against the wall of the Jacuzzi and surveyed him. Her smile was mischievous, her head full of schemes. She couldn't even help it. They came to her unbidden.

"What does it depend on?"

"You."

"What can I do to change your mind?" he asked.

"I need you to give me something."

"What can I give you that I haven't already?" He didn't seem unhappy. It was more like he was willing to give in to her demands even though he had said earlier that he liked her because she didn't want anything.

But he'd thought she wanted money. That was where she had been going wrong all along. Withholding sex wasn't the key to keeping him interested. For a time, that had worked, but she wasn't Anne Boleyn. She couldn't wait six years for her crown. She needed him to give her the one thing she would never give out again.

"None of what you've given me compares to this."

"You didn't like what I gave you?" he asked skeptically.

"I loved everything," she purred. "But that's not what I want from you."

"Tell me, and it's yours."

Here goes nothing.

"This right here." She tapped his chest on the left side twice and let her hand linger. "Your heart."

Hugh's smile was victorious. "You stole that with a smile the first time I met you."

Smooth.

He circled her small waist and crushed his lips to hers. This wasn't a kiss like anything she had ever had with him before. They were always intoxicating and pushing boundaries, but this was…claiming. He held no more hesitancy. It was as if she had proven her worth to him.

She pushed her hands up his chest and around his neck. They couldn't seem to get close enough. There was nothing between them but flimsy bathing suits and a world of secrets. Neither of which seemed to matter in this moment with his lips on hers. Here was everything she had ever wanted—a wealthy man who wanted to take care of her and her body. Here, she could finally forget. Here she could live in this fairy-tale fantasy and dream of a better future than her traumatizing past.

Hugh scooped her up, out of the water, and pressed her back against the deck. It was frigid, but a heating lamp was positioned in the corner. He viciously ripped at the strings on her top and brought her breast up to his lips. She groaned as he sucked and bit at the beaded nipple exposed to the elements. He touched her body as if it were the last thing he was ever going to do. He admired it, worshiped it, as if he needed it to keep living.

He kissed his way down her stomach and to the top of her bikini bottoms. He slipped a digit under the material and flicked against her clit. Her body jerked in his touch. Suddenly, she wasn't cold anymore, not at all.

Her bottoms disappeared in much the same manner as her top, and soon, she was stripped bare in front of him. His breath was hot against her core as he spread her open before him. His fingers entered her, and her body responded in turn to his touch, making her back arch off the deck.

Fuck. I'm horny. She hadn't had sex in almost a month. She needed him inside of her right now.

But he didn't seem to care that she was ready. He wanted her to be beyond hot and bothered.

He claimed her clit with his tongue as he pumped in and out of her. She shook beneath him, and when she thought she couldn't hold out any longer, her body released all around his fingers.

"Oh God!" Her limbs felt like pudding, and she trembled all over.

"You're hot as fuck, Bri, moaning as I made you come all over my face and fingers."

Her core pulsed at his words. "Fuck me," she practically pleaded.

"I intend to."

Hugh hopped out of the Jacuzzi, picked her up off the deck, and carried her into the master suite. She didn't even consider protesting. She couldn't wait. If he were half as good with his dick as he had been with his fingers, then she would be in for a *long* night.

After he laid her out on the bed, she scrambled under the covers, and he dropped his swim trunks. She stared with a giant smirk on her face. She wanted him inside of her right fucking now.

She rubbed her legs together in anticipation.

"None of that," he said. His hands pried her legs apart and spread her wide for his view. "That's better. No reason to obstruct my view of dessert."

"You haven't had your fill?" she teased.

"I'm not sure I ever will." He crawled into bed on top of her and kissed her again. "I'm certain I could have dessert every single night and still be ravenous."

"I feel like that could be arranged."

He smirked and then pressed his dick up against her. "Let's start with tonight."

She nodded and rocked her hips up to meet him. He slipped easily into her, and she dropped her head back.

Shit. She stretched like a glove around him.

"Fuck," she groaned.

"You feel so fucking good," he bit out.

"Yeah."

That was all she managed to say before he reared back and thrust into her. Her legs shook with the effort. She felt like lava was coating her veins, reaching out from her center, to spread through her body all the way to her fingers and toes. Sweat beaded on her forehead as their bodies met in time over and over again.

Why have I ever kept myself from this? It was utter perfection.

He captured her lips in a searing kiss, and she threaded her fingers through his hair. She couldn't hold out any longer. Her body exploded, and she screamed out loud enough that if they'd been anywhere else, she might have awoken the neighbors. He came right after her, grunting, before collapsing into a heap.

She had rendered him speechless. He breathed heavily and kissed her. All of her scheming had been worth this moment. It was pure bliss. She felt content, almost happy. It had been a while since she had gotten close to that.

THIRTEEN

"I'M NOT READY TO LEAVE," Stacia whined. She plopped her empty coffee cup down on its saucer and sighed dramatically. "I can't believe first semester is already over."

"Me either," Bryna agreed.

"It went by so fast," Trihn said.

"At least I'll see you in Miami for New Year's Eve," Stacia said.

LV State had won the conference championship in San Francisco last weekend, and that meant they would be going to the play-offs. Bryna had spent the past week in her final exams, and now, they were all waiting on grades before starting Christmas break.

Trihn bounced up and down. "I am so excited that I got a ticket to the game! I can't wait to celebrate our win and bring in the New Year with you girls."

"We'll sneak you onto the field," Stacia promised. She gave Bryna her best pouty face. "Are you *sure* you don't want to come and stay at my parents' house for break? I know my dad is the USC coach and still pretty pissy about their loss, but we could own the city!"

The last place Bryna wanted to be was L.A. for Christmas. She officially hated Christmas and didn't even want to see her family. After the disaster that was Thanksgiving, she couldn't brave her once favorite holiday for a stepfamily sham.

"Thanks, but no. I'll be fine here."

"What about Brooklyn?" Trihn offered. "Snow. Ice-skating. Shopping."

"Pass. I had enough snow while skiing with Hugh."

"Who isn't such a stranger anymore, huh?" Stacia nudged Bryna's arm.

Bryna winked. "Definitely not a stranger."

"So, why aren't you spending break with him?" Trihn asked.

She just shrugged. The thing was complicated with Hugh. She assumed he was spending the holidays with his wife—even though he hadn't said that, of course.

"He's swamped with work. Resort season around the holidays is packed until after New Year's, so we're not planning to get together until then."

"Oh, well, at least you'll have the football guys to keep you company," Stacia said. She giggled at the end, and that made it perfectly clear what kind of company she thought Bryna was going to be keeping.

"What about the football players?"

"Didn't you hear? Coach Galloway said they all had to stay here during break to practice. I think a lot of parents are flying into town to celebrate the holidays with the guys since they can't leave," Stacia explained.

"That's bullshit!" Trihn cried.

"For real," Bryna said. "Can they do that?"

"I don't know, but they are," Stacia said

"Huh. If I get bored, maybe I'll call Andrew up and see if he's forgiven me yet." Bryna laughed lightly at the absurdity of it all.

She knew Andrew was sleeping with other people, but then again, so was she. Maybe if he realized they had just been fucking, then they could make this work again.

"You have a death wish." Trihn shook her head.

"Yes," Bryna agreed with that. "Anyway, I won't be bored. Vegas is never boring."

She was wrong.

She was so bored over break. With her friends gone for only a week, she found herself bored out of her mind. Between everyone at school leaving, Hugh being swamped with work, and her refusal to see her family—especially since Pace was planning to move in right after New Year's—she didn't have much to do. She had thought Vegas could never be boring, but it was all tourist shit, and the flood of tourists drove her mad. She could only see so many proposals, bachelor and bachelorette parties, and weddings before feeling sick.

The Saturday before Christmas, she decided she couldn't stay in any longer. She needed some outside civilization. Donning a pair of ripped tight jeans, a deep-red sheer top, and her leather jacket, she went to Posse, hoping Maya would be working.

When Bryna entered the building, her mouth nearly dropped open. It was dead. The club where they spent all their time during the school year was basically empty. It made sense that if there weren't students on campus, then it wouldn't be as packed.

She walked over to the bar. She felt like a loser, coming to the club alone at this time of year. She could be anywhere, and she had decided to stay in town. She had thought it would help her escape, but instead, she was left with too much time to think about what had happened this time last year.

Maya wasn't working either. Some guy—she hadn't caught his name—made her a dirty martini with three olives. She handed him cash. She doubted she would be here longer than one drink. If this was what it was going to be like for another week, then she was considering packing up and heading out of town. It wouldn't matter where she went as long as it was away from here.

She took her drink and wandered out onto the patio. A small group of people was playing a round of beer pong at a nearby table. That was how sad the place looked. She leaned back against the metal railing and watched the game. The group was really into it, screaming, and chanting for their team, and Bryna felt very separate from everything.

She pulled out her phone to try to distract herself. Maybe tonight hadn't been a good idea.

"Hey."

Bryna looked up and right into the face of Eric Wilkins.

She sighed. *Great.*

"Hey," she said.

"This place is a graveyard."

"Yep," she said, popping the P at the end.

"What are you doing here?" He leaned back, next to her, uninvited.

"Drinking." She held up her mostly empty glass.

"Yeah, but in Vegas. It's Christmas break. Shouldn't you be at home?"

"No," she said automatically. "I hate Christmas."

"Who hates Christmas?" he asked in shock.

"Me obviously. That's what I just said."

"I mean, I'm dying to be home in Dallas. My mom is probably making Christmas cookies, making the house smell like home. I'm sure the tree is all decorated, and presents are piled high for my younger brother and me. My dad can never decide between ham and turkey, so most of the time, my mom makes both."

There was laughter in his voice and joy in his memories. It made Bryna cringe away from him. She had never known a childhood like that.

"Sounds like a Hallmark movie," she responded dryly.

"Yeah, or Lifetime, but that's home." He shrugged as if it were completely normal. "What's your Christmas usually like?"

"Used to be all right before my parents got divorced. Last year, I went to Saint Barts with a guy. I lied and told my family I would be with my mother and then going to New York with Gates," she admitted.

"Why?" he asked.

"Because it was better than watching my stepmother try too hard. My father wasn't home anyway. Plus, my mom didn't even call. This guy cared about me, so I went."

"I see."

She glanced away from Eric and closed her eyes. She had no idea why she had even told him that. She hadn't told anyone about this shit before. Maybe it was because she knew he was completely nonthreatening, and he wasn't the type to spread rumors. He might be an ass to her, but she didn't forget he had been worried about her enough to intervene after homecoming when no one else had.

"Hey...do you want to get out of here and get some food?" he asked a minute later.

She couldn't resist being catty to him. "Oh, are you asking me out?" she joked. She knew he wasn't. She wasn't his type after all.

Eric shook his head. "Forget it. I was trying to be nice."

Bryna sighed dramatically as he walked away. "E, I was just kidding." She left her drink on a nearby table. "Let's go."

"Okay," he said. "Where to? What are you hungry for?"

"Don't laugh," she said. "But…ice cream."

He looked like he was trying to hold it in, but he ended up laughing. "Ice cream?"

"I said not to laugh." She swatted at his arm.

"I didn't realize girls like you ate ice cream."

"What? Now, I can't like good food?"

He shrugged. "I mean…you're pretty small."

"I have a fast metabolism, and cheer is a hefty workout. I love ice cream."

"All right then. Ice cream it is. I know a good place."

Bryna piled into Eric's Jeep as he drove toward the Strip. She couldn't believe she was actually sitting in Eric's car. *How did we go from arguing constantly to me telling him my life story to going to get ice cream together?* It made little sense to her. The only thing she could think was that she was comfortable with him because she was alone, and she knew he had no intention of hitting on her. It wasn't often or ever that she came across a guy like that.

He parked at one of the hotels, and they walked through the smoke-filled casino out to the Strip. The lights were bright, and people were everywhere. There were so many tourists. She couldn't even handle it.

"Where are we going?"

"Sugar Factory," he said, pointing out a building next door.

They walked through the doors and were promptly seated in the dining room.

"Just dessert menus, please," Eric said to the hostess.

"Sure thing." She dropped them on the table and then disappeared.

Bryna opened her menu. There were dozens of options—everything from ice cream to cake and cookies to fondue, waffles, or milkshakes. There was even a hundred-dollar sundae with twenty-four scoops of ice cream and a thousand-dollar fondue with real gold and a bottle of Dom Pérignon included. It was dessert heaven.

"Hi. Welcome to Sugar Factory. Can I get you something to drink?"

"Water is fine," Bryna said. "But I'm ready to order. You?"

Eric nodded.

"I'll have the banana split," she said.

"All right. Do you want two spoons?"

"Um…no. I plan to eat it all by myself."

The girl looked at Bryna as if she couldn't decide if it was sarcasm or not.

"Yes. An extra spoon would be great," Eric interjected. "I'll have a strawberry milkshake."

"Sounds great." The lady walked away with the menus.

Bryna eyed Eric suspiciously. "You're not getting any of my banana split."

"It says on the menu it's made for two to eat. There is *no* way you can pack away an entire banana split like that."

"Want to bet?" she asked. "It's my favorite. And caramelized bananas. I mean, come on. That's screaming my name."

He snort-laughed. "I'll take that bet. You pick up the tab if you don't finish every last bite."

"Oh, please. At least make it fun."

"Fine. When I win, you have to hang out with me again…and be this girl, not the one from school."

She rolled her eyes. "I don't know what that means, but I'm going to eat it all anyway, so deal."

They chatted aimlessly until their food came out. Bryna's eyes were as big as saucers when she saw how enormous her banana split was.

"Having second thoughts?" he asked.

"Definitely not. I don't back down from a challenge."

She dug into her split. She was glad she hadn't had dinner and was basically living off of her dirty martini at the moment. Otherwise, she wasn't sure this was actually going to happen. As she worked on the dessert, they talked about football and their undefeated season.

"I wished I were playing," he admitted. "I'm still on the team, but it's different, being on the sidelines."

"But you said you could play."

"I could," he agreed. "But I wouldn't do that to my parents. They were freaked out when I hurt my knee. At first, the doctors didn't know if I would walk. It was not a good time in my life. I recovered remarkably well, but I don't want to go back into something I'm good at if it could kill me. I'm still young and smart. I can do something else."

"Coach? Is that the dream job?"

"Of course. That's the goal even though so few people make it to the top. Coach thinks I have the right eye for it. That's why he agreed to train me after I busted my knee," he told her. "What about you? What's the dream job?"

She shrugged. "I don't know. I guess I always assumed I'd marry into money."

"You're not serious," he said in disbelief. "You're smart and in college. You have to have some dreams, right?"

She stuffed another bite of the banana split into her mouth to keep from answering right away. Her dreams had always been so muddled by everyone else's expectations of her. She didn't know how much of what she wanted was from herself or her parents.

"Sometimes, I think film," she said. She had never said that out loud. "When I was younger, I used to watch clips and piece them together for my dad...when he was around."

"Cool. So, are you a film major?"

"Um...no. I'm undecided. I don't think my father would take me seriously if I told him I was in film even though he was in film here."

"Why not?" Eric asked.

"I've never really shown interest in it. Plus, I don't want to seem like I'm riding his coattails."

"If you like it, you like it. You have to decide to do it and not give a fuck about what anyone else thinks. I thought you were already pretty good at that."

Bryna crinkled her nose and shoved another bite of the banana split into her mouth. She was almost finished, but the more she sat around and talked with Eric, the more she thought it might be nice to hang out with him over break. She had been bored out of her mind, and he was actually pretty good company—when he wasn't acting like a douchey hostile football player.

She got down to her last bite and just stared at it. "Maybe I will change my major then and see how film suits me."

"Killer. That sounds like a great idea. At least, once you've tried it, you'll know if it's for you." Eric then looked at her bowl. "I can't believe you only have one bite left. I never would have guessed you could finish that whole thing."

She smiled and then pushed the bowl over to him with the one remaining bite in it. "I didn't finish."

"It's only one bite."

"I lost. This was fun. Let's hang out again."

FOURTEEN

Be there in five.

Bryna checked the text from Eric and fiddled with her Harry Winston B in anticipation. They had gone to get lunch earlier this week, and it had been pretty chill. Since everyone was getting back into town on Saturday so that they could fly out to Miami the next morning, Eric had made plans for Friday night. She didn't know where they were going exactly.

All she knew was she enjoyed Eric's company far too much—so much that, if he weren't gay, she would have already hooked up with him. Then again, if he weren't gay, she wasn't sure she would be as comfortable with him. It was a conundrum.

With any other guy, going out on a Friday night would certainly mean it was a date. And since this was their third time hanging out this week, it'd usually mean a whole hell of a lot more than that. She wasn't used to this. She had never had guy friends who didn't want to fuck her.

It was such a strange relief—and also just *strange*.

At least it gave her something to think about, other than her botched Christmas holiday. She had spent the entirety of Christmas Day drunk off her ass. Her mother hadn't called once. Celia had called, but Bryna had ignored it. When her father had finally phoned her, all he'd wanted to know was why she hadn't returned Celia's call and claimed they had something important to discuss with her. It'd made her even happier she wasn't home for the holidays to hear this stupid discussion.

Eric knocked hard on the door, twice.

She popped it open and smiled. "Hey."

"You ready to go?" he asked.

"You didn't say where we were going." She followed him out the door.

"I know. Just get in, Hollywood."

Bryna walked to his car, plopped down into the passenger seat, and arched an eyebrow. "Hollywood?"

"You call me Cowboy."

"Well, you drawl your words," she pointed out.

"No, I don't." He actually looked offended.

"Yes, you do. It happens all the time, especially when you're angry."

"So, it must just be around you then."

Bryna shrugged. "As long as you admit it."

"Whatever," he said, drawling dramatically.

A smile crept up onto her face.

Eric drove the short distance toward the Strip, and she drummed her fingernails on the door.

"You know, I think I've been on the Strip more this week with you than all last semester," she said.

"I know. I never come out here either. It's always so busy, and it's so much easier to go somewhere more local."

She nodded her head. "Like Posse. It would be great to go to Carnival Court all the time, but the tourists kill it."

"Yeah. I thought about this other place for tonight, and I heard this location is pretty fun. Plus, I have a friend who works there, so she hooked me up."

"Okay. You have me curious. Where are we going?" she asked.

"You'll see."

Eric parked outside The Cosmopolitan, and they took the escalators up to the fourth floor. They walked out to the pool on the balcony. In its place, she found a full-on ice-skating rink. The seating had been converted into private fire pits for groups. People were roasting s'mores and drinking hot chocolate. All the while, fake snow filtered down around them—in the middle of a casino pool in the desert. Her mind was blown.

"Ice-skating?" she asked in disbelief.

"I thought it would be fun."

"I had no idea something like this was here."

"Well," he said, "I hope you know how to skate."

He handed his two tickets to the lady at the front, and she gave them a card to rent skates and assigned them a fire pit.

"Of course I know how to skate. I have my own pair of skates at home."

"These will have to do for today."

Eric held up a pair of blue plastic skates with straps that hooked on like ski boots. They were hideous.

"I am not going to put my feet in those," Bryna said.

"Oh, yes, you are." He grabbed a second pair off the table. "What's your size?"

"Six and a half."

"Here you go." He pushed them into her hands.

She held them away from her like she was going to get infected. "I draw the line."

"Where's the girl who downed nearly an entire banana split?"

"That's different. This is bad footwear. I prefer Christian Louboutin." She pointed down at her boots.

123

"Get over it," he said dismissively.

Then, he walked away toward their fire pit, which they were sharing with two other couples, who were clearly on dates. She had no other option but to follow him with the repulsive boots in her arms.

Eric nodded at the other people next to them, and they smiled in that dreamy state of adoration for their significant other. She wanted to gag.

She watched him start to put on his skates. "I'll have you know, I'm doing this under protest."

The skates looked even worse on her feet.

"Are you happy?" she asked.

"Let's see your moves, Hollywood."

In these skates, she didn't have any moves. She was better at skiing than ice-skating. She thought it should have come naturally since she had a dance, gym, and cheer background, but she couldn't keep her balance well enough on a thin blade.

Eric didn't seem to be having any of the same difficulties. He skated backward, so he could face her and taunt her bad skating skills. "I thought you said you were good at this."

"I said I had skates at home. There's a difference. Now, stop distracting me," she grumbled.

She got the hang of it after half an hour, and they spent a good deal of time on the ice. The skating worked up both of their appetites, so they ordered food from the rink eatery—grilled cheese, tomato soup, hot chocolate, and s'mores. The hot chocolate might have been some of the best she had ever had.

When they went back out to skate again, some kids were racing each other around the rink. One rammed right into Bryna's back, and she stumbled into Eric. He tried to grab her, but she slipped out of his grasp and landed hard on her ass and hip.

"Ugh," she groaned, lying flat on the ice. Her leg was already throbbing. "That's going to bruise."

Eric tried to hold in his laughter but wasn't able to do so. "You look hilarious, sitting down there."

"Thanks, jerk. Why not help me up?"

"Sorry. Sorry," he said.

Once she was on her feet again, she could feel her leg and hip swelling. *This sucks so bad.*

"You know...your pants are soaked."

"Are you checking out my ass?" she asked.

"I can't help it when you have a giant wet spot on it." He only laughed harder when she glared at him. "Come on. Let's dry you out at the fire pit."

Twenty minutes later, her pants were dry again, but she was stiff and sore. She was certain she was going to have a disgusting bruise on her leg for the game next week. She hadn't even gotten it in a fun drunken accident.

They agreed to pack it up and go home after that. She needed to ice her leg if she wanted to stunt next week. Plus, it was already getting late.

They had made it halfway through the casino before a passing waitress stopped them.

"Eric?"

Bryna was surprised to see a very pretty girl in front of her. She had dark brown, almost black, hair piled up into a high ponytail, and with a round tray tucked under her arm, she was decked out in skimpy clothing that matched the other casino servers.

Her dark eyes were wide in confusion. "What are you doing here?" the girl asked.

"Oh...hey," Eric said. He sounded uncomfortable. "We just left the ice rink."

"We?"

"Yeah. Sorry. Audrey, this is Bryna."

With disdain, the girl set her eyes on Bryna. Audrey seemed to size Bryna up in a split second before clearly deciding she was a threat.

Why does the name Audrey sound familiar? Bryna knew she had heard that name before.

Then, it hit her. This was Eric's psycho ex-girlfriend whom Stacia had told her about at the beginning of the semester. No wonder she looked pissed. Bryna knew she was a threat to almost everyone's boyfriend—or husband, for that matter. At least in this one singular case, she wasn't actually doing anything wrong.

"Hey," Bryna said, politely extending her hand. "Nice to meet you."

Audrey stared down at her hand as if it were a viper ready to strike. She didn't even take it.

Bryna left it out until it was awkward and then dropped it. *So, that's how it's going to be?*

"Did you take *her* to the ice rink?" Audrey demanded.

"Yeah, we just left."

Duh. He had said that.

"I hooked you up with the fire-pit tickets! Those are hard to come by," Audrey cried. Her eyes were as round as saucers, and she looked hurt.

Maybe Audrey had assumed he was going to take her or something, which didn't make sense. *Why would he have asked her to get him tickets for the fire pit if he were going to take her?* They could have just gone together. Also, as far as Bryna knew, they had been broken up all semester. *Why would he have taken her at all?* Either way, it was pretty awkward.

"I know. Um…thanks," Eric said.

He was not handling this well. He seemed completely out of his element when talking to Audrey. Bryna had never seen him like this before.

"I didn't realize you were going to take another girl on a date with those tickets. Un-fucking-believable, Eric. I wouldn't have gotten them for you if I'd known. This is absurd."

Eric shuffled his feet. "Audrey, I appreciate you getting me the tickets, but Bri and I aren't—"

"Official," Bryna finished for him.

"What?" he asked. He looked at her in confusion.

Bryna wasn't having any more of this shit. She had heard this girl was crazy, and the bitch was proving it. Eric was a nice guy, and he was clearly in over his head. He needed help from a *real* bitch.

"We're not official yet," Bryna said. She slipped her hand into Eric's and leaned against his arm. She made sure not to look up at him to see his reaction. "But thanks for the ticket, Aubrey. It was an amazing date."

"It's Audrey," she spat. She glared at Eric. "Can I talk to you—alone?"

"Sorry," Bryna said before Eric could speak. "We're really on a tight schedule. We still have a *long* night ahead of us." She even giggled for good measure. "So nice to meet you though."

Bryna dragged Eric away from Audrey before he could do any more damage. He must really not want people to know he was gay if he had gone as far as dating that crazy chick. She wondered what had happened between them.

When they made it outside, she dropped his hand, and they walked the rest of the way in silence.

It wasn't until they were seated in his Jeep, driving back across town, when Eric spoke again, "What was all of that about?"

Bryna smiled. "It seemed wrong to let your psycho ex talk to you like that. You were too nice."

"How did you know she was my ex?"

"I've heard the rumors."

"Great," he grumbled. "I don't even want to know what those say."

"I thought it was easier to pretend this was a date than to have her be so fucking annoying—not to mention, desperate and needy. I can't believe you let her talk to you like that. I would have knocked her down a few more pegs if I wasn't so ready to get out of there," Bryna rambled on through Eric's silence.

"You know," he said after a minute, "you're not the person I thought you were."

"Thank you?" she said questioningly.

"Seriously, you're cool as shit. You should let other people see this side of you."

"I have to keep up my reputation."

Eric laughed as he glanced over at her. "Maybe people wouldn't be so scared of you if they saw you fall on your ass while skating."

"First of all, I didn't fall. That shithead kid rammed into me. And second, who said I didn't want people to be afraid of me? It keeps them in line."

"It just seems to push them away."

"Sometimes, that's better," she admitted. It was how she always lived her life, and it seemed to be working.

Eric parked the car outside of her condo. He angled his body, so he was facing her. She looked up at him, wondering what he was thinking because he sure as hell looked like he was thinking about something. Normally, she would be anticipating the kiss to come...or more. But not with Eric.

"What happened to you?" he asked finally.

"What do you mean?"

"I know this fun-loving girl is in there, but she's not who you show to the world. You seem like you're holding something in, so you don't let yourself fully relax. I don't know why that is."

"Life."

"Maybe." He didn't sound convinced. "Is it your parents?"

"No." Her parents had fucked her up, but this newfound guard she had put up around her heart to prevent anyone from getting to know her was new, fresh.

"Was it that guy you mentioned? The one you went away with last Christmas?"

"I don't want to talk about him."

"Sorry. I didn't mean to pry."

Bryna cracked open the door and hopped out of the Jeep. She winced when her leg hit the ground. "I had a good time tonight," she told him.

"Me, too. You know, you're not going to be able to hide this girl from me now."

She raised her eyebrows. "We'll see." She walked toward the door.

"Bryna!"

"Yeah?" she asked.

"Thanks."

"For what?"

"For what you said to Audrey."

"Yeah, well," she said with a faint smile, "thanks for getting me through Christmas."

FIFTEEN

"SPEND NEW YEAR'S WITH ME," Hugh said into the phone. "It's been too long since I've seen you."

"I would love that," Bryna said in a slight panic.

The football team was leaving in two hours for Miami. There was absolutely no way she could stay in town to see Hugh. So far, their relationship had worked out with her schedule. He was always here during the week or when she didn't have cheer. She had missed practice once to go to Lake Tahoe with him, but the play-offs were a different story. And it wasn't as if she could say she had cheer. He didn't know she was still in college.

"All right. Let me get my secretary on the phone."

"Hugh," she said before he could get off the phone, "I already have plans. I'm going to Miami with my girlfriends."

That, at least, was partially true.

"Well, I could be in Miami in a couple of hours. It's a longer flight."

She could not let her friends meet Hugh. There were too many things she was hiding for that to end well at all.

"It's actually a girls' weekend. We've had it planned for a while." She cringed.

She hoped this worked. In two weeks, there would be no more football to contend with all her time.

"I see." He sounded disappointed. "How about next weekend?"

She had to bite the bullet. "I'm going to the national championship game in Phoenix. It's something I do with my dad every year." She swallowed. *Two truths and a lie.* She was playing with fire.

"Football?" he asked skeptically. "You're into football?"

"Yeah."

"You don't seem like that type of girl."

What was with every person trying to put me into a box lately?

"I am."

"Okay. I really want to see you, Bri. I have your Christmas present. I had to find the right thing to get you, so I didn't have it when we went to Tahoe."

She smiled and let the tension leave her shoulders. On the outside, football probably seemed like the last thing she would be into. Plus, a Christmas present!

All the convincing she needed.

"How about the weekend after?"

"Bri!" Stacia screamed. She dropped her bags and sprinted across the short distance to where Bryna was standing. She full-fledged jumped into Bryna's arms.

Bryna winced as Stacia's weight hit her hip and was so glad cheer had given her the strength to hold people up...even crazy friends.

"I missed you *so* much," Stacia said.

Bryna laughed and dropped her back to the ground. "I missed you too."

"I so wish Trihn could fly with us."

"Yeah, but she's flying in straight from New York."

"Still."

"I know. She should have taken up cheerleading," Bryna said.

"It's never too late."

"Yes. I'm sure back handsprings and toe touches are right in her artsy repertoire."

"Well, we'll work on her for next year." Stacia locked elbows with her and dragged her over to her own stuff.

Stacia directed one of the male cheerleaders to grab their bags for them, and then she pushed their way through the line of people waiting to board the charter plane for the play-offs. Stacia yammered on the entire wait about her Christmas vacation.

The girls finally got on the plane and walked down the aisle.

"So, maybe I can convince someone to switch seats with you, so we can sit together," Stacia said.

"Hey, Hollywood."

Bryna stopped in her tracks and found herself staring into Eric's hazel eyes. He had a smirk on his face.

"Who is Hollywood?" Stacia asked.

"Saved you a seat." Eric nodded his head at the aisle seat next to him.

Stacia stared at her, wide-eyed in anticipation. Last anyone had checked, Bryna and Eric hated each other. They bickered like children.

"I'll pass," Bryna said dismissively.

He grabbed her arm before she could walk away. "I said you couldn't hide," he whispered.

Even Stacia probably hadn't heard him.

"I'm holding up the line. Go on ahead, S. I'll catch up," Bryna said.

Stacia looked uncertain but decided to keep walking back to her seat. Bryna moved out of the aisle, and the line moved again.

"What is all this?" she asked.

"You like the aisle seat."

"Are we friends?"

Eric gave her a look that said, *Stop acting dumb.* "You can't erase the past two weeks. I had a good time. You had a good time. You're going to have to come to terms with the fact that we're friends now."

Bryna shrugged noncommittally. "I'll see what I can do."

"Start by sitting down."

She laughed but followed his directions. "You're bossy."

"I didn't want to sit next to Beth anyway. She drives me crazy."

"And I don't?"

"Most of the time, you do, but it's different." He plugged in his headphones and relaxed back.

At this point, Bryna knew she could probably get up and leave to go sit with Stacia. She could even feel Stacia's eyes on her, wondering what was going on, but Bryna didn't mind Eric's company. She would be with Stacia all weekend.

Five long hours later, their flight landed in Miami, and the teams were quickly separated onto buses that would carry them to their hotel before the game.

Stacia scurried up to Bryna. "What the hell was that?"

"What?" Bryna asked.

She had known this was coming. It wasn't as if she and Eric were dating or anything. They were friends who had hung out a couple of times over Christmas break. It was nothing she needed to hide. She just knew the rumors would surely follow.

"You're friends with Eric now? You two totally hate each other. You're like oil and water. You don't mix."

"Yeah, I got that, Stacia."

"So, spill. What the hell happened?"

"We hung out over break. No big deal." Bryna stared straight ahead.

This really was no big deal. Stacia needed to keep her voice down before the entire squad drilled Bryna for answers.

"Okay, team!" the coach said, getting all the girls together. "Let's get over to the hotel. We have practice and dinner, and then you're free for the evening. However, that does not include alcohol of any kind. If you leave the premises, please take someone with you, and report back in by midnight at the latest! I will be checking to make sure you all are in your rooms, and nothing nefarious has happened."

"Pleasant," Bryna said.

"We will talk about this later," Stacia said.

After three hours of grueling practice and a quick dinner, the girls were finally released.

Neal had flown in from Tucson for the game and to meet Trihn. They were staying at the same hotel as the team. Stacia and Bryna met them in the lobby, and then they walked out to the beach together. The sun had set over the ocean, and the skyline was bathed in oranges and pinks.

"So, talk!" Stacia cried to Bryna.

Trihn looked at them in confusion. "What did I miss?"

"Bryna is friends with Eric Wilkins. Like *friends*," she said dramatically.

"Wait, what?"

"We are not anything more than friends."

"I thought you hated each other," Trihn said. "How did friends even happen?"

"We ran into each other at Posse and went to get ice cream."

Stacia gave her a knowing look. "You hung out with a guy and only got ice cream? Give me a break."

"I'm serious. Nothing happened. We just hung out a couple of times, but he's not interested in me at all. It's not a big deal." Bryna glared at her friends. She hated explaining herself.

"Wait, a couple of times?" Trihn asked.

Shit. "Yeah. We got lunch later that week and then went ice-skating at The Cosmopolitan," she confessed.

"You're dating Eric Wilkins," Trihn said.

"Oh my God!" Stacia screamed. "You're dating Eric! Mortal enemies now dating. How romantic. How does he kiss?"

Bryna stopped in her tracks. "We are not dating at all. No kissing. Nothing." She wished she could explain better, but they had no reason to believe her anyway. "I'm still seeing my hot stranger. He was out of town on break."

"Sure…" Stacia said.

She and Trihn shared a look that said they didn't believe a word Bryna had said.

"It's nice to have a guy friend, okay? I'm not worried about him making a move, so we just have fun. That's all."

"Fine," Stacia and Trihn said in unison.

The conversation changed to other topics as they wandered down the beach. Bryna was looking forward to a little bit of surf and tanning tomorrow afternoon, but her mind was still set on the upcoming rumors about her and Eric. She knew they would run rampant. They had with Andrew.

When they circled back to the hotel, Trihn and Neal walked off on their own. Bryna suspected they were going to have sex on the beach. Stacia apparently had plans for a late-night date with a nameless football player, which Bryna figured meant the same thing as what Trihn and Neal would be up to. That would leave Bryna all alone.

On her way back up to her room, she stopped one of the guys in the elevator. "Hey, do you know where Eric is?"

"Uh… in his room?"

She knew she wasn't helping matters at the moment, but they needed to talk. "Which room?"

"Coaches are on the eleventh floor. Ask someone up there."

"Thanks."

She made it up to the eleventh floor without incident, and thankfully, another guy directed her down the hallway even though he suspiciously looked at her. Cheerleaders were staying in different halls than football players and weren't supposed to be in their rooms. It was like high school all over again. But the players needed to keep their heads in the game. After tonight, there would be no more downtime for them.

She knocked on the door and crossed her arms over her chest.

"Coming!" Eric called from the other side. He answered the door in nothing but a pair of loose-fitting basketball shorts, and he looked like a fucking god.

Fuck. She glared at him harder.

"Hey," he said. "What's up?"

She ignored him and pushed him out of the way to get into the room.

"What? So, we're friends now?" He laughed

"We need to talk."

"Oh, this sounds serious." He shut the door behind her and leaned back against it. "You're pissed about the plane still?"

"No, I'm pissed that my friends think we're dating. We're clearly not dating."

"This is true," he agreed. "You're making a good case for it by cloistering yourself in my room."

"I don't date."

"Okay." He shrugged, unperturbed.

"And I'm fucking other people."

"Why are you trying to convince me?" he asked. He still looked completely relaxed against the door. He thought this was a joke.

"I'm not. I'm telling you that people are going to spread rumors."

"Don't they always?"

She sighed heavily. "Forget it."

"All right, chill. Ignore them like you usually do."

"Fine," she said. "I guess I'm going to go back to my room and shower. I feel like I have sand all over me."

"Curfew isn't for another hour," he pointed out.

"And?"

"Stay, and hang out. What else do you have to do?"

Nothing. She had nothing else to do.

Really, when it came down to it, she didn't care what people thought about her. *And if Eric doesn't care, then why should I?* It would probably help him out in the long run anyway.

In either case, it was nice having someone to hang out with where there was no competition or chance of getting hit on. This must be what other people considered a real friend.

SIXTEEN

IGNORING THE RUMORS WAS EASY to do with the national championship game on everyone's mind. LV State was sitting on top, undefeated, with everything to lose.

Bryna stood on the sidelines of the amazing new dome in Arizona. The ceiling had been retracted to let in natural light, and the grass was squishy under her feet. She had never been in a facility this impressive.

But her eyes were locked on the crowed in the packed stadium with the game going on behind her. She went through her sideline cheers with the girls as they all screamed their hearts out in hopes of rallying the already energized crowd.

LV State was down by four, and Louisiana State University had the ball. There was only enough time for one more drive, and things weren't looking good.

Bryna's base, Daniel, lifted her into the air. She had her arms up in a V. Her gold poms glittered in the stadium. There was so much noise all around her that everything else was forgotten, except for the game and the possibility of losing everything they had worked toward this year.

Daniel dropped her back down to the ground and then moved to one knee. She sat on his leg and watched the game on pins and needles.

The LSU quarterback had the ball. It was do or die. He threw it high. Her eyes followed the movement. There was no one nearby. The Gamblers still had one chance to get it back. One of the LSU players veered toward the ball.

They were going to lose. She couldn't breathe.

She felt as if she were watching the game in slow motion. She held her breath and waited for the LSU player to catch it and run it in for a touchdown. Then, out of nowhere, a Gambler got in front of the ball.

Bryna's mouth dropped open.

"Oh my God!" she yelled.

He had the ball!

As he streaked down to the end zone, Bryna jumped to her feet, screaming at the top of her lungs, "Go! Go! Go!"

Three excellent blocks brought him into the end zone. He dropped to his knee and put the ball on the ground.

The clock ran out. Game over.

The split second of silence after LV State had scored, beating LSU, was all encompassing. No one seemed to believe what had happened. They had won. Against all odds, they had won.

An undefeated season. This would go down in history.

Then, the dome exploded. The audience fell into an uncivilized riot with cheers from the LV State fans and boos from the LSU fans. People were streaming out of the stands while others pushed past security, jumped fences, and ignored the warnings from the people trying to hold them back from storming the field.

Bryna was swept into the mass of people who raced forward. She couldn't even care. They had won! They were national champions. The media was everywhere, asking players questions about the game. She could see Coach Galloway getting drenched from head to toe in Gatorade before shaking hands and speaking briefly for a moment with the LSU head coach. Then, the media, too, pulled the coaches away, anxious to hear their opinions about the outcome.

"Bryna," Eric said from behind her.

She whirled around. An electric smile lit up her face. "We won!" she screamed, launching herself at him.

He easily caught her and lifted her off the ground. Their hug was fierce and joyous, the rush of the win still fresh in their bodies.

"Two national championships for you!" she squealed in his ear.

"Feels damn good."

He slowly put her back down on the ground. Her body had been pressed tightly against his. Because of the commotion all around them, she hadn't noticed quite what it felt like to have his chest against hers. She shouldn't even be thinking about it now.

Their eyes met, and suddenly, all the noise turned to radio silence. She knew she should stop this. She shouldn't feel anything. She hated feeling. It freaked her the fuck out. But while staring at Eric, she couldn't help it. It was irrational. She clearly only wanted the one thing that she couldn't have. But she didn't know if it was for that reason or not. This wasn't supposed to happen to her. He wasn't interested. She was a cover. Nothing more. Nothing less.

Then, his lips were on top of hers. Unbelievably delicious soft, tender lips.

He was kissing her.

Eric Wilkins was kissing her.

Completely in the heat of the moment. All-consuming joy and passion from the game fueled this one singular perfect kiss.

His fingers threaded into her hair, and her body responded way too eagerly, as if she had never been kissed before. Fucking hell, it felt like it, like the world slowed, and there was nothing else other than this moment.

Then, the world came crashing down back around her.

"Fuck," she whispered. She took a step away from him. She noticed guys from the team were watching them. *Had they been catcalling at them?*

Then, it dawned on her. This had all been a cover. Everything. The kiss hadn't even been real.

She wished her lips didn't still tingle. Not that she wanted a fucking relationship. She was still digging Hugh. Eric wasn't even her type. At all.

And...fuck...

"Bri..."

"Can we go somewhere and talk?" she asked.

He nodded his head. "Yeah, let's go."

He looked uncertain about everything, and she didn't blame him. If half as much was going through his head as was going through hers, then he must be going crazy on the inside.

She knew she couldn't hold this secret in any longer. She had to let him know that she knew. She knew everything.

They veered through the crowd, back to the bustling locker rooms. Eric finally found an empty coach's room. Once they were inside, he shut and locked the door. He wasn't as cool, confident, and collected as normal. He actually looked a bit concerned. This wasn't going to be easy.

"I did *not* mean for that to happen," Bryna said.

"Yeah. Kind of got caught up in the moment."

"I know you're not interested in me that way. And I'm just getting used to our new friendship or whatever." She shrugged and glanced away from him. *Why is this so awkward?*

Ever since they had started hanging out, things hadn't been awkward. He was so easy to be around. But that kiss had changed something.

Or maybe it was all in her head. It hadn't *really* meant anything. All of the emotions had been running high from the game, and bam!

"It's okay. It was no big deal. We both got carried away," he said.

"I don't want this to change anything between us," she said immediately.

"It shouldn't have to."

"It's actually been nice, having a friend who I don't have to compete with and who doesn't want to get in my pants."

"I think your competitive nature is still intact. You did try to prove that by eating an entire banana split," he said with a rueful smile.

Bryna laughed, trying to loosen up some. "But not competition like with Stacia and Trihn. It's always about guys and money...and guys with money. With you, it's just us hanging out. I don't feel pressured to do anything or be anyone. You accept the bitch."

"I accept that you're not as bitchy as you think you are," he said.

"I wouldn't go that far. I'm still the same person."

"Maybe," he said, crossing his arms.

He still looked like he wasn't sure where all of this was headed, and she couldn't blame him. She had no idea how she was going to bring this up.

"But I wouldn't want you to feel pressured around me," he said. "I'm not that kind of guy."

"I know," she said automatically. She felt like she had her in. They were on the same page. "Oh my God, I can't hold it in any longer. I know your secret."

He raised his eyebrows. "What secret?"

She pushed her shoulders back and soldiered on. "You know." Her eyes were wide, silently pleading, *Please don't make me say it.*

"I don't think I do."

"Come on, Eric," she groaned.

"What makes you think it's a secret?"

Bryna fought back an eye roll. Of course it was a secret. "You know, none of the guys know. You're never seen with other girls. I don't know. Plus, if it wasn't a secret, then you wouldn't be asking me if it was."

He looked contemplative for a minute. "That's true, I suppose. I'm not sure how you found out, but I don't think anyone else knows."

"Don't worry. I've kept my mouth shut. I didn't want to out you if you weren't ready." She bit her lip.

"I didn't think you would tell anyone."

"I wouldn't Plus, I've known for a while. And we weren't really friends most of last semester, so I wasn't going to say anything. I think it's one of the main reasons I've been so comfortable around you. I don't do relationships. Feelings and emotions and love, if it exists at all, are completely overrated. If I'd thought you were into me, then none of this would have happened. I never would have let you get close."

She didn't need any more complications with guys in her life. It'd really worked out better for her in the end that Eric was gay. She could be herself around him, and he didn't judge her.

"You like to keep people at a distance," he said.

"Well, now, I don't have to keep you at a distance." She shrugged. "Since, you know, nothing's ever going to happen between us. But, um…that's all I wanted to say. We should probably get back anyway."

She opened the door before he could say anything else. The room was stifling. She hadn't expected it to be that difficult. He had seemed cool with her knowing, but a bit like she had put him in shock. It must be so weird for him to have someone else know that he was gay. At least she wouldn't have to hide that from him anymore.

But she wasn't sure why, in that moment, it didn't feel like as much of a relief as she had thought it would. Clearly, she needed to get laid. All this time without it had addled her mind and made her think things that couldn't possibly exist.

SEVENTEEN

BRYNA RETURNED TO LAS VEGAS on a total high. As she drove up the street toward her condo, she noticed another car in the driveway. A Mercedes SUV. *Fuck.*

She parked in the garage and entered through the side door. Inside, her condo looked like a land mine had gone off inside. There was stuff everywhere—boxes piled high, clothes strewed on the couch, and junk littered the floor.

"What the fuck is going on?"

A smile lit up Pace's face. "Hey, sis."

"What are you doing to my house?" she cried. "It's a train wreck."

"Moving in, of course."

Bryna ground her teeth. She had forgotten for one blissful weekend that her sleazy stepbrother was moving into her place. She had thought that, by forgetting about it, it would go away. But no, Pace was still standing right there in front of her.

"I can't believe you're really fucking moving in."

"I was offered a spot in the sports dorm, but I decided I wanted to be closer to my sister." He smirked devilishly. "The team understands."

"Ew. That's so nasty." She shook her head. "You know, I'm never going to be around anymore, and you'd better get all this shit cleaned up. This whole thing isn't right."

Pace shrugged. "You had your opportunity to get me not to come to LV State, but you didn't take it."

Bryna glared at him. "Yeah. Even if I had gone through with that stupid shit—which would never, *ever* happen—you would have *still* come here to spite me."

"You caught me. How could I resist coming here after they won the national championship?"

"You're a vile human being. I can't believe they even recruited you. You know, you're not going to get any playing time, right?"

She was sure he had already heard this argument, but she couldn't help one last-ditch effort to try to get him to change his mind. He could still transfer without any consequences.

"We'll see about that."

"With Blaine leaving, they're going to put Marshall in as QB, and you'll be sitting on the sidelines for the next three years."

Pace shrugged, unperturbed. "I'll believe it when I see it. I think I could take Marshall."

Bryna laughed. "Yeah, I'll believe *that* when I see it."

"Believe what?"

Bryna's head snapped around so fast that she got a crick in her neck. "Dad?" she cried in disbelief. Her eyes bugged out. She hadn't even heard him open the front door over the sound of her argument with Pace.

"Hey, sweetheart." He pulled her into a big hug.

"What are you doing here?" She hadn't seen him since Thanksgiving, and that had been tense, to say the least.

"I'm here to help Pace move in. It's good to see you. We're glad you made it safely back from Miami. What an exciting end to the game."

"It was," she agreed.

"Wish I had been there."

He could have come. She knew he could have. He was here with Pace, but he couldn't make time for her. It made no fucking sense.

"I think we got all of Pace's things moved in. I'd forgotten the size of this place. I think it's big enough for the both of you. Don't you?"

"Um, no. I don't think it is." Bryna pleaded with her father, "I need my own space. I can't share this with him."

"For now, this will have to do." He smiled brightly.

He seemed so relaxed, almost happy. She wasn't sure she had ever seen her father like this. He hadn't checked his work phone once since he came inside.

"Are you going to tell her?" Pace asked.

"Tell me what?"

"I wanted to talk to you in person about this, but you weren't home for Christmas, so now is the time," her father said.

Bryna wasn't sure what this was all about. *What does he have to tell me that's so important?*

"Come on outside. We'll talk about it there."

In a wave of confusion, she followed her father outside. Pace didn't look too pleased, and that also made her worry. He was normally smug about things.

The twins were lounging by the pool. Celia was standing near the edge of the pool, talking with them, wearing some hideous black maxi dress.

"Celia, darling," her father called.

"Lawrence!"

Celia had a huge smile on her face. In fact, she was almost glowing with joy.

That was when Bryna saw it. A lump. A round lump. Her head spun, and she reached out blindly for the first thing she could use to steady herself. Pace took her arm, and she swallowed hard.

Oh my God. No.

Her vision blurred and then cleared again. It wasn't going away. It was still there. The horrible monstrosity.

Celia was…pregnant.

"What the fuck is that?"

"We're so happy to tell you, Bryna," Celia said, walking toward them.

"You're going to have a new sister or brother," Lawrence said.

Bryna might be sick. She wrenched her arm out of Pace's and covered her mouth.

"What?" she nearly shrieked. *This could not be happening.*

"We're pregnant," Celia said.

"*You're* pregnant," Bryna corrected. "How the hell could this have happened? How the hell could you have let this happen?"

"Bryna," her father said warningly.

"I mean, how *old* are you?" she spat at Celia.

"Bryna!" he cried.

"It's okay. That's a perfectly normal reaction. Neither of us expected this to happen. It's okay that Bryna didn't expect this either. I know I'm older. It's unusual but not unheard of."

"Haven't you heard of birth control? Condoms? Getting your tubes tied? This is disgusting." Bryna whirled on her father. "You force these people into my life and then do this?" She shook her head. "I just can't."

Bryna slowly backed up, away from them. She knew they were trying to get through to her, but she couldn't hear anything. All she could see was that horrible belly.

She fled. She couldn't stand there for another minute.

Her hands were shaking, and her breath was coming out in short bursts when she made it into her cluttered living room. This shouldn't even have been possible. It was absurd.

"Hey," Pace said, following her into the room.

"Fuck off." She closed her eyes and tried to picture her life without this bullshit.

"I told them that I'd check on you."

"Mission accomplished. You can leave now."

"I don't want them to have a kid either, you know."

"Good for you," she spat.

"It's revolting. She shouldn't be pregnant at her age. And now, we have to share a sibling." He shuddered.

"Stop talking about it!" she screamed. God, it was getting worse and worse, the more she thought about it.

"I'm saying I agree with you. No agenda here." He held his hands up in surrender.

"You always have an agenda, even when you claim not to," she said.

"Not this time." He shrugged. "I knew you would respond like this. But I guess there's nothing we can do about it. Anyway, they seem happy, I guess. Maybe we should remember that."

"Or not. I'd rather them be miserable than have a baby."

"Do you really mean that?" he asked.

"Yes. Don't act surprised."

He shook his head. "Is this temper tantrum really because you don't want them to be happy? Or are you pissy because you aren't going to be his only baby anymore?"

Bryna clamped her mouth shut and glared at him. They shouldn't even be having this conversation. "Fuck off, Pace. I'm leaving."

"Where the hell are you going?"

"Away from you and this fucked-up family."

"What am I supposed to tell them?" he asked.

"Whatever you want. I don't give a shit."

With that, she left her condo. She needed time to think about and process what had happened. She had been ambushed, and she wasn't going to stand for it.

She definitely was going to need some retail therapy and then booze. Yes, liquor fixed everything.

Bryna pulled out her phone and jotted out a text to Trihn and Stacia.

SOS, bitches.

The rest of the week was hell. She spent as much time with the girls as possible and stayed far away from Pace. The last thing she wanted to think about was Celia's pregnancy or her stepbrother.

Thankfully, Hugh had arrived in town, and she could forget all about those pesky things.

She had called him after her blowup with Pace to confirm he was still coming into town. They had agreed to meet up at one of his resorts. She had never been there before, and she was excited that he was introducing her to more of his life. Ever since they had gone to Tahoe, she hadn't been as nervous about the whole thing. Everything was progressing smoothly. This was the relationship she'd wanted. No feelings. No emotions. No love. Just sex and money.

A woman greeted her at the entrance and took her straight up the elevator to the penthouse suite. The room was gorgeous, all marble-tiled floors, expensive white furnishings, and an unbelievable view of the Vegas Strip.

Hugh was seated at a large black desk in the office.

"So, this is where you work when you're in town?" Bryna asked. She leaned against the open doorway in her short black dress.

His smile was so easy and natural. He was clearly happy to see her. "Sometimes. I have an office, but people bother me there."

"Am I bothering you? Should I go?" she joked. She took a step back out the door.

"Absolutely not. You should come inside and sit your ass down on my desk."

She sauntered inside. "That might distract you."

"Distract away."

Bryna scooted past him until she was sitting on the edge of the desk in front of him. She reached back and shut his laptop. "Oops," she murmured.

He laughed.

"Is this distracting?"

His hands ran up her bare thighs. "Very."

She moved the laptop off to the side and then lay backward, taking up as much space as she could. She arched her back and let her blonde hair splay out all around her.

"Now, this is *extremely* distracting."

He pushed her legs apart and moved his hand up her body. She groaned and writhed on his desk. He had his pants around his ankles in a matter of minutes. Her panties followed, and then he was claiming her body.

It was pure pleasure.

No thinking. No confusion.

Just a man and a woman taking what they wanted.

She finished before him, and her orgasm brought on one of his own.

After cleaning up, she returned to the study to find him completely put together with two small boxes in front of him.

She arched an eyebrow. "What's that?"

"Your Christmas present," he said.

She sat back down and tried to hide her smile.

"And a little something else. Which would you like first?"

"Which would you like to give me first?" she asked.

He considered the question. "Your pick."

She licked her lips and stared down at her choices. "This one."

"Good choice." He handed the box to her.

She tore into the paper and popped the top. Inside was a plastic card with *WC Resorts* etched into one side. Her heart jumped. *Is he giving me a credit card? Were we there already?*

"What's this?" she asked.

He grabbed the other box and came around to the other side of the desk. "That," he said, "is a key to this suite."

"Oh?"

"I want to see you more, Bri. I don't know where this is leading, but I know I enjoy my time with you. I feel alive when I'm with you. I don't want to lose that feeling. So, I decided I wanted to make a plan to be here every other weekend to be with you, if you'd like, and you can have access to the penthouse and everything else your heart desires in my resort while you're here."

She couldn't rein in her shock fast enough. He was giving her an all-access card to WC Resorts—penthouse, spas, gambling, dinner, pool. Everything.

"This is so much," she breathed.

"It's not. I want you to be nearby when I'm in town. I'll have to work, so I won't always get to spend all my time with you, but I want you to have every luxury when I'm here."

"I love this. Thank you so much!" *How the hell is he going to top that?*

"I'm glad you like it." He handed her the second box.

"You give me your world," she said, holding up the card, "and then offer me another gift?"

"My world comes with a lot of them," he admitted.

She smiled and then took it out of his hands. She opened the lid and stared at bracelet inside. Her stomach plummeted. She felt sick.

Inside the box was a Harry Winston diamond tennis bracelet with a B that matched her necklace. The necklace Jude had given her.

"What is it?" Hugh could obviously see her disgust.

She pulled back the sickness threatening to overwhelm her and reminded herself that this was an unbelievably expensive gift. She should be thankful that he had been thoughtful enough to match the jewelry she wore on a regular basis. The necklace was her reminder, but he would never and could never know that.

"Nothing. It's lovely. Will you put it on for me?" she forced out.

He clasped the bracelet around her wrist, and she pretended to admire the thing. It was beautiful—if only it didn't reek of Jude.

"You seem tense." Hugh kissed her shoulder.

"Sorry. I've had a taxing week." She swallowed hard and decided to blame it on something else. "My stepbrother moved in with me. He's a deadbeat, and he basically has nowhere else to go. Since my dad owns the house, he decided my stepbrother had to stay with me."

She felt dumb, admitting it all. But wasn't part of all this gold-digging thing to have the guy support her? It would be nice to have the penthouse to disappear to when she needed to escape from Pace.

"That does sound stressful."

"You've no idea."

"Well, I'd offer to help reduce that stress." He brought her lips to his again. "But I do have some work to finish. Why don't you take that card down to the spa and try not to let anything bother you? I promise you a stress-free weekend."

That was exactly what she needed. One goddamn weekend without stress. She wasn't sure that was going to be possible with her new scarlet letter staring back at her. Just another notch in the belt.

EIGHTEEN

"I'LL NEED THAT PAPER TURNED IN ON FRIDAY. Don't forget!" Bryna's film professor said at the end of class.

Bryna packed up her MacBook into her Kate Spade case and carried it out of class. A lot of her classmates stayed behind to debate the finer merits of their latest assignment, but she couldn't really relate to any of her classmates. She was already happier in her intro film class than she was in any of her core requirements, but that didn't mean she wanted to stay after class for discussions. People already thought the only reason she was in the class was because of her director father anyway.

Besides, she had plans to meet Eric for lunch this afternoon. Her schedule ended after noon, and he had a light load this semester. It ended up that they both had a break on Wednesdays. She was supposed to meet him at the sports complex after the end of his class.

She made it across campus and into more familiar territory. Pulling open the double doors to the sports complex, she walked to the room where he was supposed to be but found it empty. She pulled her phone out and saw she had a text from Eric, saying he was downstairs, meeting with the coach.

She shrugged and took the stairs down to Coach Galloway's office. She found Coach and Eric standing in the hallway, talking to a man with his back facing her. He looked familiar, but she was sure her eyes were playing tricks on her.

Then, Eric noticed her. He smiled brightly and waved. "Hey, Bri. I'll be just a minute."

The guy they were talking to jerked his head around. They made eye contact across the short hallway, and everything stopped. No wonder he had looked so familiar.

It was Jude fucking Rose.

Everything in her world screeched to a halt. She was staring into the utterly gorgeous face of Jude Rose. It was like the last year fell away from them, and she was the young high school girl staring at a married man, thinking he loved her. She couldn't breathe or think. Everything felt muddled, like she was wading through water.

She could tell Jude was shocked to see her. They hadn't seen each other or spoken since he walked out. He had chosen Felicity. He had chosen to stay with his wife and son. Part of Bryna had understood why he had done it, but it didn't cure the wound opening in her chest at the sight of him.

Bryna stumbled backward as she came back to her senses. "I'll wait outside," she gasped.

She hurried out of the hallway, bounded back up the stairs, and leaned against the wall. Her breathing was ragged. She was struggling to keep from letting tears fall. She hadn't even cried when he left her. Tears didn't exist in her life. She didn't cry. She hated crying. Whenever she had thought about the moment she might meet Jude again, whenever she had allowed herself that moment of self-sabotage, she had thought she would be smooth and cool. But she wasn't.

She couldn't have gotten out of there fast enough. Seeing him felt as if she had shrapnel under her skin. No matter which way she moved, it kept digging deeper, trying to pierce her heart.

She knew she shouldn't feel anything for Jude, but she couldn't seem to help it. She couldn't get it together. He was everything. He had been everything when they were together, and he occupied her thoughts even now. She still wore his motherfucking necklace. But he had deceived her and left her powerless. Now, she craved the control he had stolen from her.

Jude shouldn't be able to shatter all of that control so easily.

"Goddamn it," she muttered.

At that moment, Eric appeared at the top of the stairs. "Hey, are you okay?"

"Yeah. Fine." Her voice was shaky. She knew she didn't look fine. She turned her face away from him. God, she probably looked like shit.

"Bryna," he said softly, "what's wrong?"

She shook her head. "I really don't want to talk about it. Let's just go."

She shouldered her bag and rushed toward the exit without giving him an opportunity to object. Eric followed her because he had no other option. As they walked to his Jeep, he looked like he wanted to say something, but he didn't. For that, she was grateful. She needed a little more time to get herself together.

They found his car in the parking garage a couple of minutes later, and she took a deep breath before taking the passenger seat. He revved the engine but didn't leave.

"So, are you going to tell me what that was all about?" he asked.

"No," she said.

"Are you sure? Usually, when your upset, you go into a drunken rage. Do we need liquor?"

Bryna looked him squarely in eyes. "No, I'm fine. No liquor necessary."

He sighed disbelievingly. "All right. What do you want for lunch?"

"I'm suddenly not hungry. Let's go…somewhere else."

"I can make something at my place," he offered.

"Sure."

Eric rented out a house on the east side of campus. It looked nice from the outside. She hadn't known what to expect, but the inside was nice, too.

"Do you live by yourself?" she asked.

"Yeah. I'm on a stipend from the university after my injury, and they cover everything," he explained.

She glanced out the back glass door and saw he even had an in-ground swimming pool. "They hooked you up."

"I know. I'm pretty lucky." He grabbed things out of the fridge. "You said you weren't hungry, but I'm grilling hamburgers. Should I make you one?"

She shrugged. "I guess."

She crossed her arms over her chest and followed him outside. She sat on a cushioned bench and tried to return to her normal state of being. She felt as if she had been drugged.

Eric started up the grill and surreptitiously glanced at her. "So, are you okay? You seem kind of…"

"What?"

"Emotional."

Bryna bit her lip. If she didn't stop overanalyzing everything, she was going to break down in tears.

"You don't have to tell me if you don't want to, but I know something happened back at school. I just don't know what."

Maybe she should tell him. No one else knew, and it was her burden to carry. She was worried about what Eric would think of her when he found out everything. It was weird to worry about that. He didn't seem as if he would judge her. Their friendship was such a tenuous new thing though, and she didn't want to fuck it up.

"So, you remember that guy I told you about?" she asked. "The one I went away with for Christmas last year?"

"Yeah?"

"He was a real asshole," she admitted. "We dated for a couple of months when I was a senior. We spent so much time together, but it was a secret relationship. No one knew we were together. I thought we were so in love. I couldn't see that the fun mystery of it all was from him holding on to a lie and keeping me at arm's length. Turned out, he was married and still seeing his wife when he had told me he was separated...and he had a kid to boot."

Eric looked disgusted. She shouldn't care what he thought, but she did.

"Jesus," Eric said. "He was married with a kid, and you never knew? Shit! What a fucking asshole!"

Bryna steeled herself for what she was about to say next. "Yeah, well, you were meeting with that asshole today."

Eric turned to stone. "What?"

"His name is Jude Rose, and he's the best sports agent in the industry. I'm guessing Blaine is signing with him, and that's why he was on campus."

Eric's mouth dropped open. "That asshole was Jude Rose?"

"Yeah." Bryna looked away, uncertain. "I didn't know he was a sports agent either at the time. It was a whirl of lust and luxury. He seemed to get me, but he was really playing me."

"I'm sorry," he said wholeheartedly. "I can't believe that happened to you."

"I was a willing participant."

"You can't be a willing participant to that level of deception. You were in high school, for Christ's sake!"

"I don't let it rule me." She tried for confidence. "I'm in control now. I know what I want, and he showed it to me in a rather explicit way."

"What do you mean? What is it that you want?"

"What I told you all along. You didn't believe me, but I want someone to take care of me like he did. I want all the luxury and none of the baggage."

"No offense, but you sound like a gold digger, which is absurd, considering who you are."

"There are worse things to be." She shrugged. "And who am I anyway? Any money I have comes from my father, who is also forcing me to live with my pervy asshole stepbrother. I can't live like this forever."

Eric's eyes went wide. He didn't like Pace. She knew that much, but there was something else in his eyes that she couldn't place. *Pity?*

"This guy really fucked you up, didn't he?"

Her silence was answer enough.

"I'd kick his ass if I could," he said.

"Don't bother. I could have buried him, but I didn't. I wanted to come out of this on top."

"You were hurt in a relationship. I can understand that. You don't have to put up this act for me."

Bryna shook her head. "It's *not* an act, and I'm not hurt. I'm finally seeing things clearly."

"All right," he said.

But she knew he could *never* understand. *How could he?*

Her phone buzzed noisily in her pocket, and she plucked it out. The text message was from a number she didn't recognize, but it had an L.A. area code. She frowned. This felt eerily familiar.

"Hmm…" she murmured. She opened the message.

Are you free?

"Well, that's interesting."

"What?" Eric asked.

"I just got a message from the devil himself."

NINETEEN

"ARE YOU GOING TO ANSWER HIM?" Eric asked.

Bryna shrugged. "I guess."

He gave her an exasperated look as she typed back a response.

Who is this?

She was pretty sure it was Jude, but she had deleted his number out of her phone long ago. It was possible it was someone else. She just doubted it. After seeing him on campus, she had done nothing but think about him. Perhaps it was vanity to think he had been doing the same.

Bri, you know who this is.

With proof before her, joy sparked in her belly with the new knowledge.

Do I?

She knew she was playing coy, but she wanted him to say it. She wanted him to admit that it was him and that he couldn't stop thinking about her. It was sick and twisted, but she couldn't deny it.

Yes.

His answer was so resolute, but another message followed quickly behind it.

I wasn't expecting to see you today.

I noticed. Why are you texting me?

Let's meet up.

She ground her teeth together. Honestly? Just like that? She could tell in one text message that he wanted to start everything up all over again. A year down the drain, and all for nothing.

So, you saw me for a whole two seconds, and what? The temptation to cheat on your wife was too great?

I just want to see you.

No. I haven't heard from you in a year. You made your bed, and now, you have to lie in it.

"Ugh," she grumbled.

"What's he saying?" Eric flipped the burgers and tried not to look too interested in her conversation.

"He's being…himself." The next buzz sent her scrambling back to find out what he'd said.

You're not the least bit curious about what I have to say?

No.

Yes, she was insanely curious. *Why now? Is it because he's in Vegas and his wife isn't here to watch over him? Is it ease of access? Or does he have something legitimate he wants to say?*

She cursed her heart for hoping. Hope was the drug of the weak.

Liar.

That one word cut like knives.

That's your repertoire.

I'd say we share the talent.

Ugh! Why am I even considering this? Why am I even allowing him to have this conversation with me? After everything, he was weaseling his way back in.

What do you want?

To see you. To talk.

Talk? Honestly? How do I know this isn't a lie? A trap?

She knew who he was. Jude never wanted to just talk, and being near him was toxic. This very conversation was bad enough. Seeing him would be the equivalent of Hiroshima.

> *What does it matter? You're considering it by talking to me. Give in to your curiosity. I have a hotel room nearby. Meet me.*

She shook her head. He would never change. She knew she shouldn't even consider going. But then again, she wasn't seeing anyone. Not really. That also had never been their problem.

She hated second-guessing herself, and she hated wondering what-if. What-if had never done anyone any good. She needed to put this all behind her.

Fine. Send me the address.

Bryna tossed her phone into her purse at her feet. "Speaking of the devil, guess I have to cut our lunch short."

"So, you're really going to go see him? After everything you told me?" Eric asked.

"Yep." She stood and stretched out her legs. "It probably doesn't make sense to you."

It didn't make much sense to her, except that she was drawn to Jude and too damn curious not to go.

"No. It doesn't make sense. Do you think this is a good idea?"

"Probably not."

"And you're going to go anyway?"

"Yeah," she confirmed.

"What's the likelihood that you'll walk out of this *less* fucked up?"

She considered the question. "I'd guess it's a one-in-a-million shot."

"And you're still going to go?"

"Pretty much."

"How exactly do you plan on getting there?" he asked. His arms were crossed over his chest. His hamburgers were forgotten on the plate he had rested them on.

"I guess if you don't take me, I'll have to walk there myself," she told him defiantly.

He sighed. She could see he was as resigned as she was.

"All right. Can I take you, and when he inevitably pisses you off, kick his ass?"

"You're not going to fight me on this?"

"I'd love to. Trust me," he grumbled. "But arguing with you is like trying to move a mountain. You're set on this."

"Yeah, I am."

"Promise to be careful."

Bryna shrugged. She was never careful. Life was too short. It was better to live dangerously and recklessly or not at all. She had every right to give Jude a piece of her mind, an opportunity that had been robbed from her for a year. He had taken so much and given nothing in return. She deserved this moment.

This time, she wasn't naive enough to think that he cared about her or that she loved him. She wouldn't be caught off guard with his presence like she had been on campus. She was too smart to be trapped in his snare.

Eric clearly wanted to argue with her more, but he didn't. He didn't pressure her to do the right thing. He didn't try to tell her that seeing Jude would be the wrong move. He didn't even say anything about the nerves in his posture. He must seriously think she was going to die after one interaction with Jude. She was stronger than that.

She would have to be.

Eric and Bryna made it to the hotel where Jude was staying. It was a five-star hotel off campus, and Eric knew where it was without her telling him. He drove up to the entrance to let her out.

She took a deep breath.

She started to get out, but he reached out and grabbed her arm.

"Hey."

"Yeah?" she asked.

"I hope you know what you're doing."

"Me, too," she whispered.

"I'll wait for you."

She shook her head. "No. I can't ask you to do that."

"You didn't ask."

She smiled. "Thanks for being a good friend, but I'll be fine. I don't know how long I'll be."

"Call me when you're done then."

"I will." She shrugged off his arm. "Don't worry about me."

He didn't think she was fine on a good day, and today was far from that. She almost felt a pang of regret for putting him in this position, but it disappeared quickly.

Bryna entered the hotel and took the elevator up to Jude's room. Her hands were shaking when she reached his door. She took a few deep breaths until her body was calm and relaxed once more.

She repeated the mantra in her mind that had so often calmed her before, *I am queen. I am queen. I am queen.*

She knocked.

Someone shuffled around inside the room, and then the door was opening. She'd thought she was prepared. She'd thought this wouldn't affect her like earlier when she hadn't expected him. She had been wrong.

The breath whooshed out of her lungs at the sight of him. *God, he's beautiful.* Up close, words didn't do him justice. Dark hair, all-knowing dark eyes, those lips, that jaw—it was too much. He looked perfect in a suit. His tie was missing, and the top button had been undone. Her stomach fluttered.

She would not break. She could do this.

"Bri," he said. He seemed to taste her name on his tongue.

She wished it had made her cringe, but it only drew her in.

She was fucked.

"Come on in."

He opened the door wide, and she entered his suite. It was modest for his tastes, but she suspected he would only be here for the night. He would have gone more extravagant if he had to actually spend any time in the hotel. He clearly hadn't been expecting visitors. He was a man of many pleasures and liked to showcase them.

"I knew you'd come."

He walked up behind her. She could feel his presence so close to her. She forced herself to remain still. She was not intimidated.

"I've heard that before," she said coyly.

He laughed lightly in her ear. She felt powerless in that moment, pulled into his enthrallment. She both loved and hated the feeling. This was why she had gotten with Hugh in the first place. She wanted the power. She could have her own exhilarating moments without the inevitable destruction that could follow.

"You know," he whispered, "I'm glad you're here."

His hand slid across the small of her back. His touch was like an electric current under her skin. It would be so easy to lean into him. She could let him sweep her away in his tempting dance. But she knew she couldn't, not if she wanted to make it out of here intact.

"Let's not." She stepped away and faced him. "I might be only a year older, but I'm infinitely wiser. I'm not going to drop at your feet over your seduction techniques."

"Oh, how I do love you on your knees though."

Bryna glared at him. This was not how she had envisioned the conversation. Though she hadn't really known what it would be like anyway.

"Stop it," she snapped.

"You're right, of course," he said, clearing the distance. "You're so over it all." He flicked the diamond necklace that he had given her.

She defiantly raised her chin. "Oh, you like my scarlet letter?" She held up her wrist where the bracelet Hugh had given her a couple of weeks ago was attached. "Looks like I've gotten another."

Jude seemed surprised at first, and then his cool demeanor returned. "I see you've upgraded."

"That is an understatement," she said. She couldn't keep the malice from her voice. "If this was all you wanted to say to me, then this was a total waste of my time."

"You know why you came here," he said. He stepped toward her, walking her backward. "You didn't give a shit about what I might say. You came here because you haven't seen me in a year."

"I thought I would find an ounce of a decent human being, and I was wrong."

He grabbed her around the waist. Her body distinctly remembered the feel of his touch. She wanted nothing more than to let those memories wash over her. She could drown in the memories.

"Stay here with me," he said. His words weren't even pleading. They were a demand, as if he thought he had any right to demand something from her.

His mouth was on hers a second later. She gasped, and his tongue slipped into her mouth. He tasted amazing. Her whole world surrendered. This was what it was supposed to be like, yet it was all wrong. She hated herself for enjoying it.

She roughly pushed him away from her. "How dare you! Jesus Christ! I cannot believe you're trying to fuck me right now. You are married. You have a kid! If she knew you were here right now, you would never see the light of day again. I could bury you."

Jude seemed unperturbed. "Oh, Bri, you wouldn't— even if you wanted to."

"You're an asshole." She was shaking again. She couldn't seem to stop.

All the emotions she'd buried deep inside herself were breaking free. Everything felt too real.

"You ripped my life apart and left me without a word, and all you got was a slap on the wrist for your behavior. I should have known better than to think *you* would act like the grown-up in all of this."

She glared at him. She was disgusted. In him. In herself.

"Bri, come on," he said as she stormed toward the door.

This had been a mistake. A horrible mistake. Seeing him had fucked everything up rather than making everything better. She had thought it would be bad but not like this. Not like she had a gaping wound in her body.

"Don't," she snapped. "Leave me alone. Call your wife, and forget this entire thing."

She rushed out of the room and down the hall. Jude didn't follow her. She didn't know why she had expected him to. It wasn't in his nature to be kind or caring or loving. He'd wanted her to come to his hotel room to have sex. No consequences for him. He had never once thought about what it would do to her.

She couldn't keep it together.

She fished out her phone and fumbled through her contacts to find Eric's name.

He answered immediately. "Bryna, are you okay?"

Tears streamed down her face. "No," she admitted. "Will you come get me?"

"I'm waiting for you outside."

"You waited?" she asked. She didn't know how long she had been inside with Jude, but it had been a while.

"I had a feeling you might need me to."

She brushed the tears off her cheeks with the back of her hand. "Thank you."

There he was, waiting in his Jeep out front just as she had left him.

She sank heavily into the passenger seat.

"I'm guessing that one-in-a-million shot didn't happen?"

"No, it didn't."

She leaned across the car and rested her head on his shoulder. He didn't protest as more tears leaked from her eyes.

"You were right. It's worse now," she whispered.

TWENTY

LIFE WAS A BLUR.

One big, hazy blur.

The weeks following her unfortunate meeting with Jude, Bryna felt like she had been transported in time. She was back to those first couple of weeks after Jude had walked out of her life. She was a zombie. A total mess.

Even her tired mantra couldn't save her from the crippling depression. She walked through classes, cheer practice, parties, all of it with the pretend ease she normally ruled with. But she didn't feel it, and she didn't care.

Trihn and Stacia tried to pull her out of her funk, but they didn't know what had happened. Any help they had was belied by their ignorance, and she refused to clue them in. They were busy with their own lives. Trihn and Neal were sickeningly cute together, and Stacia seemed to have some new guy she wasn't talking about yet. It left Bryna with too much alone time, and thus, she spent a lot of her afternoons at Eric's place, avoiding Pace.

Even Hugh had seemed to notice a change in her mood. She could only fake so much with him. She had tried to be positive and upbeat for Valentine's Day, which had landed on one of the weekends Hugh was in town. But all it had done was remind her of the Pink Charity Benefit where Jude had left her.

Two more weeks had passed in no time, and she was on her way back to Hugh's resort where she anticipated spending the weekend relaxing at the spa and shopping before locking herself away in his penthouse when he wasn't working.

She made it upstairs and found Hugh sitting on the balcony, staring out at the Strip.

"Hey," she said with a smile.

He frowned when he saw her. That wasn't normal.

"What's up?" she asked.

"I hate seeing you like this."

"Like what?" She raised her chin and tried to fall naturally into her own self-confidence. She walked over to him.

"You seem off."

She smiled and shrugged her shoulders. "I'm fine. Really."

"Yes. Well, in either case, I decided I wanted to get you a little pick-me-up."

Bryna smirked, wondering what he had in store for her.

"First, I have to do some work in the area. Will you drive with me?"

"Of course. You know I'm yours on the weekend."

"Hopefully, all the time." He circled her waist and kissed her lips.

She let herself relax into the kiss. It was only in these moments when she could forget. She craved them.

She didn't want to think about the fact that Hugh had said "all the time." They'd never discussed their relationship. She'd thought it was pretty clear what they were doing. But he seemed more...attached every time they were together. She enjoyed their being around him, and she liked Hugh. But it wasn't *love* or anything. This was too good for him to fuck it up with real emotions.

They took the elevator to the valet station. He had a metallic-blue Ferrari convertible waiting for him, and her mouth dropped. *God, I'm such a car whore.*

"Oh my God, she's beautiful."

He laughed. "I thought you might like it."

"Like? Love. This is the definition of perfection."

"You're right. I'm looking at it."

She felt his hot and enticing gaze on her. She sauntered toward the passenger seat and let him check out her ass.

"Where are we headed?" she asked.

"I'm looking at some real estate."

"Oh, exciting," she said. Sitting in the plush leather seat did a lot to lift her spirits.

He sank in the driver's seat, shifted into gear, and peeled out of the resort. She wished she were the one controlling the stick shift, but on some level, she was.

As he took the highway east, the wind whipped her hair all around her face. It was refreshing, finally getting the warm weather back. They meandered through a neighborhood not too far from her condo right now. Her eyes wandered over all the beautiful two-story houses. Each one was a little bit different, and she liked the elegance and diversity in her desert home.

Hugh stopped outside of a house with a *For Sale* sign up in the yard.

"I like it," she said immediately.

"Let's check out the inside."

They walked up to the front, and Hugh punched in the code to enter. He let her in first.

The walkway was massive with a huge staircase leading up to the second story. She looked straight out through the glass French doors that opened up to a balcony. The kitchen was top of the line, all stainless steel appliances, granite countertops, and a big bay window surrounding a breakfast nook. The living space was outrageous with a sunken living room that connected to the dining room and office. Upstairs, there were three full bedrooms. The master took up half of the house with one enormous walk-in closet and a waterfall shower that could have been its own private lagoon.

"Wow," she murmured once they finally made it outside.

The backyard had a landscape swimming pool, complete with a waterfall, lazy river, and twin hot tubs.

"This is epic. You should definitely get it," she said.

Hugh held his hand out, and she walked back toward him.

"Here."

She looked down and saw a key in his hand. "What's that?"

"I got it for you."

"Got…what for me?" she asked, astonished.

"The house."

Her jaw dropped. "You…got me a house? I thought we came here to look at real estate for you for, like, an employee or friend or relative or something."

"Well, surprise."

Her eyes surveyed the incredible house in stunned silence. Hugh had gotten her a house. She didn't know what to say.

He pressed the key into the palm of her hand. "You have been so out of it lately. I figured it must be related to things at home. You mentioned you were having difficulties with your stepbrother. I wanted to do something special for you." His lips were tender when they met hers. "I hope you like it."

"I love it."

This was more than she could have ever imagined when she'd started this with him. *A house? A fucking house? Shit!*

"Good."

She beamed at him. "Thank you. I'll never be able to thank you enough. What do I need to do?"

"Seeing that smile back on your face is thank-you enough. Don't worry about anything. I paid for it in cash. Your name is on the contract, but I have my accountant handling taxes and upkeep. I wanted this for you."

"This is insane," she said, unable to keep from smiling.

He laughed. "A little. All you have to do is furnish it. Maybe we could do that together," he suggested.

"Absolutely," she squealed. *I have my own house!* She pulled him closer and planted a very thankful kiss on his lips. "We'll have to christen every room."

Sunday afternoon, Bryna left Hugh, so he could fly back to Vail. They had ordered a good deal of furniture together, but it would take a lot more work before her new house was all in order. She still couldn't fucking believe it. The only way to make it real would be to tell everyone she knew.

She dialed Trihn's number and waited for her friend to answer.

"B! You've resurfaced from your secret weekend arrangements," Trihn joked.

"And what an amazing secret it has been, but I think it's time to clue you guys in."

"Hot stranger?"

"Oh, yes. Big news. You and Stacia are going to flip when you hear this."

"Ah!" Trihn screamed. "I'll call her, and we'll meet at my place?"

"Sure. Be there in ten."

Stacia was already at Trihn's off-campus apartment when Bryna parked her Aston Martin on the street. She jogged up the first flight of stairs, and Trihn let her inside.

"Oh my God!" Stacia cried. "Look at you! You actually look happy. I have my bestie back."

Bryna laughed. She felt like herself again. The past month of depression had seemed to wash off of her in one afternoon. It wasn't that she had forgotten about Jude's devastation, but she had renewed purpose. Things with Hugh were on the right course, and the irony wasn't lost on her that she had gotten the house because of her distress over Jude.

"It's good to be back. So, you both know I've been seeing Hugh, my hot stranger."

"Yeah," Trihn said.

"For so long! We're dying to get details," Stacia said.

"Well, he's a resort owner."

Stacia's mouth dropped open. "For real?"

Bryna nodded. "Oh, yes. I mean, I've gotten luxurious things from him, but today took the cake."

"Better than the Alexander McQueen dress and the Harry Winston bracelet?" Trihn asked. "This should be good."

Bryna produced the key out of the front pocket of her purse. "This."

"Gah!" Stacia cried. "What does it open?"

"Let me guess!" Trihn said. "A car?"

"Does this look like a car key?" Bryna asked.

"No. A fancy hotel room?" Stacia guessed.

"A safety deposit box," Trihn said.

"Oh my God, no. You're crazy."

"Tell!" Stacia said.

"A house!" she squealed.

Both girls jumped up in shock.

"A house?" Trihn asked.

"Yes! And on top of that, he's letting me furnish it however I want."

"Are you moving in together?" Stacia asked.

Bryna wrinkled her nose. "No. Please. He doesn't even live in Vegas. He flies in most weekends to see me. This is mine, and he's covering everything! So, I figured, once I have it all in order, we should throw a huge party!"

Stacia jumped up and down with excitement, and Trihn turned up the music she was streaming from the LV State radio station. Like lunatics, the girls danced around the room to the song that was playing. The DJ's voice filtered through the station at the end.

"God, I love his voice," Trihn breathed. "I'm a sucker for an English accent. It was the best part about modeling in the UK."

"Totally," Stacia agreed.

"I'm happy to announce the international debut of America's sweetheart's first single," the DJ said, his thick English accent making every word delectable. "This is 'Homesick' by Chloe Avana."

Bryna's jaw dropped. "Chloe Avana?"

"I *loved* her in *Broken Road*," Stacia swooned.

Bryna rolled her eyes. Yes, Chloe was her ex-boyfriend Gates's costar in the smash hit *Broken Road*. And Chloe was the girl he had slept with after Bryna had broken up with him over the phone. When he had come back, he had pretended like they hadn't broken up, and he'd forgotten to mention that he'd slept with Chloe. Bryna could have fed him to *People* magazine, but she had done enough damage in his life.

Chloe's career had exploded over the past year. She had starred in another movie last year, and she'd be starring in two more blockbusters scheduled for this year. Now, apparently, she had dropped a record, too.

Jesus!

"I officially love this song," Trihn said. She swayed her hips in time with the catchy techno backbeat. Growing up, she had danced most of her life, so when she got going, she was a sight to witness.

"Ugh! Turn it off," Bryna complained. She wished it weren't so catchy.

"You're nuts. I love it!" Stacia said.

"Okay. You listen to her then. She's sweet and all, but I've had enough of her for one lifetime." Bryna sure knew how to hold a grudge. "We'll plan later. I'm going to head over to E's."

"Wait, what?" Trihn shrieked.

"Eric's?" Stacia asked.

"Yeah," Bryna said.

She hung out with Eric all the time now. She had gone from hating him to wanting to spend all her time with him.

"You are *so* dating him!" Stacia said.

"No, I'm really not."

"Admit it, Bri," Trihn said. "You're with him so much. You two go and get food together. You spent Christmas together."

"That's called dating, honey," Stacia remarked.

"You guys don't understand."

"Then, help us understand." Trihn crossed her arms over her chest and incredulously looked at her. "Because everyone thinks you two are dating."

"Oh my God!" Bryna cried. "He's *gay!*"

TWENTY-ONE

"WHAT?" Stacia and Trihn cried in unison.

"Yes. Okay? Eric is gay. One hundred percent not interested in girls. Last time I checked, I'm a girl. He's not into me. Thus, we are not dating."

"No way!" Stacia said. "I don't believe you."

"Yeah. I'm with the cheer slut. I can't see someone like Eric being gay," Trihn agreed.

"What does that mean?" Bryna asked defensively.

"Nothing. I didn't mean it like that. I meant, he has an ex-girlfriend. He totally hits on you," Trihn said.

"Yeah, an ex-girlfriend who was a cover and a girl who is a friend, who is a cover." Bryna pointed at herself. "We talked about it. He's cool with me acting as a cover."

"I just...wow," Stacia said. "You're serious?"

"Yes, I'm serious!"

"I'm so shocked." Trihn sat down heavily on the bed. "I for sure thought that you two were dating behind everyone's backs and hiding it poorly. He seems to ground you. I thought you were perfect together."

"Nope. Nothing mushy going on. You both know I don't believe in love, emotions, and other disgusting things. Eric and I are just friends."

"Wow," Stacia repeated.

"But you two have to *swear* to never breathe a word of this. Not even to Neal, Trihn. Eric's obviously not out and not ready to be. Football players are hard enough to be in charge of. I wouldn't want any of their prejudices to interfere with his coaching. He's still a great coach."

"I won't say anything," Trihn said automatically. "You have to worry more about the big mouth over here." She pointed her thumb at Stacia.

Her blue eyes went wide. "I'm horrible at secrets, but I promise not to say anything. If I do, you can cut me off from the cheer world."

"That would be the end of her," Trihn confirmed.

"Okay, good. Not a word of this. I couldn't stand you two saying that Eric and I were together any longer." Bryna shouldered her purse. "I'm going to head out now."

"Tell Eric we said hi," Stacia said.

Bryna shook her head. "Sure."

Trihn walked her to the door. "You know, I'm still really surprised. I thought he was into you."

"I never get that vibe, and it's for the better."

"Well, I hope you find someone who stirs emotions back into you. I know you've been hurt. I can tell." Trihn placed her hand on Bryna's shoulder. "We're here for you. Maybe...let people in every now and then."

Bryna bristled under Trihn's scrutiny. Letting people in was what had caused all of her strife in the first place. She didn't mind Trihn and Stacia. She had never had friends like them before, but guys were a big *no*. It was easier to get everything she needed from them and keep them at a distance. She wasn't making the mistake of letting anyone get close to her like Jude again. Look what it had done. One afternoon with Jude, and she had been a mess. Never again.

"I appreciate it, Trihn. But I've got it all figured out."

"I know you do," she said, letting Bryna walk out the door. "But sometimes, when you let people into your heart, it doesn't automatically equal heartbreak."

"I'd have to have a heart to break," she said.

Trihn's laughter didn't reach her eyes. They both knew Bryna wasn't joking.

Bryna left Trihn's apartment and drove across town. She hadn't told Eric she was coming over, but she didn't think Eric would care. Spring practice would resume soon, and they would have less time to hang out. That made her frown, but then she reminded herself that she had a whole new house to herself.

She entered through the unlocked front door and found a pitcher of margaritas hanging out in the blender.

"Eric?" she called.

No answer.

She poured herself a glass of margarita and then carefully walked out the back door. There Eric was, in nothing but swim trunks and Ray-Ban Wayfarers. He had a notebook out in front of him and a half-empty margarita on the table. He looked...god-like.

Fuck me sideways. He's so freaking hot. The hot ones are always gay.

When she padded out toward him, he glanced up from his notebook.

"Oh, sure. Pour yourself a glass. I wasn't going to drink that."

"I knew you made a double batch just for me." She beamed.

"You're nothing if not predictable."

She laughed. "Yeah, right. What about me is predictable?"

"You're here"—he gestured to the pool area—"every Sunday afternoon like clockwork."

"I'm here all the time. That's not fair."

"Life isn't fair, Hollywood."

"Well, that's the damn truth." Even though a half-dozen lounge chairs were around the pool, she sat down right on the edge of his seat. Half of her body blocked his sun, and she lounged halfway back on his lap. "Ah, this is the life."

He looked down at her from over the top of his Wayfarers. "You're chipper."

"The universe has been very nice to me today."

"Is that so?" Eric asked.

"Mmhmm. I am now the proud owner of a new house."

He tilted his head to the side, and it was all she needed to know that he thought she was being ridiculous.

"A house? How the hell could you afford to buy a house? Or did your dad finally budge and let you out of you living with Pace?"

"No, he didn't, and I didn't buy it. It was given to me."

"Someone gave you a new house? How exactly did you acquire this property?"

"Hugh."

"Is…"

"The guy I'm seeing," she finished for him.

"Digging, you mean. I know those words are kind of similar, but they mean slightly different things."

"Sure. Seeing, digging—whatever. Same thing."

"So, this poor sap handed you the keys to a house?"

"Yep. Pretty much." She tipped half of the margarita back in her mouth. "Like I said, this is the life."

"I feel so bad for this guy." Eric closed his notebook and set it down next to his drink. "He has no idea who he's dealing with."

"Oh, please," Bryna said, dismissively waving her hand. "Don't get all judgy on me, E. He likes it, and he knows exactly what's happening."

"And do you?"

"Of course," she purred. She closed her eyes and soaked up the sun. "I always know what I'm doing."

He snorted at her comment. "Sounds like someone needs a reality check."

All of a sudden, Eric was moving. His arms slid under the crook her legs and then her shoulders. She didn't even have time to wriggle out of his grasp before he was hoisting her into the air and cradling her against his chest. He was smirking, and she knew that was *not* a good thing.

"What the fuck?" she cried. "Oh my God, what are you doing?"

He walked toward the edge of his pool.

"If you get me near that pool, I will murder you."

"This is for your own good."

"Eric!" she screamed.

But it was no use. Without another thought, he effortlessly tossed her, completely clothed, into the crystal-clear water. Her body crashed through the still water, and she sank under.

Holy shit!

She clambered for the surface, sputtering, as her head popped out of the water. "It's fr-freezing, you asshole!"

But Eric wasn't listening to her. He was doubled over, laughing hysterically. His laughter was infectious, and even though she was pissed at him, she suddenly couldn't stop laughing either.

"What did you just do?" she asked.

She swam to the edge of the pool and lifted her shaking figure out of the water. Her dress was ruined. It was silk, and now, she was going to have to toss it. Not to mention, her hair and makeup that she had just had done at the spa earlier this afternoon was beyond ruined. Hundreds of dollars had gone down the drain, all with one throw into the pool.

"You should see yourself right now," Eric got out between laughing. "My ribs. Christ, it hurts."

"I don't want to hear it. I'm the one soaking wet."

"You look like a drowned rat."

"How flattering," she said. She shook her head, and more laughter pealed out of her. She didn't even know why it was so funny. She was freezing and wet, but she couldn't stop laughing. She tried to pull herself together. "Well, here's your reality check, Cowboy. I'm not afraid of a little water."

She reached behind herself and grabbed the zipper on the back of her dress. She dragged it to the base of her spine. The material was sticky and hugged her frame. She pulled it off her shoulders and over her breasts. She wiggled it over her hips and then let it land with a wet squish on the floor. That left her in nothing but a soaked sheer white La Perla bra and thong set.

She spread her arms wide. "I'm not afraid, and you've now ruined a four-hundred-dollar dress. Let's play."

He swallowed and averted his eyes. "I'm not getting in that water."

"You can dish it out, but you can't take it?"

His eyes shot back to hers, and for a second, it was as if he were checking her out. But she knew he wasn't. He was probably embarrassed that she wasn't embarrassed. She knew she had a rocking body. Nothing to be ashamed of.

"I'll go get you some dry clothes."

"Oh, come on, E. They're just boobs!"

He rolled his eyes and then walked inside. All the humor of the moment was gone. *What a buzzkill.*

She grabbed her dress, downed her margarita, and then followed him inside a minute later. She walked right into the kitchen and refilled her glass. Eric was upstairs long enough that she finished half of another margarita before he returned.

He offered up a pair of sweats and an oversized T-shirt. "Best I could find."

"Thanks. I'll swim in these, too," she joked.

He didn't look at her once when she hopped off the kitchen counter and tugged on his clothes. Man, she would never have guessed that he was a prude. All the time, he was around sweaty football players who changed clothes in the locker room. This couldn't be half as bad. Maybe it was the Texan in him.

He laughed when he saw her in his clothes. "You look ridiculous."

"This is all your fault."

"You're right. I did not think this through."

"Plus, now, I'm cold *and* tipsy." She held up her half-finished glass. "I don't think the margarita is helping with my body temperature."

"Probably not." He stood stiffly and shrugged.

She had given him the perfect opportunity to offer to warm her up, and he hadn't taken it. Clearly, she was losing it if she'd thought for a second that he was acting this way because he was interested. Any other guy would have jumped all over her.

"Anyway, I'm throwing a party once I get the house furnished. A big kegger. We'll invite the whole team."

"Sounds like a plan," he said. He leaned against the kitchen counter and seemed to relax more now that she had changed the subject. "We're going to need a lot of booze to get them all drunk."

"I think we can handle that," she said with a smirk.

TWENTY-TWO

"THIS PLACE IS KILLER," Trihn said.

Bryna smiled brightly. Yes, her new house had turned out to be incredible. She absolutely had to agree. She had spent the last couple of weeks furnishing the house until it was absolutely the most beautiful, elegant, and perfectly lived-in place she had ever seen. Hugh had even surprised her last weekend with a stunning Swarovski crystal chandelier.

Of course, she didn't think people could tell quite *how* lavish it really was with nearly a hundred football players and the entire cheer team crowding into the house and her backyard.

"Yeah, I'm mad jealous," Stacia agreed.

"As you should be," Bryna said.

She was happy the weather was holding. They were supposed to have storms, but not a lick of water had hit the earth in more than a month. That meant the weather was gorgeous. It also equated to an even worse drought for the desert.

At least they got to benefit by using the awesome pool, which required wearing swimsuits. Bryna's was a strappy blue-and-white color block that made her look exceptionally tan. Her hair was pulled off her shoulders and into a messy bun on the top of her head. She had a drink in her hand and was ready to party.

She would recognize the voice of the next person who walked through the door anywhere.

Eric was standing there with Andrew and a few other guys from the team. They were all in swim trunks. Andrew had already stripped out of his shirt—or maybe he had never worn one—but Eric had on a tight-fitting LV State shirt.

"Hollywood!" he cried when he saw her.

Then, he was barreling into her stomach and hoisting her over his shoulder.

She screamed and sloshed some of her margarita on the hardwood floor, "Eric! Put me down!"

He laughed even harder and twirled her in a circle. A bunch of people were laughing at them as she was being held helplessly in his arms.

"Anyone want a take?" he asked, offering her ass for everyone's view.

"Oh my God! I will kill you! I will murder you and cut you up into little pieces!" she yelled.

"All right, all right," Eric said. "No spankings for you tonight."

"She clearly deserves it though," Trihn joked.

Bryna was placed back on her feet, and she smacked Eric on the arm. "You ass!"

"At least I didn't throw you in the pool."

"Again!" she snapped.

"Right. Again," he said, heading toward the back door with a big smirk on his face.

He was out the door with the team a minute later, and she was left there, shaking her head at him.

"And you think he's gay?" Stacia asked quietly next to her.

Bryna gave her a fierce look. "Shh!"

"Sorry! Sorry!"

"And yes, I know he is."

Trihn intervened, "Let's go dance! Neal is already in a bad mood about coming to another party."

"Why?" Bryna asked.

She shrugged. "No idea. He would rather be at home, sketching or something. We need to loosen him up with some liquor, and he'll be fine."

Bryna started drinking again when the girls disappeared to go dance. She had hired the DJ from the radio station for the party. Apparently, he did that kind of stuff on the side. So far, so good.

She was about to go join them when the last person she'd wanted to see breezed through the doorway.

Pace.

"Excuse me!" she snapped. "Who said *you* were invited?"

Pace smirked. "Hey, sis."

"Don't call me that."

"Your boyfriend invited the whole team. Last I checked, I'm on the team."

He seemed pretty pleased with himself.

Bryna looked around. "Who here has a boyfriend?"

"You, of course. Think you can hide that you're dating Eric?"

"We're not dating."

"Sure," he said disbelievingly. "How is it going though, really?"

"We're not together, but it's so cute that you're clearly jealous."

"I mean, at least you picked the complete opposite of the last one," he said.

She knew he was referencing Jude, and she shuddered.

He leaned closer toward her. "Speaking of, does the new man know all of your deep, dark secrets?"

He looked like he had her there, and she stood her ground.

"Actually, he does. Not that it's any of *your* business"—she pushed him away from her—"but we're not together, creep."

Pace looked genuinely surprise. She was glad she had thrown *him* off.

"He knows about Jude?"

"What? Like it's a big secret? Yes, he knows. Now that the interrogation is over, you can leave."

"But I'm just getting started," he said. "How exactly did you get this house?"

"What does it matter? I'm away from *you*, and that's all that's important to me."

Realization seemed to dawn on his face as he took in the luxury so many others had missed. "Slipping into old bad habits, are we?"

"Fuck off!"

She knew he loved riling her up, but she couldn't help from getting upset. His very presence angered her. It made her think about her father marrying that whore who was now fucking pregnant. She hadn't seen them since they moved Pace in, and she didn't want to hear shit about the new baby they were having.

"You know I'm not leaving."

"Then, stay the fuck away from me."

Pace laughed and walked away. "I'll find someone else to take home tonight," he threw over his shoulder.

Bryna shuddered. *Poor girl.* Pace was awful. She hated that he was here at LV State. She had been avoiding him at all extremes, spending so little time in her condo, but still, he was *around*. The whole thing put her in a sour mood.

She needed a drink. She definitely needed a drink. She wished she could bleach the thought of Pace with a girl out of her brain. Actually, the thought of Pace at all made her feel like she had bugs crawling under her skin.

She wandered into the kitchen and poured herself another margarita when a conversation drifted up to her from the open window. She glanced outside and saw Eric was talking to a bunch of the football players he had arrived with.

"So, you're banging Bryna," Greg said as if it were a fact. He hadn't even questioned it. He'd just assumed it. Greg punched Andrew in the arm and laughed hysterically. "Dude, you guys are pussy brothers now."

Andrew looked sullen and made some snide remark that Bryna couldn't discern.

Hmm. So, the guys were going to have the same conversation with Eric that her girls had recently had with her. Too bad he couldn't use the real reason they weren't fucking rather than having to hedge around the issue.

Eric chuckled. "Nah, man. We're just friends."

Greg snorted and made some crude pelvic thrust. "With benefits."

Ugh! Why does Beth like him?

"Nope," Eric responded. He tipped back his beer and seemed totally relaxed.

"I've seen the way you two are together," Greg said. "Picking her up and offering to spank her ass. I'd be all over that."

"Yeah, well, I'm not you."

Andrew rolled his neck, clearly agitated. "I've smacked that ass."

Eric and Greg both turned their attention to him.

"Yeah, before she started making out with everyone in Posse instead of you," Greg said, laughing maniacally. "I've heard she's fucked half the team since you, dude."

Andrew glared at him.

But it was Eric who spoke up, "I don't think so. Bryna is pretty picky. She wouldn't settle for any dipshit."

"Picky?" Andrew asked. Even he sounded disbelieving. "I think you have the wrong girl."

Eric shrugged. "She has expensive taste. I don't think she'd slum it with anyone."

Greg still looked doubtful. "Either way, dude, you can't just be friends with a chick like that."

"Especially not Bri," Andrew said.

Bryna swallowed hard. She knew what people thought about her. She had always known. Honestly, it had only gotten worse since she came to college. But knowing what people thought was different than hearing it. It made her blood boil. It made her want to go down there and demand to know all the people they thought she had slept with. Because the total since last summer was a big whopping two—Andrew and Hugh. That was it.

Assholes.

At least Eric had stood up for her.

"Well, I don't think that's true. Bryna and I aren't dating, and we're not fucking, so I guess we're friends," Eric said.

"So then, who are you fucking?" Greg asked. "Can't spend all this time with that hot ass and not get your dick wet."

How pleasant!

She couldn't help but be interested in Eric's answer though. Not like he was going to tell them the truth.

Eric hesitated for a few seconds. "No one. I'm too busy with school and coaching. It's like having two full-time jobs."

"No one is *that* busy," Greg said.

Eric shrugged and brushed it off. "I guess I am."

The conversation shifted to football talk, and Bryna figured she had eavesdropped enough. She took her margarita outside and migrated toward where Eric was standing with the guys. Greg punched Andrew and then tipped his hat in the opposite direction. They were both long gone before she reached Eric, who was now standing all alone.

"Wow. Seems like I know how to run them off."

"They're dicks." Eric took another swig of his beer.

"That's true." She playfully looked up at him. "So, apparently, I'm picky, I have expensive taste, and I wouldn't slum it with just anyone. I've never heard so many compliments come out of your mouth in one go, E."

He groaned and rolled his eyes. "I should have known you had somehow been listening in. I never would have defended your honor."

"Yes, because I am a damsel in distress and need you to defend my virginal virtue," she joked.

"*Virginal virtue?*" He immediately doubled over and laughed. "Those are two words I'd never use to describe you."

Bryna shrugged. "I own it."

"You do."

"Anyway, what is this I hear about you being too busy to date?" she teased. Her buzz was starting to hit her, and it felt glorious.

"Yep. Too busy." He shrugged. "I'm not interested in anyone anyway."

"Oh, I understand that." It was funny how they were able to have these private conversations in the middle of a crowded party, and no one would think any differently. "Just like the guys giving you a hard time about us not fucking, the girls have been doing the same with me."

"Seriously, did you hear everything?"

"Hard to miss it when you all were so loud." She poked at him. "Anyway, you don't have to hide anything from *me*. I know all your deep, dark secrets. You could tell me if you were dating someone."

She fluttered her eyes at him. He didn't talk about that kind of shit, and she was damn curious.

"If you know all my secrets, then you know that shit is too complicated."

"Suit yourself," she said. "Everyone needs to get laid."

"I think you do that enough for the both of us."

"Hardly," she said.

She could never have enough sex. She was already horny again and wouldn't see Hugh for another week.

"I'm like Scarlett O'Hara. I need to be fucked and often and by someone who knows how."

"I believe the quote is *kissed*," he said, trying to hide his laughter.

"Yeah, but I'm modernizing. You know she was just a slutty gold digger and pissed because she couldn't marry her cousin."

"At least she gives me hope that you won't *always* be this crazy," he said.

"She gives me hope that I'll always be beautiful. She's the queen of resting bitch face."

Eric shook his head and habitually pushed a stray lock of hair off her forehead. "You already know you'll always be beautiful, Bri. One day, you might let people see that it's more than just skin deep."

TWENTY-THREE

BRYNA FELT A BLUSH CREEP UP to her cheeks. She had no idea why. She never blushed. "Well, I've clearly fooled you into thinking so," she quipped.

He rolled his eyes and retreated. "Come on, drunkie. Let's get you back to your girls. I can't steal you away from your very own party."

They retreated back to the center of the party where she did technically belong. Though she hadn't minded hanging out and talking to Eric. She pretty much never minded that now.

The word had gotten out about the party, and soon, it was jam-packed with all sorts of students and not just jocks. Bryna was too far gone to even care at this point. The more, the merrier.

As night fell and intoxication took over, everyone lost themselves to the party as quickly as they'd lost their inhibitions. People were dancing on the lawn, fondling each other in the pool, making out in corners. All-around debauchery had ensued.

She grabbed Eric out of the crowd and forced him to dance with her, Trihn, and Stacia. He obliged them after she'd pleaded with him. It was wonderful when he couldn't refuse her.

"Is Neal ever coming back?" Bryna asked into Trihn's ear. She was in the middle of the sandwich of dancers.

Trihn shrugged with a heavy sigh. "I don't know. He's been so weird all night."

"What the fuck? It's a party. Tell him to come party."

"I don't know. He doesn't really like the scene."

"The scene?" Bryna asked in exasperation. "This is college. Welcome to the scene."

"I know. He's so ridiculous. He thinks you and Stacia are bad influences."

"What? Is he your mother now?"

"I don't know."

Trihn stopped dancing in the middle of the lawn. She looked drawn. She always wore all her emotions on her sleeve. Even though she was a strong, powerful woman with success in her own right before she'd even turned eighteen, she still let everyone else's feelings influence her. Sometimes, Bryna wanted to shake her and tell her not to take that shit, but she could only do so much. So, she would be here to support her friend.

"Maybe you should talk to him," Bryna suggested.

"He's just sitting over there." Trihn pointed at a lawn chair.

"It'll help."

"Come with me?"

"Of course."

Bryna knew she wasn't the type of person to bring along when a gentle touch was needed. Trihn must be really pissed off.

Bryna leaned her head back on Eric's chest and murmured in his ear, "We're going to talk to Neal."

"Everything okay?"

"No. He's acting like a dick."

"Want me to come with?" he asked.

She stared up into his hazel eyes and smiled. She was drunk, and she could feel it by the way her body was responding to his nearness.

"Phrasing. Are we doing phrasing?" she joked to clear her mind. She straightened up.

Eric laughed. "Let's go, Bryna."

Trihn grabbed her hand and dragged her out of the crowd of dancers. Bryna's other hand slipped easily into Eric's, and he followed. Once she was out of the crowd, she quickly released him.

"Hey," Trihn said, standing in front of Neal.

He had his cell phone out and seemed to be aimlessly scrolling. "What's up?" he asked.

"Do you want to go dance?"

"You know I really hate crowds."

"Oh," she said. Trihn looked back at Bryna with her eyes wide.

Bryna probably shouldn't intervene, but she couldn't help herself. "Then, why are you at a party?"

He looked up at her from his phone. "Because my girlfriend told me I had to go since you're her best friend."

"I did not say you *had* to go. I wanted you here!" Trihn said.

"Yeah, and that translates into me having to show up to another mindless party with a bunch of jocks who hate my very existence," Neal complained.

"No one hates you!" Trihn cried. "You're blowing this way out of proportion."

"Right," he said dismissively. He looked back down at his phone.

Bryna glared at him. "Maybe you should talk to your girlfriend instead of ignoring her."

Neal pushed himself to his feet in one quick move. "Maybe you should mind your own fucking business.

You're the only reason she comes to these fucking things. She's not a party girl. She's an artist."

Bryna stared at him as if he had grown horns. "Why can't she be both?" she spat.

"You force her into these situations. I have no idea why she's even friends with you and Stacia. You're forcing her to be this person she isn't."

"No one is forcing me to do anything!" Trihn said.

Bryna couldn't take it. "The Trihn I know is most definitely a party girl, but she's also a model, an artist, a fashion guru, a hopeless romantic, a dancer, and so much more. If you can't see that, then you're missing out."

"Whatever," he said.

"If you can't see that, then maybe you should leave," Trihn said impulsively. "You don't want to be here with me anyway."

"All right. I guess I will then," Neal responded. He glared at the trio of us standing there and stalked toward the door.

"Oh my God," Trihn cried. Tears immediately burst from her eyes. "What the hell have I done?"

"You told that loser to shut up and get the fuck out!" Bryna said.

"No. Ugh! I don't want to break up. I can't do this." She looked like she was going to hyperventilate. "I'm going after him."

"What?" Bryna asked. "He was just an ass."

"I need to talk to him."

Trihn turned and ran after Neal. Bryna shook her head and followed her into the house. Eric was close on her heels. Trihn caught up to Neal at the door and pleaded with him.

Eric put his hand on Bryna's elbow. "Hey, maybe we should give them some privacy. She's kind of a mess."

Bryna anxiously looked at her friend. She hated seeing Trihn suffer like this. *Why would she grovel for a guy who had insulted her because he didn't want to be at a party? So ridiculous.*

"Yeah, sure," she agreed reluctantly.

They took a step away from the door and went into the living room. It was packed with people, and someone had used a table for beer pong. The cleaning service was really going to be earning their money after tonight.

Bryna stole beers for them from the beer-pong pitcher. She passed one to Eric and chugged.

"Whoa!" he said, reaching for her drink. "Maybe slow it down."

"I'm thinking I need to get fucked tonight," she drunkenly told him.

He raised his eyebrows. "What?"

"Yeah, I'm horny as fuck."

"You're undoing all the progress I made by claiming you're picky."

She sighed dramatically. "Fine. I'll let *you* be picky then. Who can I fuck?"

"I am not going to choose your next victim," he said tightly.

"I'm not a black widow or something," she slurred. "I'm not going to eat them up and spit them back out."

"You kind of are."

She shrugged. "I kind of am."

She didn't care though. That wasn't what sex was about. It was about getting off. If she could have someone to satisfy that deep need, then she would be good.

"I think maybe you've had enough," Eric said.

She hadn't even realized she was still drinking the beer in her hand.

She held it out behind her, so he couldn't take it. "I've had enough when I say I have," she teased. "And I definitely have not had enough."

"Hand it over." He darted out way faster than her slow reflexes and grabbed the beer in her hand.

She didn't let go though, and the glass tipped, spilling the contents on her mostly naked body and all over the floor.

"Gross!"

Eric cursed. "You're a mess," he grumbled. "I'll get something to clean you up with."

Bryna had to stand around in the middle of the living room with her legs drenched in beer. It was disgusting. She was going to need a serious shower and exfoliator to get this shit out of her perfect fucking skin.

Her eyes wandered the crowd of people while she waited and landed on a girl standing in the hallway between the kitchen and living room. She appeared to be lost or looking for someone. That was when Bryna placed the pretty brunette. *Audrey, Eric's ex-girlfriend.*

Bryna ground her teeth together. *Bitch. What the fuck is she doing here?*

When Eric noticed Audrey, he looked startled. He was holding a towel in his hand for Bryna, but as soon as Audrey saw him, she began speaking animatedly to him. Bryna wished she knew what the bitch was saying. On instinct, she hated the woman, and she wanted Audrey out of her fucking house.

She took a step toward Eric and Audrey, but he put his hand up in front of him. Audrey stopped talking and glared at him. Then, he was walking back to Bryna. She tried to remove the scowl that had been on her face, but she didn't think she hid it well. He looked confused when he saw her.

"Sorry about your legs. I didn't mean to spill beer on them," Eric said.

He bent down and wiped sticky beer off her legs. Bryna glanced up and met Audrey's gaze. She looked horrified. Bryna wondered what it must look like to Audrey to see Eric touching her. It made her giggle.

Eric looked up at her again. "What?"

"Nothing. Just thanks," she said.

"For spilling beer on you?"

She giggled again. *A fucking giggle.* "For helping to clean me up."

He furrowed his brows and stood. "You're drunk."

Then, without a thought in her head, she leaned into him and planted her lips on him. Her mind was empty. The only thing that existed was this kiss. She remembered the feel of his lips from the national championship game. She had told herself it was an act, but he had perfect lips. It wasn't fair.

She didn't even want to acknowledge the other thing that seemed to be snaking up through her body. Jealousy. It'd flared up without warning. She wanted Audrey to watch. Bryna knew she couldn't have him. She had no shot. But seeing his ex had pissed her off, and she didn't care how irrational it was.

It could have been seconds or minutes, but suddenly, she was wrenched away from him. Eric was holding her at arm's length. He didn't look happy.

"You're drunk, and you're not thinking."

"I feel like I am."

"No," he said roughly. "You're drunk and horny, and I'm here. You would never do this otherwise. We both know it's never going to happen."

The rejection felt like a slap in the face. It was Posse all over again, with him telling her she was *that* girl. Her cheeks heated with anger, and she wanted to bite back a smart retort, but for once, she was rendered speechless.

Eric turned around and saw Audrey still standing there, watching. As soon as their eyes locked, she darted for the door.

"Fuck," he groaned. "I have to go talk to her."

"Eric," Bryna whispered, "you don't have to go."

"I do. Try to sober up. I have a feeling you're going to regret this in the morning."

He left her standing there.

All she could think was that she didn't live with regrets. Then, Jude's face popped into her mind, and the liquor she had been holding in threatened to come back up.

It was going to be a long night.

TWENTY-FOUR

BRYNA ROLLED OVER IN BED and threw her arm over her eyes. "Ugh," she groaned.

Last night had veered horribly off course. She was hungover as shit, and the only thing she could remember was the look on Eric's face before he'd left the party. *What the fuck is wrong with me?* She knew she needed to go talk to him about what had happened. She couldn't stomach the thought of him being upset with her.

But she couldn't go like this. She needed to clear her mind before she could talk to him. Right now, she felt horribly unlike herself.

She got out of bed, threw on a black mini skirt and a flouncy scoop top to fit her mood, and quickly pulled her hair back into a high pony. She retrieved her phone and messaged Hugh.

Is it morning already?

It's the afternoon actually. Late night?

Yeah. I'm dying. I can't function.

I wish I were there to make it better.

Me, *too.*

That was a lie. Bryna was glad no one was around to see her right now. After last night, she couldn't muster her facade, and she definitely wouldn't be able to keep it together around Hugh.

Why don't you have a spa day? I'll have my assistant call ahead for you.

She smiled. That sounded perfect.

I'd love that!

I'll take care of everything. I can't wait to see you again in a week.

On her way to the spa, she called Trihn through Bluetooth. She hadn't heard from her friend since she'd left with Neal last night, and after the way things had ended, Bryna wanted to make sure Trihn was all right.

"Hello?" Trihn answered groggily.

"Hey. Were you still sleeping?"

"Why are you awake this early?" she asked through a yawn.

"It's one in the afternoon."

"Is it?"

"Yes," Bryna confirmed.

"What's up?"

"How did things go last night? You never came back to the party."

"I know," Trihn said. "I'm sorry. Neal apologized, and then we made up. He was frustrated because he didn't get into the graphic design internship with Pixar that he had interviewed for last week. It was a huge disappointment, and now, all the other summer intern positions are full."

"So, he took that out on you? And you're okay with that?" Bryna was sure she didn't hide the disdain in her voice.

Trihn sighed heavily. "I don't know. It was a stressful week, is all."

"As long as it doesn't turn into a stressful week all the time."

"You're turning into Stacia over here. Stop mothering me."

Bryna shook her head and laughed. "Hardly. I'm not mothering you. I'm letting you know that I'll chop his balls off and feed them to a blender if he keeps this shit up."

Trihn exploded with laughter. "I can't believe you. Actually, I can. You'd totally do it. Thanks for caring, B."

"Don't keep confusing me for Stacia," Bryna singsonged.

"Oh my God, I love you. I'm going back to bed."

As she pulled into the valet station, Bryna hung up the phone. She handed over the keys to her car and took the elevator up to the spa. As promised, the afternoon had been cleared for her. And she spent the next couple of hours getting pressed, buffed, waxed, blown out, and all-around pampered. She felt like a new person by the end of it, and even though she knew she would still have to face Eric later, at least she could do it feeling refreshed.

As she was leaving, the woman at the front stopped her. "Excuse me."

"Yes?"

"This package was left for you." She passed over a small gift-wrapped box.

"Oh?"

"It arrived only a moment ago."

"Thanks."

Bryna unwrapped the package and opened the box. She gasped. Inside was a diamond-encrusted Hermès Paris watch in rose-gold and black. She removed it from the case and slid it onto her wrist. It fit perfectly when she slipped it on her wrist. Between this and her B necklace and bracelet, she was dripping in jewels. She shrugged and decided it suited her.

She shot off a shocked and excited text to Hugh about the watch. She couldn't stop glancing at it. The gifts were extravagant and thoughtful—just the way she liked them.

Once she reached the ground level, she glanced out at the front door and sighed. Her stomach knotted. She wasn't ready to see Eric yet. Her confidence had been rattled after last night. The anticipation of wondering what he was going to say ate at her, and she couldn't get it to go away. She knew that going to talk to him would probably fix all of that, and she was stressing for nothing. But she never stressed over stuff like this. She hadn't since a year ago when Jude had wanted to *talk*.

Maybe a drink to take the edge off would help. She backtracked to the bar and took an empty seat. Crossing her legs, she smiled at the bartender and ordered a dirty martini, her favorite.

Bryna felt eyes on her from the guy seated two seats down from her. She glanced over at him, and he didn't look away when she made eye contact. She turned away, took another sip of her drink, and then looked back. He was still watching her rather intently. *Weird.*

"Anything I can help you with? Or are you just browsing?" she asked sarcastically.

The guy shrugged. "I figured you wanted to be admired."

"Why is that?"

"Look at you," he said as if that made perfect sense.

She looked down. Her clothes were nothing special. In fact, she was in sandals. The spa had perfected her hair, but she had gone for subtle makeup because she had no plans. The only thing that was impressive at all right now was her diamonds.

"And?"

"I see you." He turned back to his beer.

Bryna narrowed her eyes in confusion. That was a strange introduction, but it did make her curious, especially since he was good-looking and only a couple of years older than her, at the most. He was blond with dark eyes, wearing casual jeans, a T-shirt, and flip-flops. He had shades dangling from the neck of his shirt and seemed very…laid-back. *Definitely not my type.*

"Sorry," he said when he noticed her puzzled expression. "I've been out of the country for almost a year, and it's more a cultural shock to come back than to be away."

"What were you doing? Work?"

"Nah. I wanted to snowboard my way through the rest of the world. It turned into a bit more of an adventure than I'd bargained for. I'd love to tell you the story sometime," he said, leaning into her.

Hmm. Smooth. She kind of liked his easygoing confidence. It was her biggest turn-on. "I'd love that, but I have to get back to campus."

"Oh! Are you at LV State or UNLV?"

"State."

"Cool. I start there in the fall. Thought I'd rejoin the world of the overworked," he said with a smirk.

Bryna laughed. "All right. Maybe you can tell me your story next semester then."

"Definitely. If you want to give me your number, I can call you when I move in. It would be nice to know someone here."

Bryna shrugged. *What do I have to lose?* "Sure." She added her number to his phone. "It's Bryna, by the way."

The guy offered his hand. "Cam."

She smiled again and shook his hand. "Nice to meet you."

"You, too."

As she was walking away, back to her car, she couldn't keep the giddy feeling from her stomach. It was nice to meet a guy who didn't have a preconceived notion of her reputation. Actually, he knew nothing about her. And still, he had *seen* her when she didn't even look her best. It was a compliment. Even if he never called, it had been nice to flirt with him for a bit.

She left the resort, feeling as if she had done a complete one-eighty since this morning. She was in a much better mood and was ready to talk to Eric. The drive was short, and she pulled into the empty driveway.

The door was unlocked when she arrived, and she let herself in without knocking.

No margaritas this time.

"Eric?" she called.

No answer.

She wandered outside and found it also empty. She decided to try upstairs, and she heard voices. Walking toward Eric's workout room, she pushed open the door and found him lifting weights with Andrew.

Both guys were shirtless, sweaty, and hot as hell. Even though Andrew was ridiculously built, her eyes kept being drawn back to Eric. Andrew was spotting Eric on the bench press, the weights nearly resting on his chest. He heaved it back up into the air.

"Am I interrupting?" She leaned against the doorframe with a smirk on her face.

Eric glanced over at her, dropped his head again, and then put the weights back into their resting place. "What do you want, Bri?"

Andrew questioningly looked at Eric. She wondered if Eric had told Andrew anything about what had happened last night. She doubted it. They were friends, but Eric was a pretty private guy...all things considered.

"It's Sunday afternoon," she said as if that explained everything.

"Yeah?" Eric muttered.

"I'm predictable...like clockwork," she reminded him.

"Did *you* just say you're predictable?" Andrew asked. His eyes were wide in surprise.

Yeah, she wouldn't normally say that about herself, but she did spend most Sunday afternoons here.

"Shut up, Holloway," Bryna spat.

Andrew laughed and held his hands up in surrender. "I'm just saying..."

"Well, don't."

Eric didn't engage them as he sat up and toweled off. Then, finally...finally, he looked up at her. "Did you need something?"

Bryna shifted under his scrutiny and took an uninvited seat. "I got back from my spa day and thought I'd come over."

"Really?" He sounded disbelieving.

"Yeah. I wanted to check in on you."

"Come on. The truth, Hollywood."

Bryna tilted her head up. This was the truth. Mostly. "You didn't come back to the party last night." *After I kissed you.* "I haven't heard from you all day."

"And?"

"And I wanted to check on you," she repeated.

"What exactly am I missing here?" Andrew asked. He grabbed his own towel and rubbed at the back of his neck.

"Bryna is here to apologize, but she's really bad at it. She's going to need to try harder," Eric informed him.

"You're an ass. I'm not here to apologize," she said.

Andrew nodded. "I'd have to agree. That sounds unlikely. Bri doesn't apologize."

"See? I'm here because I haven't heard from you."

Eric shrugged. "Fine. If you're not here to apologize, then you can go. We're busy." He lay back down on the bench.

Andrew laughed hysterically. "You know, maybe I should go." He grabbed his T-shirt and gym bag and started for the door.

"There's nothing I'm going to say that you can't hear," Bryna said.

"Yeah, but I suddenly feel like I'm in the middle of an argument between an old married couple."

"Oh, ha-ha," Bryna spat. She couldn't believe Andrew. "You're hilarious."

"You have no reason to leave," Eric said.

Andrew shrugged. "I'm going to go anyway. I'll see you guys later. I have a feeling you'll be waiting for that apology for a while." He left, and his laughter followed him down the stairs.

"So…" Bryna said.

"Yep."

"Do you want to go get dinner or something? I'm starved."

Eric sat up with rapid speed and stared at her in disbelief. "You're really going to skirt the issue and act like nothing happened?"

"It's worked for me before."

"Hardly."

"Fine! I was drunk, and I kissed you. I didn't think it was that big of a deal." It was a lie.

She had felt bad about it all day. She hadn't meant for it to happen, and his reaction had been even worse.

"No big deal?"

"You've never kissed anyone while you were drunk?"

"Sure." He shrugged. "But usually, it was because they wanted me to."

She wanted to say that she hadn't known he wouldn't want it, but that wasn't true either. She had known and done it anyway. It wasn't her finest moment.

"Yeah. Drunk," she reminded him. "I guess I shouldn't have done it."

He tilted his chin down and observed her. "You can do better than that. Apologize like you mean it."

"You're insufferable."

Eric stood and walked toward her. He stopped when he was only a foot away from her. His hazel eyes were a mix of disappointment and frustration. "I'm your friend, Bri. Real friends apologize when they fuck up. They don't act like they're better. They don't pretend like it never happened. They don't push back when you call them out on their mistake. I realize this *friend* thing is new to you, and you're used to guys throwing themselves at your feet. But I'm not that guy. You knew the consequences and what it could cost me when you kissed me, but you did it anyway. I think I'm in the right in expecting an apology."

"I know," she said softly.

Their little game was over. Knots worked at her stomach, and she hated that she'd hurt him. Because he did look hurt. *Did he know I'd kissed him because Audrey was there? Did he know I'd been jealous? Would he still want this friendship if he did know?*

And Eric was right. He was the first real friend she'd had...maybe ever. She cared too much about his feelings, which had never happened before either. She had never cared about whether or not she hurt someone. She always avoided the confrontation or pushed them out of her life because she didn't care enough or she didn't want to deal with the fallout.

But not with Eric.

"You know?" he asked. He shook his head and walked away.

"I'm sorry," she stuttered out. "I didn't mean to upset you."

He sighed and sank into the chair. His eyes found hers across the room. "Okay."

"Okay?"

"Yeah."

"Just like that?"

"You actually apologized. I didn't think you would."

"I don't like you being upset with me."

"You were just drunk."

His eyes looked haunted, and she wondered what he was thinking when he looked at her.

"You know I can't stay mad at you." Somehow, the way he'd said it though made it seem like everything wasn't okay.

She was forgiven, but there was something more…and she didn't know what she could do to fix it.

Maybe she couldn't.

TWENTY-FIVE

THE CROWD ROARED AS THE GOLD TEAM scored the final touchdown of the spring scrimmage game. It made Bryna smile even wider because that meant Marshall had beat Pace. All in a day's work.

As the stadium emptied out, Stacia ran up to Bryna. She was decked out in a silver uniform for Pace's team, and Bryna was wearing the traditional gold for Marshall's side.

"Good game, huh?" Stacia asked.

"Yep. Good to be back. I hate that we have to wait five more months until we're on the sidelines again."

"Heartbreaking."

"Definitely." Bryna waved as Trihn hopped over the railing keeping her from the turf. "Hey!"

"Hey, guys," Trihn said.

"Hey!" Stacia touched Bryna's arm. "Can I talk to you later?"

"You're talking to me now," Bryna pointed out.

"I know but later, too. Alone?"

"Okay?" Bryna said questioningly.

"Don't worry."

Bryna raised her eyebrows. "I wasn't until you said that. What's going on?"

"Nothing," she squeaked. "We'll talk later." Then, she turned and jogged toward the locker room without looking back.

"That was fucking weird," Bryna said to Trihn.

Trihn shrugged. "Stacia is a weird chick."

Bryna gave Trihn a suspicious look. "Do you know what this is all about?"

"Even if I did, I wouldn't tell you before she did." Trihn held up her hands to fend off Bryna's likely attack. "Hear her out."

"Fine." But she didn't have to like it.

"I'll see you at Posse later. Meet you there!" Trihn said.

Bryna shook her head in confusion. She wondered what Stacia wanted to talk to her about and why Trihn wouldn't clue her in. Stacia had said not to worry, but it'd automatically made her worry.

She shook off the feeling and sought out Eric.

"Hey, everyone is heading to Posse. You up for it?" she asked him.

His eyes darted to hers and then back out to the field. "I think I'm going to call it quits tonight. I'm exhausted, and I don't feel like partying."

"What? Since when?"

Eric ran a hand back through his hair. "I have a huge test on Monday. I'm stressing it, so I'm not really feeling the scene tonight. After the spring game, Posse gets wild."

Bryna frowned. This was unlike Eric. He wanted to skip out on a party to, what? Sleep? Study? Those things could wait until Sunday or the summer.

"Is this because of what happened last time?" she asked, shifting from one foot to the other.

Things with Eric had been rocky ever since she threw the party at her house. No matter what she did, it didn't seem like they could find their rhythm anymore. She hadn't thought one kiss would fuck everything up.

"I'm not going to drink that much," she added.

"No. It's fine. I know you're going to drink more than you expect to. You always do. Go and have a good time."

"Okay," she said uncertainly.

He already seemed to be occupied with something else. She shrugged it off and headed back to the locker room to change out of her uniform. She was just on edge. Between Stacia having something to talk to her about and Eric not coming out tonight, she wasn't sure what to make of it all. But she didn't like it.

A couple of hours later, she was standing at the bar at Posse with Trihn and Neal. A bunch of the football players were already in attendance. Maya was pouring round after round, and it was clear that what Eric had said about the scene after the spring game was true. It was going to get fucking crazy.

She'd promised herself she wasn't going to get out of hand. Without Eric here, she didn't really want to anyway.

"You're not drinking like a fish, Queen Bee," Maya said. She shifted into her hip and stuck Bryna with a questioning stare.

"Yeah. I'm waiting for Stacia to get here. Do *you* know why she needs to talk to me?"

Maya shrugged her dark shoulders. "Bartenders know everything."

"And? What is it?"

"I'm not spilling." The look she gave Bryna was absolute. "That goes against the code."

"There is no code," Bryna told her.

"Oh, there's a code."

"What are you? A pirate? Should I ask for parlay?"

"Oh, you're funny." Maya shook her head. Her dark locks framed her face, and her returning smile was genuine. "You just don't know the code because you don't bartend."

"Fine. Does everyone know this secret, except for me?"

Maya smirked. That was answer enough.

"Great." This was beginning to get ridiculous. *How do I not know if everyone else does?*

"There's your little cheer slut now," Maya said. She pointed out Stacia walking in from the patio door.

She was wringing her hands in front of her. This was not going to be good.

"Thanks."

Bryna walked right up to her, unafraid. She couldn't wait around and wonder any longer.

"What do you need to talk to me about?"

Stacia's eyes widened. "Um…let's go over here."

She grabbed Bryna's arm, and they walked to a more secluded part of the club. Stacia looked seriously nervous.

"Oh my God, spit it out. This is like waiting to open presents on Christmas morning, and your parents want to actually wake up and drink coffee first. Not that we ever had Christmas like that, and I always knew my presents ahead of time, but still…"

Stacia flinched. "Sorry."

"Well?" Bryna spat anxiously.

"So, I don't want you to bug, but I'm kind of, sort of dating Pace," she said in a rush.

Silence stretched between them. Bryna was sure she hadn't heard Stacia right. Stacia had spoken so fast that it must have been unclear. She had *not* just said she was dating Bryna's creepy, disgusting, pigheaded stepbrother.

"What?" Bryna asked, her voice like ice.

"I know! I wanted to tell you in person. I didn't want you to hear it from anyone else, so I asked everyone not to tell you. We've been sleeping around, but it was no big deal," Stacia cried. "He was just another football player."

"And now, he's not?"

"No. We've been getting serious, B. I had to let you know. I know you told me not to touch him with a ten-foot pole, but I mean, I didn't think it mattered if it was just sex. That doesn't mean anything. You know how it is. Then, we hung out and talked, and he's really kind of...great."

"Great," Bryna said hollowly.

"Don't be mad."

"Why would I be mad?" Bryna asked. "I just specifically told you to stay away from him because you don't know what he's capable of, and you've been fucking him behind my back. Then, you've started dating him and come to talk to me as if it doesn't matter. Like I won't care after I moved out of my house *twice* to escape him."

"Bryna," Stacia murmured awkwardly.

"Did he tell you to tell me about this?"

"No!" she cried. "He actually said not to tell you. He was worried about your reaction."

"I'm sure."

"Come on!"

"He's totally playing you, and you don't even see it. He wanted you to be quiet about it, so he could tell me himself. It's all a fucking game with him. He wanted me to get pissed, so I'd isolate myself from my friends. It's fucking high school all over again."

"No! Bryna, it's not like that," Stacia said. Her eyes brimmed with tears.

"You don't know what you're talking about! Pace is obsessed with me. He's wanted to fuck me since he moved into my parents' house with his Valley trash mother. He's trying to get to me through you, like he did senior year when he slept with my two best friends over New Year's. This whole thing is another ploy."

"God, B! Do you think of anyone but yourself? Pace likes me, and it's *not* because of you. You sound pissed that one of your many admirers isn't fawning over you, and someone else is getting the attention for once."

Bryna's mouth dropped open. "That is *not* the case. The last person I want fawning over me is Pace. I'd be perfectly happy for you if this were any other guy."

"Fine. Don't be happy for me, but get used to it because I'm not changing my mind."

"Is this because he's a quarterback? I know you want an NFL quarterback, S. Pace is the backup."

"It's his first year," she spat. "He'll start when Marshall leaves. And *no*, it's not about that. I actually like him."

"I can't see how."

"I knew this would be difficult, but you're my friend. Can't you at least pretend to be supportive? Even if you have to lie?"

Bryna ground her teeth. "It would be a lie."

Stacia harrumphed, shook her head, and then stormed off without a word. Clearly, Bryna's reaction had pissed her off too much. Maybe if it Pace really wasn't using her, then Bryna could get used to the idea. Maybe. But it seemed unlikely.

Bryna's eyes searched the room. Stacia had stomped over to Trihn and Maya and was probably talking shit about the confrontation. But that wasn't who Bryna wanted to see. Her eyes found Pace standing next to the patio door, talking to some other football players.

She angrily stalked over to him, and the other guys scattered.

"What the fuck?"

"So, Stacia told you, huh?"

"Do you always have to try to ruin my life?" she spat.

"I don't have to try. You're really good at it on your own."

"Ugh!" she cried out. "It's just another game! Avery and Tara all over again, right?"

"No," he admitted. "I actually like Stacia."

"Oh, I'm sure."

"I told her not to tell you because I knew you'd react this way, but shocking, your *friends* don't know your past. I was saving you some anger, but now that you know, stay away from Stacia. You're not going to change her mind. We're together. The end."

Bryna screamed in frustration. *What the fuck is wrong with the world?*

She couldn't handle being out right now. This was all too much. She wasn't really pissed at Stacia. Bryna was just angry that Stacia had let Pace manipulate her so well. She had no idea what he was doing, and when she did find out, Bryna feared for her friend. She wasn't sure Stacia could handle it.

Without another word to anyone else, Bryna stalked out of Posse. She walked to her car in the parking lot and drove across town to Eric's house. She was too keyed up to go home. Eric would be able to calm her down after all of that. He always knew the right things to say.

She ground her teeth. She hoped Eric was ready to get fucked up because she wanted to down a bottle of liquor and forget the evening. Forget that Stacia and Pace were dating.

Bryna pushed open Eric's front door.

"Eric?" she called.

No answer.

She hadn't really expected one. He was probably studying. It was still pretty early, but he could be asleep.

Tossing her purse and heels at the base of the stairs, Bryna ambled into the kitchen. She dug through the pantry to find a half-empty bottle of Maker's Mark.

"Perfect," she muttered.

She grabbed two glasses out of the cupboard. They weren't crystal or fancy or anything, but they would do in a dire situation. *Good enough for now. Good enough to wash away the thought of Pace.*

She paused and decided it might not be a bad idea to take a shot first. Then, she could have a head start. Eric would understand. Unscrewing the top, Bryna placed her mouth to the bottle and let the bourbon burn down her throat.

"Holy shit!"

She replaced the top on the bottle, clinked the two glasses between her fingers, and tiptoed up the stairs. The door was closed to his room, but she could see a sliver of light through the crack at the bottom. Maker's was going to make studying *really* interesting.

She jiggled the door handle, trying to force it open with her hands full. Frustration creasing her temple, she leaned into the door with her shoulder and shoved it open as the handle clicked. Unceremoniously, she stumbled forward into the room, keeping a tight grip on the precious cargo in her hands.

Her eyes adjusted to the dim lighting, and the scene before her came into focus. A dirty brunette was bent over at the waist. Her mangled mess of hair was tossed forward across the bed, obscuring her face where it was trapped against the wad of comforter she was holding on to for dear life. Her red tank was hanging off the end of the bed. Perfect smooth hands had a grip on her waist.

Her eyes followed those hands she knew all too well, going up his arms to his bare chest and into that gorgeous face. His forehead was lined from exertion, and sweat beaded his brow. She couldn't break her eyes away as he thrust over and over into the girl crushed up against his bed.

The world tilted, and she felt the bottle drop out of her fingers. The glasses crashed to the floor, shattering as they hit the ground. The bottle collided with the floor seconds later, and amber bourbon splashed up onto her legs and soaked into the carpet.

How long have I been standing there, watching Eric fuck some other girl? Why is he fucking a girl? Why do I feel like I'm going to throw up?

At the noise, Eric stilled his movements and looked up. His eyes locked with Bryna's across the room. "Fuck!"

The girl's head popped up. Bryna's mouth dropped open.

Audrey!

TWENTY-SIX

"WHAT THE FUCK is she doing here?" Audrey yelled.

Bryna stood there, shell-shocked. She had no idea what to say. There wasn't anything to say. Yet she couldn't move. Her feet were glued to the floor.

Everything was happening in slow motion. Eric was moving away from Audrey. Audrey looked up at him in shock because he'd stopped.

Still, Bryna said nothing.

"Bri," he whispered desperately into the silence.

"I," she croaked. Her vision shifted, and all the emotions from the day crashed together as one. "I didn't know."

She wanted to run from the carnage of her life, and she had never been a runner. She had always faced life head-on and catapulted forward through adversity. But this…she couldn't face. She didn't even know why, but she needed to get out of there.

"Sorry," she muttered absentmindedly. The word tumbled from her lips, unbidden. Then, she bolted through the door.

She couldn't handle this right now. Not with everything else. Her stomach was roiling. It didn't make sense. This was Eric.

Gay Eric.

Fucking his ex-girlfriend like he was most definitely Not Gay Eric.

She took the stairs, two at a time. Her heart rate skyrocketed as she nearly tripped over the final stair in an effort to escape the reality of what she had witnessed in Eric's bedroom. She retrieved her high heels and purse from where she had left them and made a dash for the exit.

"Bri," Eric called out to her.

That was followed by a high-pitched, "Are you fucking kidding me right now, Eric?"

Bryna couldn't even think about this. Couldn't think about the fact that Audrey was in Eric's bed. Couldn't think about what this meant for her friendship with Eric. Couldn't think about why she felt like her heart was shattering into a million tiny pieces.

Pushing the door open, she stared in anger as the drought that had pervaded Vegas for so long finally cracked. The curtains opened in the heavens, and water rained from the sky, threatening to flood her desert home. But it didn't matter that she had blown her hair out or that she had on fresh makeup or that the rain might ruin her designer clothes. All that mattered was getting away.

She located her keys, punched the unlock button, and watched the lights flash at her. Bryna dove into the downpour and rushed for her parked Aston Martin. She was soaked within seconds. The water ripped at her body with a ferocity that matched her own temper. She yanked the door open to her car and tossed her purse and high heels into the passenger seat.

Eric called her name again from the front door, and she made the mistake of looking back. He stood there, silhouetted in the doorframe, in nothing but a pair of dark jeans. He hadn't bothered with putting on a shirt in his haste to get to her.

She gulped. She couldn't do this. She shook her head. Her wet hair smacked against her face. He didn't appear to care as he barreled out of his house and into the rain. He cleared the distance before she even remembered she was supposed to get into the car.

"Where are you going?" he yelled over the beating of the rain on the pavement.

"Home."

He slammed his hand against the door to her car. "Goddamn it, Bri. What are you even *doing* here tonight?"

She jumped as her door closed. She was at a loss for words. He had followed her.

"You said you were exhausted," she said.

"You said you were going to be at Posse all night."

"Yeah, well, Stacia decided to ambush me and tell me she's dating Pace, so I thought coming to get drunk with you was a better alternative."

"Stacia and Pace?" he demanded.

"At least I'm not the only one shocked by the information." She closed her eyes against the rain. "I guess I should have known there was a real reason for you being *exhausted* tonight. I didn't know you had plans." She gestured to his house.

His eyes stormed over. "Bryna—"

"I should go," she cut him off.

"No! Why didn't you run to your millionaire, Hugh?"

"Are you joking? Why were you fucking her?" she screamed, unable to hold back the rage boiling inside of her. Her hands were trembling. "You said you were gay!"

"What?" he yelled. "I never fucking said that!"

"Yes, you did! At the national championship game after you kissed me!"

He had said it…well, all but said it.

"No fucking way!"

"When you and I first met, Gates said that you'd told him you were gay!" she shrieked.

"I never fucking said that to him. He said you were trouble and a hot mess. That it would be smart for me *not* to be interested in you. I thought he meant you were a slut and a bad person. That's why I treated you like shit all last semester. Then, I got to know you, and I realized that wasn't the person you really were. It was the person you showed everyone else."

Bryna's jaw locked. She couldn't believe Gates had said that, that he had told her Eric was gay, so they would stay apart.

"Then, what the fuck were you talking about at the national championship game?"

"Audrey!" He threw his arm out at the house. "I've kept her a secret from everyone. I thought you knew we were still sleeping together."

Bryna's mouth dropped open. She stepped away from him. "You've been sleeping together this whole fucking time?"

She didn't know why it shocked her. It wasn't like she hadn't slept with Andrew and then Hugh, but still, it did. She had been so sure that Eric was gay that she couldn't even reconcile this information with reality.

"I thought you knew."

"No!" she shrieked. "No, I never fucking knew."

He reached for her, and she backed away.

"Don't touch me."

His hands went into his soaked hair, and he turned his face up to the sky. He let loose a primal growl. When he met her eyes again, he looked determined, focused. "You said you wanted a guy who could take care of you and that we would never fucking happen. You said that you would never be comfortable dating me or any guy."

"I was comfortable because you were a nonthreat! You were gay!"

"Fuck!" he cried. "I backed off because I didn't want to scare you. I wasn't sure what was happening or if you were really the person I wanted. Everything was just happening, and then you ground it to a stop."

Everything seemed to become crystal clear. The reason he had been pissed about her kissing him in front of Audrey. The consequences to her actions for that night. The way he'd seemed to notice her but kept his distance.

Fuck, I've been blind. Horribly blind.

"Why are you so angry anyway?" he asked, stepping closer to her. "Why did you break that bottle, looking ready to murder someone?"

"I am *shocked*!"

"Don't lie to me!" he yelled at her. "Tell me why."

He moved into her space until she was leaning against the hood of the car. Rain still poured down between them.

"Tell me."

"No!" she yelled. She pushed against his chiseled chest, wanting desperately to keep herself together.

"Tell me the truth, Bri." He stared at her. "Tell me it's because you want me."

"No." She defiantly shook her head from side to side as her heart beat in time to the rain.

"Well, I can't keep lying. You might be able to pretend, but I can't."

"This is insane! You were the one upstairs, bending some bitch over your bed!" she spat at him.

"I was ending things with Audrey tonight!"

"It sure as *hell* didn't look like it!"

"I couldn't do it anymore. I was ending it, and then I was going to tell you the truth, whether or not you wanted to give up the bullshit. I can't pretend anymore. I don't know what the fuck this is, but I've wanted to do this for too damn long without any excuses in our way."

"Do what?" she screamed. Her lungs felt raw.

She was so angry, and he looked furious.

Then, he pushed himself against her, buried his hands into her soaking wet hair, and kissed her lips with all the pent-up sexual tension coursing between them. She beat against his chest as he demanded a reaction from her. She hit him twice more, and then her mind seemed to forget why she was resisting. She didn't want this to stop. Slowly, she relented into his kisses.

Water poured down their faces, mingling with their kiss. She moaned against his mouth, and their tongues met in perfect unison. This was their third kiss, but for the first time, she truly savored him. He tasted like pure heaven. A touch of everything that was right in her life. He pushed her arms up around his neck and covered her body with his own. They molded together, both soaked through.

A bolt of lightning tore through the sky in the distance, and thunder crashed overhead. They both jolted at the interruption. Eric glanced up at the sky and then back down at Bryna. His smile was one of pure joy. Like he wouldn't want to do anything else or be anywhere else in that moment.

His lips were on hers again. Harder. More desperate. Seeking out the one thing that she couldn't give to anyone. Yet it was perfection. Every nerve in her body was attuned to his touch.

This was what she had always been missing.

Yet her emotions roiled through her body. *How can he kiss me like this after he'd had his dick in some other girl?* If he had wanted to be with Bryna, he'd had a million opportunities to tell her the truth. Yeah, she had said she wasn't comfortable with him, but then when she was comfortable, he could have told her the truth. The truth was at his fingertips at every opportunity. He couldn't pull this bullshit because she had caught him with his ex. She couldn't pull a one-eighty on her life when there was so much fucking uncertainty.

Bryna wrenched out of his grasp. He gave her a questioning look, and then she reached back and slapped him clear across the face. His head snapped to the side, and he ground his teeth.

"Don't touch me," she repeated. Her voice was hoarse. She held the tears back with the force from her will alone.

Eric staggered a step back in shock. She used that opportunity to grab the handle of the door, and she pulled it back open.

"Bryna, please," he begged. "Don't go. Let's try to work it out."

"What is there to work out? You said it yourself. We both know this is never happening, and you're going to regret this in the morning." She threw his words back in his face.

"Let me explain," he pleaded.

She couldn't let him. Even if she wanted to listen and make things work, she couldn't. It would never work between them. The last six months of their relationship, the supposed ease of their friendship, was all a lie. One big lie.

"You've explained enough."

She sat down in the driver's seat and then pulled out of his driveway. Her heart was beating a million miles a minute. It wasn't until she was around the corner that she let the tears fall freely. Once they started, she couldn't get them to stop.

TWENTY-SEVEN

BRYNA PULLED OVER TO THE SIDE of the road and parked her car. Shuddering deep sobs wracked her body. She had no idea she could even cry like this, that tears could even flow so freely. Her heart of ice had cracked, shattered, melted, and it was currently sitting in a puddle at her feet.

She didn't even know what she was feeling. She was so angry with Eric for sleeping with Audrey, for being with her all this time. Yet she was angry with herself for being angry with him. She had been with someone else this whole time, too, but he had *known*. She had never kept Hugh a secret from Eric. She hadn't kept *anything* a secret from Eric.

It was all even more fucked up because Eric had thought she had known all along about Audrey. And they had both kept their distance because of one stupid fucking night at Posse when she had been a mess about Jude, and Gates had pushed her and Eric apart.

Part of her wanted so desperately to turn the car around and go back to him. But the other part kept replaying the image of him fucking Audrey in his bedroom over and over again. *How can I get over that?*

"Why?" she whispered helplessly into the silent car.

For over a year, she had worked under the assumption that he was gay. She had opened herself up to him, only to have a wall slide back over her heart. Even though she had deceived herself, she still thought it was Eric's fault. If he was falling for her, he should have said something. She couldn't listen to her own heart telling her she had fallen for *him*.

Her hands were still shaking when the tears finally dried up. The rain was slowing to a drizzle. She forced herself to start driving again. She needed to get away and process.

Pulling out her cell phone, she ignored the missed call from Eric and dialed Hugh's number.

"Hey," Hugh said.

"Hey." She thought her voice was strong, but she still sounded weak and vulnerable. She hated Eric for making her like this. It went against her nature.

"Are you okay?"

"I just…need you." She didn't know what else to say.

"I'm working out of town. Is it urgent? Are you hurt?"

Only emotionally. "No."

Hugh sighed heavily into the phone. "I wish you'd tell me what's wrong. You keep your secrets so close to your heart. Just let me in," he pleaded.

If only I could tell him the truth…but what's the truth at this point? She had lost sight of it in the chaos.

She bit her lip and decided to tell him as much as she could. It wasn't like she could go into explicit detail about Eric. "I got into a huge argument with two of my best friends. I know it probably sounds dumb," she admitted softly, "but I don't think things will ever be the same. And it's all my fault."

That last part took her off guard. She hadn't even known she was going to say that, but it felt true. She could have prevented the argument with Stacia if she had accepted Pace, but the thought of doing that made her want to throw up. She could have prevented the argument with Eric if she could accept his feelings, despite what had happened with Audrey, but that didn't seem possible either right now.

"It's not dumb," Hugh said understandably. "If it has upset you this much, then it's important."

She swallowed back her tears at his words.

"I'm in Atlantic City. I'll fly you out to see me, so you can get away from everything. How does that sound?"

"Really great," she admitted.

She couldn't think of anything better than escaping the reality of her life right now. She'd had to confront everything head-on recently, and she didn't know how much more she could take.

"Good. I'll have someone make all the arrangements. Try to relax, and you'll be with me soon."

Five hours later, a car picked her up from the airport and drove her to Hugh's resort in Atlantic City. Though she had been groggy on the plane, she hadn't been able to sleep, no matter what she had done. She was even more alert in the car. She couldn't escape the images flashing through her mind or the reality of what she had been through.

When she arrived, Hugh was waiting for her in the lobby. She couldn't believe he was awake. With the three-hour time difference, she couldn't believe *she* was still awake.

"Why are you awake?" she asked.

"As if I could sleep after that call." He pulled her into his arms and kissed the top of her head. "Come on. You look like you need to sleep."

"I'm not the only one."

He laughed. "It's morning here, love. I have to work."

"Work when I leave."

"I would love to do that." They hopped into the elevator, and Hugh inserted his key to take them to the top floor. "But I can't neglect my responsibilities. It's nice to have you here. I'd travel with you everywhere if I could."

She smiled at his words but didn't respond. Her head was too clouded with other things, and she was tired.

They reached the penthouse where Hugh was staying. It was dark inside, and he didn't bother to turn the lights on as he guided her to the master suite. The bed was enormous and unbelievably inviting.

"Why don't you rest?" he suggested. "You're dead on your feet. You can tell me all about what happened when you wake up."

"Wait," she murmured. She ran her hand down his tie. "Aren't you coming with me?" She didn't want to be alone tonight even though her mind told her it was the smart thing to do. She didn't want to listen.

"You know I'd love nothing more, but I have to work."

He pulled back the covers, and she crawled into bed.

"Let me take care of you. I'll still be here when you wake up."

"Okay," she whispered.

As soon as he disappeared, fresh tears hit her anew. She didn't even know why she was crying. Her emotions felt like a tangled knot in her chest. She couldn't differentiate one from the other. She just cried and let it out—everything that pained her, everyone who had ever hurt her.

Her father.

Her mother.

Celia.

Pace.

Jude.

Gates.

Avery.

Tara.

Stacia.

Eric.

Just a long list of people who had disappointed her and people she had disappointed. They all scrambled together, their faces morphing into one, until her tears were just a cascading waterfall of her pain. She unleashed it on the world, fighting with herself for even feeling. *How dare I feel!*

The tears ached and tore at her, but no matter what she did, she couldn't escape the darkness that pulled her under.

Bryna awoke with a start.

She clutched at the sheets in a panic. Her eyes flew open. She couldn't remember where she was, and for one blissful moment, she forgot everything. Then, it came back to her, knocking into her with a ferocious vengeance.

Her heart hammered in her chest, and she waited until it returned to its normal cadence before deciding to check the clock. *3:00 p.m.* She had slept through most of the day. Sleeping had given her some perspective and made her more alert. She wrenched the sheet off the bed, wound it around her body, and wandered into the main living area of the penthouse. She didn't know who she might encounter or else she likely would have gone in the nude.

But no one was out there. The blinds were drawn, so none of the afternoon light could filter into the room. Only one of the rooms off of the living space had a light on, and she walked in that direction.

Hugh was working in an office, as she had found him so many times in his Vegas suite. It was a comforting sight. At least some things hadn't changed.

"Do you ever sleep?" she asked.

In a slow and desirous fashion, his eyes moved up her body covered in nothing but a sheet. "Only on weekends when I'm with you."

"Come to bed," she encouraged. "It's late."

"Or early. It is the middle of the afternoon after all."

She walked over to him and let the sheet slit up one leg, as if she were wearing an expensive ballroom gown. "Come to bed," she repeated.

Hugh grabbed her without pretense and pulled her in front of him, so she was seated on his desk. "I think I'll have my bed here."

He leaned forward and kissed her neck, savoring the taste to her shoulder. Then, he removed the thin sheet to expose her body to him. She didn't cover up even though she felt bare—mind, body, and soul at this point. His lips moved to her breast, and she arched against him, willing him to devour her whole.

"I want you so much more than this, Bri." He kissed his way to the other breast.

"What do you want?" She was sure she sounded like she was pleading with him.

"Everything." He leaned her backward, so she lay across his desk. "Let go with me."

His fingers trailed a line down her sides to grip her hips. His eyes roamed her body as he kissed down her navel. She sucked in a deep breath.

"I do," she murmured.

"You come to me with worries, but you are still so far away."

"I'm right here." She ground her hips in a circle as a reminder.

"I know." He sighed and sat back up before indulging.

She quivered underneath him, desperate for his touch, desperate to forget.

"I know how much you're hiding, and I don't know why."

"Hiding?"

This conversation had shifted.

"Do you think I would start a relationship with you without knowing everything I could first?" he asked.

In confusion, Bryna sat up quickly. Her stomach dropped out, and fear seemed to reign over all other emotions. *What did he know? How much did he know? And how did he know it?*

"What?" she asked.

"I've been waiting all this time for you to tell me. I want you to admit who you are. I'll still love you either way."

Bryna startled. "L-love me?"

"I know." He looked down and then up again into her eyes. "I couldn't hold it in any longer. Of course I love you. I was lost when I first met you. I don't care that you're an eighteen-year-old college student. I don't care that you told me you were going to Miami to hang out with your girlfriends when you were there for the play-off game. Did you think I wouldn't notice the coincidence? There's so much. I don't care who you are or where you came from. I'm tired of the lies."

She was slack-jawed at his admission.

"When I'm with you, I want *you*, not the illusion you've created," he continued.

"I don't know what to say."

He knew everything about her, but she knew next to nothing about him. She hadn't wanted to know. She had thought that was part of the arrangement. He was married, and she was his sugar baby. That was how this worked. She didn't *love* him, and she certainly couldn't say she did.

"I don't expect you to say anything. I'm sure it's all a shock, but I want you, Bryna," he said, using her name for the first time. "Choose me."

Haven't I already done that by flying out here?

She swallowed. There was no other choice.

"I choose you."

Hugh leaned her back against the desk and made his way back down her body. The intensity with which he consumed her revealed how much her words meant to him. She came, writhing on the table under his capable hands and practiced mouth. Her world slipped away, and she used the ecstasy of this dream to help her forget what she had left behind, to remind her why she had chosen this to begin with.

She heard a zipper, and then his pants hit the floor.

"Fuck, Bryna," he groaned.

He maneuvered himself to her opening, and she felt the building pressure when he entered her in one swift motion. He wasn't gentle with her, and she liked it. It felt like punishment. She needed it. She let it wrap all around her. She wanted him to be brutal, to fuck away her nightmares.

He rocked into her again and again, leaving nothing but the sound of their bodies slapping together in their wake. When Hugh flipped her over and forced her flat against his desk, she tried to push the image of Eric out of her mind. She had decided long ago that he didn't matter. She needed to remember it again.

Hugh gripped her tighter, and she felt her own climax building, despite her dark thoughts. Or maybe it was because of her dark thoughts. She didn't even know anymore. All she knew was that they hit that spot together. Both soared away to another place and another time, and her release left her in tatters once more.

TWENTY-EIGHT

THE NEXT MORNING, Bryna felt like hell. Even though she had slept for nearly a day straight, it hadn't helped. She had bags under her eyes from crying, and her stomach was still in her throat.

She applied a healthy dose of makeup to get rid of the side effects of her unnecessary tears. She grabbed her phone and checked it for the first time since she had landed in New Jersey. She had three missed calls and five text messages from Eric. She sighed heavily. *Great.*

She opened the first one.

> *I know I fucked up. That wasn't how I wanted to tell you that I like you. Please let me explain. I don't want to lose you.*

Bryna closed her eyes and fought back the wave of emotions that hit her. She couldn't do this. She needed some time away to think about what she wanted to do. She had chosen Hugh last night, and right now, that was where she needed to be. She deleted the other messages before reading them and tucked her phone away in her purse. She promised herself she wouldn't look at it again while she was here.

Holding back her frustrations, she walked out of the bedroom to find a huge platter set up for breakfast.

Hugh smiled brightly when he saw her. "You look refreshed."

It couldn't have been further from the truth.

"Thanks. What's this?"

"I thought we could eat together. I have some time before my first meeting. Care to take a walk down the boardwalk?"

"Sure."

She sat down and ate a pancake, some eggs, and fruit, and then they left the hotel room. The resort was right on the water, and it was teeming with high school spring breakers. It was hard to believe that had been her a year ago. She had spent her senior spring break alone. She didn't like to think about that.

"It's nice to be away," she admitted.

Hugh stepped out of the way of some kids running down the boardwalk and pulled her with him. "It is."

"I'd love to do this all the time." She felt wistful. She couldn't abandon school or the cheer team, but this was paradise.

"Well, what about this summer? Do you have plans?"

"No." She hadn't really thought about it.

"I'm opening a new resort in Barcelona."

"Really? That's amazing. Barcelona is beautiful!"

"In that case, will you come with me?"

"To Barcelona?" she gasped out.

"For the summer."

"The *whole* summer?"

"As long as you'll have me."

She couldn't believe it. Her brain couldn't wrap around it. Even after everything he had done for her, she still thought it was crazy that he would want to bring her.

"I want to take you with me—not as Bri, but as Bryna. No more secrets between us. Just you and me."

Her heart leaped in her chest. *This is what I want. Right?*

He didn't see her as a sugar baby. He saw her more as…his girlfriend. *But what else am I? When did everything spiral so far out of my control?*

When she didn't answer right away, Hugh looked concerned. "You don't have to come with me. It would be a bunch of fancy dinners, a ribbon-cutting ceremony, lots of shopping. You'd probably hate it."

Bryna laughed. "Okay. Twist my arm, why don't you?"

"I want you there with me to experience it all."

"All right. I'd love to go."

Bryna returned to campus the next day. She'd had so many missed notifications that she had turned her phone off in annoyance. She didn't know what to say to anyone, and she wasn't ready to be herself anymore. It had been nice to be with Hugh, away from reality for a bit longer.

She dove headfirst into classes the next day. On her way out of the film building, she found Eric waiting for her.

"Bri, can we talk?"

"No."

She walked toward her car, but Eric followed.

"You were gone. I went to your place. I asked around. No one saw you."

"Eric, stop."

She ground to a halt and stared into his hazel eyes. They were so full of concern that she almost looked away. But she couldn't. She needed her hard exterior for this.

"I have to process what happened this weekend. It's not going to be like a light bulb where I flip a switch, and everything is better. The more you push, the farther you push me away."

He pursed his lips, but she could tell he knew she was right.

"Well, things with Audrey are over. You have to know, I never meant to hurt you. I didn't think anyone really could."

"I'm not hurting," she lied.

Eric gave her a don't-give-me-that-shit look. He could see through her. "Okay, Bri. But think about one thing before I go. Remember when you said, at the national championship game, that you were only comfortable with me because you knew nothing could ever happen between us?"

"Yes?"

"It proves that, even then, you were thinking about something happening. You were too scared to admit it to yourself." He threw his hands out in supplication. "I'll give you all the space you need, but you've changed me as much as I've changed you. I want to give this a shot, and I'm not going to give up."

Bryna swallowed hard. "We'll see how long this lasts before you go back to her."

"Knowing you're within reach? Never."

He was so sincere. It almost softened her to him, but then the image of Audrey hit her all over again, and she couldn't do it.

"We'll see. Good-bye, Eric."

He stared straight ahead as she left. She was sure that he hadn't thought the conversation would go like that. *What had he expected? Even if I want to be with him and all would be right with the world, how could I when the thought of him touching someone else made me gag?* She had hated the idea when she had thought he was gay! The reaction was so much more visceral now.

She was pissed off all over again, and she still had to deal with cheer practice tonight. When she got in her car, she turned her phone back on and noticed that she had another missed call and a text message from Trihn that basically screamed at Bryna to answer her. It was complete with all caps and a million exclamation points.

With a resigned sigh, she decided to put Trihn out of her misery.

> *What's up?*

Trihn's response was immediate.

> *I haven't heard from you in three days, and all you can say is, "What's up?" What the fuck, Bri?*

> *I missed you, too.*

> *Come to my apartment right now! Otherwise, I will be forced to disown you—but not really. Just get over here!*

Bryna shook her head. This was why she was friends with Trihn.

> *Okay. On my way.*

Bryna drove the short distance to Trihn's apartment and was greeted with a scowl.

"Where the hell have you been?"

"Atlantic City," she answered truthfully.

She walked into Trihn's apartment and lay back on the couch. She had prepared herself for this interrogation. *God, my life has been reduced to one big interrogation.*

"What? Why?"

"Hugh flew me out."

Trihn shook her head. "That's absurd."

"Yeah. After school ends, he's flying us to Barcelona for the summer."

Trihn's eyes were wide as saucers. "Damn. You have him wrapped around your finger. Are you sure that's a good idea?"

"Does it matter?"

"Of course!"

"Can we get on to why you have really been obsessively calling me?" Bryna asked.

Seeing Eric had exhausted her. This conversation would surely only make it worse.

"Geez, you're in über bitch mode. I just wanted you to talk to Stacia."

"No."

"Ugh! I knew you'd be difficult."

"She's the one who went behind my back to date Pace, and I'm being difficult?" Bryna ground out.

"Look, she likes him. Give it a chance. You never know. It could be over by the end of the summer."

"Then, I'll wait it out."

Trihn rolled her eyes. "She was really upset after you left. What the hell happened?"

"Nothing. I couldn't be there any longer."

"And you left for Atlantic City, unplanned, and didn't respond to anyone's messages? Don't tell me that was all Stacia. Even you aren't that melodramatic."

Bryna shrugged.

"Seriously, what the fuck? I'm your friend. Stacia is your friend. And you're about as closed off as a brick wall." She raised her hands and took a step back. "I don't know how to be here for you."

Bryna sighed. Maybe Trihn was right. Maybe Bryna should tell her friend. It would be nice to actually talk to someone about it.

"Okay. So, remember how I told you Eric was gay?"

"Yeah?" Trihn asked uncertainly.

"Well, he's not."

Trihn's mouth dropped open. "I *knew* it!"

"Yeah, yeah. You knew," Bryna said with a sigh.

"Oh my God, he loves you, and you're going to get married and have babies." Trihn looked ecstatic at the possibility of Bryna being with Eric like that.

It turned Bryna's stomach. Marriage and babies were not in her near future.

"Ew. No. He was sleeping with his ex, Audrey, when I made a surprise visit to his place."

"What?" Trihn shrieked.

"Yeah. I thought that he was gay, and he thought that I knew he was sleeping with his ex-girlfriend. We got into a huge argument afterward, and I left."

"Has he tried to contact you?"

Bryna nodded.

"What did he say?"

Her heart constricted as she remembered his face. "I saw him on campus. He came to try to convince me that he and Audrey were over, but I couldn't get the image of him fucking her out of my head."

Trihn shook her head. "So, let me get this straight. Even though you've been seeing Hugh this whole time, you're angry at Eric for being with someone else?"

"Yes."

"Why?" she cried. "It doesn't make sense."

"He *knew* about Hugh. I thought Eric was off-limits. If he was interested in me, he could have said something!"

"It sounds like he thought *you* were off-limits, too. I mean, if he thought you were dating someone, he wasn't going to be like, 'Hey, forget this guy.' That's definitely not the Eric I know."

"Whatever."

"Look," Trihn said, trying to find reason. "Your anger is so misguided. You're angry because you like him. You're hurt. That's okay. Let yourself hurt, and then talk to him about it. You can't push him away forever."

Bryna closed her eyes. She didn't want to hear this from Trihn. She had made up her mind already. "I don't think I can do that. The person I was when I was with him wasn't real. It was all a facade between two people who thought they knew secrets in the other one's life."

"It's only a facade if you want it to be."

"No. I chose Hugh. I'm going to Barcelona with him this summer. That's it." She tried to sound so definite, but she knew she hadn't. Her strength was hidden beneath layers of bitchy behavior and high levels of self-confidence. All of which had been rattled this week.

"Oh, B," Trihn whispered.

"Don't pity me! It's what I want."

"Okay," Trihn said softly. She let the subject drop even though it was clear in her eyes that she wanted to say more. "But will you talk to Stacia?"

"It's going to take a while to get over Pace."

"She didn't want to upset you, and she can't help that she likes him," Trihn tried to reason.

"Psh. Yes, she can. She just doesn't see it yet."

"Fine. I can't be the middleman anymore though. You two need to make up."

"Then, have her call me when they break up," Bryna said, standing.

"You're a stubborn bitch."

"Yep," she agreed.

She felt even more like one when she left Trihn's place and saw another missed call from Eric along with a text message.

I'll stop bothering you after this. You want space to figure things out. I don't get it because every part of me is screaming to be near you. I know you feel the same. Call me an idiot for what happened over the past couple of months.

Whatever you want. But, Bri, I'll never be that idiot again. I can't imagine my life without you. I'm still the same person. I'm still your cowboy. Come back to me soon.

Bryna bit down on her lip, hard. Then, she deleted the text and promised not to look back.

TWENTY-NINE

TRUE TO HIS PROMISE, Bryna hadn't heard from Eric since that last text message. Several long weeks had gone by, school had released for the summer, and she hadn't heard one word from him. Just like she had wanted. At least that was what she told herself when her Sunday afternoons were full of finals prep rather than margaritas and on Wednesdays when she ate lunch alone instead of at his place, grilling burgers.

But none of that mattered now. She could adjust to anything. And it was for the better. She was ready to leave for Barcelona for the summer. She met Hugh in New York City with a ridiculous amount of Louis Vuitton luggage and her overused passport.

Their flight to Barcelona was smooth sailing, and they landed in the beautiful afternoon weather. A limo picked them up from the airport and transported them to the completed resort. It wouldn't officially open for nearly another month, so they were staying there exclusively until then.

Together, they spent the weeks leading up to the big ribbon-cutting ceremony lounging on the Spanish beaches, shopping, and hitting every romantic location in the city. Hugh had to work a lot, but he tried to make up for it with over-the-top evenings.

When he was gone, it gave her time to think about why she had left. Eric's face popped into her mind over and over again. She tried to forget the look on his face when he had begged her to stay, but she couldn't. And though she was still so angry with him and herself for what had happened, the distance made the reality of his actions wane.

She knew it could never be the same. Part of what had made them, *them* was a lie. But she hoped they could have a part of their friendship back. She wasn't ready to confront that now, but maybe she would be when she got back from Barcelona. Maybe.

Hugh caught her lounging by the pool during one such instance when her mind was off thinking about what she had left behind in Vegas.

"Hey, gorgeous." He kissed the top of her head.

She startled. "Oh, hey."

"You seemed far away. Where were you?"

She smiled lazily to try to hide the thoughts warring through her mind. "Just excited for the ceremony tonight. Glad it's finally here."

"And sad that it means our time together this summer is coming to a close," he finished for her.

"Oh, don't remind me."

She didn't know what was going to happen with them after this. He had said he loved her. That left a whole lot of nagging questions in her mind, questions she was trying to avoid like the plague. *What would happen from here? How could we be together when he's married? Is this going to be a permanent arrangement?* It was confusing because though she had made her decisions, she felt as if she should know more about him. She wanted to ask all the questions she had avoided before because she didn't think they mattered. But she didn't.

"You're gone again."

She laughed and tried to play it off. "No, I'm still here. How was work?"

"Everything is set up for the ceremony down to the minute details. I came to check to see if you were ready for all of this?"

"Sure. Why wouldn't I be?"

"Well, it will all be filmed. I'll be showcasing you to the world."

She swallowed. "Really? You didn't mention that."

"It's been picked up by some national and international media. I didn't want to scare you. You'll be at my side, and I'll do all the talking. You just have to be your beautiful self."

"Oh. Right." *Arm candy.* "Well, I've been in front of a camera before. So, no big deal, I guess."

She wished he hadn't kept it from her. It wasn't like she was afraid to be on camera, but it was another big step. *What the hell is he going to say if someone asks why I'm here with him?* It was all so confusing.

"If you're not comfortable, I can have you in a strategic position off camera." He pulled her hand up to his lips and lightly kissed her fingers. "But I want you to be with me."

"That's why I'm here. Of course, I'll be on camera with you, if that's what you want."

"Good." He smiled brightly. "You should probably go get ready then. I have a surprise for you."

"A surprise?" she asked, her face lighting up. "You're full of surprises."

"I am. I like to surprise you."

"Well, now, I'll spend all afternoon wondering."

He gave her an easy smile. Everything was always so easy for him. She wished she could push all her cares away so readily.

"Good. I'll see you at the ceremony. I can't wait to see your dress. Are you sure I can't look ahead of time?"

"I've spent a lot of time keeping this secret from you! You can't look now."

He backed away with his hands up. "Of course. I'll allow you to surprise me this once then."

A couple of hours later, Bryna was refreshed with her hair pulled back into a severe twist and her makeup dark and smoky. Her dress was an exquisite floor-length racerback Dior creation, hand-beaded in bright reds, with a slit that reached to her upper thigh when the panels separated. It was both elegant and sexy.

When she walked out of the room, the look on Hugh's face made the whole ensemble worth it.

"Now, how am I supposed to keep my hands off of you through the entire ceremony?" he asked.

She smirked, triumphant. "You'll have to give it your best shot."

"I am going to have a lot of jealous colleagues."

He offered her his arm, and she fit her hand into the crook of his elbow. His lips landed on hers, tender and thoughtful, filled with all the love he professed to her on a regular basis. She still hadn't returned the phrase, but every time he kissed her, it was as if he didn't need to hear the words. He acted as if he could taste them.

They walked together down to the entrance. Hugh shook hands with a few people in the lobby while a bunch of people gave her the side eye. They knew she had been there with him the whole time, and still, they skeptically looked at her. Hugh didn't even seem to notice. He grabbed her hand once more, and they walked out to the crowd of people and up onto a platform.

Then, Hugh started his speech. She stood next to him. Cameras flashed everywhere. It reminded her of the red carpet she had been on countless times with her father and Gates. All of the eyes should have made her feel better, but suddenly, she felt worse. She enjoyed this, but she didn't love Hugh. She didn't know if she would ever love him. She liked him. She liked their time together, but she didn't feel that spark.

But he kept saying it. He kept saying it like love existed. Love was laced with poison, and each time she drank from the bottle, she died a slow, painful death.

The applause jolted her out of her thoughts. Hugh reached forward, holding up some impossibly large gold scissors, and cut the ribbon. There were a series of pictures, and then everyone was herded inside to the ballroom. A huge after-party was being held in all the hotel ballrooms to celebrate the new resort. Hundreds of people flooded in behind them, and Hugh smiled at them all, greeting them and thanking them for coming to the resort. He was an eternally gracious host.

"Come on, while everyone's distracted," he said. He took her arm and pulled her out a side door to a deserted balcony overlooking the city below.

Bryna leaned her elbows against the railing and let the breeze kiss across her skin. "That was a lot of people."

"And everyone was watching you."

She glanced over at him and laughed lightly. "You were the one giving the speech."

"Hey, I would have been watching you, too, if I could have."

"You see me all the time."

"But not in this dress." His hands slid down her hips.

"No. I normally wear less."

Hugh smiled and then took a calming deep breath. He actually looked…nervous. *That's odd. He's never like that.*

"I have your surprise."

She arched an eyebrow. Suddenly, her nerves tingled up her back in warning. She didn't even know why, but it hit her hard.

He swallowed and then pulled out a flat blue velvet box from his jacket pocket. Her eyes locked on it.

"I told you earlier that I wasn't ready for you to leave me after the summer. The truth is, I don't want you to leave at all. My life is complete with you in it. I enjoy waking up every day and finding you beside me. I haven't felt like this in a very, very long time."

Her ears were ringing. She could barely hear what he was saying.

He opened the box, and inside was a stunning Harry Winston collar necklace of exquisite diamonds. It looked as if it weighed a ton, and it shined so bright that it was almost blinding. Her hand went to her mouth in shock.

"I love you. I know you've been kind of distant, and we haven't even been together for a year, but this feels too real to me. I want it to be real for you. I didn't know what your dress looked like, but I figured that diamonds matched everything. You always wear your B, but I wanted you to wear something of mine tonight."

"Hugh," she breathed.

She shook her head. *How is this happening?* He had all but said he wanted to marry her. Besides the fact that he was already married, she was only fucking eighteen years old. This couldn't be real.

"I just…"

"Let me put it on for you."

"Wait," she said.

She put her hand out and touched the necklace. She couldn't do this. She had thought this was what she wanted. She had thought all the glitz and glamour would make up for what had happened with Jude. He had created her, and she had let herself fall into this trap. *But by letting Hugh think I love him, am I any better than Jude in the end?*

She didn't want to lead Hugh on. When it had been fun and carefree, she had assumed they were both on the same page. But this wasn't a game. This was someone's life. And it had lost its luster. She no longer wanted to be the person Jude had created.

"What? What is it?" he asked with so much concern in his voice.

"I don't think I can do this. I don't get where you think this is headed." She looked up into his eyes. "I mean…you're married."

Hugh's shock was evident. He snapped the box closed, nearly biting into her hand, before she snatched it away.

"What are you talking about? I'm not married!"

THIRTY

BRYNA'S JAW DROPPED. "What?"

"Why would you think that?"

"I...I don't know."

She really didn't. She had thought Hugh was like Jude and that everything was the same. But after his confession of love for her and this new revelation that he wasn't actually married, she was scrambling to find a reason for her actions.

Hugh's expression only darkened further. "Did you believe this whole time that this was acceptable behavior for a married man? Did you think I'd sleep with you and tell you I love you if I were with someone else?"

Bryna opened and closed her mouth, unable to form words. She had thought those things. She had thought them the whole time. It hadn't even bothered her even though she knew it should have.

"Well? Is this what you think of me? You believe I would deceive you so thoroughly…and my wife at that." He shook his head. His anger had gone from simmer to full boil in under a minute.

"No. I don't know. It…wouldn't be the first time I've been with someone like that," she whispered.

His narrowed eyes and clenched jaw told her that was the exact wrong thing to say. *Fuck.*

"So, you've done this before?"

"I…" She swallowed and tried to hold herself up. She couldn't believe this was spiraling. "I didn't do it intentionally."

"But *this* was intentional with me?"

Bryna cringed. It had been intentional. She had plotted their relationship out with practiced precision from the get-go.

"Christ, it was."

"Hugh…"

"No." He held his hand up to silence her.

She clamped her mouth shut.

"I don't want to hear your excuses. I thought, with your past, who your father is, your previous relationship with Gates Hartman, your trust fund—"

"You know about my trust fund?" she asked in shock. This sounded like he had done more than a background check.

"I told you, I covered my bases. I didn't want to be made a fool of." He stared at her, plainly stating she was making a fool of him at the present moment. "What did you expect to happen, Bryna? I screened you. Our first few dates were to ensure this wouldn't happen. It seems that being around actors much of your life has made you a pretty adept one. Do you even care about me?"

And there it was. Under all the anger and carefully controlled businessman facade, the hurt was showing through.

"Yes," she said, her voice wobbling.

"But you don't love me?"

"No," she whispered.

He looked as if she had slapped him. "How could you, when you thought I was cheating on my wife to be with you?"

His question was rhetorical, and she kept her mouth closed. She didn't want to do any more damage.

He tore away from her, walking the length of the balcony in a fury before returning to her. His hands were fisted at his sides. "I don't understand. We're in Barcelona together. I've brought you halfway around the world. I've introduced you to all my business associates. I put you on fucking television at my side!" he yelled. "Didn't you think more people would be concerned about my actions? Didn't all the signs point to me being available? And why the hell didn't you *say* something?"

His desperation ripped through her.

"I don't know. I...thought everyone was in on it." As soon as the words had left her mouth, she realized how bad it made her sound.

"Yes, they're all in on it," he said coldly. "Because my wife is dead."

Bryna covered her mouth. *Good God, what the hell is wrong with me?*

"If you had done your research as I had, you would know she died nearly five years ago."

"I'm...I'm so sorry."

"Yes. Well," he said, waving away her pity, "I thought I was moving on."

"With me," she whispered. She truly felt like a horrible person.

"Yes, with you! I've given you the world, and you've spit in my face," he exploded. He ground his teeth together, trying to restrain himself. "Have you been with others while we've been together?"

Bryna looked away, not wanting him to see the guilt in her eyes. She had finished things with Andrew before sleeping with Hugh. But she'd kissed Eric three times since then. She might have only initiated it once, but she had wanted more. She would have done more if things had been different.

"Christ," he said, stumbling back a step. "You have, haven't you?"

"No! No. I haven't slept with anyone."

"Then, what did you have to think about?" He didn't let her answer before barreling forward. "Is this why you came to see me in Atlantic City? Is that why you were upset? Were you with someone else?"

"I was upset about my friends, like I told you. One of them is a guy, but we were never together. Actually, I thought he was gay up to that point."

Hugh grabbed his hair in frustration. "I don't know what to say about any of this. I thought we were working toward something. Now, I'm terrified to find out what you wanted from me if you didn't love me."

Bryna looked away.

"Was it the money?" he spat in disgust. "I've had people want me for it before, but I thought you were different."

She couldn't respond. At first, it had been the game to have the power, to have the thrill of someone showering her with goodies like Jude had. But then, over time, it had gotten worse. She'd wanted more. She'd basked in the rush of getting everything. But it wasn't just the money. She had cared for him. She had thought they had an agreement. She had thought he knew what he was getting into. Now, this…

"Say something!"

"No! It wasn't just the money. It was you, too…I liked being with you, too."

"Not *just* the money," he murmured, stunned.

She covered her face with her hands and took a steadying breath. "That's not what I meant."

"Sir," someone called, interrupting their argument, "it's time for your speech."

"I'll just be a minute," he said, not turning around. His eyes were hard. "When I get back…you should figure out exactly what you *do* mean."

Hugh left her alone on the balcony. The door closed behind him.

"Fuck!" she yelled into the silence.

She closed her eyes and tried to piece herself back together. Things hadn't just spiraled out of control with her accusation about him being married. It had plummeted to the bottom of the Mariana Trench.

What the hell am I going to say to him? Everything he had said hit too close to home. She had been digging him. Though she had never clarified, she had thought they were on the same page. Now, it looked like they hadn't even been reading the same book.

She was trying to figure out what to say to him when her cell phone went off in her purse. She jolted out of her thoughts and stared down at it in shock. She had forgotten that she even had it with her. No one had called her all summer. She had received messages from Trihn online but not phone calls.

She pulled the phone out of her purse and saw her dad's number. *What the fuck?*

"Hello?"

"Sweetheart! I'm glad I could reach you. I don't know what time it is in Spain."

How does he even know I'm here? I hadn't told him before fleeing the country. Maybe Pace.

"Hi, Daddy," she said uncertainly. "It's midnight."

"Honey, Celia went into labor. I really need you to come home."

"What?" she asked. "You want me to fly back from Barcelona for the baby?"

"Bryna," he said, surprisingly sweet, "I know you don't approve of this. I know you don't approve of Celia or Pace or what happened with your mother. But I don't want you to blame the new baby for those things. She's going to be your half-sister. Your baby sister."

Her heart constricted at that word.

"She's completely innocent in this, and I want her to grow up knowing her sister. I need our family together even though we haven't been much of a family lately."

"Lately," she mumbled.

"Since your mother left."

"Yeah…left."

"We're not perfect. No family is. But without you, we're not even complete. I'm not going to command you to come back. You're almost nineteen-years-old, and you can make your own decisions, but I want you here. Celia wants you here. We love you. What do you say?"

Hugh's face appeared at the door, and he still looked pissed. *Great.*

She took a deep breath. "I'll have to think about it and get back to you."

"Thank you for at least considering it. We hope you come back. Your birthday is next week, and I know we'd all like to celebrate together."

She was stunned as she hung up the phone with her father. The new baby, her father acting like…a father, him wanting to celebrate her birthday—she didn't know what to make of any of it.

"Well?" Hugh said. He crossed his arms and looked at her.

She could see all the love and devotion underneath the tension in his shoulders.

Bryna sighed. "I don't think I can say anything to make this better. I didn't want to hurt you. I thought we were on the same page. I thought this was what I wanted, but I guess it's not." She hated the look of pain that crossed his face. "My stepmother just went into labor in Los Angeles…"

"Then, maybe you should go to L.A. to be with her."

She swallowed, hearing the dismissal in his voice. "Yeah, I guess I should."

Hugh closed his eyes and released a deep breath. "Here." He held out the box with the necklace. "Keep this."

She stared at it, slightly horrified. "I can't take this."

"I'm not going to return it or give it to someone else." Their eyes met across the distance between them. "And I'd say you've earned it."

Bryna flinched at his harsh words as he placed the necklace in her hands. "I wish it hadn't turned out this way," she told him truthfully.

"Yeah, well, I was the idiot who fell for it."

"Hugh," she whispered.

He shook his head. "I really don't want to hear it. Take your spoils and go."

She pushed the box back into his hands. "No. I don't want it. You shouldn't give it to me. I don't deserve it."

"Fine." Hugh flung the box over the balcony.

Bryna's mouth dropped open. She looked over the side and listened to the crunch as it hit the ground four stories below them. "I can't believe you just did that."

"It was worthless." He turned his back on her and looked out at the city. "Just go."

She tilted her head, refusing to acknowledge the wobble in her chin at his words. She deserved his anger. But it was for the better that it was ending. She couldn't keep living this life, and she didn't want to hurt him. He was a good guy. He needed to find someone who could love him back just as fiercely.

As she staggered out of the ballroom to pack for her journey back to Los Angeles, she wished that she could have been that person for him. But once again, she found it was all one big lie.

THIRTY-ONE

AFTER SIXTEEN HOURS IN FLIGHT and three layovers, Bryna finally landed at LAX. She was exhausted and probably needed to sleep for a week straight, but she was home. The crisp Los Angeles air hit her full-on, and she soaked in the warm early morning sunshine.

Home.

A cab drove her through the insufferable traffic that she definitely hadn't missed and straight to the hospital. She had no idea what she looked like. She was carting around her carry-on, and she felt totally run-down. The only good thing about all of this was that she had mailed the rest of her luggage to her parent's house, so she wouldn't have to deal with it.

A nurse directed her to the hallway where Celia's room was. Bryna's father was standing in the waiting room. The twins, Lacey and Kacey, were sprawled out on sofas. One was reading on a Kindle while the other played video games. Both were completely checked out.

"Hey, sweetheart," her father said.

She fell into his arms, and he hugged her tightly against him. For a split second, she felt like a kid again. Her daddy could fix anything. He could make the hurt go away. She had always been a daddy's girl.

He kissed the top of her head. "It's good to have you home."

"It's good to be home," she said.

Her dad stepped back and smiled down at her. "Celia's excited for you to meet your sister."

Bryna's hands were sweating. Through all of this, she had tried not to think about what exactly she was coming home to. She knew nothing about babies. Growing up, she hadn't had a younger sibling. She didn't know anyone who had been pregnant where she would have to be around a baby. The whole thing made her anxious.

"Don't worry. You'll be fine," he said, as if reading her mind. "There were some complications at first, but everything is okay now. Go on in and see them while they're both still awake."

"All right," Bryna said.

She was resolved to do this. She took a deep breath and then entered the hospital room. Celia was lying in bed. She looked exhausted, but she was holding on to a small bundle in her arms and didn't even seem to notice her own fatigue.

"Bryna." Celia looked up at her with a wide smile. "I'm so glad you came."

Bryna shrugged uncomfortably. "Dad said there were problems?"

"I'm almost forty. It was expected. What's important is you meeting your new sister."

Celia offered Bryna the baby. She noticed how nervous Bryna was and showed her how to cradle the baby in her arms. Bryna was still shaking and freaked out, but she wasn't going to drop her. The baby was so little. That would do some serious damage.

"What's her name?" Bryna asked.

"Zoe Ava."

"Hi, Zoe," Bryna cooed.

Shit. She did not just fucking *coo* at a baby. *Who the hell is this person inhabiting my body?*

"You're such a little thing," she said to Zoe.

Celia laughed. "She's actually perfectly healthy. Seven pounds and three ounces. Simply beautiful."

"Fatty," Bryna joked.

Zoe stared intently back up at her.

Celia shook her head. "She likes you."

"She'd better," Bryna said, not taking her eyes off of the baby. "I'm awesome."

Celia laughed again. "You're good with her. I knew you would be."

"I don't like babies," Bryna said to Zoe. "But you're family now. I guess I can't let you turn out like the rest of them." Bryna frowned at her own joke. She had wanted it to be funny, but all things considered, it wasn't even true. "On second thought, we should get you a nanny who speaks a couple of languages. Then, you can talk circles around your mom and dad and turn out better than all of us."

Celia's eyebrows drew together. "Are you okay?"

"I don't know," she admitted.

"I know we haven't gotten along in the past, and I pushed you too hard to try to be a family. But I truly only wanted the best for you. It might not seem like much, but I want to be family for you, and that doesn't mean anything more than this right here, if you don't want anything more. Know you are always free to talk to me…maybe just as a friend, if that's easier."

Bryna didn't take her eyes off of Zoe. She couldn't look up at Celia with all of her sincerity. This was the woman who had ruined her life and wrecked her parents' marriage. Bryna was here for the baby. Yet Celia had sounded so heartfelt.

Zoe fussed, and Celia held her hands out to take her from Bryna. Once she was cuddled back against her mom, Bryna took a deep breath and sat down on the chair next to the bed.

"Tell me what happened with my dad. I only know the aftermath. Divorce, and boom, new mommy."

"Oh, Bryna," Celia said with so much sympathy in her eyes that Bryna had to look away.

"I need to know the truth."

"I met Lawrence on set. I was working for a production company at the time. It was a coincidence that we ran into each other. Everyone was afraid of him so I ended up bringing a lot of stuff to him. I was doing errands that were a bit beneath me actually," she said, remembering the incident with a smile. "I was there the day Olivia served him divorce papers. He made everyone else go home, but I didn't know until it was too late. I'd been there myself, and I couldn't leave him. So, I offered to take him to lunch. In a million years, I never thought it would lead to this," she told Bryna.

"So…you didn't even date until after Mom divorced him?" Bryna asked in surprise.

"Of course not! Well, I didn't even really know him. Then, I got to know him, and we fell in love. Neither of us expected it. We both had kids who were nearly adults. We were both divorced. We never thought it would work. But then, one day, we decided that the past was the past. What was important to us was our kids and being happy. We knew everything else would work itself out." Celia smiled down at little baby Zoe. "And it has."

"So…you love him?"

"Love him?" she asked with a giggle. "We have a baby together! Of course I love him. I've never loved anyone more."

"But how did you know?" Bryna asked.

"That I loved him?"

"Yeah."

"Oh, wow. No one has ever asked me that before." She looked up thoughtfully contemplating the question. "I don't know really. I can't place it exactly, as if there were a moment when I didn't love him, and then suddenly, I did. I couldn't go a day without thinking about him. I always smiled at the thought. I stopped being able to imagine a life without him in it, and I was okay with that. I just knew. There was no going back."

Bryna looked at Celia with uncertainty. *How could it have been that easy? Nothing is that easy.* She had put so much effort into all of her relationships, and they hadn't panned out at all. *If love is effortless, then how am I supposed to find it?*

"Okay…"

"You know you don't have to find love at eighteen."

"Almost nineteen," she reminded Celia.

"Yes…almost nineteen either. Look at me. I didn't find it until I was almost forty!"

"Hmm…that's true. Thanks."

"Anytime, Bryna."

Bryna stood and reached down to lightly pinch baby Zoe's cheeks. She had a lot to think about. "You're cute, little missy. You must have gotten that from me."

Celia laughed. "Probably. She's lucky to have a big sister like you."

"Maybe I'll come see Zoe again."

"I'm sure she'd love that."

Bryna and Celia shared a smile.

On her way out, Bryna shook her head in confusion. She'd had a completely civil conversation with her stepmother, and it hadn't been terrible. Actually, it had been perfectly normal. She had no idea what had just happened.

"How was my little girl?" her dad asked once she was outside the room again.

"Good. I think she probably wants to see her dad though."

He smiled brightly and then rushed back into the room. It was as if he were twenty years old again. Zoe had reenergized him just like Celia had when they got married. *Why didn't I see it before?*

"So, you like the baby."

Bryna turned around in a rush and saw Pace walking toward her.

"I'm surprised," he continued, "that you came back from your vacation for this. After you were so adamantly against it, I didn't think you'd show."

"Yeah," she said. She didn't have it in her to argue with him right now.

"Aren't you going to gloat?"

"About what?" she asked.

"Barcelona? This strange life you're leading?"

Bryna arched an eyebrow. "No. There's nothing to gloat about. I'm glad summer is almost over. How is Stacia?"

"You're asking about Stacia?"

"Yes. I miss her," she said plainly.

Pace softened at the mention of Stacia. A rare genuine smile touched his lips, replacing his typical sneer. "She's good. She misses you, too."

"So, you're still together then." She had suspected as much since she hadn't heard from Stacia at all. She had only heard about Stacia through Trihn.

"We've been together all summer. She lives here in the city, you know."

"Right. Her dad is the USC coach."

"Her dad is…something," he said uncertainly. "A bit controlling."

"I'm not surprised. Has to be hard to try to control all that wild child in her."

"Yeah. She's fun that way." He smirked.

There's that asshole again.

"Ew. I can't. Gross."

Bryna walked away from him. She'd thought they were working toward a civil conversation, too, and then he had brought that shit up.

"Hey," he called, following her. "Do you think you could talk to her?"

Bryna narrowed her eyes, wondering what the catch was. "Why?"

"She's still upset that you're mad at her. I don't like to see her like this," he admitted.

"I'm not going to talk to her because I care about what you say. Let's make that clear."

He nodded.

"I'll do it because I care about Stacia. You just happen to be associated with her at the moment."

"Fine."

"Fine!"

Bryna left the hospital lobby and took a cab back to her father's house in the Hills. She dropped her luggage in her old room and stared around with a small smile on her face. It felt surreal to be back home. She hadn't been back since Thanksgiving, and she hadn't even realized she had missed it.

She had been missing a lot these days. Like the truth behind her parents' divorce and how Celia and her father had gotten together. She had blamed it all on Celia. It was the easiest thing to do. But after what Celia had said at the hospital, Bryna wasn't sure what to think. Maybe she had just been taking out all her anger on her stepmother. Either way, she had lost her mother, but that didn't necessarily make it Celia's fault. That revelation softened Bryna's resolve for a minute.

She shook her head. She couldn't deal with all of that today. Maybe her family was a little less fucked up now. It was an improvement. Something to think on later.

Right now, she needed to talk to Stacia.

Here goes nothing.

"Bryna!" Stacia yelled into the phone. "Oh my God! You're calling me! From Barcelona!"

"Actually, I'm in L.A."

"What? I didn't know you were back."

"Yeah. I actually got back into town this morning," she said. "Do you think we could meet up? I want to talk."

"Oh. Oh, yeah. Sure. Um…I'm at the beach in Santa Monica actually with some friends from high school. You're welcome to join us if you want. Of course, if you'd rather me leave and come to you, I would totally understand that."

"No, Santa Monica is fine. I haven't driven in a couple of months, and I'm dying to use a stick shift again."

Stacia laughed. "I would say I get that, but stick shifts and I do not get along."

"You're missing all the best cars then." Just the thought of taking one of her dad's cars out on the road made her skin tingle with excitement.

"I'll let someone else drive me around in them."

Bryna shook her head. "Typical. Anyway, I'll be there soon."

Even though she hadn't spoken to Stacia in months, it had been so easy to fall back into their normal banter. Bryna wasn't entirely sure what she was going to say to Stacia about Pace, but she couldn't keep putting it off. She wanted her friend back, and they needed to work out their differences. They couldn't do that through a wall of silence.

She threw on a bathing suit and then walked out to her dad's garage. Her hands skimmed over the row of beautiful cars, yet her eyes were drawn to the cherry-red Porsche 911 GT3 convertible. It handled like a dream and her father would kill her if he knew how fast she took it out of the house. But it wasn't supposed to be locked up. It needed to be set free.

The drive to Santa Monica wasn't long enough for her taste. She might need to drive up and down the Pacific

Coast Highway to release some more of her pent-up energy.

The valets were salivating at the chance to drive the thing. She tossed the keys to the guy who would have the pleasure.

"Don't hurt my baby," she said.

He nodded, awestruck, and she walked out to the beach. Finding Stacia took a bit of time, but eventually, she located her friend's enormous hot-pink umbrella that gave Stacia's position away on the beach.

Bryna stripped out of her tank top and stuffed it into her oversized Dolce bag. One of the guys sitting next to Stacia nudged his buddy next to him when he saw Bryna. They were both ogling every inch of her Spanish sun–kissed skin.

Stacia didn't seem to notice as she sprang to her feet and rushed toward Bryna. "You're here!" She pulled Bryna into a big hug. Stacia dusted sand off of her and motioned for them to walk down the beach. "I'll be right back," she called to her friends.

Once they were a sufficient distance away, Bryna spoke up, "I saw Pace earlier."

"Yeah?" Stacia said uncertainly. "He didn't tell me you were back."

Bryna shrugged. "I didn't exactly tell him. I went to see the new baby."

"Really? Pace told me that Celia had her baby. Little Zoe? Is she adorable?"

"She is actually."

"I know neither of you were thrilled she was having another kid."

"We weren't, but it's hard to hate a baby. She didn't do anything, you know?" Bryna laughed. "It's not her fault my family is fucked up."

"So, did you come back for the baby? Trihn said you were supposed to be in Barcelona all summer."

Bryna wasn't sure she was ready to talk about what had happened with Hugh. The baby had been an excuse, but the reason she'd left was Hugh. She had a lot to think about before she would be prepared to tell her friends about her adventures.

"Change of plans," Bryna said.

Stacia grabbed her arm and stopped her in her tracks. "Bryna, I'm so sorry! I shouldn't have blindsided you about my relationship with Pace. He warned me that you wouldn't like it, but I had no idea it would be this big of a deal!"

Bryna waved her hand. "I know. It's okay."

"It is?" Stacia asked in confusion.

"Yeah. I guess it is."

"Why? You make me nervous."

"I don't like Pace. I don't think he's a good person or has good intentions. I've known him for too long not to know the tricks he likes to play. The last thing I would want to happen is for you to fall into one of them, but he does seem to legitimately care about you, I guess." Bryna smiled at her friend. "I've had an…eye-opening summer, to say the least, but I'm not suddenly a different person. I don't have to like Pace. You do. I have it on good authority that you would dump his ass if he treated you poorly."

Stacia laughed. "Trihn?"

"Yeah. Plus, I don't think he's worth losing a friend over."

Stacia threw her arms around Bryna, and they hugged on the beach. "Seriously, what happened to you this summer? Trihn told me about Eric and then Barcelona…"

"I feel like I put a lot of effort into what is supposed to be an effortless exterior. I don't want to do that anymore." She shrugged. "I don't know if it makes sense, especially since the head bitch isn't vacating her throne. I want to try to live for a new me."

Bryna hadn't realized how true the statement was until it left her mouth. It took so much time to maintain this personality that people associated with her. Her friends, Eric, Hugh—they all saw a different side of her. At this point, she didn't know which one was the real Bryna. It had been a soul-searching summer, and she was ready to move on.

"Well, I love the new you. Let's get back to my friends. We have so much to catch up on."

Bryna bit on her lip. She had one more thing to do before she could completely start fresh again. One more burned bridge.

"I'd love to." She longingly looked out at the beach. "But I have someone I need to visit."

THIRTY-TWO

THIS WAS GOING TO BE a whole hell of a lot harder than talking to Stacia.

Gates.

She hadn't stopped thinking about him since he had kicked her out of his premiere during her senior year. He was her first real boyfriend, her best friend, and one of her biggest mistakes. She hadn't spoken with him since that night nearly a year and a half ago when she did what she thought was irreparable damage to their relationship.

He had told her he loved her, and she had told him to fuck off. It didn't exactly leave her in an inspiring place to get back into his life.

Things weren't perfect between them. They never had been, but in a way, they were the only ones in each other's lives who really *got* each other. She had taken advantage of him. He had gotten swept away by her. They were horribly wrong for each other. Too similar in most ways. Both had egos larger than the Pacific Ocean. But as much as she'd wanted it to seem like she didn't care that she didn't talk to him anymore…she cared.

Bryna didn't even know where to begin initiating this contact. Some part of her wanted to show up at his place and force him to talk to her. But that was the part of her that allowed herself to imagine his rejection. The other part of her knew that calling would be the right choice…even if he didn't answer…even if he didn't want to see her.

She got back into the Porsche, replaced the convertible top, took a deep breath, and dialed his number.

She waited an interminable amount of time before the line clicked over.

"Well, that's a name I haven't seen in a while."

"Hey, Gates," she said. It was surreal to hear his voice.

"What can I do you for, Bri?" he asked.

She could tell that he was going to be difficult, and she didn't blame him.

"The tabloids say you're in L.A."

"You follow the tabloids now?" he asked.

She only knew he was here by chance after scrolling through a tabloid on the plane. She normally didn't follow them.

She was suddenly nervous about this whole thing. But it was Gates. They had known each other too long. She could do this.

"What are you up to right now?"

"Cut to the chase, Bri. I don't have all day for this," he said, his voice cutting like ice.

"Can I come over? We need to talk," she said quickly.

"Is this Bryna Turner? I haven't heard from her in over a year and I'm confused right now."

"Gates, don't be a fucker."

He laughed at her outburst. "Oh, there she is."

"Yeah. Same old me," she said dryly.

"Seriously, what do you want?"

"I just want to talk, honestly."

"Am I going to want to hear what you have to say?" he asked, clearly cautious.

After all this time, what could I possibly say to change his mind about me? Maybe nothing. But if she said nothing, then nothing would change. And hearing his voice confirmed how much she wanted things to change. She had been able to rely on him for everything, and even if she didn't want anything romantic with him, she still wanted his friendship. That was worth something to her. She hoped it still was for him.

"You know, I'm really busy," Gates continued.

"Cut the shit. I wouldn't have called if it wasn't important, and you know it. If I know you at all, you're probably sitting around in your boxers, playing Xbox."

After a minute, he responded, "Damn. You know me too well."

"Yeah," she mumbled. "I did."

"Okay. Fine. I'm too damn curious now. Come on over. This'd better be good."

"It is," she murmured before disconnecting.

At least...she hoped so.

The drive to Gates's place was easy. She pulled up to the attendant, he cleared her through the gate, and she drove up to his mansion. It was enormous and far too much for someone his age. *But who am I to talk?* She had a house of her own that she hadn't even worked for. At least he had this because his movies had taken off.

When she knocked on the door, she was unsurprised to see him wearing dark jeans and a fit red polo. His dark brown hair was spiked up in the front, and his blue eyes were apprehensive. His hesitant smile wasn't the one that he used for the cameras that made all of America melt. But he still looked like her Gates, and he was still gorgeous.

"Hey," he said.

She cleared her throat and looked away from his bright blue eyes. She'd fallen victim to them a time or two in the past. "Hey."

"I guess...come in."

"Thanks," she said, bypassing him and walking into the living room.

"This is weird," Gates said once he joined her.

"Yeah. A bit."

"I mean...have you ever seen the downstairs to my place?"

Bryna shrugged. "I honestly don't think so."

"Yeah. We mostly occupied the bedroom."

"Yeah."

An awkward silence fell between them. It had never been there before, but the time apart and the unfortunate circumstances surrounding the dissolution of their friendship had forced the wedge between them. There was so much that needed to be said, and it all hung between them.

"Anyway," she whispered.

"I never thought I'd hear from you again," he said, breaking the barrier.

"I know. I never intended to call."

His eyes narrowed. "Then, why did you?"

"It's complicated."

"Well, you asked to come over here." He walked to the couch and plopped down.

His posture showed that he was uncomfortable with what was going on, and she didn't know how to make this easier. This wasn't her forte.

She barreled forward, not wanting to lose her nerve. "So...remember that time you told me you loved me, and I didn't believe you?"

Gates glared at her. "The night you told me to fuck off at my own premiere the day before Valentine's Day? Then, I didn't hear from you ever again? How exactly do you think I could forget that?"

She took a steadying breath and sat down across from him on the coffee table. "Apparently, I make a habit of it."

"A habit of what?" he asked curiously.

"Not believing people when they tell me they love me, not realizing they love me, and royally fucking up everything in the aftermath."

Gates looked taken aback at that. "Ah, I see. So, who was the victim this time?" He sounded bitter.

"Hugh Westercamp," she answered honestly. She couldn't lie to Gates. *What good would hiding the truth do now?*

Hugh was out of her life by her own choice, and any damage she could do to his character had already been done to his heart.

"The hotel executive?" he asked in disbelief.

"That's the one."

Gates whistled under his breath. "Damn. You've upped your game."

"I did," she agreed. "But I've decided to give it up."

"What? Hugh?"

"No. The game," she told him.

He laughed until he realized she wasn't joking. "Bri, come on. You've got to be kidding, right? Games are in your blood. You live and breathe scheming. You always have."

"You're right," she acquiesced easily. "But when I play games, I hurt people." She looked him directly in the eyes now. "I hurt you, and I'm sorry about that."

Gates didn't say anything for a minute. He stared at her, speechless. She knew she wasn't good at apologies. Until Eric, she hadn't even really apologized to anyone. It wasn't who she was, but she had wronged Gates by letting this gap between them continue, and she needed to make amends.

"Did you just apologize?"

"I should have a long time ago. I know I told you we were broken up, but the line was fuzzy. I could have handled it better."

His jaw dropped. "What the fuck happened to you?"

She laughed at his shock. "I guess…I saw the light."

"I guess is right."

"I'm still me. I can't change the head bitch, but I wanted to apologize even if you don't want to talk to me or be friends again. I had to let you know that I still want that even though I know I don't deserve it."

"I don't want that," he said immediately.

She tried not to flinch at his harsh words. Of course he didn't want that. "All right. Well, I said what I came to say." She stood and hurriedly started toward the door.

"Hey," he said, catching her arm before she could run off. "I said I don't, but what I meant was that I shouldn't. I shouldn't want us to be friends again."

"Great clarification," she said sarcastically.

"Look, I dreamed of the day this would happen, and you never came to me. I couldn't go to you. I tried to move on. But I guess I've realized I should have gone to you a long time ago. I loved you, Bri. I knew you hated hearing it. I knew you didn't feel the same way. Yet I pushed, and that wasn't fair either. We've both done some pretty shitty things to each other, but we've been friends for a long time."

"We have," she agreed.

She was shocked that he had said those things. She never would have guessed that he felt this way about what had happened.

"It's been hard without you."

"No one to keep your ego in check?" she joked.

"You're ridiculous," he said.

But he was laughing. Suddenly, all the tension that had been between them seemed to leave his shoulders. She didn't think they would be perfect, but she was willing to try.

"Are we cool?" she asked.

"It's a start."

"I can live with that." It was more than she had expected.

"Come on, you." He directed her out through the back door and to his pool.

Her mind immediately went back to a different pool where she and Eric used to hang out with margaritas and burgers she couldn't always eat. It made her sigh as she lounged back on a chair.

Speaking of Eric...

"Now that we're kind of on the same page," she said, narrowing her eyes, "you put me in quite the bind last year."

"How? I wasn't even around!"

"Do you remember when we went to LV State for my campus visit?"

He shrugged. "Sure. You got trashed."

"That night, you told me that Eric Wilkins was gay!" she spat. "And you told him that I was a slut and to stay away from me!"

Gates looked at her and then busted out laughing. "Holy shit! I forgot all about that."

"I can't believe you did that!"

"Hey! I never said he was gay! You inferred that. And, at the time, I didn't want anyone else near you."

"Yeah, well, thanks for the heads-up. Jesus. I spent the last year thinking he was gay, and now...he's not."

She looked away from Gates, but she was sure he had read her expression. They had known each other for too long that even a little distance couldn't change that.

"So, you like him."

"No," she said fiercely. She didn't know what she felt for Eric. She still couldn't get the image of him with Audrey out of her mind even if she knew it was irrational since she had been with someone else the whole time. But she missed him, and that sucked. "It's complicated."

"Everything always is with you."

THIRTY-THREE

BRYNA RETURNED TO LAS VEGAS on cloud nine. She'd road-tripped with Stacia up I-15 a week early, and both girls were happy to return to cheer practice. It worked Bryna's lax summer muscles and kept her mind occupied. By the time classes were starting again, she was ready to face school once more, but this time, it would be with a bright new outlook.

After talking with Celia, Bryna had been feeling a strange calm about her family life that she couldn't remember existing since middle school. Baby Zoe had made an impact. Not that everything was peachy keen. She still hated Pace and had been avoiding him like the plague while at home. But now that things were back to normal between Bryan and Stacia, Bryna knew she would be seeing a lot more of him. And as much as she despised the way he treated Bryna, she knew he was as much a product of their parents' marriage as she was.

And now she had Gates back. Things were still a little weird between them. She had expected as much, but at least they were talking. It was better than the alternative.

She walked into her film history class with a bounce in her step that she had never had before and a genuine smile that she couldn't wipe off her face. She recognized a few familiar faces from her intro class last semester. She ignored their stares. She had gotten them last semester, too, because of who her father was. It had isolated her in the class, but she hadn't cared then, and she certainly wouldn't care now.

With her head held high, she took a seat in the middle of the lecture hall and pulled out her MacBook. She hummed to herself as she scrolled through pictures from this week at cheer. She felt the seat next to her shift, and she grumbled under her breath. Of all the places for someone to sit in this huge auditorium, some person had to sit right next to her.

She glanced up to make some snide remark about it, but it stalled on her tongue. "You."

He lazily smiled down at her. "Hey yourself."

"It's Cam, right?" she asked uncertainly.

She had briefly met him inside Hugh's resort last semester. She had given Cam her number on a whim, but he'd never called. She hadn't even thought about it since then. But now that he was in front of her again, she remembered why she had given it to him.

"That's right. And you're Bryna? I knew I recognized you."

"You never called," she accused, looking up at him through her lashes.

"And I bet it broke your heart."

"You've no idea."

"Well, I'm here now. Who could have guessed we'd have a class together?"

She tilted her head and licked her lips. "So, are you a film major?"

He shrugged. "I'm kind of in between. Acting. Film. I like them both. I wouldn't mind getting into either. I'm in an acting class, too. Are you?"

She shook her head. She had no desire to act…ever. She belonged behind the camera, like her dad, not in front of it, like her mother. Not that she was about to say that to someone she had just met. With some luck, he wouldn't find out that her father was Lawrence Turner for a very long time.

"Too bad."

Bryna smiled at that. She liked this. This was easy. See? She could be normal and flirt with regular college guys. Trihn and Stacia would be proud.

"It would be nice to know someone else around here."

"Oh, yeah? I'm the only person on campus you know?"

"Well, I have a roommate, Carl, but I wouldn't say I *know* him."

"And you know me?" she asked.

He leaned forward and smiled. "I'm getting there."

She laughed lightly. "Well, you'll need more than one class to get to know me. I'm a woman of many mysteries."

"I'm a pretty good judge of character." His eyes swept her face. "I'd say you're only as mysterious as you want to be."

"Guess you'll have to find out," she murmured.

The professor walked up to the front of the room.

"Oh, I intend to," Cam said under his breath.

Bryna tried to pay attention in class, but it was the first lecture of the new term, and she knew nothing important would happen until the next class. Instead, she tried to figure out what to make of Cam. He was hot—tall, blond, dark eyes. But he definitely wasn't her type…even though he was a charmer. He had a laid-back attitude that didn't mesh with her high-strung type-A personality. He was almost a little sloppy in jeans and a T-shirt with flip-flops. He looked like he would be more comfortable on a snowboard or a surfboard than in Las Vegas. Yet that was all a part of the appeal.

She was still thinking about it when the class was dismissed, and he followed her out of the room.

"Well, see you on Wednesday," she said with a smile.

"Hey, are you free?" he asked. "Do you want to go get something to eat?"

She smiled. It was nice to be treated like any other girl for a minute. No one else in this school did it. And when she had gotten here last year, that was exactly what she had wanted. *Strange how much had changed in a year.*

"I'd love to, but I have cheer practice."

"You're a cheerleader?" He couldn't keep the surprise from her voice.

"Yeah."

"Oh. I wouldn't have guessed."

"Is that a problem? It's not like we always carry around pom-poms or something," she said.

"Not a problem," he said automatically. His lazy smile was back on his face. "I'll see you on Wednesday."

"All right. See you then."

As she turned away to walk to the sports complex, she smiled to herself. It wasn't as if she had a date. All he had asked was if she wanted to get food after class. Of course he was cute and seemed interested in her. Maybe if she stopped trying to scheme and calculate his motives, then she could just enjoy the moment.

She walked into the complex, and her stomach turned to knots. This place made her think of Eric. She hadn't spoken with him yet. She knew she needed to. There was a lot left unsaid between them, but she had wanted to ride out her high for as long as possible.

She hurried to the cheer locker rooms before she could run into him, and she changed into her workout clothes. This would be a good practice. It would clear her mind of everything that kept floating around up there.

And it did just that.

The team had spent hours perfecting sideline cheers, working on stunts with the new girls, practicing dances, and working their bodies into the ground. By the time they were done, Bryna's muscles were sore, her legs felt like Jell-O, and she was all-around exhausted. She even stuck around to take a shower at the sports complex instead of waiting to go home. She had taken too much time off this summer, and now, she was paying for it.

She threw on a pair of Nike running shorts and a tank top, diffused her hair until it was in loose beachy waves rather than her normal stick-straight look, and then exited the locker room. Almost everyone else had already left, but she could still hear the football players rumbling around outside. This time of year, they would work until there was no more daylight, and then they'd turn on the field lights and keep working.

She rounded the corner and stopped dead in her tracks. She had been hoping to avoid this for another day, but fate didn't seem to allow it.

"Bri," Eric said.

His voice. God, his voice.

She kept her face impassive. "Hey."

Four months. After four very long months without him, she had almost forgotten how hot he was. She had always thought it wasn't fair that he was gay with those features. Now, her mind had to skip over that assessment she had made so often and remember that he was most definitely *not* gay.

"How was your summer?" she asked when he didn't say anything.

He stared and drank her in. "Who cares? You weren't in it."

"Eric," she said.

She shook her head but didn't look away. His hazel eyes trapped her, even from this distance.

"We can't do this right now."

"If I keep letting you decide when we can talk, we never will. You can't pretend that nothing happened."

"I'm not, all right?" she said, her voice a little too loud. "I'm not pretending anything. I know perfectly well what happened."

He stormed over to her. "Then, talk to me. I'm still me, you're still you, and that means we're still us. Just the way we were. You can open up to me."

"I did. I told you I needed space. The thought of you touching someone else made me nauseous, and I needed to process. What part of that did you miss?" she yelled.

Yet, she didn't step away from him. She couldn't. At this point, she could smell him—musky and all man with a hint of something purely Eric. She hadn't even recognized it until he was standing before her, but it was just…him.

"None of it. Not a single thing."

His hand reached up and swept her hair off of her face. He left it resting on her neck, and her pulse raced.

"I like your hair like this. Natural," he murmured.

She swallowed hard. All of the brand-new happy Bri feelings vanished from her mind. There was only this moment with his eyes and hands and lips.

Then, those lips were touching hers, and everything went cloudy in the most perfect way. Never had she imagined their conversation would lead here. She had imagined arguing, fighting, a whole lot of yelling, and storming out the door. But his kisses were intoxicating, and she was awash with the drunken feeling.

He grabbed her hand. "Come with me." Then, he pulled her away.

A protest rose up in her throat, but he didn't stop as he wove her through the hallways and into a back locker room. It was dark and deserted. No one came back here this early in the season, and even if the football players did, they wouldn't be done for another couple of hours. But that didn't explain why Eric was here…

She opened her mouth to ask him, but he pressed his lips to hers, and all coherent thought vanished once more. *How did he do that?*

He pushed her back against a locker, and his hands slid under her tank top to touch her skin. She gasped into his mouth, every nerve responding to him, to this. She hadn't been touched in over a month, but it wasn't just that. She knew it. It terrified her. She should stop. But his tongue was massaging hers, his hands were on her skin, and his body was covering hers. This was Eric. Her body was *screaming* to let it happen.

"E…"

"Please," he breathed against her lips. "Tell me to stop, and I will, but you want this. I want this."

"I…" She didn't have the words.

She didn't know what she wanted. Everything was so confusing, but this right here made perfect sense. Eric made perfect sense.

His hands slipped all the way under her shirt. His thumb flicked against the soft unlined bra she was wearing, and her body arched into him.

"I've thought about doing this for months." He kissed her throat, and his other hand grabbed her ass. "I've thought about how you would taste, how your skin would feel against mine, what this would feel like." He grabbed her leg, hoisted it around his hip, and pressed against her.

Her body responded like a lit match.

"Tell me you've thought about it, too."

She had. She most definitely had fantasized about what he would do to her if he weren't gay. But she had kept herself from getting too lost in a fantasy that would never come true. She hadn't wanted to feel, and now, it seemed all she was able to do.

"I've thought about it," she admitted.

He sighed as if he hadn't been sure, and she had confirmed everything for him. He continued with renewed purpose. He lifted her shirt over her head and tossed it to the floor. His hands traveled the length of her body, admiring every inch of it. His fingers ran teasingly along the inside of her shorts, and she squirmed against him.

She couldn't take it any longer. Her fingers found the hem of his shirt and yanked him closer. She wrenched his shirt off next, exposing his chiseled chest, and she reclaimed his lips.

The energy crackled between them. In seconds, her shorts were in a pile on the floor. Then, she tugged down his zipper, and his pants slid over his hips. Eric grabbed her other leg and forced her body back hard against the locker digging into her back. She ignored the feeling. There was so much pent-up energy between them that she couldn't stop this train ride even if she wanted to, and her body was absolutely saying not to stop.

Their breath mingled, and their eyes met. Something passed between them that she couldn't even begin to explain. But it was powerful and terrifying. Her heart constricted as she opened herself to him in a way she never had to anyone else before.

He filled her in one swift motion, claiming her body. When he moved, she closed her eyes and slammed her head back into the locker. Their bodies melded together fiercely, desperately. It was perfection. Her nails clawed into his skin. His grip on her hips tightened. She was sure there would be bruises. But neither of them stopped.

Bodies smacked together. Eric picked up the pace, and sweat beaded on his forehead. She could feel it slicking her own back in the hot locker room, undoing the shower she had just indulged in. Her body didn't care what she was giving up for this, and she was giving up much. She knew it.

As he hit the right spot with her yells filling the space and his orgasm following right after, she knew that something had truly cracked inside her. And she couldn't go back to not feeling. Yet emotions like this only brought pain, not the joy and happiness she had been feeling for the past month.

Eric dropped her legs back to the ground and rested his forehead on her shoulder. "Fuck, Bri."

Her heart was still racing in her chest, but she didn't say anything. She didn't know what to say. She was shaking, actually terrified of what this was. It wasn't supposed to be like this—hot and cold and full of extremes and heartbreak. It was supposed to be effortless, and things with Eric had always been complicated.

She reached for her clothes and righted herself. "I should go," she murmured.

"Wait, what?" he asked.

He touched for her, and she spun away from him.

"What's wrong?"

"Everything." She covered her face, heaving in a deep breath.

"That was incredible. There was nothing wrong with that," he said.

She could hear the pain in his voice.

"I can't do this! Don't you understand? We can't be together!" she yelled. It made no sense with what she had just done, but she was pushing all of that aside and giving in to this terror welling inside of her.

"We can. We can be together. We just were." He gestured around the locker room.

"No." She shook her head. "This isn't how this works."

"Why?" he yelled right back. "Why can't it work? You wanted this. You wanted this to happen between us. Can you look me in the eye and say you don't have feelings for me?"

She stared at him and clenched her jaw. "That's the point, Eric. I do. I do have feelings for you. And I shouldn't. It scares the shit out of me. You're dangerous, and you are only going to break my heart. I...I don't trust myself when I'm with you."

"You can't really mean that," he said, uncertain, his voice losing its edge.

"I do. I mean it wholeheartedly."

She swallowed hard and then brushed past him, leaving the locker room. Her whole body was humming from what had happened, yet she had tears falling out of her eyes, tears she couldn't control or explain.

This is the right thing. That was what she kept telling herself through the tears.

THIRTY-FOUR

THE HOUSE WAS EMPTY.

Cold.

Lifeless.

What had once brought her so much happiness left her with a bad taste of desperate materialism. Everything from the hardwood floors to the Swarovski chandelier to the pool out back and the rich furnishings within made her feel slightly nauseated.

Every day, all it did was bring back memories of Barcelona. The look on Hugh's face when she'd asked about his wife. His very dead wife. His anger and rather valid accusations. The ease with which he had thrown that necklace over the balcony just to show how little money meant to him. She could still recall exactly what he had looked like when she said she didn't love him. It made her cringe all over again.

She couldn't change it now. She didn't love him. She had cared for him, but she had been selfish from the start.

Young, selfish, and stupid.

Just like she had been with Eric. Her heart constricted, and she stumbled up the stairs to her bedroom. It was immaculate, all classic whites and blacks, just as she had left it. Yet it didn't even feel like hers. It felt like a version of the person she had contrived for Hugh out of the person she had become after Jude left her. Looking around, she didn't even know why she had ever thought she wanted this.

She shivered at the depressing chill that wracked her body. She hated feeling like this. Vulnerability was not her norm. But she couldn't bring back the self-assurance she wore like a second skin.

Thinking about Eric only made it worse. She had never been good at turning down sex, and when he had approached her, all of her desire for him had exploded into that one singular moment. It was a year of pent-up energy that had cracked open like fireworks in the night sky. But she couldn't let it happen again. She didn't want to lead him on or hurt him.

Jude had hurt her, and though Eric was far from Jude, he had the same ability to completely and utterly wreck her very existence, taking this semblance of control that she still clung to like a life raft and leave her drowning in the middle of the ocean.

God, I need to get a grip.

She clawed her clothes off her body and threw them in a pile in the corner of her room. Even though they reminded her of how she had let Eric fuck her in the locker room, she smiled at the mess. Then, she stepped into the giant waterfall shower and turned it to scalding. She stood under the spray until her body was pink and tender, letting the water wash away all remnants of what had passed between them.

She took time to blow her hair out, making it pencil-straight, and forced out the memory of him fingering the wavy tresses with such care. The person he had kissed wasn't even her. It had been someone who was both mentally and physically exhausted that she hadn't even taken time to do her hair. She couldn't let herself do that again. Once she was finished, she slipped into a pair of black designer jeans and a black crop top.

There. Now, she felt more like herself. Except for this house. It still haunted her. She was slowly suffocating under the weight of Hugh's presence here.

She had to get out. Picking up her phone, she dialed Trihn's number.

"Hey!" Trihn said. "How was your first day back?"

"Eventful."

"I bet! I'm in this new art class with Neal, and it's amazing! What are you up to?"

"I'm at home." She bit her lip, debating if she could do this. "Do, uh…do you think I could stay with you?"

"Like, at my apartment?" Trihn asked, confused.

"Yeah. I mean, for the night. I can't be here for another second longer."

"Sure. Of course. What's wrong with your place?"

"Everything." She sighed heavily. "It feels like the walls are closing in."

"Sorry, B. Do you want to come over now?"

"Yeah. Let me pack a bag. Thanks, Trihn."

She laughed lightly. "What are friends for? Of course, I never thought you would want to stay with me since you have that huge mansion, but Stacia and I have plenty of space at the new apartment!"

Bryna hadn't felt left out when Trihn and Stacia decided to move in together. It'd made sense for them to do that. She had always liked her space, and with the guys she had been interested in, it was better to not have any roommates. Now, she was kind of wishing she had been included, a feeling she was not familiar with.

After she hung up, she quickly packed her Louis Vuitton carry-on and strode out of her house. She locked it up tight and immediately felt better. It was official. She couldn't stay there any longer.

The drive to Trihn and Stacia's new apartment was easy enough. She made it through the front gate, parked next to Stacia's SUV, and took the elevator to the top floor. Trihn answered on the first knock and beckoned her inside.

The place was cute and way bigger than it looked from the outside. It took up nearly the entire top floor of the building with four bedrooms and baths and direct access to the pool. It wasn't Bryna's dream house, but look where that had gotten her. The apartment was cozy and warm, which was more than she could say for the house. More importantly, this place was full of her friends.

That meant it had to be better.

"Okay. Spill. What's going on?" Trihn asked.

She looked at Bryna in that knowing way. Sometimes, it felt like Trihn could read her mind, and after what had happened with Eric, Bryna was really glad that she couldn't.

"Nothing. Everything." Bryna took a seat on the couch and tossed her bag at her feet.

"Well, I can tell. You look pretty run-down," Trihn said, taking the seat across from her.

"Wow. Thanks!" she said sarcastically.

Stacia bounced into the room. Her blonde hair swished around her face as she walked. "Hey, B!"

"Hey."

"You know what I mean," Trihn said. "You look out of it. Not your normal pep."

Bryna shrugged. "I don't know. It's just the house."

"Is it Hugh?" Stacia asked. She bit her lip and looked uncertainly at Trihn. "I know you were stressing since you came home from Barcelona, but I thought things were better."

"They were," she said softly. *Then Eric happened.* "I just feel off. Like I can't live in that house anymore." She looked down at her manicure. "I think I'm going to sell it."

Both girls gasped.

"What?" Trihn asked.

"But it's perfect!" Stacia cried.

"Yeah. It was," Bryna agreed. "But now, it's a reminder. It doesn't feel right."

"Man, it's worse than I thought," Trihn said. "It sounds like you're having an identity crisis. Soon, you're going to shed your designer clothing and give up the Aston Martin."

"Whoa!" Bryna held her hand up. "Don't get carried away. I just don't want to always be reminded of what I did to get that house. I hurt a good man, and it didn't feel good for either of us."

"I know. I was joking. Mostly. I don't like you like this, and if the house makes it worse, then you shouldn't stay there."

"So, are you going to move back into the condo?" Stacia asked.

"And live with Pace? Over my dead body!"

"Oh," Stacia said.

Trihn laughed. "Good luck with that, Stacia."

"Baby Zoe might make me understand Celia a bit better, but it doesn't excuse Pace's behavior. And I can't live with him again." Bryna shuddered at the thought.

She had reluctantly spent time with Pace at home over the summer break, and it'd felt like a repeat of senior year. He'd had no respect for personal boundaries, and they'd continually butted heads. He was better when he was around Stacia, but only because he'd tiptoe around her, and she'd keep him in line. At least that was a blessing.

"Why don't you stay here?" Trihn offered. "We would have included you if you didn't already have a place."

"Wait, really?" Bryna asked. She had never expected them to offer her a place to stay. She had figured she would need to call her dad to see if he would get her a new place or dip into her trust to rent something while she worked it out.

"Yes!" Stacia cried. "Definitely!"

"Are you guys sure? I mean, I know you probably wanted the extra space."

"We're sure! We don't need the extra space. We'd rather have you," Trihn said.

"That's right!" Stacia agreed. "You won't change our minds now."

Bryna smiled. *How could I say no?* She didn't even want to say no. She felt like she had missed a lot while growing up without having real girlfriends or siblings. Trihn and Stacia were making up for it by a long shot.

"All right. I'll do it!"

Stacia jumped up and down and threw herself at Bryna, tackling her with a hug. "This is going to be so much fun!"

"We need to go out for drinks to celebrate," Trihn said. "Take it easy, S. You're suffocating her."

Stacia laughed and flopped down next to Bryna with a giant smile on her face.

"Drinks sound great," Bryna agreed.

"Do either of you care if I invite Neal? We haven't spent much time together since I've been back. He's been a little weird actually."

"Sure, I don't mind," Bryna said. "Weird, how?"

"I don't know. Just busy I think."

Bryna narrowed her eyes. *What kind of guy would ignore his girlfriend after being apart for nearly the whole summer?* But by the look in Trihn's eyes, she didn't want to talk about it anymore. She was upset, and she tended to internalize that.

Trihn stood to make her phone call.

Stacia turned to Bryna. "Don't worry. No Pace tonight," she volunteered.

"Good."

"He's still at practice," she said dreamily. Her love for quarterbacks knew no bounds.

Bryna colored at the thought of football practice. She couldn't help but think about Eric. She knew he must have dipped out of practice early, so he could wait for her after cheerleading got out. There was no way that run-in had been an accident.

And she…couldn't believe she had slept with him. She had wanted to. So bad.

No. She needed to stop that train of thought right now. She had made up her mind. She wasn't going to sit around and give him the opportunity to break her heart. She liked it the way it was.

"Do you hear them?" Stacia whispered.

"What?" Bryna asked. She hadn't been paying attention.

Stacia nodded her head toward the other room. Bryna strained to hear Trihn's conversation.

"Yes! I want you to come. I haven't seen you. I miss you," Trihn said.

She sounded frustrated, and Bryna watched her pace the kitchen in irritation.

"I know you don't like partying, but Bri needs me, and we're celebrating. So, I'm not going to stay in tonight."

Pause.

"This is a part of my life! God, why don't you get that? I'm allowed to like going out and drinking as much as the artsy side of me."

Bryna cringed for her. This was an ongoing argument. She didn't like that they were still fighting over the fact that Trihn liked to go out and have a drink. It wasn't as if she was going out to fuck a bunch of different guys.

"Yes, I'm aware it's a *Monday*," she said. The anger in her voice was seeping through. She clenched her hands into fists. "Fine. Stay in then. Only alcoholics go to the bar on Mondays, right?"

Pause.

"Yeah, I'll see you later in the week. Bye."

Trihn hung up the phone and stormed back into the room. Stacia and Bryna tried to pretend like they hadn't heard.

Trihn waved them off. "I know you were listening. Neal isn't coming. I don't want to talk about it. Let's go get a drink."

They nodded, seeing that she didn't want another argument, and then followed Trihn out of the apartment.

They drove over to Posse with Chloe Avana's new single being the only thing to break the silence. The DJ announced her upcoming national tour, and Bryna rolled her eyes. Things were better with Gates now, but she couldn't stop her aversion to Chloe even though the girl had really done nothing wrong, except for being in the wrong place at the wrong time on her rise to fame.

Posse wasn't completely dead for a Monday night. It was usually pretty chill, but there was still a cloud of businessmen and college students on the premises. They wandered up toward the VIP lounge in search of Maya.

Maya was standing behind the bar with a group of men in suits in front of her. She was sashaying her hips, making small talk, and pouring drinks like a pro while seemingly flirting with them and keeping a perfect distance. She knew exactly what she was doing.

Her eyes lit up when she saw the three of them walking toward her. She gave them a look like she could use a welcome reprieve from the guys who were surely going to tip her generously. She passed them their drinks and then walked over to the girls.

"Bri!" She leaned over the counter and kissed her cheek. "Trihni! Stacia! It's good to see my girls. I missed you this summer."

She was already throwing together drinks for them—a dirty martini for Bri, amaretto sour for Trihn, and something fruity for Stacia.

"I missed you, too," Bryna said before taking a big gulp of her drink.

"We all did," Trihn agreed.

"You just missed the drinks," Maya said.

"Those help," Trihn said with a wink.

"One of these days, you're going to have to take a night off and come out dancing with us, Maya!" Stacia said.

"One day," she agreed. "But not today. Anyway, I think there's one for you here tonight, Bri."

"One what?" she asked. Her mind was still elsewhere, and she didn't catch up with what Maya was insinuating until she tilted her head toward the businessmen.

"I know how you like them." Maya smirked. "The one on the far side of the bar is totally your type."

All three girls looked over at the same time. Maya was right. He was completely her type. He was tall with dark hair and an awesome charcoal-gray suit. He had money and power and liked both in large quantities. She could tell that even from this distance, even without seeing his face or knowing anything else about him, other than the cut of his suit and his posture in it. Her body immediately responded to it, and all she could gather was that it was confused as hell. She liked guys like this, but it also made her stomach turn. After Hugh, she couldn't look at a guy like that the same.

"I don't know if I'm up for that," Bryna said.

"What? He's got your name written all over him," Maya said.

"She had kind of a…bad summer," Trihn explained. "Maybe another night."

Maya shrugged. "Okay, but I think you're missing out. He's a higher up for Google."

Bryna shrugged. "Let's just dance."

She placed her drink on the counter, unfinished, and veered for the dance floor. She didn't want to get drunk tonight. She tended to act like an idiot while intoxicated.

She was here to celebrate moving in with her friends and to not think about Eric—at all.

She let her body go free and forgot her struggles. The music was loud. Her friends were close. All felt right. She danced until her legs were shaking and her face was flushed before breaking away from the floor in need of some water.

She tried to flag down Maya, but she was busy with a group of customers who had walked in. Bryna leaned back against the bar and fanned herself as she waited.

"Can I get you a drink?" someone asked from behind her.

She turned around and found herself face-to-face with the hot businessman they had been eyeing earlier. He was even more handsome in person. She was shocked he worked for Google. *Are tech guys suddenly getting hot?*

"Just water. It's hot on the dance floor."

"I think I can manage a water."

She smiled. "But can you afford it? It's pretty expensive."

"Most valuable thing in the world," he replied.

"Hmm…and I always thought that was diamonds."

He laughed and nodded at her necklace. "Seems you have that covered."

She shrugged and glanced away, suddenly feeling uncomfortable.

"I'm Rick," he said, offering her his hand and drawing her attention back to him.

"Bryna."

"Nice to meet you."

Maya returned then and looked triumphant as she saw Bryna talking to Rick. "Dirty martini?" she asked.

"Just water."

Maya arched an eyebrow but complied.

"Are you sure you don't want anything else?" he pushed.

"Really, I'm fine."

She purposely glanced down at his left hand. No ring. Not even an indentation. Maybe he wasn't a bad guy.

But that didn't even matter, did it? It wasn't that she should be looking out for the bad guys. They should be looking out for her.

Maya left her water on the counter and refilled Rick's scotch glass before disappearing with a smug expression on her face.

"Do you want to dance or maybe go somewhere more private to talk?" he suggested.

She sighed. "I know where you think this is going, but it's not. I'm not the kind of girl you want to talk to privately. I'm dangerous."

He raised an eyebrow. She had only managed to intrigue him.

"I like dangerous."

"I'm a gold digger," she said flatly. "The jewels you're admiring me for are from someone else. If you stick around, I'll manage to get some out of you, too."

He stepped back in surprise at her frankness.

She pulled the Harry Winston B necklace off and held it in her hand. She couldn't believe she was still wearing it after all this time. It was her signature look, yet what it symbolized wasn't even her anymore.

She left him alone and confused. She didn't have an explanation. It turned out she did idiotic things completely sober, too.

"What happened?" Trihn asked as Bryna approached her.

"Here." She handed Trihn the B necklace, which she took in confusion.

"What?"

"That's not me anymore," she said. "I can't even look at it."

She was getting rid of her last piece of Jude. It felt like shedding her skin and starting fresh. Now, she needed to find someone who could see her as she was now, not as she had always allowed people to see her. No director father. No gold-digger status. No slutty reputation.

Just someone with no expectations.

She didn't know what that meant for her, but it wasn't an older guy in a suit, thinking he could buy her body with a few drinks.

THIRTY-FIVE

THE NEXT DAY, Bryna put her house on the market. She called a moving company next to take only the things that were truly *hers* to the new apartment. Everything else she was planning on leaving.

She didn't know how long it was going to take. She had never sold a house before. But after only two weeks, she had an offer on the table and was set to close on the place. It was terrifying but a relief that everything had happened so quickly. She would be signing the papers this afternoon in between class and cheer. It was supposed to be quick and painless.

She walked into her history of film class on edge. Her mind was caught up in the paperwork and what her intentions were after that.

Cam dropped into the seat next to her with a smile just as class started. He still sat next to her every day, and they flirted. It was nice since after the fiasco at Posse, she had been avoiding most other guys. She was spending more time focusing on her studies. She had done fine freshman year, but cheer and guys and money and booze had made her lose focus. She figured if she was only really concerned with cheer that would leave her with a lot more time to bring her GPA up.

Her professor left them with a mound of homework to do at the end of class. But she couldn't think about that right now because she had to leave to go sign the closing papers.

She stuffed her work back in her bag and was on her way out when Cam caught up with her.

"Hey, I know you're busy with cheer or whatever after school, but what about this weekend?"

She stopped in her tracks. "It's the first home game."

"Oh. Okay," he said, clearly disappointed. "Never mind then."

Is he asking me out? "Wait," she said before he could walk away. "That's just Saturday though."

His smile widened at her words. "Yeah? Good. You're always super busy. I thought I'd never get a free moment with you outside of class."

"Well, I haven't exactly agreed to that moment yet," she teased.

Cam laughed. "That's true. Do you want to go out with me Friday?"

"I'll see if I'm free," she joked. She pulled out her phone and pretended to scroll through her calendar.

"Now, I'll never get on the schedule."

She playfully bumped his arm. "I'm just kidding. I'm free. What do you have in mind?"

"Dinner and a movie?"

This wasn't a normal thing for her. She didn't do these typical dates, but there was a first time for everything. This was what she wanted anyway—a fresh start with someone interested in her for her.

"That sounds great."

She left campus with a feeling of accomplishment. Here was a totally normal college guy asking her out. She could do this without all the extra baggage from her past.

Signing was as easy as they'd explained it would be. She had to sign and initial about a million pieces of paper and hand over her house to total strangers, but by the end, it was a done deal. No going back now.

A check was issued directly to her, and the sum made her head spin. Hugh had paid a small fortune for the place. Not that he had cared at the time. Money didn't matter to him. That she had come to figure out the hard way.

She didn't have much time before she needed to be back on campus, but she had to take care of this. She drove out to the WC Resort. The receptionist called for the hotel director when Bryna explained that she had something for Mr. Westercamp.

The hotel director was short and impeccably dressed. "How may I help you?" she asked.

Bryna held the envelope out to the woman. "This is for Mr. Westercamp. It's secure and he's expecting it, but it cannot be mailed. I trust that you will deliver it to him."

The woman warily eyed her. "You're Miss Turner, right?"

Bryna stilled. "Yes?"

"I thought so." She took the envelope from Bryna. "I can't assure that he will open it, but I will deliver it."

"Thank you." She turned to leave. That was all she had come for.

She didn't need a guarantee that he would open it, but she didn't want the house on her conscience anymore. Hugh should have his…investment back.

Bryna hurried out of the hotel, not liking the weight of it around her. She carried a lot of guilt for what had happened between them, and she didn't need the reminder.

She got in her car and drove to the sports complex for practice. She arrived only minutes before she was supposed to be there. She rushed into her uniform and threw her hair up into a messy ponytail.

Stacia appeared at her side as they walked out of the locker room. "Where have you been?"

"I had to take care of some business with the house."

"Is it gone?"

Bryna nodded stoically.

Stacia touched her arm. "I'm sorry."

"You didn't do anything."

"I know. But I'm still sorry."

Bryna sent her a half smile. "Thanks."

"Also…Eric stopped me earlier."

Bryna slowed her pace. She still hadn't told the girls what had happened between her and Eric. She didn't know what they would think, and she kind of wanted to keep that moment to herself. "What did he want?"

"He said he needed to talk to you."

"I can't," she said automatically.

"Are you going to tell me what happened?" Stacia asked.

"No," Bryna said honestly. "But I have a date on Friday with a guy in my film class."

Stacia wrinkled her nose in disgust. "Oh God, an artsy guy? Please don't tell me that you are turning into one of *those*! I can only handle Trihn like this."

"He's not an artsy guy," Bryna said defensively. "I'm a film major. Would you call me artsy?"

"No. Fashionable."

"Exactly. He's cute and nice, and he wants to take me to a movie. It's different, and it sounds easy. I need some of that in my life right now. Not Eric Wilkins."

"Okay. I guess that's good then. But what do I tell Eric if he asks me about you? I can't lie to him, Bri!" She actually looked conflicted about the whole thing.

"Don't lie. Tell him just what I told you."

Because maybe if he heard that she was dating…he would stop pursuing her. That was what she wanted after all…

Right?

Friday rolled around faster than she'd thought possible, and she had nothing to wear.

She stared at her closet stuffed full of clothes and couldn't decide on a single item. When she had asked Cam where they were going, he had just smiled and said she could dress casually.

The only thing she had ever done casually was sex.

After about a hundred outfits, she had on a short black skirt, a flouncy tank top with some cleavage for good measure, and a pair of cute sandals. She felt dressed down for a date, but this was what he had said after all.

She wasn't sure she even felt comfortable in her skin, purposely dressing like this on a first date, but this was Cam. She was sure it would be fun.

The knock on the door made her dart out of her room. She shooed Trihn and Stacia away and then opened the door.

"Hey," she said brightly.

"You look great," he said, surveying her.

"Thanks. You, too."

He had on jeans and a green polo with the flip-flops he always wore to class.

"Are you ready?"

"Yep." She shut the door behind her and followed him out to his car. "Wow. Is this yours?"

It was a classic black Mustang from the sixties. She wasn't as familiar with older cars because her father preferred new supercharged sports cars. She knew enough to know this thing was beautiful and in mint condition.

"Yep. All mine."

"I love her. I'm usually more of a Ferrari-Porsche kind of girl, but this is beautiful."

"Thanks. All original parts. My dad owned her first."

"Incredible," she mused. "I'd love to drive her!"

"You drive a stick?" he asked, surprised.

"Since before I could walk."

He smiled and opened the passenger door for her. "Then, maybe I'll let you give it a spin, if you're lucky."

"I'm always lucky," she said.

She sank into the seat and let him close the door for her. *A perfect gentleman.* Cam got into the driver's side and then drove them away from the apartment.

It wasn't far before he was pulling over onto a side street for the restaurant—if the thing he parked in front of could be considered a restaurant. It was a food truck that was basically a trailer with a window and menu on the side. There was a patio outside with picnic tables and some benches, all of which were already full. Plus, there was a line around the block. So, at least that was a good sign. Though she was skeptical.

"Hope this is okay. A friend of mine discovered this place. I swear, it's the best food in town."

She had been to the Eiffel Tower Restaurant, so she highly doubted that.

"Yeah. Should be interesting," she said. She hoped she'd sounded convincing.

They got in line, and after a good half-hour wait, they made it up to order. Cam got them two burritos, which seemed to be the signature item, chips and queso, and two beers. She stared down at her aluminum can but made no comment. This was fine. She drank beer at house parties. This wasn't any different.

Another couple vacated their spots, and they found a space to sit on a bench. Cam set the burritos down in front of them, and she took a long swig of the beer. It was cold and refreshing in the Vegas heat. She wasn't sure what to make of the burrito wrapped in aluminum foil. *Did people actually eat like this?*

Cam was already removing the foil and digging into the burrito. He looked like a mask of pure joy.

"This is so amazing, Bryna. I can't wait for you to tell me what you think."

She swallowed. He was so happy. It had to be good. She hated being skeptical. She needed to relax and live in the moment.

Taking a deep breath, she peeled back the foil and took a small bite of the burrito. It was everything—full of spices and tender chicken. There were a million things inside, and she could hardly distinguish the mush, but it was amazing. Flat-out best burrito she had ever had in her life.

"Oh my God," she murmured.

He smiled triumphantly. "I told you so."

"I would have never guessed this heaven was on a beat-up truck in the middle of nowhere."

"I know. I'm glad you like it."

"Learn something new every day."

"You've never eaten from a food truck before?" he asked.

She shook her head. "Not in L.A."

"They have them in L.A."

She shrugged. "Not where I live."

"Well, you should get out more!"

"I am."

She meaningfully looked at him, and he smiled bigger.

They finished their food and piled back into his Mustang. She was still in shock about the food truck. She was used to good food but usually fancy food. She'd had a chef growing up, and burritos hadn't exactly been on the menu.

She was so lost in thought about the burrito experience that she almost didn't notice when they pulled up to the movie. Her eyes widened.

"A drive-in?"

"Yeah. They show all the best movies. I thought it would be better than some blockbuster."

"I haven't been to one since I was a kid. My dad used to take me before he—" She cut herself off. She didn't really want Cam to know who her dad was yet. "He just worked a lot."

"Sounds like my dad."

"What are we seeing?" she asked, quickly changing the subject.

"*Casablanca.*"

"Good choice."

Cam paid for their tickets and bought them popcorn that she had no intention of eating, and then they found a spot near the center of the place. People were staring at his car, and she didn't blame them. It was a classic.

They snuggled in close together as the movie started, and Cam rested his arm across her shoulders. She had always loved *Casablanca*. It was a film her mother used to play on repeat when she was younger. Bryna knew every line, but it didn't stop her from admiring the beautiful work.

Cam's tentatively laced their fingers together. She tilted her head and rested it on his shoulder, whispering the lines under her breath.

"So, you've seen this one before, huh?"

She nodded. "It's one of my mother's favorites."

"Good."

As the closing lines rolled through, Bryna felt a tear come to her eye, just like Ingrid Bergman's as Humphrey

Bogart delivered his famous line, "Here's looking at you, kid."

As Ingrid turned to walk onto the plane, Cam tilted Bryna's chin up to look at him. He brushed his nose against hers. His lips were so invitingly close, yet her thoughts strayed to the closing of the movie where Ingrid left the man she loved, at his request, to be with another man. It felt just like love...heartbreaking.

"I'm going to kiss you now," Cam whispered, breaking her from her thoughts.

"I'm surprised you haven't already."

"I wanted to make sure you were okay with it."

She smiled. No one had ever checked to make sure before. "I'm very okay."

His lips met hers, soft and tender. It was a question wrapped in the uncertainty of how she would respond. She pressed her lips harder against him, wanting to forget, to not think about anything in that moment. She wanted to get swept away and lost in his lips. She wanted a kiss that would make her mind go blank and the world tip.

And it was a good kiss.

Cam pulled away, and she hoped the guilt wasn't on her face for thinking of another kiss in his stead.

He kissed her on the cheek once and then pulled out of the drive-in with a satisfied smile on his face.

Her mind was still lost on that kiss. It had been good. He was nice and sweet. They got along. Everything seemed to be going in the right direction. It wasn't what she had expected out of the date, but that was for the better. She couldn't keep doing the same things and expect different results. Like with Hugh. Or Eric.

She shut her mind down. She was not going to think about Eric anymore.

Cam drove up to the gate of her apartment complex and punched in the code to get in. "I had a great time," he told her as he rounded the corner.

"Me, too," she said with a smile. "Do you want to..." She trailed off when she saw the car in front of their building.

A big, shiny Jeep.

Eric's Jeep.

THIRTY-SIX

"DO I WANT TO…" Cam prompted.

She had been about to invite him up, but there was no way that was happening now. If Eric were up there, they would be walking into a land mine. "Do you want to walk me to my door?"

"Of course."

She couldn't tell if he was disappointed. She didn't know him well enough to judge his mood in that way. Maybe he still thought she would invite him inside once they got up to the door.

He parked, and she walked around to his side. They walked hand in hand into the building. The elevator ride was charged. She could tell he wanted to say something more but was waiting for her move. Yet she couldn't make the move. She couldn't produce the invitation with Eric one step inside her apartment.

Well, she could, of course. She could walk right inside with Cam and pull him into her bedroom with a smirk. The old Bri would have done that in a heartbeat. Less than a heartbeat. But she didn't want to hurt Eric. She cared about Eric. They were friends...of sorts before she had found out that the basis for that friendship was based on unsubstantiated lies.

So, no flaunting the new guy yet. It was one date. She would give it some time.

"I'd love for you to come in," she said hesitantly. "But I'm not sure I'm...ready for this yet."

"Oh," he said. He seemed surprised. "That's okay. We can take things slow."

"I'd like that." Even though she had never gone *slow* a day in her life.

"I want to do this again," he said. "Maybe next week?"

"Ambitious. Asking for another date at the end of the night."

"I like being around you. You're beautiful and sweet and make me smile."

Sweet? Shit! Had anyone ever said that to me before?

"Well, you're in luck. I like you, too. But...I can't do next week. It's an away game."

He laughed softly. "I'll always be competing with football. How about this? You name the time, and we'll go whenever you're free."

"That sounds good."

He placed his hand on her cheek and slowly kissed her. "Good night," he whispered against her lips.

"Night."

She waited until he disappeared around the corner and into the elevator before breathing regularly again. She turned around and braced herself for what was about to happen. Her thick skin would be needed for this encounter. She couldn't be soft and pliable. It was hard enough, adjusting to that with Cam, someone who didn't know her at all. Eric would eat her alive with that attitude.

She pushed open the door and walked inside with her head held high. Eric was seated on the couch, watching some horrendous Kardashian show with Trihn and Stacia. It was almost comical.

With concerned wide eyes, both girls looked over at her at the same time. Eric's expression was entirely different. He looked ravenous, and it was so painful that she almost looked away.

"Hey," he said, standing before anyone else could say anything.

"What are you doing here?" she demanded, closing herself off. "Aren't football players holed up out of town?"

"I'm not a football player anymore, Bri. Remember?"

"Right. Career-ending injury and all. Still doesn't explain why you're in my apartment."

"Um," Trihn murmured, "we'll go to our rooms or something. Come on, Stacia."

"No need. Eric was just leaving."

"No, I wasn't. I'm not leaving. So, let's go to your room where we can talk," he said.

Trihn and Stacia shifted uncomfortably. She knew they were wondering what she was thinking, but she couldn't pull her eyes from Eric. He looked run-down with circles under his eyes and a five o'clock shadow. He still had on his LV State coach's polo and khakis. His hair was a little rumpled, but it was sexy. Not that she was thinking of him like that at all. She needed to look away.

"You're so damn stubborn," she said.

"Me?" He took a step toward her in a fury. He was breathing heavily, and then he stopped himself and took a breath. "Sorry," he mumbled to Trihn and Stacia. "Let's go, Bri. We need to talk."

"I have nothing to say to you."

"Second door on the left," Trihn told him pointedly.

Bryna glared at her. "Thanks."

Trihn shrugged and gave her a mischievous look. Eric walked down the hallway, and against her will, she followed behind him into her room. This wasn't a good idea. In fact, this was the opposite of a good idea.

He slammed the door shut behind her and then pushed her back against it. She was taken off guard as her body collided with the door. He grabbed her face in his hands, and then his mouth was on her. Possessively. Achingly desperate and demanding. Tension, sweet tension, rippled between them. It was like it had a life of its own. Suddenly, her hands were wrapped up in his shirt, drawing him closer. His hands dug into her hair, crushing them together. His tongue flicked against hers, and she groaned into his mouth.

No. Wait. No. This wasn't supposed to happen.

She shoved him with all her strength and took a step away from the door. Her heart was ricocheting throughout her chest, and she didn't know if there was enough oxygen in the room to keep up with the gasping breaths she was taking.

"What are you doing?" she cried breathlessly.

"Kissing you, goddamn it!"

"You can't just kiss me!"

"I just did. And you wanted me to kiss you. I can't fucking pretend with you. Why are you pushing me away?"

He took a step closer, and her back pressed into the door once more. Part of her waited for his lips to be on hers again, and she told herself there was no reason to be disappointed when it hadn't come.

"I was on a date tonight!" she spat.

"Stacia mentioned that."

Bryna narrowed her eyes. "That couldn't have anything to do with you being here?"

"Of course it does. What the fuck, Bri? You're dating now? Who is this guy?"

"Yes, I'm dating! And it's none of your fucking business who I date."

"We slept together!"

"And I told you, we couldn't be together!" she yelled back. "So, it still means you have no opinion on the matter."

"How can you say that after that kiss? You're afraid of being hurt. I know you. I know what happened with Jude."

She cringed at the name.

"I was there for you that day. I saw what you were like. I know this Hugh guy did a number on you, too. I know your family fucked you up. Let me be the one to put it all back together."

"Don't you see? You won't put it back together. Whatever you think this is, is a lie. I was only around you because I thought *this* could never happen. I don't want this at all."

"What do you want then?" he demanded. "Stacia said you're not digging that douche anymore, and now, you're dating some film student? This isn't you."

"Maybe I don't want to be me anymore!" she cried. She threw her hands out and shook her head. *Why is all of this so hard for him to grasp?* "All I do is cause people a lot of problems. I get called a bitch and a slut, and I've never cared before, but I'm not a slut. For once, it's nice to be with a guy who doesn't treat me like one."

Eric looked sad at the accusation. "I never did."

"You fucked me in the locker room!"

"That's not because you're a slut, Bryna," he said softly. He took a step toward her as if he could make her understand. "It's because I'm crazy about you. When you're not trying so hard to be someone else, *this* works." He gestured between them.

Bryna rubbed her forehead in frustration. "I can't do this tonight. I don't want to fight. I came back from a date, and you're ruining it." She sighed and looked back up at him. "You should go. I want us to be friends again, but it doesn't seem like that's going to happen. So...just go."

"You're right," he said finally. "We're not just friends. I want so much more than that."

He leaned down and softly kissed her on the lips. His hands cupped her face, and she unconsciously leaned into him.

"I want this."

"Eric," she whimpered.

His hand went to her heart.

"And this."

He kissed her again as his hands moved to grab her hips. He pulled her flush against him. "And this."

Then, his hands climbed up her short skirt as he pushed her back against the door. "And this."

"St-stop," she whispered feebly.

"Tell me you don't want this. I know you do. I can feel it." His fingers dug into the soft flesh of her inner thigh.

"I do...but..."

He drew circles up her thigh, closer and closer and closer. She closed her legs against him. She couldn't...

"Why must you fight me?"

"Please," she whispered as he spread her legs farther apart again.

As his finger trailed along the line of her thong, she wasn't sure if she was even fighting him anymore.

"Please..." She didn't know if she was asking him to stop or begging him to keep going.

"I want you, Bri." His mouth was hot against her throat.

His finger dipped under her thong and pressed against her wet core. She groaned at the feel of him and how riled up she already was.

"I know," she murmured incoherently.

His touch made her whole body quiver.

"Your body, mind, and soul. Do you want me to take your body?"

She shook her head, but the word that tumbled out of her mouth came as a shock to her, "Yes."

He sighed with relief, kissed her shoulder, and then took a reluctant step backward.

"Eric?" Her vision seemed to clear all at once. She realized the spell he had cast on her and what she had been about to do. Suddenly she felt cold and empty all over again, trapped in this vortex of lust and sin that she couldn't escape.

"Then, let me in. Your heart isn't frozen or black, like you seem to think. You opened it to me before, and I want it again."

"I can't," she said softly, woodenly stuck to the door.

"We're hanging on the edge. Jump."

She shook her head. "The problem with jumping is that you're as likely to end up broken as you are to being saved."

"Fine," he said, shaking his head in dismay. "I'd rather take a chance on being broken. I guess you have to make up your mind on what you want."

He grabbed the door handle, and she moved out of the way. He opened it and left, and she watched his retreating back as he headed down the hallway.

"I already have."

THIRTY-SEVEN

ERIC WAS A CONSTANT THOUGHT in the back of her mind.

Bryna didn't know what had happened that night or how she had lost control so easily. That wasn't supposed to happen. She was trying to move on with her life and make good decisions. But being around him perpetuated the darker side of her personality. She wanted and wanted and wanted when she was with him. She couldn't get enough, and that was dangerous.

So, she avoided him during games and on the plane for away games and at the hotel and practices and everywhere else she saw him. She knew he was waiting for her to make up her mind, but it was so clear that she had already decided.

She'd chosen Cam. They had gone to lunch a couple of times after class, he'd message her a lot, and they'd chat online. It was real, stable, and normal. She liked where it was going even if they were moving at a glacial pace.

Of course, that was her doing since she had told him he couldn't come in that first night, and he'd agreed to take things slow. It wasn't bad. Her body was just on fire.

Cam was coming to the next home game and then they were going out with her friends afterward. She was excited for her friends to finally meet Cam, but she wasn't sure how she felt about sharing him yet. She had never really dated anyone before who the girls could meet. Another new experience.

The night before the home game, she was lounging around the apartment with Trihn when the doorbell rang. Trihn hopped up and answered it. A minute later, she returned with an envelope.

"Um…this is for you." She held it close to her chest.

Bryna raised her eyebrows. "Oh, yeah?"

She reached for it, but Trihn kept it away from her.

"It says Westercamp."

"What?" Bryna asked, suddenly chilled.

"Yeah. It looks official, and a courier delivered it."

Bryna snatched the envelope from her friend and tore it open. "Oh my God."

"What?" Trihn asked anxiously.

The check she had left at the WC Resort fell out of the envelope and onto the coffee table in front of them.

"He returned it," Bryna breathed.

"The check for the house? Oh my God. What are you going to do with it?"

"I…I don't know. I thought I was doing the right thing by returning it. I never thought he would give it back to me."

"You were doing the right thing," Trihn said. She reverently held the check between her hands. "This is an absurd amount of money. You can't keep it."

"No. I never intended on keeping it. I just wanted him to know that I didn't want the money," she said, still shocked. "Do you think he thought I was throwing it back in his face?" Just the thought of that made her queasy.

"I don't know," Trihn said honestly.

"Oh God." Bryna was horrified.

He couldn't think that, could he? She hadn't wanted to hurt him in the first place. She had returned the money for the house as a gesture to show that she had cared about him and that it hadn't been just about the money. In fact, she didn't even need the money, and he should have taken it back. The last thing she'd wanted was for him to think that she had sold the house to spite him or something equally horrible.

"It's okay, B," Trihn said. "That wasn't your intention."

"I know. I know." She took a deep breath. "I have to figure out how to fix this."

"You will. We'll figure it out."

Bryna nodded. She carefully replaced the check in the envelope and put it in a safe in her room. She didn't know what she was going to do from here. She had thought she was doing the right thing. Once again, it'd backfired in her face.

Changing into a slip, she crawled into bed and hoped she would dream up a solution.

The next day, Bryna didn't have an answer, but at least she would have a full day of football to keep her mind occupied. It was a gorgeous day with the sun beating down overhead. Her muscles were strong and ready for the cheers and stunts that were ingrained in her mind. She had a smile plastered on her face as the Gamblers easily whooped their opponent.

Halfway through the game, Coach Galloway pulled out the starters, including Marshall, and Pace went in as quarterback.

Stacia jumped up and down next to Bryna with excitement. "My boyfriend is in as QB!"

"I can see that," Bryna said dryly.

Her base, Daniel, rolled his eyes, and Bryna fought back laughter.

"Mission complete," Stacia said.

Bryna shook her head and returned her focus to the game. She hated admitting that Pace looked good out there. She knew from Stacia's rants and her own general knowledge of Pace that he wasn't satisfied as the backup. She could see why, too.

Even though Marshall was better, Pace was still really good. He could have been starting at almost every other school, but he had chosen LV State to mess with her. She wondered if he now stayed for Stacia or if he had a bigger agenda she hadn't yet discerned. Either way, she wasn't going to let him know that she thought he was good at anything. He had stopped his harassment for the most part, and she wanted to keep it that way.

When the game ended, her eyes turned to the stands to try to find Cam. Trihn had promised she would bring him down onto the field afterward. She heard someone clear his throat behind her, and she turned to find herself staring up in the most perfect hazel eyes.

She took a step back to give herself some distance and tried to ignore how good Eric looked in his coaching outfit.

"Hey," she said softly.

There were a lot of people around. Thousands of people. And the only person she could focus on was right in front of her. She had a problem. A major problem. And his name was Eric Wilkins.

"Are you going out tonight?" he asked brusquely.

Bryna tensed. "Yeah."

"With the new guy?"

"Yeah."

Eric simply nodded. "Okay." Then, he turned and walked away.

Bryna looked over her shoulder momentarily to see if she could see Cam or Trihn, but it was still too crowded for them to get on the field. She raced after Eric and grabbed his arm to stop him.

Sparks flew threw her hand upon contact, and she hastily removed it. Touching him was dangerous. "Wait…why?" she asked.

"I was deciding whether or not to stay in tonight."

"Are you *staying in* like last year?" she asked. The image of Audrey popped into her head, and she hated herself for remembering that day.

"No. I'm staying in because of you. I told you I was done with her. We're done. It's that simple." He sighed. His eyes silently pleaded with her.

"Why? I'm not giving you a reason. I'm not giving you hope."

He tilted his head and assessed her. A slow smile crept onto his face. "I have hope. You're talking to me now, and I remember the way you kissed me, the feel of your skin, that look in your eye—"

"Stop!" she said desperately. She realized how close together they were, and she took a hasty step backward. She hadn't even known they had moved toward each other like magnets.

"See? There's still hope."

"Eric…"

"But I'm not going to torture myself. You said no and stop, and I'm not forcing you into anything, Bri," he said. "I do have to tell you that I think you're making a big mistake."

He walked away before she could respond. Not that she had any idea what she would have said. Things with

Eric were…complicated. She didn't want complicated tonight.

"Hey!" Cam said from behind her.

She nearly jumped out of her skin as she turned to face him. He pulled her into a quick hug. She hoped she had composed herself.

"Hey, you!"

He released her. She noticed Trihn and Neal behind her. Trihn nodded her head and gave her a look that said she had seen Bryna with Eric. She shrugged lightly. Their unspoken communication.

"Who was your friend?"

"What friend?" she asked.

"The guy you were talking to."

"Oh. Nobody." She needed to change the subject. "How did you like the game?"

He shrugged. "It was football. Neal is pretty cool though. He filled me in on this Posse situation."

Oh no! Bryna knew exactly what Neal thought about Posse and their entourage.

Bryna narrowed her eyes. "What exactly did he say?"

"Just that I should expect to drink and dance all night."

She breathed out in relief. "Sounds about right."

"Should be fun."

"I think so." She smiled as he laced their fingers together. "I have to change, and then we can head out."

Bryna hurried after Stacia to go into the locker rooms. Trihn jogged after her, leaving Neal and Cam all alone to wait for them.

"What was that all about?" Trihn asked.

"What was what about?" Bryna asked innocently.

"That whole thing with Eric."

"There's nothing with Eric."

"There clearly is," she said, placing her hand on Bryna's arm to stop her. "I don't want you to get hurt again. Talk to me. What's happening? Do you really *like*

Cam? He doesn't seem like your type, and I don't want you to lead him on if you're not interested."

Bryna wrenched her arm away. "I'm not leading Cam on. I like him. We have fun together."

"Then, what is going on with Eric? And don't say nothing."

"Nothing," she said automatically.

Trihn glared at her, and she sighed.

"We slept together."

"What?" Trihn shrieked.

"Shh!"

"Sorry. What? You slept with Eric? When? Why is this the first I'm hearing of it?"

"It was at the beginning of the school year before I went out with Cam. It was the first time we saw each other since last year, and I don't know. Things just exploded."

"Literally."

Bryna shoved Trihn. "Yes. Literally. Jesus. Then, I couldn't stop thinking about how I was trying to be this new person, and the person I'd been around him was a lie. Everything got jumbled. I don't want to be with someone who I was only comfortable around because I thought he was gay for over a year."

"Are you *sure* that was the only reason you were comfortable?" Trihn asked meaningfully.

"Yes! I just…" She shook her head and tried to get all her thoughts together. "I want this to be easy and effortless. I want to be strong, Trihn, but it seems like the harder I try to be strong, the weaker and more vulnerable I become."

Trihn grabbed her and hugged the breath out of her. "I know just what you mean."

Bryna hugged her back. She was glad she didn't have to explain any further.

They headed into the locker rooms, and Bryna changed into more appropriate clothing for Posse. When they returned, Cam and Neal were standing with Pace at the entrance to the locker rooms. The sight of them all together made her uneasy.

"Ready to go?" Pace asked impatiently.

Stacia bounded over to him and snuggled up into his arms. "I'm ready."

Bryna barely restrained herself from gagging. Trihn sent her a sympathetic look. She wasn't fond of Pace either. She hadn't witnessed firsthand the bullshit he had put Bryna through, but she'd claimed that she got a bad vibe from him. Bryna couldn't agree more.

The group proceeded to Stacia's SUV, which was the biggest vehicle between them. It wasn't far to Posse. They could have walked from the football stadium, but it was nice to have a car nearby regardless. Pace took the keys from Stacia and revved the engine as everyone else piled in.

She couldn't believe she was willingly hanging out with Pace. It felt so wrong. Bryna tried to tune out his bullshit about how he should be the new starter for the team after getting playtime on the field. She ground her teeth and leaned into Cam. He put his arm around her shoulders in response.

"If only Coach didn't have such a stick up his ass for Marshall," Pace droned on. "Speaking of, you know who has been in a shit mood lately?"

"Who?" Stacia asked, enraptured.

"Eric."

Bryna jolted slightly and looked up into Pace's eyes in the rearview mirror. They were mischievous. She knew he had brought up Eric on purpose. Trihn swiveled around to check on Bryna. Bryan's eyes widened slightly, telling Trihn not to give Pace the satisfaction of a reaction. She didn't want Cam to notice.

"He has been yelling at everyone and biting our heads off for dumb shit. I think he needs to get laid. We're all determined to find him a new girl."

Neutral. Completely neutral.

"Bryna, you're close with him, right? Maybe you could talk to him."

"No," she said flatly.

"Come on. You guys were joined at the hip last year. Maybe you could recommend someone we could hook him up with," he teased.

"Shut the fuck up, Pace," she growled.

He had an uncanny ability to get under her skin like no one else.

At her outburst, Cam stiffened next to her. She could see that he was looking at her curiously from the corner of his eye. She couldn't make eye contact.

"What?" Pace said. He raised his hands from the steering wheel as if he were innocent. "I thought since you two were...*friends*, you could get him to chill."

"We're not friends."

Trihn slapped Pace on the back of the head. Stacia whispered animatedly to him at the front of the car. From the backseat, Bryna couldn't hear her, but she was glad that at least it shut him up even if he had said more than she wanted.

The car was suddenly stifling, and she was internally screaming, *Let me out of here!*

THIRTY-EIGHT

BRYNA WAS MORE THAN HAPPY when they pulled up in front of Posse. Pace parked the car, and she hurried outside where she could breathe. She couldn't believe Pace had brought that shit up in. He had been trying to start something, and she was going to murder him in his sleep if he didn't get his shit together.

Cam followed behind her, and they all started toward the entrance. They made it inside before Cam said anything.

"So...who is Eric?" he asked slowly.

She sighed. She'd known this was coming. "He's just a...guy friend of mine."

"But you said that you weren't friends."

"I know." She looked up at him and wished that she could tell him everything, but this was all new, and she didn't want to scare him off. "He's a guy I used to hang out with a lot last year."

"Is he the guy from the game?" Cam asked intuitively.

"Um...yeah."

"Did you two date?" he asked.

She shook her head. No, they hadn't dated. They had just been inseparable, and now, they were...nothing. Something. Complicated.

"Okay," he said uncertainly. "Should I be worried?"

She shook her head again. "You have nothing to worry about," she reassured him. Anything that might have been with Eric was never going to come to fruition.

"All right. I really like you, Bryna. I don't want any surprises. You know you can tell me anything."

"Of course," she lied through her teeth.

He smiled as if he had gotten through to her. "Let's go catch up with your friends then."

Bryna sagged with relief that he wasn't going to ask any more questions. She wanted their relationship to be simple and fun like it had been since their first date. She knew introducing him to her friends was going to make things a little difficult, but she had never planned on bringing up Eric.

They walked over to the bar. Maya was working and showing off her black skin in a tiny black bra top and high-waist jean cutoffs.

Bryna whistled at her as she approached. "Looking hot tonight!"

"B!" Maya squealed. She leaned across the bar and kissed her cheeks.

"This is my date, Cam," she said to Maya.

The girl had a tendency to push hot older guys on her, so she wanted to make it clear from the get-go that it wasn't happening tonight.

"Nice to meet you. I'm Maya." She reached across the bar and shook his hand. "What can I get you?"

"Nice to meet you, too. Just a Bud Light is fine."

Maya nodded and passed a beer to him. She worked on a dirty martini and handed that one to Bryna. She was going to need to sip this because she wanted to keep her cool tonight.

"Oh my God, B, I almost forgot to tell you. The whole club is abuzz about it. Guess who is up in VIP, asking for you?"

Bryna's eyes went wide. Not good. Hopefully, it wasn't some guy. She couldn't think of any who would be asking for her specifically by name, but she never really knew what could happen.

"Um, who?"

"Gates Hartman!" Maya cried.

Bryna relaxed. "Oh! Gates." She breathed out heavily. "What is he doing here?"

"Wait, like the movie star?" Cam asked. He looked between Bryna and Maya like they were speaking gibberish.

"Um, yeah. We're close friends from home."

"You're close friends with Gates Hartman?" he asked in disbelief.

"Yeah, how come I didn't know this?" Maya asked with a pouty bottom lip.

"Sorry. We fell out of touch after *Broken Road* released and got back in touch this summer."

Cam opened his mouth and then closed it. She wondered what he was thinking. She was kind of laying a bomb on him.

"Where exactly are you from?"

She sighed. Cat was out of the bag. "Beverly Hills."

His eyes widened. "Wow. Okay. Beverly Hills and Gates Hartman. I think I need to process this. What do your parents do?"

Bryna blushed. She couldn't meet his eyes. She had been dreading this very conversation. Everyone else already knew who she was, so she never had to tell anyone that her mom was a famous actor and her father an even more famous director.

"My dad is Lawrence Turner."

"The director?" he sputtered.

"Yeah."

"So, your mom is Olivia Bendel."

She nodded.

"And I took you to a food truck."

Bryna laughed heartily. "Yeah, you did."

"I feel kind of like an idiot."

"Don't! It was fun. I had a really good time."

He shook his head and stared at her with all new focus. She hoped it was a good thing.

"I can't believe this. I grew up watching your dad's movies, and your mom's movies are classic."

"Don't tell her that," she joked.

"No. I didn't…that's not what I meant."

"This is still me though, Cam. You don't have to explain yourself. I haven't suddenly changed because you know who my parents are." At least she hoped not.

"I know. Right. Of course not. Just a surprise."

"Yeah. I try not to lead with that. It's a bit intimidating." She shrugged. "Come on. I'll introduce you to Gates."

"How do you know him again?"

She bit her lip. "He went to high school with me, and we've known each other for a long time. He's a close friend of the family."

She didn't mention that they had dated for over a year and that he was her first real boyfriend. Those things were behind them, and all that mattered was that they were friends. Gates wasn't trying to get back with her. That ship had sailed.

"I have to admit, I haven't actually seen any of his movies, but I know of them."

"That's fine. He's more than his movies."

Bryna took his hand, and they climbed the stairs to VIP. The bouncer ushered them inside. Once she crossed the threshold, she was tackle-hugged by a rather drunk Gates.

"Babe!" he cried, picking her up and swinging her around.

"Gates, put me down!"

He laughed and obliged her. "Surprise!"

She shook her head and sent him an exasperated look. "What are you doing here?"

"I had a free weekend and thought I'd come spend it in Vegas with my favorite girl."

"You're ridiculous and drunk."

"Pleasantly tipsy," he joked.

"Gates, this is my...Cam," she said, stepping back so that he could see she had another guy in tow.

Gates held his hand out. "Hey. Nice to meet you."

Cam nodded his head as they shook and assessed each other. "You, too. Bryna was telling me that you guys went to school together."

"Yeah. We go way back. Bri's awesome when she's not acting like a total bitch. You know what I mean?" he asked.

He nudged Bryna, and she put her hand on her forehead.

Dear God, Gates!

"No. I guess I haven't seen that side of Bryna."

"There's another side?"

"He's joking. Aren't you, Gates?"

"Yeah. Totally. Where are all your hot friends?" he asked.

"Downstairs. Want to join the masses?" She was thankful for the change of subject.

"Sure. Think people will recognize me? I brought a baseball hat."

She shook her head. "It's packed down there already since it's a home game weekend. I think you'll be fine."

"All right. Let's go." Gates fell into step next to Cam and asked him a million personal questions. Gates was a very energetic and talkative drunk. He was so much more chill when he was sober.

She wasn't sure what Cam thought of him. He kept sending her furtive looks as Gates continued to talk. They made it back downstairs and over to her group of friends. Gates hugged Stacia, who he had hung out with some over summer break. Trihn had never met him, and Bryna thought Trihn was going to faint.

"He's even cuter in person," Trihn whispered to Bryna.

"I know."

She beamed. Everyone was getting along. Despite the one Eric hiccup in the car, this all seemed to be going better than she'd anticipated.

Gates grabbed her around the middle. "Let's dance," he whispered in her ear.

She gave him a meaningful look, and he sighed.

He let her go and then looked up at Cam. "Hey, Cam. Do you mind if I borrow your girl? Dance floor is calling my name."

"Uh…sure. I don't really dance anyway," Cam said.

He looked at Bryna for confirmation, and she shrugged.

She wanted to dance. If Cam wasn't going to dance, then it would be fine to dance with Gates.

She would take some assurance just in case. "Trihn, Stacia, come on."

"Oh!" Stacia cried. "Queen Bee leading the way tonight."

Stacia smacked Trihn's ass as she passed by and beckoned her on the dance floor. Bryna got lost in her friends' silly behavior. They shimmied and swayed and shook their asses in time with the music. It was like freshman year all over again before any of them had been dating anyone and they had just been carefree.

Gates came up behind her, grabbed her hips, and ground against her. They moved like one fluid motion. She had known him for way too long, and she'd had sex with him way too many times not to automatically get his rhythm. Stacia moved behind him, and Trihn was in front of her, bent over at the waist, doing unbelievably dirty things with her body.

Bryna dropped her head back in laughter as she shook her ass. She rested her head on his shoulder and threw her hands up in the air, getting carried away with the music.

"Missed you," Gates breathed into her ear.

"I missed you, too," she said. "This is fun."

"You should be careful with me, Bri. I think that guy really likes you."

"I like him, too," she said hesitantly. "He's nice."

"Yeah. Then, you should probably switch out with one of your girls. The way your body is moving…"

She swirled her hips around against him, and he groaned.

"You're killing me here."

"The great Gates Hartman reduced to nothing by little old me?" she joked.

"You're having too much fun with this. I'll have you know, I've fucked a whole lot of celebrities since you."

She turned around to face him and winked. "No one does it like me."

His eyes confirmed what she was saying. "That guy isn't your type."

"He's not," she said, unperturbed.

She glanced over at Cam. He was talking to Neal and Pace and not even paying attention to her.

"But I think it's good."

"If you say so." Gates's hand returned to her hips, and he drew her in closer. "Get over here."

She giggled and pressed herself up against him. Their movements were completely in sync, and they danced like that through the next three songs. Her eyes drifted over to Cam, and she saw he was staring intently at them now. She bit her lip as she decided to just dance through the end of this song and then go back to spend time with him.

Then, her stomach plummeted. She took a step back from Gates. "Shit!"

"What?"

"Eric," she whispered.

He walked right up to Cam and put his hand out.

Oh no. No, no, no. She didn't even say another word. She bolted toward them.

What the hell?

He had said that he wasn't going to be here.

She roughly grabbed Eric by the arm, and he staggered back a step.

Fuck!

He was drunk off his ass. She normally wouldn't have budged him a step.

"What are you doing?" she snapped.

"Hollywood!" he crowed.

She crossed her arms and stood her ground.

"I was introducing myself to my friend, Cam, here."

"Bryna?" Cam said.

He looked confused, and she didn't blame him.

"I'm sorry," she murmured to Cam.

"I'm not really sure what's going on here." Cam's face was set in a stern line.

She couldn't read him. She didn't know what he was thinking, but she didn't think it was good.

"Well, let me tell you what's going on," Eric slurred.

"Another time," she said. She latched on to his arm and pushed him in the opposite direction. "I'm so sorry, Cam. I'll be back in a minute."

"Okay. And then you'll explain what all of this is about?"

"Bri doesn't explain herself to anyone," Eric said. "Least of all, herself."

"Jesus Christ, Eric!" Ignoring Cam's look of confusion, she hauled Eric away from him before Eric could do any more damage. She dragged him through the door to the patio and as far away from anyone else as she could possibly get. The place was packed, so it had been a feat.

"What the fuck are you doing here?" she cried, shoving his drunken ass backward and into the side of the building.

"Came to make friends," he joked.

"You said you were going home, and you weren't going to torture yourself! You asshole!"

"I'm not torturing myself. But fuck if I'm going to sit at home either. I'd rather make better use of my time."

"How the hell is this a better use of your time?" she demanded. She planted her hands on her hips.

"I'm assessing the competition." He shrugged, and that signature smile graced his lips. "Seems meager at best."

"Oh my God!" She shook her head and took a step back from him. "You're drunk and being an ass. You should go home."

His hands reached out and grabbed her hips. He was more deft than he had appeared seconds before. She stumbled forward against him, and in a second, he had her flipped around, her back pressing into the building and his hands pinning her to the spot.

"Come home with me."

She stopped breathing for a second as she stared up into his face. It was so raw with emotion. His eyes were so hungry for her. "No," she murmured. "I'm not playing right now. Let me go."

"You're going to need to do better than that. There's none of the Hollywood spunk in your voice." He leaned forward and rested his forehead against hers. "Be here with me right now. Don't be with him. Don't be with anyone else."

His lips hovered inches from hers, and she promised herself she wasn't fantasizing about kissing him—the memory of what his lips tasted like, the feel of them moving against her, the way everything else shut down.

"I'm here with my…Cam," she managed to get out.

"But not your boyfriend," he said. He sounded triumphant. "It's never bothered you before to kiss other guys…fuck other guys when you didn't have a boyfriend."

His fingers pushed up into her hair, and he dragged their lips together. She could taste the alcohol on him. Whiskey. Dear God, it was like a shot of adrenaline to her system.

Yet she shoved him away.

"This is different. I'm not the same girl that I was when I did those things. I want to be different. I want to be…good. Fuck, I don't know. Stop making this so damn difficult. Just go home! You're drunk and making a fool of both of us."

She stormed away from him because she knew if she stayed another second, he would kiss her again. He did every chance he could get now. It was like a drug neither of them seemed to be able to quit.

It terrified her. She wasn't still angry with him for what had happened with Audrey.

She was angry with herself. For falling for him when she had promised herself she wouldn't. For putting her heart in his hands without even knowing she had done it. For giving him control over her with just a touch.

She had given those things away once before, and it had ended in catastrophe. She couldn't love him.

She sucked in a deep breath. Love wasn't supposed to exist.

THIRTY-NINE

WHEN BRYNA WALKED BACK INSIDE, she ran into Gates.

"Hey, what happened? Where did you go?"

"Eric is back there. I hate to ask, but will you make sure he leaves? He's drunk and causing a scene."

"Yeah, I will. But what's going on? Are you with Eric now? What about that other guy? What's his name?"

"Cam," she volunteered. "No, I'm not with Eric. He's just…I don't know."

"Hmm…I think I understand. Let me go talk to him."

"Thanks, Gates." She gave him a hug and then back to Cam.

He was waiting for her at the bar. He had his arms crossed, and she could tell now he was pissed. She hoped he hadn't seen her with Eric outside. She hadn't meant for any of that to happen. But she never meant for anything with Eric to happen, but he kept weaseling his way back into her life over and over again.

"Hey," she weakly said to Cam.

"What's going on, Bryna? I feel like the girl I've been hanging out with over the past month disappeared tonight."

"I'm still here. We're still getting to know each other. I don't know everything about you," she said. "I have some baggage...I guess. It's not all going to fix itself overnight."

"Well, I don't expect it to, but I didn't think I'd get bombarded with ex-boyfriends."

"Eric isn't my—"

"And Gates?"

"Um...yeah, we dated."

"I thought as much," he said, looking away. "It's fine. I know everyone has a past. I have a past and ex-girlfriends. I just want to be prepared when they come up and introduce themselves to me or you start basically having sex with them on the dance floor."

She opened her mouth to object, but what he had said was the truth. She hadn't wanted all of this to come out tonight, but it wasn't as if she could hide it all forever. If they were going to date, then he needed to know.

"I guess you've seen the worst of me tonight." It was a lie.

She hoped to God he never truly saw the worst of her. Her gold-digging status wasn't *that* well-known. Most people just thought she liked to date older guys. That wasn't so crazy.

"Come on. Why don't you dance with me then?" she asked.

He shrugged. "I don't dance much but okay."

They went out onto the floor and spent the rest of the night there. Gates resurfaced sometime later and nodded his head at her. That must have meant that he'd gotten Eric into a cab. She breathed a sigh of relief and was glad the rest of the night would be uneventful.

Cam offered to drive her home. He hadn't been drinking in a while, and they still had to walk across campus to his car. She went to the restroom before leaving, and on her way out, she ran into Pace.

"Hey," he said with a smile.

"Were you waiting for me?" she asked, suddenly suspicious.

"No. Just happened to run into you. I like Cam."

She narrowed her eyes. "Why?"

"He's a nice guy."

"And?"

"And nothing, Bri," he said with a smug smile. "He's just nice. Seems good for you."

Her guard was immediately raised. "What the fuck did you do?"

"Nothing! Christ! I can't say I like the new boyfriend? Don't jump down my throat."

He disappeared inside the men's restroom, and she glared after him. She didn't trust him to be so cavalier. He had looked way too pleased with himself. She bit her lip, trying to figure out what he might have done. *Had he told Eric to come to Posse? No, Eric knew better than to listen to Pace. Had he said something to Cam?*

Grr. I don't know.

She walked back to Cam with her head full of all the schemes Pace could have enacted. She knew if it were herself, a million things could have happened. He could have seen her and Eric kiss. He could have videotaped her dance with Gates and sent it to TMZ. He was probably the one who had told Cam that she and Gates had dated. She didn't know what else Pace might have done, and it made her nervous.

Cam took her hand as they left the club. Their walk across campus was silent. Presumably, she should have been enjoying his company, but she was too caught up in what Pace could have done. Maybe that was what he had wanted all along. He could have totally been bluffing. She nearly groaned with frustration.

If Cam recognized her mood, he didn't say anything. She got in his Mustang, and he drove the short distance back to her apartment. As they walked up to the top floor, he wrapped an arm around her waist and squeezed her side. It brought her back to reality, and she instantly felt bad for letting her mind wander.

"I had a good night," he said once they reached the door.

"Me, too. Despite some of the setbacks."

"Water under the bridge."

His lips touched hers, and she felt this weird sensation creeping through her stomach. It felt like sewage was being poured directly into her gut. She had never felt like this before. Horrible. Awful. Wretched.

Not from the kiss. The kiss was fine. But it was something else…

Guilt.

She had let Eric kiss her earlier. She had wanted that kiss. She had craved it. And now, she was here, kissing Cam, and it felt…wrong. Like she shouldn't be doing it. She and Cam weren't even official. They weren't boyfriend and girlfriend. She should have no reason to feel guilty about what had happened. But she couldn't help it.

She backed away into the door and fumbled for her keys. "I think I'm going to go to sleep," she said into her purse. "I'm pretty exhausted."

"Right," he said. He looked down at the ground and then up at her uncomfortably. "Are you sure? I could come in and keep you company."

"A different night. I'm just so tired." She yawned for dramatic effect.

"Okay, Bri," he said the name ironically. It didn't fit right on his tongue. "Night."

With that, he turned and walked away.

Then, there was this other weird emotion. Pain shot through her chest, and her stomach flipped uncomfortably. She felt her mouth go dry, and her head pounded. She bit her lip and thought about walking after him, but she didn't.

Regret.

Goddamn it.

She turned the key into the lock and pushed her way into the apartment. But she couldn't stop thinking about what had happened tonight. She couldn't go to sleep like this. Not now. She changed into some more comfortable clothes and then went out to her car.

She didn't know what she was going to say when she showed up, but she knew she needed to say something. She couldn't leave it like that. There was so much unsaid. She sighed and drove across town.

She parked in front of his house. His car was in the driveway, and a light was on inside, so she knew he was home. She knocked twice, and when no one answered, she let herself in.

"Hello?"

The TV was on downstairs, but she didn't see him. She heard the toilet flush in the bathroom, and then Eric walked out.

When he saw her, he stopped in his tracks. He was shirtless in nothing but a pair of basketball shorts. His hair was tousled, and he looked like he might have been sick, but he wasn't drunk anymore. He'd sobered up.

"Bri?"

"Hey," she said. She dropped her bag next to the couch and sat down. She tucked her feet up to her chest and leaned her head on her knees. "Do you think we could just sit for a minute?"

"Uh…yeah." He walked over and plopped down on the other side of the couch. He rested back naturally. His eyes were on her, still disbelieving that she was in his house.

"I'm glad you made it home safely," she murmured, looking at the floor.

"Gates talked me down. That was your doing?"

"Yeah."

She sighed and met his gaze. Their eyes locked, and a million emotions crackled between them.

"Why are you here, Bri?"

She shrugged. "I wanted to check on you."

"And?"

"I feel something," she murmured. "Guilty."

"You feel guilty?" he asked curiously.

"I shouldn't have kissed you. I'm dating Cam."

Eric's face screwed up with disgust, and he looked away. "I don't understand you. You're dating, doing all of these normal things, living this new life, and you don't want me in it."

"I can't seem to help having you in it. A year ago, you hated me, and now, I can't seem to stop kissing you."

"I didn't hate you. I didn't understand you. Similar to how I feel about what you're doing now," he said. "But about this kissing thing…"

"We can't do it anymore."

He shook his head and stood in a fury. "Just tell me what the fuck is wrong. Is it Audrey? Is it that you thought I lied to you? Are you scared? I was here for you all along. I deserve to know the real reason you keep pushing me away."

She shook her head. "Please, don't make me do this right now."

"Then, when?" he yelled. "I got drunk and came to Posse to try to get your attention. You sic your ex-boyfriend on me and tell me to go home. What more can I do to show you that I care? Tell me how to fix this." He reached down and hauled her up by her shoulders. "Tell me."

"Nothing! There is nothing you can do to fix this. I just want the guilt gone, Eric."

She couldn't even meet his eyes. She didn't know how to let him in. Before, it had been so easy, completely nonthreatening. And now, every time she let him in, she felt like she was breaking in half. Even worse, she wanted to break in half.

"I said I wouldn't be one of those guys who fell at your feet. You're just a girl, Bri. A beautiful, smart, funny, amazing girl but just a girl." He stepped back. His eyes were dark and stormy. "I can't keep this up. I can't keep waiting for you to see what's in front of your face. I know you too well, and I know that you're lying to me and to yourself. You drove across town in the middle of the night after your new boyfriend dropped you off to come check on me? It's not adding up."

"I drove across town to check on my friend. He left, drunk off his ass, and I wanted to make sure he was home alive."

Eric growled deep in his throat. "Don't feed me bullshit, Bri. I'm not like everyone else, and you know it. I could see through your bullshit long before we were even friends. Don't think you're fooling me now."

"I'm not trying to."

"Yes, you are. You're trying to fool everyone. You think this new you is somehow better. But I saw this side of you while you were still the head bitch of LV State. You don't have to act with me."

"I'm not acting!" she cried.

"You know what? Just get out. Go home. Go back to your guilt about kissing me even though I'd put money on the fact that it's guilt over kissing him." He walked to the door and threw it open. "Get out, and don't come back until you can be honest with me. I promise not to see you again or try to convince you otherwise. Just get the fuck out of my house."

Bryna gaped at him, but he didn't look like he was going to budge.

"Fine," she spat angrily.

And with nothing else that she could do, she walked out the door. He slammed it shut behind her, and she jumped at the force of it.

Eric was gone.

FORTY

BRYNA WALKED THROUGH THE NEXT FEW DAYS in a hazy blur with a self-destructive streak she hadn't encountered since she last saw Jude. She didn't want to think about that night with Eric, yet she couldn't stop thinking about it. It had spun completely out of control. She felt out of control, soaring through a vortex without hope of escape.

And it would only get worse when she saw Eric. Every day, he'd walk past her like nothing had happened. She understood his anger. She would have understood him ignoring her or giving her the cold shoulder. But he didn't do that.

He was perfectly nice. Almost too nice. He didn't tease her or flirt with her or try to convince her of anything. He acted as if nothing had ever existed between them. Nothing at all.

It was unbearable. She hadn't known it would be.

Part of her dreaded those fake few seconds of his time, but then her heart would still skyrocket when he walked in the room.

Even worse…she was doing this to herself.

She could change it. All she had to do was swallow her pride and say something to Eric. But she didn't know how. She wanted to make it better, to go back to the way they were, but she knew he wouldn't be satisfied with that. They had crossed a line somewhere along the way, and then she had run headlong in the other direction. Fear paralyzed her.

"You're drooling," Stacia whispered.

"Am not."

"Eric does look good today, B. But shouldn't you be drooling over your boyfriend?"

"He's not my boyfriend."

"I was talking about Cam," she joked.

"I know." She tore her eyes from Eric. "Stacia, can I ask you a question? I know how Trihn would answer, and that's why I haven't asked her."

"Shoot."

"What would you do if you realized that you made a terrible, terrible mistake and didn't know how to fix it?" Bryna bit her lip, and her eyes drifted back to Eric.

"What would I do if I had slept with Eric and then pushed him away, all while dating someone else?" Stacia mused.

Bryna rolled her eyes. "We didn't sleep together while I was dating Cam. We kissed once or twice…or three times."

"Hmm…Trihn would tell you to march over there right now and confess your mistake."

"I know."

"I think you should probably fix your other… problems first." Stacia placed her hands on her hips "I can't tell you what to do, B. You kind of do whatever you want anyway, but I can say that Eric was a really good friend to you. Could you imagine your life without him?"

"No," she admitted.

"Could you imagine it without Cam?"

Bryna was silent. It was answer enough.

"Thanks, S."

"Anytime."

Bryna took a deep breath and walked the short distance to where Eric was standing, talking to a new cheerleader, Bethany. She was a doe-eyed freshman and was staring up at Eric with hero worship. She was going to need to cut that out.

"Hey," she said.

"Bryna," Eric said.

She bit her lip. She hated this formality between them.

She turned and stared at Bethany until she squeaked and ran away. Her reputation preceded her. She expected Eric to make fun of her for scaring off the freshman, but he didn't say anything.

"Can I talk to you later tonight?" she asked.

"You're talking to me right now."

"I know. I mean…can I come over and talk to you?"

"I'll be here late," he said noncommittally.

"What about after practice?" she pushed.

He looked like he was struggling for neutral. "If you must."

She breathed out a sigh of relief. "I thought you might ignore me."

"No, I'm not ignoring you."

"Good. Then, I'll see you after practice."

"This better be worth it," he said before turning and walking away without another word.

At least she had gotten a reaction.

She left and headed straight for Cam's house. They were supposed to be studying for their huge film midterm, but she had all week she had claimed that she was too exhausted from cheer to come over. Tonight, she had *promised* she would come over since she had been avoiding everything for over a week, and last weekend was an away game.

Cam seemed surprised to see her when she knocked on the door. "Hey."

"Hey."

"Are you here to study? I wasn't sure I'd ever see you again outside of class."

"Yeah. Fall semester is so hard with football."

"I'm glad you're here."

He let her pass, and she hurried inside. She took a seat on the couch and pulled out her homework. She knew that she needed to say something. She needed to work up the nerve to do it. She had never been in this situation before.

When she had broken up with Gates, it had been over the phone and more of a joke to him than anything. He hadn't taken it seriously. With all the other guys she had dated, things had just fallen apart. This wasn't like either of those situations. Cam was a nice guy. She couldn't just let it lapse, but she didn't want to lead him on. She wasn't as into this as she wanted to be.

Cam sat down next to her. He looked so happy to see her, and she felt horrible about what she was about to do.

"Cam, I…"

Then, he was kissing her. Not like he had kissed her before. No hesitancy. No subtly. He was kissing her with a ferocity that she would never have guessed he possessed until that moment.

"Whoa!" she said. She pushed him back a bit and wrenched backward. "I, uh…thought we were doing homework."

Cam groaned. "Come on. You don't need to study."

"I need a good grade on this exam."

"You're Lawrence Turner's daughter," he said condescendingly. "You're going to get a good grade in *film*. Even if you don't, who cares?"

Bryna stiffened. "*I* care." *How dare he!* She hadn't passed her film classes because of who her father was. She'd passed them because she was smart and worked hard. "My father has nothing to do with this."

Cam sighed heavily. "You don't even *need* a film degree. Considering your connections, you could break into film however you wanted to."

"I probably *could* if I had any interest in using my parents' success to get ahead, but I don't." She narrowed her eyes.

"I would. I think it makes sense. Everything in this world is about who you know." He didn't even seem to notice her rising temper. "Anyway, the test isn't even until Friday. You'll be fine if we have a little fun tonight."

His lips were on hers again, and she tried to push him back.

"Cam, no."

"Just shut up. I know you want this." He used his extra weight to push her backward into the couch.

"I don't want this!"

His hand slid up her shirt, and her skirt slipped up her thighs. His lips were on her neck, forceful and demanding in a way she had never seen in him before. His body was pressing his weight into her. She couldn't believe this right now.

This was not Cam.

"What happened to us taking things slow?" she cried.

"Fuck slow, Bryna!" he growled. "We've been dating for a month and a half. We haven't done more than kiss. I'm tired of slow."

He sat up in a fury, and she hastily scooted backward, away from him.

She yanked her skirt and shirt down. "What happened to 'whenever you're ready' and you didn't mind?" she spat.

She didn't care that she had been about to break up with him. This was unacceptable. She wanted answers. *Had he been waiting for a time to ignore what I want to try to fuck me?*

Maybe she wouldn't have been angry if this was what she had really wanted, but the thought of sleeping with him made her sick.

"That probably went out the window when I found out you were playing games with me!" he yelled. He shoved away from her and crossed the room. His hands were in his hair.

"Games?" she asked in disbelief.

This was honestly the first relationship where she hadn't been playing games. Games were her norm. *Here I am, trying to do right by Cam, and he's accusing me of playing games? What the fuck?*

"Yes! What the hell do you think this is? You're hot and cold. You bring your ex-boyfriends around while we're going out and still expect me to believe this good-girl act? Please. I'm not an idiot."

"You clearly are because none of this is an act. I have no idea what you're talking about. Gates and I have been long over, and Eric and I never dated. They're not even relevant to the fact that you tried to force yourself on me."

"Force myself?" he snapped. "From what I hear, you give it up to anyone who wants it."

"What?" she cried. "Who the hell told you that?"

"Your own brother! I know the truth now. You were trying out some experiment with me, but you normally like to slut it up. I thought if everyone else was getting some, then I should too."

Bryna stared, slack-jawed. "You know...I was coming here to break up with you, and I felt bad about it. Thanks for proving that I've made the right choice."

She grabbed her bag off of the ground and stuffed the papers for the class back inside.

"You're breaking up with me?" Cam cried. "What the fuck?"

She slung her bag over her shoulder and turned to face him. "You wanted the slut that my stepbrother totally made up to fuck with you, then you'll get the real Bryna.

I'm Queen Bee. A downright class-A bitch. I was never ashamed of it. So, I'm not going to sugarcoat it for you any longer." She walked up to him and dangerously narrowed her eyes. "You were a total mistake. I see that now. You're just a jackass disguised as a nice guy."

FORTY-ONE

BRYNA HAD BEEN STARING at the world upside down and under water, and she had just broken the surface.

Her head felt clear.

Her eyes were wide open.

Walking out of Cam's place was like having a weight lifted off her shoulders. She couldn't believe that Pace had gotten to him and sabotaged her all over again.

Oh, wait. Yes, she could. *The motherfucker!* At least, this time, she had wanted an out. *Who could have known that Pace's meddling would give it to me?*

She hadn't expected this to be the outcome. She had thought Cam was a good guy. She wasn't used to dealing with this breed of asshole. She wasn't sure if he had been biding his time to hook up with her or if Pace had manipulated him so thoroughly. Maybe it wasn't even his fault.

Ugh!

Either way, it didn't really matter. Pace hadn't made Cam try to force himself on her. No one had made him ignore her when she told him to stop. She clearly hadn't been into it. Then, things had gone from bad to worse.

She had thought that she could reinvent herself, but apparently, that was impossible. She never thought her reputation for being a slut and playing games would hit her so squarely in the face, especially considering she had been doing the exact opposite of *both*.

She wanted to go confront Pace about what had happened, but she wouldn't give him the satisfaction. That was what he wanted.

What she really needed to do was leave here and go see Eric. Of course he wouldn't be finished with practice for another hour at the earliest, but it didn't matter. She would wait.

He had waited for her after all, even when she had been a gold-digging bitch and when she had pulled a one-eighty and tried to be a good girl. But she didn't have to dig or be this good girl when she was with him. She just had to be herself. And that was a person she had been too afraid to be.

On her way back to the apartment, she texted Eric.

Let me know when you're home.

She didn't receive a response, and she hadn't thought she would get one while he was occupied. The wait was endless. She was glad that Trihn was at Neal's that night, and Stacia was cramming for a test with a friend from her class. All Bryna did was pace relentlessly and check her phone over and over again.

It dinged, and she jumped out of her skin.

Home.

She sighed in relief. She wasn't sure if he would actually respond. It didn't matter that it was just one word. She would take it.

The drive across town felt endless. She was so jittery that her stomach was doing flip-flops, and she couldn't keep her legs from bouncing.

She pulled up to his place and saw his Jeep in the driveway. She jogged up to the front door and knocked twice. He never answered the door, but she figured she would try since they were on such uneven ground. A couple of months ago, she would have walked in and been having margaritas with him without even thinking about it.

When Eric didn't answer, she pushed open the door. The downstairs was empty. Only the hall light was on.

"Eric?"

"Up here," he called from upstairs. "Give me a minute."

She took the stairs two at a time and walked into his room to find him coming out of the shower in a plain white towel. His hair was wet and messy. There was still that dewy shine to his toned body. She couldn't help but look.

"Oh…"

"Are you just going to stare?" Eric asked when he noticed her watching him in the doorway.

"Should I not?" She arched an eyebrow.

"I guess it depends on what you're doing here."

"Margaritas?" she joked.

Eric rolled his eyes, unamused. He grabbed some clothes out of his drawers and threw them into a pile. "I'm going to change. Let's get this over with when I get back."

"Okay," she whispered.

It only took him a second to change in the bathroom. He dragged a towel through his wet hair and then hung it up on a hook on the door. His hair was still tousled, and she reminded herself she had no right to touch him. She was in the wrong, and she needed to make this right.

He crossed his arms over his chest. "Let's have it."

"I broke it off with Cam," she said in a rush.

"And?" he asked.

He didn't even look surprised. Maybe he had been expecting that. *Had he known I was going to do it even before I had?*

"And…I'm here."

Eric shook his head. "It doesn't work that way. You can't jump ship and expect me to welcome you back with open arms."

"I know."

"I'm not really sure you do." He leaned back against his dresser. "You being single doesn't change or excuse your behavior."

"You're right." She held her hands up in defeat. What she had done was bad, and she didn't blame him for being pissed at her. "I deserve your anger, but will you let me explain?"

"If you think you have a good enough explanation for the past couple of months, then go ahead."

Bryna took a deep breath and let everything go. She couldn't keep holding this in and pushing him away. She couldn't be scared anymore.

"I thought a fresh start was what I needed after Hugh." She looked down at her feet. She hated this part. "You know, I thought he was married and that we were just having a good time. I thought we were on the same page. But we weren't. He wasn't married. Actually, he wanted to marry me."

Eric sucked in air through his teeth. Their eyes met, and she nodded. *Yep.* Sounded as horrible out loud as it had back in Barcelona.

"He wanted to marry me, and I was playing him. I'll never forget the look on his face. I broke his heart."

"Jesus."

"I was Jude," she gasped out. "I tricked Hugh into loving me, and for what? A million dollar house, some jewelry, and a few trips?"

"That house was worth a million dollars?" Eric sputtered.

She nodded. "Yes. I sold the house and tried to return the money to him. He sent it back to me without a note. In either case, everything with Hugh wasn't worth it. The money wasn't worth hurting him."

Bryna sat down on the edge of the bed and tried to judge Eric's reactions. She knew him well, but he was guarded. He wasn't ready to let her back in. She didn't blame him.

"So, I stopped. I pumped the brakes and said fuck it. I was going to leave the Queen Bee behind. Cam was an opportunity to forget all of that."

"Because he didn't know you," he accused.

"You're right. He didn't. He thought I was someone else completely. I wanted him to think I was this other person. I wanted to fool myself into believing it. But you made me realize that I couldn't. So, I went to dump him tonight, and I guess Pace had filled Cam in on the old Bryna." She shuddered at the memory of him pushing her back into the couch.

"God, does everyone listen to what Pace has to say? I can't believe anyone would believe a word that came out of his mouth."

"I know. Trust me."

"We'll see about that," he said.

"Yeah. So, then, he tried to force himself on me."

"What?" Eric cried. He pushed himself away from the dresser in a fury.

"Yeah. When I told him no, he accused me of playing games with him."

"Fucking prick. Just the thought makes me want to go over there and murder him."

Bryna smiled at his reaction. Eric was pissed at her for everything that had happened, and he still wanted to pummel Cam. That was a good sign.

"I don't think you could get away with murder."

"He should feel lucky then."

Bryna shrugged. She despised what Cam had tried to do, but she had already ended everything related to him in her mind. "I wasn't trying to play games with him, but he was right. I was. I was with him—"

"I don't need to hear this." Eric turned and walked away.

"Not physically. We never did more than kiss."

He looked back at her in confusion. "Really?"

"Yes." She sighed. "I was with him, but my heart was here with you."

"You can't come over here and say that shit to me," Eric said gruffly.

"Why? It's the truth," she spat. "You asked me why I pushed you away. At first, I thought it was Audrey. As hypocritical as it sounds, I felt like you lied to me by sleeping with her."

"That does sound hypocritical."

"I know. But when I came back to school and saw you, my world exploded in the middle of this transformation. I was scared and stubborn and refused to admit it."

"Admit what?" His eyes begged for more.

"You know," she whispered.

"No, I don't. You think I'm going to let you off the hook without finally admitting your feelings for me?"

She narrowed her eyes. "Look, I'm trying here!"

"You're not trying," he cried. "I'll tell you when you're trying!"

"Don't yell at me!"

"You put me through the ringer. You rejected me over and over again. You can't walk in here and finally explain everything that happened this summer and think it'll all be okay! It doesn't work that way."

"I know that! I don't think it works that way. Fuck!" She jumped up and paced away from him. "I'm trying to talk to you." She held her hands out in supplication.

"Then, keep talking because I don't see how this pertains to me at all. You fucked up with two other guys and pushed me away. That's all I've gotten from your little story."

"You're going to make this difficult, aren't you?"

"Yes. I said make it good."

Bryna took a deep breath and slowly let it out. She needed to get her thoughts under control. This wasn't going at all how she'd thought it would. Not that she had expected Eric to fall at her feet. He had sworn he would never be that guy. She didn't want him to be that guy. She just needed to lay it all out there.

"Let me start over," she told him. "After Jude, I didn't want to feel. I thought emotions and love were stupid things made up to torture people. I swore, I would never let myself fall apart again like I did with Jude. He ruined me."

She fiddled with her fingers but kept eye contact. Eric needed to know she meant it.

"But without even trying, we fell together. You and I. Not easily. We fought. We argued. We yelled at each other. You didn't put me on a pedestal. You treated me like I was a normal person. Not a queen or a bitch or a slut. And without even knowing it, I fell head over heels for you."

"You did a good job of showing it," he said sarcastically.

"I know. This hasn't been easy for me. I mean, I was fucked up long before Jude. My parents' divorce kind of shattered my world. I thought my stepmother had come in and ruined everything for me, but I talked to her after she had Zoe, and it turned out that I had been wrong about a lot of things. I think, in my own way, I showed you I cared. That night Audrey showed up at my house? I kissed you because I was jealous."

Eric raised his eyebrows. "I figured as much."

"I've never been jealous or guilty or regretful. It's all because of you."

"Oh, good. I bring out the worst in you."

"God, that's not what I meant." She ground her teeth together to try to keep herself from biting back at him. "I ran. I was scared. Yep, I did it. What I felt for you…feel for you, I didn't want to feel. I tried to escape it, but I couldn't."

"What do you feel? You still haven't said exactly."

"I've never done this before."

"Tell me, or walk, Bri."

Every time he pushed, she'd dig her feet in. She should just tell him, but for some reason, she couldn't get the words out. They were there on the tip of her tongue, but they were just out of reach.

"Stop being so pushy! I'm here! That's what you wanted, right?"

"I wanted honesty." He gave her a demanding look.

"I want to be with you," she said in a rush.

"Why? Two weeks ago, you claimed you didn't want to be near me. Why now? What changed?"

"Because even when I'm not with you, I want to be. Seeing you brightens my day. Hearing you call me Hollywood or Bri feels right. I miss margarita Sundays and having lunch with you on Wednesdays. I miss seeing you at parties and being myself around you. I even miss our arguments. I don't have to dig or be a good girl with you. I can just be myself. No matter what, it always comes back to you. It's because I don't want anyone else. I just want you."

He smiled smugly. "That's more like it."

"Cocky asshole."

"Pretty much, but you just said you liked that."

"It wasn't expressly listed," she said.

"I added it to the list."

Bryna looked at her feet and debated where to take it from here. There was still so much that needed to be said and that they needed to work out.

"I don't care if we have to take things slow," she told him. "We weren't dating before. I know I have some making up to do."

"Hmm…" he said, taking a step toward her. "Slow might work as long as I get to use all that make-up time."

"A solid month of making up," she offered.

"A month? Please! You walked out last semester."

"You were sleeping with someone else!" she reminded him.

"So were you."

"This isn't helping," she said. "You're arguing with me about last semester when I'm over here, telling you that I'm in love with you."

FORTY-TWO

SHE LOVED HIM.

Bryna's hand flew to cover her mouth at the same time his dropped wide open. She hadn't known she was going to say that. She hadn't even officially realized that was what she was feeling. But now that it was out, she couldn't take it back. She didn't want to take it back.

Love was something she had never wanted to feel again. But with Eric, she couldn't help it. He drove her crazy, and he put her in her place, but he cared for her. He wasn't purposely malicious, and even when she wouldn't fight for herself, he was there fighting for them. He had known what she needed long before she did. She had taken a while to get there.

"You love me?" Eric asked in surprise. He walked over to her, and she met his gaze.

"Yeah, I do. I guess I've known for a while. I didn't want it to be true with my past, but I can't fight it. I love you."

"You have a weird way of showing it."

Bryna smacked his arm. "Ass."

He grabbed her arm and then hauled her against him. In an instant, his lips were on hers.

It was like diving into a swimming pool on a hot summer day. The world silenced all around her.

His lips were soft, sensual, and all-consuming. There was nothing else in that moment, other than the feel of him against her. Her body pressed into his, and his arms wrapped around her waist. She brought hers around his neck. She was clinging to him breathlessly.

It felt like coming home.

She had been denying this for so long. Now, she had no reason to. She shouldn't have waited. She had been stubborn and idiotic to push him away. She had never felt this complete release with no expectations and no complications.

Just Eric.

His tongue caressed her bottom lip, and she shivered all over.

He smiled against her mouth. "You love me," he whispered.

"Yes."

"I love you, too."

She met his gaze, and all the pieces fell into place. This was where she was meant to be. Not with someone who valued her for her looks or her body. Not with someone who bought her happiness with gifts or someone who only liked her because of who he thought she was.

Just Eric, who loved her for exactly who she was.

Suddenly, the temperature skyrocketed. All the pent-up energy from their time apart hit a crescendo. There were no barriers. Nothing kept them from one another, and they both realized it at the same moment.

Eric pushed them backward, crashing into the bed. His hands went up into her hair and brought their lips together harder, more desperate. Her fingers worked at the hem of his shorts, and she was aching to claw them off of him.

"I need you out of these clothes," he said.

Fuck!

They were on the same page.

"Yes," she agreed. "Now."

He grabbed the bottom of her shirt and yanked it over her head. She hastily removed her shorts while he ripped his own clothes off his body. She ran her hands down his toned chest. He had a rocking body, and she wanted to investigate every inch of it.

He groaned at the feel of her touching his skin and kissed her again. "Get on that bed," he commanded.

She scrambled backward, not caring in the slightest how sexy she looked. He was staring at her as if he had never wanted anything else more in his life. And in that moment, she felt sexier than she ever had before. It was through his eyes that her body came alive.

Eric followed her onto the bed, and the feverish pitch that their desire hit sent sparks through every nerve in her body. He traced his lips across her shoulders, down the sides of her stomach, over the curves of her hips, and lingered on her thighs. His lips worked their way back up. He kissed her knee once, slowly and tenderly, as if he wanted to remember the way her body felt, treasure the memory, and ingrain it in his mind.

She trembled as he worked his way back up her thigh, stopping when he hit her thong. His breath was hot against her skin, and she imagined all the things he would do with that mouth. It only made her body awaken more to his touch.

As she angled her hips nearer to his mouth, he chuckled lightly against her skin. "Let me savor you," he said.

Bryna groaned, but she wasn't really complaining.

Eric kissed up her flat stomach and to her breasts barely hidden beneath a thin layer of sheer material. He opened the hook and eye and tossed the bra to the floor.

"That's better," he groaned.

Her breasts were on full display, and he seemed to revel in every last inch she was showing.

"You've seen them before," she teased.

"Don't remind me."

He pushed his growing erection against her core at the thought. Her head dipped back, and she squeezed her legs around him.

Fuck! I want him.

"That day was like torture," he said. His hands began massaging her tits. "You stepped out of that dress, soaking wet, and all I could think about was what I wanted to do to keep you soaking wet."

"Fuck," she cried.

She greedily rubbed herself against him. His words were doing the trick well enough on their own.

His tongue flicked her nipple, and her whole body spasmed.

"Oh God!"

"I had to go upstairs to try to calm down. I was rock hard," he said, shoving against her again, "and terrified you would notice. I wasn't supposed to have that kind of reaction to you. But fuck, your body."

He brought her nipple into his mouth and sucked on it, long and hard. As moved to the other one, his hand pinched the bud tight, causing her to jump. His tongue swirled and energetically stroked her into a frenzy.

"Fuck me, Eric. Just fuck me," she begged. "Oh my God, I need you inside me."

He looked up at her with that beautiful smile. "I'm just getting started."

He pinched her nipple, and she trembled.

"So, you like that. Good. I want to know everything you like. Every time I touch your body, I want you to think about me doing this." He brushed his finger against her erect nipple. "And this." He dragged it through his teeth. "And this."

Eric moved his mouth lower and lower until he was kissing the line of her panties. He dragged them off of her body, letting his fingers glide the length of her legs. Then, he grabbed her hips, pulled her flat on the bed, and spread her legs before him. He buried his face between her legs, and there was nothing but the touch of his tongue, the eagerness of his mouth, and the waves of pleasure coursing through her body.

She was holding on by a thread. He brushed her clit with his tongue, and her whole body shook with her lack of restraint. She was not going to be able to keep this up. Her body was already turning to putty.

His fingers skimmed up her leg and then down the length of her lips. She was already so wet and easily coated him.

"Fuck," he said against her skin.

She was a goner.

He slid his fingers in and out of her, and he had to use his other arm to hold her body down. She felt herself coming undone. She couldn't hold out any longer. It was as if he already knew exactly how to work her. He knew her body like he knew her mind.

She came hard at the insistence of his fingertips and the tip of his tongue. She honestly wasn't sure if she had ever come this hard. She was swimming in a sea of euphoria. Her body was coated in the stars. Her mind was basking in the glow of the sun. She was away—far, far away—where nothing could reach her as she rocketed through the sky.

She must have cried out because suddenly Eric's mouth was on hers. He tasted of her, but she didn't pull away. She felt blissfully alive, endorphins hitting her body with the force of a bulldozer.

"You're amazing," he said.

"Me? You're the one who made me orgasm," she muttered.

He laughed. "I like you like this."

"You can make me like this…anytime."

"I plan to."

Eric stripped out of his boxers and settled himself between her legs.

She put her hand out to stop him. "Wait…don't you want me to make you feel good?"

"This is going to make me feel very good," he said as he slid inside her without protest.

He buried himself deep until she was completely full. Her body contracted all around him.

"Next time," she whispered. Then, she lost her train of thought.

"Next time, I will fuck you, too. And the next time and the next time."

"Okay," she agreed.

He laughed into her neck. "You agree so easily. I could get used to this."

"You'd better."

He lovingly kissed her neck once and then started up a slow pace, testing her. She gripped his muscular back, digging her fingernails in. He felt incredible. This was a thousand times better than when he had taken her in the locker room, and that had been mind-blowing. But this time…he was hers.

It blew her away that Eric Wilkins was hers. She had idolized him as a football player, thought he was gay, hated him, become friends with him, and then fallen in love with him. It all felt…surreal. Here she was, not just fucking Eric, but making love with him. This was terrifying in the finality of it, but she wanted it. She wanted him.

Sensing her emotions, Eric picked up the pace. He slammed into her relentlessly. As she felt him getting closer, he wrapped his arms around her back and hauled her up into a sitting position. Then, he worked her hips, so she was bouncing up and down on top of him. He pushed into her so deep that she didn't think she could hold out any longer.

"Oh, fuck," she cried.

"Come for me, Bri," he demanded.

"Come with me."

And they did. Her whole world tilted, and suddenly, as if it had always been that way, it started to revolve around this wonderful man. He held her in his arms as they both came down from their climaxes and lightly kissed her all over. First, on her hair, then her forehead, cheeks, chin, nose, and finally, her lips. Featherlight kisses that promised so much.

He pulled back to stare into her eyes and then smiled. "I love you," he reminded her.

"I love you, too."

He looked relieved.

She nudged him. "I'm not going to change my mind."

"Well, certainly not after that," he joked.

She sighed and lay back on the bed. "I feel amazing."

"I feel like I'm going to need another shower."

She looked up at him with mischief in her eyes. "I could help with that."

They spent the rest of the night locked in each other's arms, making up for lost time. They knew that not everything would be fixed between them so easily, but this was the first step.

Bryna woke up the next morning to light filtering in through the window. Her body was pleasantly sore but utterly content. She opened her eyes to find herself in Eric's bed. A smile touched her lips, and she relaxed back into the pillow.

Memories of last night washed over her, and her body heated at what had happened. The clearest thing of all was her confession. She loved him. She had *told* him she loved him. Even when she had thought she felt that for Jude, she had never told him. Now that she was looking back on it, she wasn't sure she had even loved Jude. She had loved the idea of Jude. *How could I have loved someone I knew nothing about?*

Eric was different. She knew him completely. He was the person she always wanted to run to when times got tough. He made her feel safe, whole, happy.

His arm was wrapped around her waist, and he tugged her tighter against him as if refusing to let her go. She didn't fear that when he woke up things would be different or that he would push her away after the haze of the night was gone. This just felt right.

She slightly shifted her weight, and he groaned.

His lips touched her shoulder, and he squeezed her once more. "Morning."

"Hey." She entwined their fingers together.

"You feel nice in the morning. I'm going to stay in bed and have you for breakfast."

"I think I could allow that."

He kissed her again. "I'm glad you're still here."

She turned around to face him. "Where would I go?"

"Dunno. I was worried last night was a dream," he said with a cocky smile, "and I'd wake up to find I'd imagined you here."

"I'm not going anywhere."

"It would have been one hell of a vivid dream."

"How vivid?" she purred in his ear.

"Let me show you."

Eric gripped her hips and pulled her effortlessly on top of him. She realized he was already hard for her. They had slept in the buff, which made this really easy. He eased back inside her. She was tender from all their activity last night, but the pain soon disappeared as pleasure took over.

When she finished, she fell against him, panting.

He kissed her forehead. "I could get used to this," he whispered.

"Me, too."

After they both cleaned up, they crawled back into bed and lay in each other's arms.

Bryna was struck with how completely *normal* it was. There was no awkwardness. There was no wondering whether they would go out for breakfast or if she should just hurry out. There hadn't even been a question of whether or not they would make love again in the morning. It had just happened. Just like them.

"So, where do we go from here?" she asked him, her head resting against his shoulder.

He ran his hands through her hair contentedly. "Let's take it one day at a time. I don't want us to rush out and tell everyone what's going on yet. I'm going to keep you all to myself for a little bit longer."

"You want to hide me?" She was mostly joking, but the fear pricked at her regardless.

Eric laughed, reading her question for what it really was. "No. But I want us to get to know each other again as a couple without the public scrutiny of the entire football team and cheer squad."

Bryna nodded. "That's true."

"As long as you're mine and there's no more running away, then it honestly doesn't matter to me what we do."

"No more running away," she agreed.

"Good. Then, we'll figure it out."

"Unfortunately, I still have to get to class today," she told him.

"Skip it." He held her in place against him.

She giggled and kissed him. "I wish I could, but I can't."

"Okay. Then, come over right after class before practice."

"I will," she promised.

She reluctantly disentangled herself from Eric's arms, put her clothes back on, and headed home to change before she had to be on campus. Stacia and Trihn were both in the living room when she arrived.

Both of their eyes widened in surprise.

Trihn arched an eyebrow. "That must have been one hell of a study session with Cam last night."

Stacia giggled. "I want to hear all the details."

"We broke up," Bryna told them.

It felt great saying it out loud. That felt like a lifetime ago compared to what had happened with Eric last night.

Stacia gasped.

But Trihn smiled. "About time."

"Yeah, it was," Bryna agreed. She walked over to the couch and plopped down. "Cam found out that I used to sleep around or dig or whatever, and he tried to take advantage of me."

"What? Did you knock him out?" Trihn asked.

"What a douche bag!" Stacia cried.

"I know. I couldn't believe it, honestly. He seemed like such a nice guy, and he didn't know my reputation. But then as soon as he did, all went down the drain. So, I dumped him."

"Good. He deserved much worse than that," Trihn said.

"Yeah, like a swift kick to the nuts," Stacia agreed.

Bryna laughed and nodded.

"Where were you all night then?" Trihn asked.

"So...afterward, I went over to Eric's."

"Yes!" Stacia cried.

They both looked at Stacia questioningly.

"What? A football player or an artsy guy? It's not even a choice."

Trihn narrowed her eyes. "Thanks!"

"Hey! I'm just saying."

"Tell us about Eric," Trihn encouraged, ignoring Stacia's barb.

A smile came to Bryna's face, unbidden. Eric had that effect on her.

"We're kind of keeping it on the down-low right now, so you can't say anything to anyone, but I think we're together. We got into a big argument about everything that had happened between us. After I explained that I wanted to be with him, he came around to the idea. I told him I loved him," she confessed.

"Aw," Stacia crooned.

Trihn smiled brightly. "Finally! It's about time."

Bryna giggled. "You're so right. It's about damn time."

FORTY-THREE

WHEN BRYNA WAS WITH ERIC, time seemed to fly. All the best things in the world were tucked into the hours she spent at his house, lost in his arms. And just as good was the fact that she had her friend back. When they weren't lying around in bed in a state of ecstasy, they would hang out by the pool, have margaritas, grill burgers, and generally enjoy each other's company. There were still some lingering problems from their separation, but they were working through it one day at a time.

Without even realizing it, the away game against Colorado was upon them, and the entire team would be flying into Denver. Since the team still didn't know about their relationship, she and Eric had agreed to drive to the airport separately. She was sure some people had suspected by the way they acted around each other, but their relationship was in its infancy, and they didn't want the scrutiny.

Stacia and Bryna arrived at the airport in Stacia's SUV. They grabbed their bags out of the trunk, and then Stacia locked up. As they walked inside, Stacia had a bounce to her step.

"I cannot wait to fuck Pace in the hotel room," she said.

Bryna cringed. "That's disgusting. I can't hear you talk about him like that."

"Come on, B. He's not your real brother! And you're going to do the same with Eric anyway."

"Shh!" she chided. "People don't know yet."

"Sorry. Sorry. But you are, right?"

"I don't know. We'll see."

"That's a yes," Stacia said.

They checked in with the cheer coach, and then they were ushered on the plane, which had already been open for seating. Stacia walked on first, eager to get to her seat next to Pace. Bryna didn't know where her seat was, nor did she care. She had every intention of sitting next to Eric. This was their first away game together since last year, and there was no way she was going to sit next to anyone else even if it made people more curious.

As she walked down the aisle, she noticed someone was seated next to Eric. It was Bethany, the freshman girl who had been talking to him after practice that one day. Whatever she had said, he seemed to find funny because he laughed at her, and she giggled. Bryna's temper went from zero to sixty faster than a Bugatti.

She took a deep breath and reminded herself that Eric loved her and that she had no reason to be pissed off. But she was. It was just the fact that this girl thought she could flirt with him. Bryna had never felt such intense jealousy. Even though they weren't out as a couple, he was hers now.

"Ahem," Bryna said. She crossed her arms and stared down at Bethany with the best bitchy Queen Bee look she could muster.

Bethany's eyes widened. Clearly, she knew to be afraid.
"Hey, B," she said.

"You're in my seat," Bryna pointed out.

"Oh." Bethany looked down at her ticket. "It says I sit
here."

Bryna took the ticket out of her hand and then passed
the one she had been holding back to Bethany. "Now, it
doesn't. Scoot along."

"Um…" Bethany looked at Eric, hoping he would say
something so that she could stay sitting next to him, but
his eyes were locked on Bryna. He looked amused. "Eric?"

He turned his attention back to her and shrugged.
"Bryna normally sits here."

"I've sat here the last two games."

"Yeah. She sat here every game before that."

Bethany scrunched her eyebrows together as if she
didn't get it.

"You're new," Bryna said. "You'll figure it out."

"Okay. Well, I'll see you later," she said to Eric with a
big smile before disappearing down the aisle with Bryna's
ticket.

Bryna sank down into the seat and turned to look at
him. "So…you were going to sit there and flirt with her?"

"I wasn't flirting with her. We were talking."

He gave her a serious look, and she wanted to bite her
tongue, but she wasn't one to let things go.

"You were laughing at whatever she was saying, and
she was trying to stay seated next to you. Flirting."

"I was laughing because she's a little slow. I have no
interest." He lowered his voice and leaned forward toward
her. "You're really cute when you're jealous."

Bryna wrinkled her nose. "Cute?"

He laughed and reached down for his headphones. "I
know you love that word."

"You use it on purpose."

"I'm going to do a lot of things later on purpose, too."

Their eyes met, and her stomach flipped.

"I like where this is going."

"You'll like it more later when I sneak you into my hotel room."

She raised an eyebrow. "Last time I was in your hotel room, I didn't have to sneak in there."

"Coach is trying to crack down on pregame fun, and you're my fun. So, we'll have to be more careful," he told her.

"Sneaky. I like it."

She leaned toward him, eager for a kiss, but he gave her a look.

Later.

They weren't officially out to everyone yet, and she had completely forgotten while trapped in his gaze. She covered by reaching for her own headphones.

"Ugh!" Eric said.

Her head snapped up. "What?"

"Your fucking stepbrother."

"Pace?" She glanced around and saw that he and Stacia were only a couple of rows behind them. "What about him? I mean, besides everything."

"I can't stand the sight of him, knowing his part in what happened with Cam," he said, his voice low and dangerous. "Did you ever confront him about what he did?"

She shook her head and turned away from Pace. She wasn't happy about the fact that he had manipulated Cam into thinking she was a slut he could use. She didn't know what exactly Pace had said. Even though she always thought the worst of him, she didn't want to believe he had actually convinced Cam to hurt her...to try to sexually assault her.

"No," she said softly. "Just let it go. He's not worth it. Plus, Stacia is happy. We made amends about her and Pace this summer. I don't want to start anything and risk my friendship. She is more important to me than Pace."

"He got you attacked!" Eric growled.

Her eyes widened. "Keep it down."

"Sorry. It infuriates me."

"I don't think he *knew* it would lead to that. Trust me. I don't want to defend Pace, but I don't want to get into it with him."

Eric nodded and tore his attention from Pace, but he didn't look happy about it. She could see he had murder on his mind. She didn't know how to quell it or even if she really wanted to. Pace had it coming to him, for more than what had happened with Cam. He was a little shit, and his actions had far-reaching consequences.

The flight was easy enough, and soon, they were transported a couple of miles from campus to the hotel where they would stay for the night. They were all instructed to stay in their rooms and not make a disturbance. A special announcement was made about anyone getting in serious trouble if found in a room with a member of the opposite sex.

Bryna shrugged it off, as did everyone else. Most of the girls were dating someone or at least sleeping with someone on the team. She didn't understand what the big deal was.

"Big plans tonight?" Stacia whispered amidst the group of students congregated in the lobby waiting to be dismissed.

Bryna shrugged. "You?"

"I was wondering if we could use our room…if you're going to see E?"

She bit her lip. "You haven't told Pace that Eric and I are together, have you?"

Stacia bounced lightly from one foot to the other. "I'm sorry!" She covered her face and shook her head. "I'm so bad with secrets. I only told him, and I made him *swear* not to say anything to anyone, not even you! He hasn't said anything. I promise. I'd kick his ass if he told anyone."

Bryna sighed heavily. "Great. Just great, S."

"I know. I'm horrible. I tried, but I'm so bad, and he's so good at figuring it all out anyway."

"I guess you can use our room, but if it somehow slips that I'm with Eric and I get in trouble, you *know* I'm blaming him for this, right?"

"No way, B. He would never do that."

Bryna rolled her eyes. *Why is Stacia so naive when it comes to Pace? Is it just that he is a quarterback or is it something more?* She didn't get it. He was pretty evil, all things considered.

She hadn't told Stacia about Pace's part in what had happened with Cam, and she really wanted to do it in the moment. But somehow, she didn't think Stacia would believe her. Stacia hadn't listened any other time Bryna had told her about Pace's deceit.

Her eyes found Pace's in the crowd. As if sensing her eyes on him, he turned to look at her.

A smug smirk crossed his face, and he raised his eyebrows in question. *Yes?*

She pursed her lips and flipped him off across the room. He tilted his head back and laughed. *Great.*

"Tell him that if he rats me out about Eric, I will tell the coach that he's in our room," she told Stacia honestly.

"You would rat me out?" she gasped.

"I think it's a strong incentive for nothing to go wrong tonight."

"You really think he would do that?"

"Positive."

"Okay. I really don't," she said. "But be careful if you're that worried."

Be careful. But she made no suggestion to stay in instead.

The girls brought their bags up to their room, and Bryna waited for her signal from Eric to sneak into his room. She hadn't even done this in high school. No one had cared enough for her to have to sneak around. But she wanted to spend the night with Eric.

A knock at the door jolted her, and Stacia rushed over to open it. Pace strode in like he owned the place. He seemed surprised to see Bryna.

"No late-night rendezvous with the new flavor of the week?" he asked.

Stacia smacked him. "Be nice."

Pace kissed Stacia hard on the lips, but he never agreed to be nice. Bryna knew he wouldn't be nice to her. They had too much animosity between them. Not to mention, she was pretty sure he still wanted to sleep with her...Stacia be damned.

Her phone dinged.

Ready.

Eric. Finally. Time to get away from her fucking stepbrother.

"Just remember," she said, stepping up to Pace and poking him hard in the chest, "I don't trust you. So, if you do anything to fuck this up, you're hurting Stacia, not just me or you."

"I don't have any plans, *Bri*."

She glared at his use of her nickname. "You always have plans."

"Oh, we're so much alike, sis."

"Stop antagonizing her, Pace," Stacia said. "Go on. Pace isn't going to do anything."

"Good."

Bryna left the room and headed up a couple of floors. She knocked on Eric's door. Her stomach was knotted, knowing there would be consequences if they were caught, but she was also excited. The danger made it enticing.

Eric opened the door and pulled her inside by the middle. He slammed the door shut, swept her off her feet, and carried her to the king-sized bed in the middle of the room.

"I missed you," he said into her hair.

She turned her face and kissed him with a sigh. "I missed you, too."

Their bodies melded together, and she forgot all about her argument with Pace. As she got lost in Eric, all the warnings left her mind. This was how it was supposed to be.

Knock. Knock. Knock.

Bryna blearily opened her eyes and looked over at the clock. *6:00 a.m.*

"Fuck!" Eric cried.

She was still in his room. She had passed out. "Shit! Who is at the door?"

"I don't know. Throw some clothes on, and go into the bathroom or something. I'll go find out what's going on."

Bryna hastily changed and rushed into the bathroom. *How old am I?* She was a fucking adult. She didn't need rules about what she could do at night.

Eric cracked open the door, and she heard him speaking to the person on the other side. "What's up? It's six in the morning."

"Sorry, Eric. Coach wanted us up and at a morning meeting in half an hour. He wanted me to let you know."

Eric wiped his eyes and nodded. "All right. I'll be there. Thanks, Coach Morris."

Phew. Just one of the assistant coaches.

"Sure thing."

Eric closed the door with a sigh. "Jesus, that freaked me the fuck out."

"Yeah, these new regulations are insane," Bryna said, coming out of the bathroom. "For a second, I thought that Pace had given us away, and we were in some big trouble. I actually had the weirdest dream that I snuck out of the room while Coach was investigating. I ran downstairs and turned Pace in for his deceit. It ended before I found out what happened to him though."

Eric laughed. "You have an active imagination."

"You're right."

He pulled her into a hug. The adrenaline was wearing off, and she felt really tired again. She had to be up soon to get ready for the game, but she still felt exhausted.

"I guess Pace didn't do anything bad this time around."

"Maybe he's learned his lesson," Eric said, but he didn't sound like he believed it. "Go on back upstairs, and get some rest. I'll see you at the game."

He kissed her long and hard. Each kiss had a hint of desperation. It was like they both wanted to ensure that if this was the last kiss they ever had, it would be perfect.

Bryna scurried out of Eric's room and went upstairs to get a little bit more sleep. Pace was gone when she arrived, and she was thankful that it was just she and Stacia.

When they woke up and were getting ready for the game, Stacia glanced over at her and asked, "Everything okay last night?"

"Yeah. Surprisingly."

Stacia smiled bright. "See? We both were just having a good time. Nothing to worry about."

Bryna relaxed and tried to believe Stacia. "I hope you're right."

They were driven over to the field early that morning. It was a noon game, and the sun was bright overhead. This game was important if they wanted to make it to another conference championship. They had already lost to Oregon earlier this season at home.

Nothing seemed to go as planned, not a single thing in the game. Bryna had never watched so many things go wrong in one game. It was like watching a live update of her love life over the past year. Injuries, bad calls, dropped balls, missed field goals. Everything that could happen, happened.

There it was. The final score. Loss.

They had lost to Colorado.

It was a crushing blow. After an undefeated season last year, no one was prepared for two losses so early in the year.

The team left the field with heavy hearts. The Colorado fans were cheering loudly in the stands. They had all stayed to watch last year's national champions be brought low.

Eric came up beside her but didn't say anything. She knew they were both frustrated with what had happened.

Stacia was in front of them, trying to console Pace. His objections to Marshall were getting louder and louder and drawing attention. The last thing they needed was for a camera to catch what he was saying.

"None of this shit would have happened if they'd put me in as quarterback. Marshall fucked up this game. He lost it for us," he spat viciously.

"We can't change it now," Stacia said.

"We can change the fucking coaching staff being up Marshall's ass. He's not Blaine. He's not going first round at the draft. Figure your shit out and work it out. Put me in instead."

Stacia opened her mouth to say something more, but Eric lost it.

He grabbed Pace by the collar and threw him up against the cement wall. "Shut your fucking mouth."

Bryna's eyes bugged out, and she glanced around to see if any media were in the tunnel. It looked clear, but fuck, they could get in so much trouble.

"Get off me!" Pace growled.

They were nearly an even match. Eric had about an inch on Pace, but Pace was still in pads, so he looked bigger than Eric at the moment.

"You're a worthless piece of shit. If I had it my way, the coaching staff would never put you in as quarterback.

You have to prove yourself before you get playing time, and you don't fucking deserve it after what you did."

Bryna grabbed Eric's arm and tried to pull him back. "Eric, stop! What if someone sees? Stop it!"

Stacia tried to get between them. "Eric, let him go now."

Eric pushed off the wall and took a step away from Pace, but they were in a standoff.

"I don't know what the fuck you think I did, but you and I both know I deserve playing time over Marshall."

"I don't believe that at all."

Pace laughed. He looked between Eric and Bryna. "Have you been listening to Bryna? Is all of this because you're banging my sister? So has everyone else, Eric."

It happened so fast. Bryna hadn't even seen it coming. Eric swung and punched Pace right in the face. They were on top of each other in an instant. Bryna and Stacia desperately tried to get between them, but when two giant football players over six feet tall want to fight, there was nothing they could do to stop them. A few of the other guys rushed over and tore them apart. Marshall was one of them.

He grabbed Eric and hauled him away. "What the fuck, E?" Marshall asked.

"He's pissed because he's banging my sister and listening to her drivel," Pace said. He was holding his face. Blood was pouring out of his nose, and it looked like he had a busted eyebrow.

Eric seemed perfectly okay. He had gotten the jump on Pace.

"You got her fucking attacked, you fucking asshole!" Eric yelled at Pace.

"What are you talking about?" Pace asked. His eyes landed on Bryna.

"After what you said to Cam, he physically attacked Bryna."

"What did you tell Cam?" Stacia asked. Her voice was suddenly flat.

"The truth," Pace spat. He was still so riled up that he hadn't heard the warning in Stacia's voice. "That Bryna is a slut and fucks around and likes to play games with people."

Stacia glared at him. "You went behind my back and behind her back to tell Cam that shit? He almost raped her!" she cried.

"What?" Pace asked, shocked. He turned to Bryna. "Seriously?"

"Yeah," Bryna whispered. *Great. Now all of her dirty laundry had been aired to the football team.*

"I never believed her when she said you fucked with her life on purpose," Stacia said. "Now, I get it. I don't understand it, but I get it. I can't be a part of that. You hurt my best friend."

"Stacia, I didn't know he would do that."

"And you didn't care!" she yelled back. "Then, you won't care as I walk away."

Bryna stared on in amazement as Stacia turned and left. Pace looked stunned.

"I didn't know," he said to Bryna.

"Too little, too late," she said.

Then, she jogged after Stacia and wrapped an arm around her shoulders. She released the tiniest of sobs that Bryna knew was sure to turn into a waterfall once it really hit her that she had lost her quarterback.

FORTY-FOUR

THE NEXT WEEKEND, the team won a stunning victory at home. It was Halloween, and the annual Slutfest party was being thrown at a house the cheerleading captain, Lauren, had rented for the event. It was one of the biggest events of the year, and people had been talking about it all week. Lauren had promised that she was going all out this year, bigger and better than ever before. Reportedly half of the student population had been invited.

"I don't want to go," Stacia said.

"You need to get out and stop moping around about Pace," Trihn said.

"I'm not moping. I'm mourning."

"You're not mourning. Nothing died!" Trihn reminded her.

"It feels like it."

"It'll be fine," Bryna said. She finished applying fire-red lipstick and then turned to her friends. "The party will be so big that you won't even see him. All right?"

"What if I want to?"

"You don't," Trihn said. "He's an ass. Think about what he did."

"I know," she murmured. "But…this sucks."

Stacia had been like this all week. She'd cried herself to sleep every night, and Bryna had seen that she had a dozen missed calls from Pace on her phone. She felt bad for Stacia. She hated seeing her friend in pain, but she was glad Stacia had taken the blinders off. He wasn't a good person. Stacia needed to drop him from his pedestal, preferably on his head.

"You're going. That's the end of it," Bryna said, putting her foot down. "Now, I'm going to head over to Eric's. I'll meet you guys there."

Stacia's bottom lip popped out. "Have fun with your football player."

"Eric doesn't play football anymore. He isn't defined by what he does. He's defined by the kind of person he is. He is good and kind and valuable without the title," Bryna said. "That is the kind of person you deserve, too."

Trihn and Stacia stared at her in shock. A year ago, she would never have said anything like that. In fact, she would have laughed at someone who had said that to her. A lot had changed in a year.

She smiled at her friends and then exited the apartment.

She was in an excellent mood by the time she arrived at Eric's house. This was their official coming-out party. She liked to call it that, considering their history. After the blowup at the game last weekend, everyone had found out they were dating, but they still hadn't really been seen together as a couple yet. Tonight was the night.

She walked into Eric's house, unannounced, and found him lounging in the living room, watching *The Avengers.*

"You're not dressed up," she said. She placed her hands on her hips.

They had both agreed to dress up.

His eyes crawled over her body, and his jaw dropped. She appreciated the look as she had gone all out in a bright red devil costume, including a red corset, boy shorts, and garter with mile-high heels, horns, and a tail.

"You didn't either," he joked.

"You're hilarious."

"Queen Bee is out to play tonight." He hopped off the couch and straight toward her.

He moved in for a kiss, and she darted out of the way.

"Lipstick."

He laughed. "All right. I don't have to kiss those lips then." He kissed down her throat while his hands grabbed her ass.

"Dear God, we're never going to make it out of this house, are we?" she asked.

He met her gaze. "Do you want to? I'm not going to be able to keep my hands off of you all night as it is."

"I think this will be fun to witness," she teased. "Now, what the hell are you wearing anyway?"

"I'm Coach Galloway." He pointed at the name on his shirt.

She glared at him. "You stole one of his shirts and are basically going as yourself? That's not dressing up, Cowboy."

"All right. I hate dressing up, but you look hot."

"Jerk."

He looked her up and down and seemed to be considering something. "I do have a great idea for a costume."

"What's that?"

"How about you be the devil on my shoulder?"

He scooped her up before she had a chance to realize what he'd said, and he effortlessly hoisted her onto his shoulder.

"Oh my God, Eric, put me down. Right now! What the hell is wrong with you?" But she was laughing.

"Come on, Hollywood. Devil on my shoulder." He adjusted the weight so that one arm was holding both of her legs to keep her from moving.

"I get the joke! Now, put me down."

"I don't know about that." He playfully smacked her ass. "I have a pretty awesome view right now."

"I'm going to kill you."

"I don't think you're exactly in a position to say that," he teased.

"You just wait."

He laughed and righted her once more. "You're so feisty."

"Damn right I am," she snapped.

He grabbed her face, and ignoring her protest about the lipstick, he kissed her long and hard. The world slipped away, and she remembered all too well why she and Eric were a perfect match.

He released her and wiped his mouth off with a laugh. "You were right about the lipstick."

She leaned into him. "I can think of a time you would want it on you."

"Oh, yeah?" he asked, intrigued.

"When it makes a circle around your cock." She winked.

"How about we skip the party, and you show me exactly what you mean?"

Bryna giggled again. "You can't get out of going out with me, but I promise to be a very bad girl later."

Eric drove them over to the Slutfest party in his Jeep with the promise to stay sober enough to drive them home. Lauren had ensured everyone that there were a ton of rooms for her friends to stay the night if they got drunk, but neither of them wanted to do that when they had a big comfortable bed at Eric's house.

True to Lauren's word, the house was already slammed with people when they arrived. They fought their way through the crowd. A couple of kegs were out back, and there were coolers full of Hunch Punch. Eric scooped Bryna out a glass and grabbed a beer for himself before they ventured back inside to find their friends.

Music was blaring from the surround-sound speakers. Bryna caught the eye of the DJ, and he waved. It was the guy from the radio station that she had used for her party last semester. She thought his name was Damon or Damien or something. She waved back before leaving that room behind.

They ran right into Stacia and Trihn as they entered the house.

"There you are!" Bryna cried.

Stacia looked hot in a slutty referee costume, but Trihn had surprised them all with her outfit. She had gone all out in a cheerleading uniform. She was wearing Stacia's black-and-gold Gamblers top and a tiny little skirt with plain white shoes. Her ombre hair was pulled up into a high ponytail, and a huge gold-and-silver bow took over her head. She looked gorgeous. It was also crazy to see Trihn in a cheerleading uniform. She was model tall and filled out the uniform like a champ, but it was so not her normal edgy look.

Eric even laughed when he saw her. "I get it," he joked.

Trihn shrugged and uncertainly looked back at Neal. Bryna knew that Trihn and Neal had had *another* argument about the party. She was sure that he wasn't pleased that, on top of the party, he also had to deal with her looking like a cheerleader. Bryna truly thought it was only a matter of days before Neal would be kicked to the curb, but Trihn had insisted that this was the only problem in their relationship.

"What are you dressed up as?" Bryna asked Neal.

His eyes met hers with disdain, and Bryna plastered a fake smile on her face.

"I don't dress up for Halloween," he told her.

"Let me guess. It's supposed to be a sacred night for the dead to walk the earth again. All Hallows' Eve and Dia de los Muertos and all that," she said.

"No," he said dryly. "It's just dumb."

"Did you have a childhood?" she asked. It was pretty sad when she was the one asking that question.

"Do you consider this childhood?"

"There's candy."

"Hey, man, I get it," Eric said, breaking the tension. "I'm not dressed up either. It's better to just have the women dress up anyway."

Neal smiled at Eric, but Bryna wasn't sure he agreed with that either.

"Why don't we go get a drink?" Trihn suggested. She practically dragged Neal away from them.

"God, what a buzzkill," Stacia said. "I mean, I'm sad, but he drains the life out of her."

"And the rest of the room," Bryna agreed.

"Oh, shit!" Stacia squeaked.

Bryna's eyes followed hers, and she saw Pace walking into the room.

"Um…" Stacia mumbled. She grabbed the closest jock to her and ground her body on him.

Bryna wasn't even sure she knew his name, not that it mattered.

Pace looked furious and stormed toward Stacia.

Bryna cut him off before he reached her. "No."

"Get out of the way, Bri."

"No. You need to let her be."

Pace glared down at her. "Look, I didn't know that shit with Cam was going to happen, and I fucking took care of it."

"What do you mean, you took care of it?" Bryna asked in confusion.

"I returned the favor from Eric." He pointed at his eye where the bruising was still healing from where Eric had punched him.

"You beat him up?"

"Roughed him up a bit."

"Why?" she asked, confused.

"You drive me nuts, Bryna. Our family is fucked up. You put me through hell in high school. Being around you makes me want to tear my hair out, but…" He grumbled under his breath, looking away.

"Wait, what did you say?"

"You're still technically my family, I guess, if only by marriage. I can fuck with you. No one else can fuck with you."

Bryna stared up at him, perplexed. "You have a conscience?"

"Fuck no!" He glared down at her. "I just want you to talk to Stacia for me."

"Are you kidding me?" Bryna asked. "After everything you've done, beating up Cam doesn't change this shit. You threatened to come to school here if I didn't sleep with you. You told Felicity about Jude. You plot to sabotage me over and over again when I have done *nothing* to you. You deserve what happened with Stacia, and you should stay away from her."

He looked like he wanted to say more, but she turned and left. Eric gave her a questioning look, but she shook her head. He didn't need to fight her battles for her.

Stacia seemed fine now that she was occupied.

Bryna downed the rest of her drink in a hurry. "Let's go get another."

When she threw back the second one just as fast, Eric got worried. "Maybe you should slow down."

"Maybe I shouldn't," she said, pressing herself against him.

"You play dirty." He ran his hands down her sides. "I want to get you out of this costume. People have seen us together. Can we leave now?"

She giggled and took another sip of her drink. "Maybe."

"Eric!" Andrew called from behind them.

Bryna turned around and saw him strolling over to them with Marshall, and a few of the other guys from the team in tow.

"Hey, man," Eric said without his normal enthusiasm.

"Dude, so this is really happening?" Andrew gestured between Bryna and Eric.

"Yep," she said confidently.

"He laid Pace out for her, so I would say so," Marshall said. His smile was genuine as he shook Eric's hand. "Happy for you, man."

"Yeah, but I just don't understand," Andrew said. He swung his beer around, clearly tipsy.

"Let it go, Andrew," Marshall said.

"I mean, aren't you all wondering how they're actually dating when Bryna just likes to fuck?" Andrew asked.

Bryna's eyes darkened. She was truly the devil in that instant. "You're right, Andrew." She held her hand up before Eric could barrel into his friend. "I do like to fuck. I just found someone better at it."

"Oh," all the guys said at once.

Andrew turned a deep shade of red at her comment. "Be ready for her to run scared, bro."

Eric stepped forward. "I recommend that you leave. Bri is with me now. Anything else that you say about her will come back tenfold from me."

"I mean…whatever, man. If you want my sloppy seconds…"

Bryna threw herself in between Eric and Andrew. "He is drunk and an idiot," she reminded Eric. "Not to mention, jealous. Very unbelievably jealous. It is not worth your time or anger."

Eric took a deep breath and then stepped back. "You're right. Sober him up, and get him out of here."

Eric grabbed her hand without a word and pulled her through the party. She finished off her third glass of Hunch Punch on the way up the stairs to the second floor. She was staggering from the booze as they veered toward an empty room.

He pulled her inside, shut the door, and locked it. "I think I want to find out what's under that costume now."

"You already know," she said. She ran her hands down his front. "Don't be upset about those guys. I know what my reputation was. It's just me and you now, right?"

"Yes. I just want to kill everyone who talks about you like that," he told her.

"You wouldn't have a football team to coach. And who cares? I'm with you now."

He smiled and kissed her all over again. He walked her backward toward the bed. She climbed up there, but he turned her around and bent her at the waist. He reached out and stroked her through the thin layer of material that covered her body. She heard his pants hit the floor, and then he was peeling back the boy shorts.

"I've been thinking about getting you out of this outfit all night," he groaned.

The head touched her opening, and her body tightened in response.

"Take me then," she told him.

And he did. He plunged inside her. From that angle, he hit her so deep, and she cried out. She hoped no one could hear her over the music, but she didn't care.

Eric grabbed her with one hand on her shoulder and the other one on her hip, and then he pumped into her. It was exhilarating and wonderful. All the anger about what the guys had said fueled him. He drove into her over and over.

His fingers tangled into her hair, and he yanked her head backward. She moaned at the feel of it. *God, I like it rough.*

"God, I love when you moan and scream," he said.

She moaned louder. He was delivering after all.

Their bodies were perfectly matched. She couldn't stop herself. She released and felt her walls contracting around him. He grunted and jackknifed into her as he came viciously.

She lay there, panting for a minute, before cleaning up in the adjacent bathroom. Her hair was a hot mess. She finger-combed it, but anyone looking at her would know that someone had been pulling it. But she didn't care at this point.

She turned to find Eric all put back together. The anger from earlier had dissipated. He looked euphoric.

"Want to get out of here?" he asked.

Bryna laughed. "We haven't been here that long."

"But I'm thinking of taking all those clothes off again already, and I'm not sure I'll have the patience to find another room."

She was still high off of her orgasm and maybe a little more than tipsy. All the alcohol seemed to hit her at once, and she took an unsteady step forward.

"What was in those drinks?" she murmured.

"Everclear."

"My whole body is woozy. I can't feel my head."

Eric looked frightened. "In a bad way?"

"In a drunk way." She bumped into him. "I want to dance!"

He laughed. "Okay, but no more drinks, crazy."

She nodded her head, but she wasn't sure if she was agreeing with him. Another drink didn't sound *that* bad.

She took his hand, and he started down the stairs in front of her. She was watching her steps, so she wouldn't slip in her heels when Eric stopped suddenly. Bryna fell into him and latched on to his arm to stay steady. *Whoa!* She was way drunker than she thought.

"Why'd you stop?" she slurred.

"Uh…let's go this way."

He tried to move her off to the right, but that was when Bryna saw what had stopped him short.

Audrey.

FORTY-FIVE

BRYNA MADE EYE CONTACT with Audrey across the few feet that separated them. She hadn't thought about the fact that if Lauren was inviting everyone from school to the party that it meant Audrey would show up. She had been at Bryna's own party at the house that Hugh had purchased for her. But it hadn't clicked that she might be here today.

"What the fuck, Eric?" Audrey cried. She closed the gap between them.

Bryna wrinkled her nose. The last time she had seen the bitch, Audrey had been on all fours on Eric's bed. Just the thought made the liquor in her stomach turn.

"Audrey, don't do this tonight. Just go back to your party," Eric encouraged.

"Are you joking? I can't believe you're with this whore now!" Audrey yelled loudly.

It was loud enough that nearly everyone in the immediate vicinity looked over to see who she was talking about.

"She's not a whore," Eric said calmly. "And we're going to walk away and pretend this never happened."

"You can't be serious. You're scared of golddigging jersey-chasers, and you've settled for the biggest bitch of them all?" Audrey accused.

"You have no fucking clue what you're talking about," Eric growled.

"I might be a bitch, but that does not make me a gold digger or a jersey-chaser," Bryna spat.

"You're known for both, and you want me to think it's a coincidence that you've chosen Eric?"

"He's not even a football player anymore!" Bryna yelled at her.

"Somehow that negates his multimillion-dollar trust fund?" Audrey yelled back.

Bryna's mouth dropped open. "His what?" She looked at Eric in confusion. *What the hell is she talking about?*

"Audrey," Eric said in warning, "that's enough."

"What is she talking about, Eric?" Bryna asked.

"It's not enough. I hate to see you like this." The tone of Audrey's voice changed when she looked up at him. She sounded soothing, like she wanted to reach out and touch him. "You shouldn't have to debase yourself by dating her. You told me yourself that you would never be interested in a slut like her. You said she was the worst kind of human imaginable."

"You said that?" Bryna asked. Her addled mind couldn't keep up with everything that was going on.

Did Eric really say those things about me? And what the fuck is Audrey talking about? A trust fund? He's from Dallas. He wants to be a football coach. How the hell would he have that kind of money?

"No, I did not say that."

"Now, you're lying?" Audrey asked in disgust. "You've really lowered your standards."

"You jealous bitch," Bryna spat.

"Fuck off, Audrey. You're proving me right for every reason that I left you in the first place," he said.

Then, he pushed Bryna through the crowd without a backward glance. They made it out the door and to his car before she blew up.

"What the fuck was all that about, Eric?"

He sighed and sank into the driver's seat. "I don't know. I never expected her to show up and try to sabotage me."

"She's a fucking twat."

"That…is true," Eric agreed.

"Let's go back to your place." Bryna crossed her arms and sank back into the seat. She had a lot to process. She didn't know what to make of anything Audrey had said. *Had she acted like a major bitch because I was now dating her ex-boyfriend? Is anything she had said actually true?*

Eric drove back to his house and parked the Jeep. Bryna got out without a word, and he followed her inside. She felt ridiculous, having this conversation in a slutty devil's costume, but things needed to be said now.

"So…did you say all those things?"

"No."

"You never called me a slut or the worst human imaginable?"

Eric sighed and ran a hand back through his hair. "Okay. Yes, I said those things, but I didn't know you then. Once I got to know you, I realized you were nothing like that person."

"God," Bryna grumbled. She sat down on the couch and pushed her hands up into her hair. "I'm drunk, and it's Halloween. I don't want to be doing this right now."

"I'm sorry." Eric sank to his knees before her. He pulled her hands away from her face and stared deep into her eyes. "If I could take back the things I said about you

411

and all the other cheerleaders, then I would. It was a total dick move."

"I know, I know," she breathed. "We were both under the illusion that we were different people at the time."

"Exactly." He seemed to breathe a sigh of relief.

"But I don't get the other stuff. What the fuck is with Audrey? What was she saying about a trust fund?" she asked in confusion.

"That…is complicated."

"Well, we have all night."

He nodded and took a seat next to her. "I met Audrey my freshman year and thought she was perfect. I trusted her implicitly from the start. When I blew my knee out, she was there for me every single day. She went to therapy with me. She encouraged me and helped me heal. I'm not sure I would be as strong as I am without her."

Bryna nodded. "Then, I guess…we're all in her debt."

"She would want you to think that. She sure holds that over my head. But she didn't do it for me. It took me a long time to realize that. Even after I broke up with her, I still went back to her, thinking maybe I was wrong, until she would do something again that made me realize that I was right."

"Why did she do it?"

"She did it because she wanted a football player. When I decided I wasn't going to risk playing anymore, she freaked the fuck out." His voice was soft, as if recalling a recent injury. "She went on a rampage and talked to the coaches, the therapists, my parents—I mean, everyone— begging them to convince me otherwise. She wanted to get her paycheck at the end of all this, and when I refused to give it to her, she turned into a lunatic."

Bryna's mouth opened and then closed. On some level, she could see Stacia doing the same thing. "Maybe she just cared about you?"

"No. She cared about herself."

"Then, why did you keep sleeping with her?" she asked.

"Guilt mostly." He sighed and looked sad. "In my head, I *knew* that she was using me. I mean…I knew what she wanted from me at least. But she was there for me. She took care of me. She helped me so much. It's hard to erase someone like that from your life, especially with a constant reminder from her."

"I think that makes sense. It's hard to let go of your past. That is something I'm very aware of."

He smiled forlornly. "I couldn't really escape it, so I would say horrible things about people who were after someone for what they had, and I thought you were no different. But when I got to know you over Christmas last year, things changed. Everything changed." He reached out and stroked her cheek. "You changed my world."

She smiled. "You changed mine, too."

"The other thing is…I wasn't a hundred percent honest."

She stiffened. "About what?"

"What Audrey said about my trust fund is true."

"You have a multimillion-dollar trust fund?" she asked in a whisper. It was strange to think she wasn't even as eager as she once would have been. Her heart would have soared with her good fortune, but this was Eric. He could have had nothing, and she would still love him.

"Yeah." He awkwardly looked away. "It's weird to talk about. It's not really *me*. But my family is big money oil. They have been for generations."

"Oil," she whispered.

"Yeah. There's a good chunk of land in the middle of nowhere with my name on it."

Bryna laughed. Once she started, she couldn't stop.

Eric looked at her warily. "Why are you laughing?"

"I have no idea. It's just…you have a trust fund?"

"Yeah?"

Bryna wiped her eyes where tears were forming. "I find that hysterical. After all this shit I've gone through, somehow, I ended up with someone wealthy."

Eric stiffened. She realized how harsh her words sounded as soon as they had come out of her mouth. That wasn't how she had meant them.

She reached out and grabbed his hand. "It was never about the money. I have money. Digging was about power and control. What I realized was that I didn't need that at all. I needed an equal. I have no interest in your money. I love you. I loved you before. I love you now. I'd love you penniless."

He raised his eyebrow. "Really?"

"Well, I'd give you a few pennies, but yes. This doesn't change anything. You're still you. I'm still me. We're still us."

He smiled. "I like that."

"Me, too," she said before kissing him.

The next morning, Bryna awoke with a wicked headache. Whatever had been in that Hunch Punch was something fierce. She swallowed down what felt like a bottle of Tylenol and a gallon of water. After a few extra hours of shut-eye, she felt mostly whole again.

Eric was downstairs, studying, when she resurfaced.

"What time is it?" she said.

He checked his watch. "Two."

"Jesus."

"Yeah. I was going to come wake you, but you seemed like you needed the sleep."

"Thanks." She took a seat next to him at the table.

"Margaritas?" he offered.

She laughed. "I know it's Sunday, and I'm all for our margarita Sunday, but I think I'm going to have to pass."

His eyes met hers across the table, and she saw fear reflected back to her.

"What?"

"I'm sorry about last night," he said. "I know we're good now, but Audrey shouldn't have said those things, and I should have told you sooner about my parents."

Bryna gave him a rueful smile. "How exactly would you have brought that up? 'Oh, P.S., Bri, my parents own big oil in Texas.'"

"Uh…yeah, that's about right."

"You shouldn't have to worry about talking money to me. I don't need to know how much you're worth because I already know your real worth. And Audrey was just jealous."

"I'm glad you feel that way, but I'm still sorry." He reached across the table and gave her a kiss.

"You can stop apologizing. You have no reason to apologize, and I don't need an explanation from you. We're on the same page." She nodded her head, as if that was the end of the conversation. "I do, however, have something I want to talk to you about."

"Should I be worried?" he joked.

"Horribly."

He made a face at her.

"I think I know what I want to do with the money and jewelry that Hugh gave me while we were together, and I was wondering if you could help me. That relationship is totally over, and I don't want that money and guilt hanging between us any longer. You know?"

"I know what you mean." He arched an eyebrow, suddenly curious. "What do you want to do? I don't think he's going to take any of it back."

Bryna shook her head. She didn't think so either. Actually, she knew he wouldn't. If he could toss a Harry Winston necklace over a balcony and return the check for the house without hesitation, she knew that he wouldn't take the money back now.

"I don't think so either."

"Then, what?"

"I thought I would donate it to charity in his name. Does that sound dumb?"

Eric's face lit up. "No. That sounds like a great idea."

"I've thought about a few charities, but I really don't know which one to pick."

"Hmm." Eric sat back and contemplated it for a minute. Then, something struck him, and he jolted forward. "Did you ever find out how his wife died?"

"Um…yeah. Breast cancer."

Eric nodded at her as if that were her answer.

"Oh! That's perfect. You're right. I'll donate the money through him in his wife's honor. It won't make what I did better," she acknowledged, "but maybe it will show him that I did care and didn't mean to hurt him like that."

Eric smiled at her and kissed her knuckles. "Look at you. All grown-up."

She laughed. "Not entirely, I think, but I don't want this hanging over my head. Hugh is a decent man. He deserved better."

"There's nothing you can do about the past. Do what you can to make yourself feel better now that you've moved on, and everything else will fall into place."

"You're right."

Her phone buzzed in her purse, pulling her away from their conversation.

"It's been buzzing on and off all morning," Eric told her.

"Weird." She picked up her phone and saw that her dad was calling. "Oh no."

"What?"

"It's my dad."

"Is that bad?"

She bit her lip and steeled herself for this conversation. She needed to be hard to hear what he was about to say because she could almost guarantee he was going to cancel on her. There was no other reason for him to call her the weekend before homecoming.

"Hey, Daddy," she said.

"Hey, sweetheart! How are you?"

Bryna took a deep breath. "Good. Just get it over with."

"Get what over with?" he asked.

"You know, just go ahead and tell me you're canceling."

"Bryna," her dad said softly, "I'm not canceling."

"You're not?" She couldn't keep the surprise from her voice.

"No, and I'm sorry if you think the only reason I call you is with bad news."

"We don't exactly have the best track record."

He sighed. "No, we don't, but we'll work on that. I actually called because I wanted to let you know that the whole family is going to come up on Thursday for homecoming. Celia, Lacey, Kacey, and baby Zoe, of course, are all going to come up with me. We thought that we could meet you and Pace at the condo and have a dinner with just us family."

"Really?" she asked.

She wasn't sure if she could quite process this. Her dad wanted to have dinner with the whole family, and he was coming to homecoming to see her.

"Yes, I think it would be fun. I haven't seen you or Pace since school started, and I thought we could spend time together."

"Can my boyfriend come?" she asked without thinking.

Eric's head popped up, and their eyes met across the table. Maybe proper etiquette would have been to ask Eric first if he wanted to come and meet her dad, but it was too late now.

"Boyfriend? I didn't know you had a boyfriend. You haven't mentioned anyone since Gates—"

"Yep, new guy. His name is Eric."

"Well, sure. Tell Eric he's invited. I'd like to meet the guy who is dating my daughter."

She laughed. "Sounds good, Daddy. See you on Thursday."

She hung up the phone and shrugged. "I guess you're meeting the fam this week."

FORTY-SIX

"WHY ARE YOU FIDGETING?" Bryna asked.

She brushed her hand down the front of Eric's button-down shirt. The sleeves were rolled up to his elbows, and he had on a pair of dark wash jeans. He looked down at her with his hazel eyes, trying to conceal his worry.

"Seriously, I never guessed you would be afraid of meeting the rest of my family."

"It's more your dad."

"My dad?" She raised her eyebrows. "What about him?"

"Between football and his movies, he's a legend!"

Bryna laughed and pushed him away. "He's just my dad. Football was a long time ago. You of all people should know that football doesn't define who you are."

"What about the movies?"

"He's good at what he does," she acknowledged, "but he's still just my dad. You should be more afraid that I'm introducing you as my boyfriend to my dad."

"Okay. Now, I'm more nervous."

She shook her head and dragged him out of his house. Her heels clicked against the tile, and she tucked her dark pink skirt underneath her as she slid into the passenger seat of his Jeep.

Bryna and Eric arrived at the condo early. Her dad was still a good fifteen minutes away as they walked up to the front door. Bryna felt weird about knocking on the door to the place where she used to live, but this was Pace's place now. Just another reason she didn't want to walk inside.

Eric knocked for her, realizing she was just going to stand there, staring. He kissed the top of her head while they waited. Pace opened the door a minute later. He looked between them, grunted, and then turned away.

They followed him inside. It was crazy to see the transformation of her condo. He had certainly made it into a bachelor's pad. She shuddered to think how many women had probably wandered in and out of here.

They all stood around in silence. Eric and Pace were still on unsteady ground after Eric had punched him after the Colorado game. Bryna was the last one who wanted to break the tension anyway. It was nice to have someone on her side about the whole Pace situation.

Finally, Pace broke the silence, "Have you heard from Stacia?"

"I live with her."

"Yeah, I know. I mean...has she asked about me?"

Bryna made a face. Even if Stacia had, she wasn't about to tell Pace that. "No."

He clenched his jaw and nodded. "Okay."

The knock at the door interrupted the awkwardness. Pace walked over and answered it.

Lawrence, Celia, Lacey, Kacey, and another woman holding Zoe, who Celia introduced as the new nanny, all paraded into the condo at once. They were a bustle of hugs and kisses for both her and Pace. Even the twins seemed to have some enthusiasm in their steps. It was probably because they were out of school for tomorrow, which meant no Harmony Prep for a day.

"And this must be Eric," Lawrence said. He stepped forward and shook Eric's hand.

"Yes, sir."

"Eric Wilkins in fact," Lawrence said with a smile. "You didn't tell me this, Bryna."

She shrugged. "Wasn't sure if you would recognize him."

"Wasn't sure?" he asked. "After that impressive national championship win three years ago? How could anyone forget?"

Eric laughed and stared over at Bryna before looking back at her father. "I'm honored that you recognized me."

"Of course, I did. We're all proud Gamblers here."

The guys talked football.

In the meantime, Bryna walked over to the nanny and took Zoe in her arms. "Oh my God, she's so big."

Celia smiled and walked closer. "They grow so fast."

"I didn't know you were going to have a nanny."

"That's all Lawrence. I'd keep her close to me at all times if I could. Even though she's lucky number four for me, I want her near me. It's hard being away."

Bryna bounced her little sister in her arms. Zoe laughed and cooed up at Bryna. "I could see that."

"How have you been? I feel like I haven't seen you in forever. It was nice having you home for the summer, you know."

Bryna didn't take her eyes from the baby. "It was nice being home, but I've been so busy with school and cheer."

"Of course. Not to mention, a new young man," Celia said. She eyed Eric and wiggled her eyebrows. "I see you've found some of that love that you were asking me about at the hospital."

Bryna smiled as her eyes fell on Eric, too. He was talking to her dad as if they had known each other for years. She had known he had nothing to worry about.

"Seems I have," she said.

"Bryna! You didn't tell me that Eric was coaching," her father called.

"I didn't tell you anything actually. Just that he was coming." She handed the baby off to Celia with a smile and wandered over. "Should I have told you his life story ahead of time?"

"Now, Lawrence, give him room to breathe. You just met him. Don't want to run him off," Celia said.

"I don't mind," Eric said.

"Well, we do," Celia said. "We don't want to be late for our dinner reservation."

After Celia left Zoe with the nanny, they piled into two cars and drove to a nice steakhouse near campus. It wasn't a place where many students would go unless their parents were in town. Even Bryna had never actually been there before.

They were seated at a large table for seven with Bryna tucked in between Celia and Eric. Her father and Pace were across from her, and the girls were at the end of the table.

"So, did you two meet during football?" Celia asked.

"Actually, Eric showed me around campus on my visit during my senior year," Bryna answered.

"What are your plans for the future, Eric?" Lawrence asked, leaning forward.

He gave Bryna a meaningful look, and she almost laughed. It was weird to have people interested in what was going on in her life...with her boyfriend. Her father had never really cared about what happened with Gates, but he had known him for a while, so maybe that didn't count.

"I'm waiting to hear if I got into grad school for sports management here at LV State next year. I plan on spending two more years coaching with Coach Galloway and then getting a job as an assistant coach for another university when I graduate."

Her father nodded. "Good goals. Smart."

"More than Bryna can say," Pace spat under his mouth.

"Bryna has goals," Eric said, automatically defending her.

Pace stared him down. "I'd love to hear what her *goals* are. The last I heard, they were quite...colorful."

"Pace, don't be rude," Celia whispered.

Bryna sighed and shook her head. She had no interest in being baited by Pace. "Yes, I have goals, but we're not talking about me tonight."

"I'd love to hear them," her dad said.

Bryna bit her lip. "Um..."

She still hadn't told her dad about her interest in film. He didn't even know she was a film major. She hadn't been sure how to say it without it coming off poorly. She didn't want him to think that she wanted his help or that he would need to give her a job or something. Worse, she worried he would be flippant about the entire thing.

"Go on," Eric said. He squeezed her leg under the table.

"I'm actually a film major," she said. Her back was ramrod straight.

Her father's eyes brightened. "Film?"

"Yeah. I'm in history of film this semester and took intro to film last semester."

"That's great," Celia said. "Don't you think that's great, Lawrence?"

"What do you want to do with that?" he asked. Dad mode had fled, and director mode had returned.

She hated this. This wasn't what she'd wanted.

"I don't know. It's just something I'm good at," she said offhandedly.

Eric gave her a stern look. "Bri."

"I don't need anyone to make a big deal out of it."

"I was just curious," her dad said.

"Directing, okay? I'm interested in directing, but I don't need help, and it's just an idea at the moment," she said in a rush.

Her father broke out into a smile. "That's great!"

"It is?"

"I always hoped you would be interested in directing since you never took to acting. Plus, I would never want you to get into acting. You always seemed more interested in the behind-the-scenes anyway. Makes me proud to know you want to do this, too," he said.

His smile was broad, and she saw…admiration in his eyes.

"Really?"

"Absolutely. I understand you wanting to make it in Hollywood yourself. I was exactly the same way. But if you need something, I'm here," he said.

"Thank you," she breathed, relieved.

The rest of dinner went off without any more awkward exchanges. Even Pace seemed to loosen up. He still disagreed with Eric and didn't seem comfortable, but it was the best they could get at the moment. It made her happy that not only had she been able to get everyone in one place, but they also all liked Eric, and she had even confided in her father about film. A lot of big steps in one dinner.

Her father paid the check and then drove back to the condo. Bryna had classes in the morning, so she and Eric were planning to leave early.

"Bryna, do you mind if I have a word with you before you go?" her father asked.

"Uh…sure," she said, looking at Eric.

He smiled. "Don't mind me. I'm going to play with Zoe." He took her from Celia and rocked her in his arms.

Bryna's eyes widened. She couldn't believe how small Zoe looked in his huge arms.

"Okay. It'll just be a minute."

Bryna stepped out the back door with her father. It was dark and beautiful outside. The desert heat was gone and had been replaced with a nippy chill that sank into her through her shirt and skirt. But it didn't even matter. She was out here with her dad, and she hadn't been alone with him in a long time.

They were silent for a moment, just content with the other's company. It had been even longer since that happened. She had always been daddy's little girl. After the divorce and Celia, things had changed. For the first time…it almost felt like things were coming back together.

"Bryna, I want to apologize," her father said. He turned to face her.

"For what?"

"Everything. Too much to account for, but especially for homecoming last year. Not to mention, how absent I have been from your life for the last couple of years."

"Oh," she whispered in shock.

"I should have been here for you. You wanted me here for homecoming and Christmas the year before. You wanted me to be there for a lot of things. I know I can't make up for missing those things, but I want to try. I'm sorry. This isn't the way a father treats his daughter, and I know that now."

She didn't have any words. She had never thought this day would come. Things were better between them, but like Bryna herself, her father was stubborn with his apologies.

"I had my head up my ass long before Olivia and I got a divorce. The baby has made me see that my priorities were all out of alignment. With Celia's help, I realized the damage I did by not being around." He reached out and held her hands. "I don't want to wake up and find I don't have my daughter anymore."

Tears leaked from her eyes without warning. "You'll always have me," she whispered.

"Bryna"—he pulled her into a swift hug—"I love you, sweetheart."

"I love you, too, Dad."

He pulled back and wiped the tears from her eyes. "We're going to make things right between us."

"I'd really like that."

"I know your mother hasn't reached out like this, and I know we're not on the best of terms."

Bryna snorted.

"Not on good terms at all," he clarified. "But I don't wish bad things for her and you. You're still her daughter. I don't want to be completely selfish and keep you from her."

"I don't even know the last time I *saw* Mom," Bryna admitted.

"She needs a push. I worry I would be in her same place if it wasn't for Celia. Olivia might not want to see me, but I would go with you to see her if you want. I want my daughter to have a relationship with both her parents, and if you let her, one with Celia, too."

Bryna swallowed back the tears. "You'd go see Mom with me?"

"Of course."

"That would mean everything," she told him.

"Then, it's settled."

"I've missed you," she said, grabbing him for another hug.

She suddenly felt so very young, wrapped in her father's arms. But it was right. Hearing him say that he wanted to mend their relationship meant more than the world to her. It meant she could finally start to heal.

FORTY-SEVEN

THE HOMECOMING GAME was another impressive victory. Her father was named Alumnus of the Year, and their entire family took a picture on the field at the fifty-yard line. It was a high moment for Bryna for her college career.

Her family left on Sunday, and soon, she was back in classes again on Monday. History of film was wrapping up for the semester. She had managed to completely avoid Cam since their breakup, despite having a class together, but today, she wasn't lucky enough.

She practically stumbled into him on her way out of the classroom. She glared at him. There was still some pretty bad bruising around both of his eyes. Not as bad as it must have been when Pace beat his face in. The bastard deserved it.

"Oh, hey," he mumbled.

"Whatever." She pushed past him and out the door.

He kept up with her.

She gave him a nasty look. "Back off."

He opened his mouth to say something, but then his eyes widened. Bryna turned around to find Eric walking toward her across the quad. She had forgotten that he had agreed to meet her outside of class since they had plans. He looked pissed, seeing her with Cam.

"I don't want to talk to you, and if people see you harassing me..." She trailed off.

He seemed to get the hint. "Fine," he said with a shrug.

Eric stared Cam down as he quickly turned and walked away.

"What the fuck was he doing?" Eric asked.

"I don't know, nor do I care."

"I don't like him near you," Eric said.

"He won't be near me anymore. I think Pace knocked some sense into him at least."

"Pace did that?" he asked, gesturing to his own face.

"Yeah. He must have had two black eyes."

"Good."

Bryna laughed. "I'm over it. I have you, and that's how it should be."

"That's right." Eric grabbed her around the middle and kissed her hard. When he pulled back, he smiled down at her. "Are you ready?"

Her stomach flipped, and she nodded. "As ready as I'll ever be."

They walked over to his Jeep, and he drove her across town to a large office on the third floor of a giant complex. They entered the clean white room and were immediately greeted.

"Welcome to the Las Vegas Breast Cancer Research Center. How can I help you?" the woman asked.

Bryna took a deep breath. "I'd like to make a donation."

Then, she explained everything to the lady, including the one and a half million dollar donation total.

The woman's mouth was nearly on the floor by the time Bryna was finished. She handed Bryna some paperwork to fill out. "Here you go, honey. I'm going to find my manager, so she can speak with you. Give me a second."

Bryna filled in all the information that she could and put the check on the clipboard.

A short African American woman came out of the back room and smiled at her. "You must be Bryna," she said.

"That's me." They shook hands. "This is Eric."

"So nice to meet you both. I wanted to personally thank you for your incredible donation to our center. If there is anything that I can do for you, please let me know. You are touching so many lives with this money, and with it, we will be one step closer to finding a cure to this horrible disease that continues to hurt our nation and the ones we love."

Bryna swallowed and nodded. "There is one thing you could do for me," she said.

Thanksgiving came and went.

It had been way better than it had been last year. She had spent a lot of time playing with Zoe and missing Eric. He had come back early for the game that weekend, but it had still been a long stretch without him. She was starting to realize that her life revolved around him but in a good way. He was good for her, and when she was away from him, it made her heart heavy.

When she came back to school, it was the big end-of-the-year game against USC that would decide who would go to the conference championship game.

Bryna walked back into the apartment after her classes and sank into the couch. Trihn was there, watching TV, and Stacia came out of her room.

"I have so much homework," Trihn groaned.

"So many tests," Stacia agreed.

"I wish we could spend the rest of the year watching TV and vegging out on junk food," Bryna said.

"And not gain a pound," Stacia said.

"Amen," Bryna agreed.

Trihn glanced down at her phone when it beeped. "Ugh!"

"What?"

"Neal just canceled. He was supposed to come over to hang out."

Bryna rolled her eyes. "And his excuse?"

"He has to work on his art project, and all of his paints are at his house."

"This would be valid if he wasn't a prick to you most of the time," Stacia grumbled.

"You know it's bad when the cheer slut agrees." Bryna pointed her thumb back at Stacia.

"So true." Stacia didn't even try to argue.

Trihn shrugged. "I'm sure it's perfectly valid, guys. You're so negative. I'm going to go study, I guess." She got up and walked toward her room.

Stacia sighed. "God, what a buzzkill."

"I know. He drags her down. If I knew she wouldn't kill us, I would plot sabotage."

"He sabotages himself enough already. Everything he does irritates her, and she refuses to acknowledge it."

"She'll figure it out on her own," Bryna said.

"Let's hope so."

"All right. I'm going to go to Eric's, I guess."

"You practically live there now, Bryna."

She shrugged. "I like being around him."

Stacia frowned. "Yeah, I know that feeling."

Bryna grabbed her bag and headed out of the apartment. She wished there were a way to give her two best friends exactly what she had with Eric. It would be her gift to them if she could, but she didn't think either girl would find it with Neal or Pace. They both needed someone who would love them unconditionally. No secrets. No strange distaste for their lifestyle. No bullshit.

She was halfway to Eric's place when her phone rang. "Hello?" she answered after not recognizing the number.

"Bryna?"

Her heart stopped. *Hugh.*

"Hey," she whispered.

She hadn't expected him to get a hold of her. She had figured that after she sent in the money in his name that would be the end of it. She had asked the director not to include her name on anything related to the donation. This wasn't her donation. It was Hugh's. She had just put it in the right hands.

"I just received a handwritten card from the head of the Las Vegas Breast Cancer Research Center."

"Really?" She swallowed.

He knew. He knew she had donated it. She didn't know why she was suddenly so afraid. Of course he had to know. *Who else would have donated that kind of money in his name?* She had known that the charity might send him something after the enormous donation. She'd figured he would even put it together that it was her. It freaked her out wondering what he thought about it.

"It says that a donation was made in my name for one and a half million dollars." He coughed and then cleared his throat. "In honor of my wife."

Is he choked up? She couldn't tell. She didn't know what to say. She never thought he would call her, and now that he was, she was frozen.

"Did you do this?" he demanded.

Her stomach dropped out. He was pissed. He must be angry with her. Maybe he thought she had disrespected his wife by putting it in her name. That wasn't what she had intended at all. *Fuck!* She had thought she was doing the right thing.

"Yes. Yes, I did," she managed to get out. She took a deep breath and barreled forward. "I'm sorry if you don't approve or if you are offended. I couldn't hold on to the money or the jewelry or anything any longer. It didn't feel right to me. Since you wouldn't accept it, I wanted to put it to good use though, and that was the only way I knew to somehow make all of this right."

"I'm not mad," he said softly.

"Oh."

"Touched actually."

Bryna's jaw dropped, and she had to pick it up off the floor. "You're touched?"

"It was thoughtful. I hate to say, I'm surprised, but I am."

"Well, I don't have the best track record." She sighed. "I just…wanted to do something good."

"This is good."

She knew that voice. She could almost see his smile through the phone. He was happy, pleased even.

"Thank you," he said.

Her throat closed up. She couldn't take his thanks after what she had done. "Please, don't thank me. It was your money."

"Well, thank you anyway. After all this, it was nice to see that you meant well. Maybe we weren't meant to be, but we were together for a long time. I didn't want us to leave on bad terms."

"Me either," she admitted.

"I really wish you the best. It sounds like you are in a better place than when we left."

"Things are better. I hope they are for you, too. You deserve to find happiness."

She hated the way things had been left with Hugh in Barcelona. She had deserved his dismissal. She had deserved much worse. But it was so nice knowing that it wasn't the end of their story.

Once she hung up, Bryna parked in front of Eric's house, and she jogged inside with a skip in her step. He was out back, grilling, when she wandered inside.

"Hey!" she called, hopping out the back door.

"You're in a good mood." He leaned down and kissed her. "Burger?"

She shook her head. "No, thanks. I just talked to Hugh."

Eric raised his eyebrow. "Is that so?"

"He wanted to thank me for the donation, and I guess we're good now."

He smiled. "Good. I'm glad that's not weighing on you anymore. I know you were upset over what had happened in Barcelona."

"I was. I mean, I was a bitch. Beyond a bitch. Inexcusable."

"Well, sounds like he's forgiven you, so maybe it is excusable."

"Yeah. It just wasn't at the time."

"You've changed a lot since then. I think it's okay to be forgiven for past transgressions."

Bryna bit her lip and looked at the ground. Maybe it was time to forgive one last person in *her* life. "I've been thinking about Jude."

Eric's head snapped back to her. He knew too much about what had happened with Jude. She was sure he wasn't comfortable with her thinking about him. After what had happened the last time she was with Jude, Eric likely wanted to beat Jude's face in.

"Why?"

"If Hugh can forgive me, maybe I should forgive Jude."

Eric took the burger off the grill and set it on a plate. He took his time closing the grill and turning it off before walking over to her and taking her hands.

"I'm not just saying this as your boyfriend or because I love you. I'm saying this as your friend and as someone you trusted before you trusted anyone else, but you have no reason to forgive Jude. And I think you have long put him in your past," Eric told her. "In fact, I think you put him behind when you took off that awful necklace you always wore that he gave you."

"What do you mean, I shouldn't forgive him?" she asked, confused.

"He doesn't deserve your forgiveness in that way, and honestly, he won't care if you've forgiven him or not. You care that Hugh forgave you. It just proves that the difference between you and Jude is vast."

"I know that."

"Jude is never going to change, Bri. He proved that when he was here last year. I don't think you need to do anything to make that right with him because it never will be. It is not up to you to change him. It's up to him."

Bryna took a deep breath. On instinct, she wanted to argue with Eric. If she could change, then Jude could change. But the truth was that she had *wanted* to change. She had had a rude wake-up call in Barcelona and worked on making herself better. Jude had had that same wake-up call when Felicity caught him with Bryna and whoever the girl had been before her. Still, he had advanced on her in the hotel room last year.

She hadn't felt the weight of her scarlet letter in some time. Maybe Eric was right after all. Maybe she had officially left Jude in her past, where he belonged.

FORTY-EIGHT

THE CROWD ERUPTED.

It was senior night in the stadium, and LV State was paired up against USC. This rivalry game would determine who would go on to the conference championship. Both teams were playing as if it were do or die. The crowd grew unbearably loud. The dome echoed all the voices until it was a cacophony of cheers.

The LV State fans grew quiet as the ball was snapped to Marshall. He looked twice, found his man open, and let the ball loose. It was a beautiful pass.

And then…a USC player leaped in front and snatched the ball out of the air.

Bryna's mouth dropped as everyone screamed.

No. No! This is not how it's supposed to end.

Touchdown.

USC had won. Their fans went wild.

Bryna stood there, staring at the end zone. The irony didn't escape her that this was the same way they had won the national championship last year.

Stacia's shoulders sank next to Bryna, and when Bryna turned to her, Stacia burst into tears. Real hot tears streamed down her face.

Stacia covered her face with her hands and let the sobs wrack her body. "We lost!"

Bryna patted her on the back. "We did."

"I can't believe *that* was our last home game of the year!" Stacia cried.

"There's always next year, I guess."

"Ugh! I need to get drunk and fucked tonight."

Bryna laughed. "I'm opposed to you doing either. I think you should definitely do that."

"It's more that I'm tired of fucking being alone."

"It hasn't been *that* long."

Stacia swiped at her eyes. "Whatever. I need someone to make me forget this happened. Where is that stupid brother of yours?"

"Stacia!"

"What?" she snapped. "I miss him! Don't judge me, Bri."

"I'm not judging you. But do you think that's a good idea?"

"I'll make him grovel and crawl to me on all fours, all right?"

"Ew. I don't want to know the details," Bryna said, holding up her hands.

"Just don't be mad at me. I'm horrible at staying away from him."

"I noticed," Bryna grumbled. "I won't be mad, but I will voice that I think this is a terrible idea."

"Noted," Stacia said before scampering off in search of Pace.

Bryna shook her head as Stacia left. It was such a bad idea, but she wasn't going to change Stacia's mind. She would have to figure out the consequences herself.

"What are you shaking your head for?" Eric asked. He came up behind her and grabbed her around the middle.

"Stacia is about to make a big mistake."

Eric laughed and spun her around. "So are a lot of people after that loss."

"Not me."

"For once," he joked.

"Ass!"

Eric grabbed her face in his hands and kissed the breath out of her. It was pure heaven. She could so easily get lost in that kiss even amid a crowd of ninety-thousand people.

"Well," she asked when he pulled back, "how does it feel?"

"Your body? Amazing," he growled.

She laughed. "No! I mean, how does it feel to be done?"

He shrugged. "I liked your body better."

She gave him a pointed look.

"I'm not done yet, am I?"

"No. But it was our last home game and your last game as an undergrad. You might be back next year, but this feels pretty final."

"I suppose it didn't go as expected." He looked up at the scoreboard that showed their loss.

"Two national championships in four years. Not too bad, if I do say so myself," she said.

"Pretty fucking awesome actually." He smiled down at her with all the love in his heart. "I want to soak it all in. We lost, but it's not the end. We'll be back next year, and we'll take back our title."

"Sounds good, Cowboy."

He laughed and poked her in the stomach at the nickname. "How does it feel to you? Huh, Hollywood?"

"It's not the end for me."

"It's *one* end."

"But you're my beginning, so it doesn't feel like anything is ending."

"True. We didn't make a championship game this year, but I have you, so I'd say it all worked out."

"I have to agree." She tugged him closer. "Maybe you could show me how much it all worked out."

"It sounds like you want to skip Posse tonight."

"Are you complaining?"

"Not a bit."

He grabbed her hand and dragged her off the field. The locker rooms were packed with players and coaches. Eric quickly veered away from them, looking for a place that wasn't going to be a madhouse. The likelihood of finding somewhere quiet was slim, but he seemed to know where he was going.

He opened a door to the workout room, and Bryna walked in after him. It was dead quiet. The only problem was that the building was all glass on three sides. People streamed by the room from the stadium back to their cars, completely oblivious to the fact that they were inside.

Eric ignored the crowds. It was dark outside, and the interior lights were out. So, hopefully, if anyone saw any movement, they wouldn't put two and two together.

He pulled her against him, and their lips joined together again. The kiss wasn't hesitant. He couldn't care less about the chances of getting caught.

It was just them. Here and now. And in the moment.

This was all she'd wanted. Eric was all she would ever need.

The fact that she had ever contemplated wanting something else felt like a dream, as if she had been living someone else's life for so long. Being with Eric was like coming up for air.

Speaking of coming up for air...

She pulled back and took a deep breath. Her fingers worked at the button on his khaki pants, and she slipped them down his legs. She dragged his boxers off as she slid to her knees in front of him. His eyes were wide as saucers and ravenous for her.

She grabbed his dick in her hand and massaged it up and down. It lengthened in her hand, and she ignored the hard floor digging into her knees. She would wear her bruises with pride tomorrow. For now, she just didn't care.

She slipped the head in her mouth and swirled her tongue around him. He groaned and put his hands into her hair. At one time, she would have thought that was controlling…that the guy wanted to take charge of what was going on, even as she held all the power in her mouth. Now, she knew it was a sign of affection. He was in love with what her mouth could do to him. He always came undone at the way she worked him, and she loved it when he showed his appreciation.

Her tongue licked up and down his cock until he was wet, and then she bobbed her head forward and back. Unless she opened up the back of her throat, he wouldn't fit all the way, but he didn't complain. As she stroked him, she could feel him tensing up. If it were possible, he might have even gotten bigger.

"Fuck, Bri," he grunted. "You feel so fucking good."

She smiled at his pleasure and felt herself getting worked up. She wanted to masturbate while she was at it, but she focused all her attention on him. He would reciprocate tenfold later, she was sure.

She sucked him off like a champ. He was so close. She could feel it. He would come any second if she kept going.

"Bri." Eric tried to pull her back.

She licked him again.

"Fuck, Bri. Fuck. I still want to fuck you."

She groaned as she sucked him and then stepped back. "You make it seem like a bad thing that I want to get you off."

"I fucking love it." He lay back on a bench press with his arms over his head. "Now, get on my dick."

She smirked. "How about I ride you like a cowgirl, Cowboy?"

His eyes lit up. "By all means."

Bryna removed her bloomers and then straddled his body, facing away from him. She slowly eased his cock inside of her. She was so wet from giving him a blow job in full view of half of the stadium that she easily sank all the way down to the hilt.

"Oh God," she moaned.

He gripped her hips. "I could get used to this sight."

His hands guided her up and down on top of him. Soon, she was bouncing. He was hitting the perfect spot over and over again. She couldn't even think. Her mind was lost on the feel of him inside her. Her body superheated, and she felt all the tension wash off her. She was close.

God, he's so amazing.

Her body arched as he thrust into her, pushing up and meeting her as she slammed down on top of him. She jerked a few times and then felt her body give out. She clenched all around him, and wave after wave shattered her calm.

She must have been loud because Eric clamped a hand over her mouth and pulled her backward against him. He jackhammered a few more times inside of her before coming hard.

They both relaxed, completely spent. After taking a minute to gather themselves, Eric pulled out, and they both put their clothes back on in euphoric silence.

He pulled her close and kissed her tender lips. "You know I love you, right?"

"You'd better."

"How could I not with that attitude?"

"Exactly. We're too perfect for each other."

"I mean, how many other girls are going to let me fuck them in the weight room after a football game with thousands of people on the other side of the glass?"

She arched an eyebrow. "Probably a ton of dumb sluts."

He laughed. "Fair. But I only love one of those sluts."

"Ouch. Such nice words behind that barb."

"All in jest, my love." He leaned down and dropped his lips on hers again.

"It'd better be because I love you, too."

"You are everything to me, Bri. Everything. And I wouldn't have it any other way."

FORTY-NINE

Three Weeks Later

BRYNA STOOD IN FRONT OF THE SPRAWLING MANSION her mother considered home on the outskirts of Los Angeles. Her mother had only moved forty-five minutes away from her father's house in the Hills, and Bryna realized that the last time she had seen her mother was the summer before her senior year of high school. That was two and a half years ago. It made her heart ache.

Luckily, her father was at her side. She didn't want to admit that she was scared and thought about walking away right then and there. Not that she could. They had called ahead to let her know that they were coming, but she still thought about it.

"Are you ready?" her father asked.

She nodded and then reached forward and rang the doorbell. A minute later, her mother pulled the door inward. She was every bit as beautiful as Bryna remembered her. She was a classic Hollywood beauty with shoulder-length blonde hair, bright blue eyes, a porcelain face like a goddess, and a slender figure. She was dressed to the nines in a cherry-red dress with a narrow waist and high heels. Her makeup was subtle and perfect.

This was the Olivia Bendel that Bryna had grown up with.

She startled as if she were surprised that they had arrived even though they had called to say they were coming.

"Lawrence," her mother said. Her voice crisp.

"Olivia." He smiled even though Bryna knew this was hard for him. "Good to see you."

"Likewise."

"Hey, Mom," Bryna said. She was dressed more casually in a tight-fitting chambray button-up tucked into white shorts and brown fringe booties.

"Bryna, come in. Come in."

Once they were inside, her mother reached forward and tentatively hugged her. Her mother actually seemed to have more substance to her than the last time Bryna had seen her.

She seemed a little nervous herself about what was happening. "I have lemonade in the sun room. Lawrence, you still like a whiskey and Coke, I assume?"

"Lemonade is fine with me for now," he said.

Bryna knew it had taken a lot of strength for him not to bite back.

"All domestic-like," she muttered under her breath.

Bryna and her father shared a look. They both smiled at the same time. This was the relationship she was completely used to.

Her mother busied herself with pouring lemonade and then taking a seat. She played the part of the entertainer well. Bryna would never have guessed that her mother's life wasn't as perfect as it seemed. Last she had heard, her mom was banging the cabana boy, drinking heavily, and on coke.

"So, how can I help you?" she asked politely. "This visit is most unexpected."

"You don't have to pretend with me, Mom. I'm your daughter."

Olivia pursed her lips. "What's all this about?"

Bryna looked at her dad, and he nodded his head.

"I want a relationship with you, Mom. I've had a rough couple of years. It was hard, not having you around."

"Well, if you're here to guilt-trip me—"

"I'm not," she interrupted. "Things are finally good with Dad again, and I want that for us."

"Of course," Olivia said slowly. She glanced between the two of them. "I'm not surprised you reached out to your father first. You always were a daddy's girl."

"Olivia, it's not a competition," he said sternly.

"Of course not. You've already won. Hotshot directing job. Big house in Beverly Hills. Harmony Prep. How could she say no?"

"Stop!" Bryna cried. "It's like I'm back in high school. I can't stand you arguing, and that's not why we're here."

"Then, why are you here?" her mother asked. She'd lost all her poise in that question.

She looked like Mom again. It made Bryna smile.

"Dad *wants* me to have a relationship with you. In fact, this was his idea."

"Lawrence?" Olivia asked, surprised.

"I don't want her to grow up without a mother, Olivia."

"And...your wife?" she asked.

"Celia is not her mother," he said flatly. "She's her stepmother."

"I see."

"*I* want to have a relationship with you, Mom. It comes down to whether or not you want to have one with me," Bryna told her.

Olivia sighed heavily and let a hesitant smile come to her face. "Of course I want to have a relationship with you."

Bryna took a deep breath. This was the tricky part. "I love you, Mom, but I hate to see you hurting yourself. I've been let down a lot, and I want to move forward with my life. I don't know if I can do that with your…lifestyle."

Olivia colored and looked away. "I don't know what you mean."

"Yes, you do. You're a great actress, but you can't hide drugs from people who have lived in your house for most of their lives."

Her father frowned and looked away. Bryna hoped he realized his part in all of this. He had never stopped her mother. Maybe he wouldn't have been able to, but he hadn't tried either.

"I'm not judging you. You can live your life however you want. I've made mistakes, but I don't want your mistakes, too. I want a mom," she whispered.

"I've been getting help," Olivia whispered. Their eyes met. "I had a bad accident a couple of months ago, and I've been trying to be better, for me and for you, even though I didn't think you wanted me in your life."

"I've always wanted you in my life. I just want someone who isn't self-destructive. I was self-destructive enough for the both of us."

Her mother wiped a tear from under her eye. "I can't promise it will be better today or tomorrow or next week. I've been battling this for years, but I took the first step. I'm going to therapy and drug and alcohol counseling. I'm trying."

Bryna broke out into a smile. "That's what I want. I want us to be a family again…even if our family is different."

Olivia rushed across the room and wrapped her daughter in a hug. "I'm so sorry for everything, Bryna. The absence was my fault. I want to be better. I will be better."

"I know. Me, too, Mom."

Olivia cried into Bryna's hair, and they both held each other like that for a while.

Then, her mom pulled back and wiped her tears. "We'll make this work," she promised.

Bryna looked to her dad, and he put a protective arm around her.

This was her family—a broken dad, a broken mom, a new stepmother, a jerk stepbrother, withdrawn twin stepsisters, and a brand-new baby halfsister. It wasn't perfect, far from it, but it was hers.

"We all will."

When Bryna got back to her house, her father had to rush off to work. He was a busy man, even two days before Christmas. Luckily, Eric was waiting for her when she arrived.

"Hey," he said. His whole face brightened when he saw her. "How did it go?"

"Bad."

He frowned. "I'm sorry."

She laughed. "Just kidding. It went great."

"Geez. Fucking freak me out!"

"You're too easy." She giggled. "I mean, not everything was fixed today. But it will work itself out. I'm a persistent bitch."

"I have no doubt it will work out."

"Me, too." She smiled up at him and drew him in for a kiss. "I hate that you have to leave today," she groaned.

"I know. How can I leave?"

447

"I have an idea. Don't. Just stay here. Have Christmas with me."

He rubbed his nose against hers. "You know I would love to do that, but my parents miss me, too. Have to spend some time with them."

"Maybe…I could meet them someday."

He smiled. "You will definitely have to meet them. They will love you."

"Are you sure?"

He nodded. "Absolutely."

"Good."

"I'm glad that you're going to have a real Christmas with your family though. Last year, you told me you hated Christmas, and I don't want that to be the case anymore. New memories to replace the old."

She slid her fingers around his waist and held him close. "Memories with you."

"For many years to come," he said, punctuating the sentence with a kiss. "I do have a Christmas gift for you though."

"You do?" she asked with excitement. "I didn't know you were getting me anything!"

"Gifts are a trigger for you, so I didn't want to raise your expectations of me," he joked.

"You're crazy. I already have high expectations for you."

"In that case, I'm screwed."

"I'm sure I'll love it. What is it?" she asked. She looked at his hands and then down at his pockets. All seemed to be empty.

"Come on. I'll show you."

She was intrigued. She had never gotten a present from Eric. She understood where he would be worried though. After a house, jewelry, a key to a penthouse suite, and lots of clothes, it would be pretty intimidating to pick out a present for her. Not that she needed anything. She was happy with Eric. That was what mattered.

With L.A. traffic, it was a solid half an hour before they reached their destination, which turned out to be a small ice cream shop in West Hollywood.

"Oh my God." She laughed hysterically.

She had heard of this place before, but she'd never been here. She couldn't believe he was taking her to get ice cream. It was going to turn into a Christmas tradition.

"I was going to take you to the Sugar Factory," he said as he stepped out of the car. "But then we came to L.A. to be with your family."

"The place doesn't matter when I'm with you."

"I'm glad we're on the same page."

He took her hand, and they walked across the parking lot.

A hostess met them inside. "Just two?" she asked.

"Yeah," Eric confirmed.

"This way." She walked them over to a booth in front of the windows and then handed them two menus. "Enjoy!"

"Welcome! Do you know what you want to drink?" a waitress asked when she walked over.

Eric plopped the menus down on top of each other and handed them to the waitress, unopened. "We want the biggest banana split you have."

The woman's eyes widened as she wrote their order down. "For just the two of you?"

Eric nodded.

"Good luck," the waitress said before disappearing.

Bryna gave Eric a curious look. "Why am I suddenly frightened by her reaction?"

"Because I picked this place with the guarantee that it had one of the biggest banana splits in the city." He laughed. "And you'd better eat every last bite."

Bryna leaned forward in her seat, all business. "All right. What are the terms?"

"If you finish the whole thing by yourself, then I'll pick up the tab."

"What a horrible Christmas present," she joked. "And if I don't finish it?"

"Then, you're going to have to hang out with me again."

The words were so familiar, reminiscent of their first time really hanging out. This was where it had all started. Just like this.

She stuck her hand out. "Deal. You'd better be ready to pay up."

Eric shook her hand with laughter in his eyes. "Oh, I *always* pay up."

A couple of minutes later, an enormous banana split was set down between them. Bryna's eyes were huge when she saw the size of the ice cream. It was maybe double the size of the one at the Sugar Factory. *How the hell did anyone finish this?* They would need a large class of hungry fifth-graders to even give it a go.

Bryna took the two spoons that the waitress had left for them. She arched an eyebrow and then handed one over to Eric. "Eat up, Cowboy. We're going to be spending a lot more time together."

"I hoped you might say that."

They smiled at each other and then started in on their banana split.

Much like her family, she and Eric weren't perfect. They argued. They made fun of each other. They teased and joked and sometimes even ridiculed one another. But underneath it all was bottomless love and understanding.

Bryna didn't need the money or riches or trips. She didn't need any of it.

It'd turned out that the only thing she really needed to make her life better was Eric. With him, everything else seemed to fall into place.

And as they toasted to their first year together, Bryna knew all would be well.

The End

FIND OUT WHERE IT ALL STARTED FOR BRYNA IN DIAMONDS (ALL THAT GLITTERS, #1).

http://amzn.to/1KzQJEqLink

TURN THE PAGE FOR A SNEAK PEEK OF K.A. LINDE'S NEXT BOOK COMING THIS FALL.

Struck from the Record
(Record, #4)

A standalone novel from Senator Brady Maxwell brother, Clay's point of view.

Struck from the Record

Chapter 1

"Fuck!" she screamed.

Her head fell backward into the heavy law books with an audible smack. Clay leveraged her body against the bookshelf as he thrust upward. His hands gripped her bare ass where he'd shoved the tiny green thing she considered a dress out of the fucking way. Their bodies smacked together, and her screams were growing more insistent.

Clay hadn't said much. He didn't have to. She was going to come over the adrenaline of getting fucked against a bookcase in his clerk office at the Supreme Court. She hadn't believed he actually worked there, and so he had set out to prove her wrong. Since his term as a clerk had come to a close, he figured fucking her was a fitting going away present.

"Yes, yes, yes," she yelled, loud enough that he was sure her echoes were carried down the hallway.

He didn't care. It was the middle of the night, a week before Christmas, and no one else was here. Even the diligent, annoying douche who worked for Justice Scalia hadn't been here when Clay had taken her into the building.

Clay leaned forward into her and pounded forcefully, until she reached her climax, and her screams died out. He liked vocal women, but sometimes screaming into his ear made it fucking difficult to concentrate. Now with her fucking quiet, he focused on getting himself off, which really had been the whole point.

"Jesus Christ," she said breathily. "Fuck me. You're going to make me go a second time."

"Shut up," he said forcefully. He hauled her off the bookshelf, walked her over to his desk, and threw her back down on the scattered mess that he would have to deal with later this week.

She groaned. "Make me." Her eyes glistened. "Choke me."

His eyebrows rose. He'd expected the girl to be a slut, but he hadn't anticipated kink.

Whatever. I'm in.

His hand reached out and wrapped around her throat. Her eyes fluttered closed in pleasure. He hadn't even done anything. He was just holding her like a doll he was about to shake around.

With his hand positioned at her throat, he drilled into her at a bruising pace. She was making mewling noises, and with him in complete control of her, he found them hot. This was a better view too. He could stare at her tits. She had a seriously nice rack. That was why he'd let her question him when he'd said he worked for the Supreme Court. It was fun to have people look at him in disbelief. Much better than when they recognized his name.

He was close at this point. Without asking if she was about to hit her second climax, he tightened his grip on her body and came inside of her. He shook as he finished. His breath was coming out in heavy bursts. It had taken more effort than he normally expelled with her screams still ringing in his ears.

He removed the grip on her throat and was surprised to find a red handprint where he had been holding her. He must have been clutching her harder than he thought. She probably would like if she ended up with bruises.

Clay pulled out and trashed the condom. He turned his back on her and adjusted his black suit. After this rendezvous, he'd have to send it to the dry cleaners.

When he faced her once more, the girl was still lying on the desk. He gave her a once over in appreciation of her mostly naked form, still laid out, and unable to move. She looked spent and exhausted, but it was time for her to get the fuck out of his office.

"All right. Let's go," he said briskly.

She sat up on her elbows and gave him a seductive look. "What about round two?"

"I appreciate your vote of confidence," he said sarcastically. "I might be Casanova, but I don't have another one in me right now."

"Well, come on, Casanova. Let's go to your place, and we can have seconds and thirds. I'm suddenly ravenous." Her eyes glittered with excitement. Her body was still flushed from the vigorous fucking.

"I don't think so," Clay said, suddenly bored. It had been fun when it was a challenge. He liked challenges, but this was too easy. He could pick up any girl at a bar if he wanted to. *At least put some fucking effort into it.*

She pouted, but had enough dignity to not say anything else. She immediately covered herself up and followed him out. He got her safely into a cab, and then took his own back to his townhouse. Once it reached their destination, he absentmindedly threw the driver a twenty. His place was convenient as it was only short distance from his work. He enjoyed the bachelor feel to the place, but tonight it felt cold and uninviting. Maybe he should have taken up that girl on her offer. As soon as the thought hit his mind, he knew that he never would have gone through with it.

He had spent his life constantly on the edge between recklessness and complete control. He had a game plan— top of his class at Yale, clerk at the Supreme Court, federal judge, attorney general. Thinking of it both excited him and made him feel sick. He wanted to live up to the man his father expected him to be, but following the mold made him crazy. It was a double-edged sword. A line he constantly skirted.

That girl had been an immediate pleasure, a reckless pleasure…not one needed to indulge in a second time to discover anything more about her. She had been a treat for completing his clerkship and moving one step closer on his path. But tomorrow, he would have to clear out his desk and get serious about deciding which private practice offer he would accept to begin in January.

He had been staring at the three offers for over a week now, and they would be expecting an answer by Christmas…maybe New Year's at the latest. He would push it back if he could. Recklessness was creeping up into his game plan all over again.

But not tonight.

He shrugged out of his suit coat and walked to his wet bar. He passed over the hard liquor and cracked open a beer. He'd already had a few drinks tonight, but the beer didn't seem to quench his thirst. He knew it had something to do with his clerkship coming to a close. Another thing completed on a checklist. It didn't seem fulfilling in the way it had when he had been accepted.

Clay stood and fished his cell phone out of his pocket. Maybe he should go home to Andrea tonight. It might be nice to get out of the city for a bit. Spend some time in a real house, even if it was in the D.C. suburbs and not at his place in Chapel Hill.

He dialed Andrea's number and waited for her to answer. It clicked over to voicemail. He scowled down at the phone. "What the fuck?"

Then it almost immediately lit up again.

"Can I help you?" Andrea asked curtly, when he answered the phone.

Clay cracked a smile. *There's my bitch.* "Hey babe, I'm coming home tonight. Are you there? I'm tired of the city."

"And what was her name that made you so tired?" she asked. Her voice was high and musical just like he had always found it these past fourteen years they had known each other.

"Should I remember?"

And he didn't. He didn't even know if he had bothered asking for her name. It hadn't mattered at the time. Had she been blonde or brunette? Everything about her was a mystery except the feel of her ass in his hands, the sight of her scrunched up green dress, the way the material stretched tight across her rack, and the red imprint on her throat. Everything else was a blur.

"Your standards are slipping."

"I'm still with you. Can't be that low." Clay smirked.

"I'm out of your league, honey."

"Always have been," he agreed easily.

"Why do I put up with you anyway?" Andrea sounded bored, not irritated. She was never irritated with him. Not really. She didn't give a shit what he did. Just like he didn't care what she did in her spare time.

Clay had met Andrea on Hilton Head beach when he was almost thirteen years old. They had spent every summer together on that beach until her parents finally split up after their sophomore year of high school. Six long years of endless arguments and limitless pampering to make up for the fights jaded Andrea's soft heart. By the time they met up again at Yale their freshman year of college, they were both very different people.

Romance was wasted on them, and so they had entered into an arrangement of a lifetime. They could do whatever they wanted, but at the end of the day, they would be together. Guard their hearts. No feelings would get hurt. They wouldn't turn out like her parents, and he wouldn't have anyone in his life to disappoint for his behavior. It was perfect.

"You don't put up with me. You enjoy it. It's all my charm."

"Oh right," she drawled. "That Maxwell charm. It does have a certain appeal."

"Every appeal," he said confidently. "So, are you home? I'll grab another cab and drive out there."

Andrea made a tinkling giggle. "Do you think you're the only one who can have fun, Clay Maxwell?"

A smile spread across his face. "You're bad, and it turns me on."

"Well, you'll have to do something about it by yourself. I won't be home tonight. I have…other plans," she said breathily, for his benefit, he was sure.

His body itched with the sudden challenge she was posing. Andrea always seemed to do this. He could fuck so many other girls, and then one little giggle from her made him want to claim her all over again. Not as his girlfriend or his wife. He shuddered at the very thought.

She was just a continual challenge. She was beautiful with long blonde hair, bright blue eyes, and a tall lean frame that he knew intimately. But every time he thought he had her figured out, every time he was sure she was going to do one thing, she would do something else. She liked to play games, and he liked her games.

Because at the end of the day, he knew exactly where her head was in all of this. It wasn't seeking out a Harry Winston engagement ring. It wasn't demanding an *I love you* before bed. It wasn't a scowl for his philandering or the way he treated his brother or innumerable other reasons. It was just an arrangement for two people who cared about each other…in their own way.

"Pray tell me, love. Who is the lucky bastard?" Clay asked.

He was already throwing his coat back on and changing from his light blue tie into a purple striped bowtie. Andrea came from old Southern plantation money, and his family could stretch their lineage back to Thomas Jefferson himself. They had been in real estate in the Triangle area of North Carolina for just as long. He was a Southern boy through and through, and if there was one thing Andrea couldn't resist, it was when he acted like it.

He pressed the phone into his ear, as he expertly tied the bowtie.

"He's no one you know," she told him.

"I know everyone."

"Not this one."

"Stop teasing me."

She giggled. "Oh, but you don't really want me to do that, Clay. You probably want me to describe him on the phone. Should I start with his suit or how big I think he is?"

"Always good to know your competition," he said, adjusting the tie one more time.

"Well, I don't have time. I have to get back to my game. I don't want him to think I have a doting boyfriend at home waiting for me."

Clay snorted. "Doting. Sounds just like me."

Andrea was silent for a moment, and if he couldn't hear the bar noise in the background he might have thought she had hung up on him. "Sometimes it's not that far off," she said quietly.

"Right," he said with a laugh. "Doting, Andrea?"

"You're an ass."

"Yeah. You've always known that. Now, I'll show you doting. Where are you?"

"Don't ruin my game, Clay," she said without conviction. He could hear the tell tale signs of excitement in her voice. He was sure she was pouting on the other line to look like she was upset. Poor schlup.

"I would never," he lied.

"I don't ruin yours."

"You do if you can help it. Now tell me," he demanded.

"Fine," she said. "But you better bring you're A-game. He's a keeper."

"Don't I always?"

She told him the bar she was at. It wasn't far from his place, which made him wonder if she had picked it hoping for this outcome. She was conniving, and he wouldn't put it past her.

Clay felt emboldened. His melancholy from his apartment evaporating as he left to chase down his girl.

ACKNOWLEDGMENTS

GOLD is a project that I have been working on for several years now. It wormed its way into my mind while I was working on another, but it wasn't until I wrote *Diamonds* that I realized how different this book really needed to be to show Bryna for the woman that she becomes—from golden girl to gold digger to maybe even a little grown-up. Thank you for coming along this ride with me as Bryna finds her way through it all.

As always, there is a long list of people who helped make this book come to life. You all mean the world to me, and I wouldn't have gotten to this point without you. Jessica Carnes, Bridget Peoples, Rebecca Kimmerling, Lori Francis, Katie Miller, Diana Peterfreund, Mariah Dietz, Christine Estevez, Christy Peckham, Katie Ross, Jessica Sotelo, Corinne Michaels, Lauren Blakely, Gail McHugh, Kendall Ryan, Emma Hart, Pepper Winters, Jenn Sterling,

Mary Ruth Baloy, Daniela Padrón, Sarah Hansen of Okay Creations (for the badass cover), Jovana Shirley of Unforeseen Editing (for the incredible editing and formatting), and all the bloggers and readers who gave up their time, which they could have been using any other way, to read this book!

I also have to thank my husband (ahhh!), Joel, for sitting through the madness of writing this book in the midst of wedding planning. I know that couldn't have been the easiest thing in the world. Also my sister Shea who loved *Diamonds* and always encouraged me to keep going through the hard parts of *Gold*. Much love to my writing puppies, Riker and Lucy!

I hope you all enjoyed Bryna's story and will stay tuned for the next book in the All That Glitters series, *Platinum*, which follows Trihn! ♥

ABOUT THE AUTHOR

USA Today bestselling author K.A. Linde has written the Avoiding series, the Record series, and the Take Me series as well as her new adult stand-alone *Following Me*. This is the second in her four-book All That Glitters series. Book one, *Diamonds*, debuted on the *USA Today* Bestsellers List.

She grew up as a military brat traveling the United States and Australia. While studying political science and philosophy at the University of Georgia, she founded the Georgia Dance Team, which she still coaches. Post-graduation, she served as the campus campaign director for the 2012 presidential campaign at the University of North Carolina at Chapel Hill.

An avid traveler, reader, and bargain hunter, K.A. recently moved to Chapel Hill, NC, with her husband, Joel, and two puppies, Riker and Lucy.

K.A. Linde loves to hear from her readers! Feel free to contact her here:

kalinde45@gmail.com
www.kalinde.com
www.facebook.com/authorkalinde
@authorkalinde

46910934R00261

Made in the USA
Lexington, KY
20 November 2015

09 - LE BALTHAZAR – BIÈRES QUÉBÉCOISES

Dans le domaine de la micro-brasserie québécoise, ce bar constitue un tournant. Il ne sert rien d'autre que de la bière artisanale québécoise : 32 sortes en fût et 70 en bouteilles. Et c'est plein de monde le soir. Ai-je besoin d'en dire plus ? Jadis disponibles seulement dans des débits spécialisés fréquentés par les connaisseurs, nos meilleurs petits brasseurs sont désormais accessibles au grand public. Finie la marginalité, la bonne bière se démocratise. Comme le disait un célèbre personnage de télésérie québécoise : « La game vient de changer. » Le Balthazar peut accommoder 200 personnes à l'intérieur et 85 personnes en terrasse.

195, promenade du Centropolis

10 - SALON SACO

Pourquoi des clientes viennent-elles de l'autre bout du Québec pour se faire coiffer ici ? Parce que Luc Vincent est une vedette de la télévision (notamment grâce à l'émission de Jean Airoldi) et un expert du « changement d'image ». Il dirige un salon affilié à un grand nom de la haute coiffure : le Britannique Richard Ashforth. Ce dernier forme ses affiliés à travers le monde (il y a une vingtaine de salons Saco) pour les initier aux modes émergentes, de manière à leur donner une longueur d'avance sur la compétition.

1671, boulevard de l'Avenir

09